Sophie Hannah was born in Manchester in 1971. She is currently Fellow Commoner in Creative Arts at Trinity College, Cambridge. She has published three collections of poetry. This is her first novel.

# gripless

## Sophie Hannah

ARROW

Published in the United Kingdom in 1999 by
Arrow Books

3 5 7 9 10 8 6 4 2

Copyright © Sophie Hannah 1999

. The right of Sophie Hannah to be identified as the author
of this work has been asserted by her in accordance with
the Copyright, Designs and Patents Act 1988

First published in the United Kingdom in 1999 by
Arrow Books Limited
Random House UK Ltd
20 Vauxhall Bridge Road, London SW1V 2SA

Random House Australia (Pty) Limited
20 Alfred Street, Milsons Point, Sydney,
New South Wales 2061, Australia

Random House New Zealand Limited
18 Poland Road, Glenfield,
Auckland 10, New Zealand

Random House South Africa (Pty) Limited
Endulini, 5A Jubilee Road, Parktown 2193, South Africa

Random House UK Limited Reg. No. 954009

A CIP record for this book is available from the British Library

Papers used by Random House UK Limited are natural,
recyclable products made from wood grown in sustainable forests.
The manufacturing processes conform to the environmental
regulations of the country of origin.

Typeset in Melior and Sabon by MATS, Southend-on-Sea, Essex
Printed and bound in Norway by
AIT Trondheim AS, 1999

ISBN 0 09 9280353

# Acknowledgments

I would like to thank the following people:

For being the first readers of the first draft and making brilliant suggestions: Adèle and Jenny Geras, Dan Jones, Suzanne Davies, Chris Gribble, Gisela Striker and Isabelle Thomas.

For answering factual queries and helping with research: Adrian Wright, Ian Tomlinson, Ivan Hare, Catherine Barnard and Neil Strickland.

For general support and encouragement: Norman Geras, Johnny Woodhams, Michael Schmidt, Peter Salt, Hilary McDonald, Rachel Hanlon, Simon Brett and the Tonbridge School Totleigh Barton party of 23–28 March 1998, Tony Weir and all my colleagues at Trinity College.

For allowing me to use their computer when I was too busy writing to be sociable, and for bringing champagne: Mel, Christine and Lewis Jones.

For looking after the book once it was written and having its best interests at heart, sometimes even before I did: Lisanne Radice, Jane Gregory, Suzanne Amphlet, Victoria Hipps and everyone at Arrow.

I know I've left out someone crucial – thanks to them as well.

*Part One*

# Chapter One

## The Downsizing of the Readership

Are you in love? If you're not in love at the moment, don't read this book. Put it back on the library shelf, on the bookshop display table. Maybe read it at some future time when you are in love, but don't read it now. If you're not in love, you won't like it. It won't like you.

This is not a gimmick. You think it must be one, don't you, because what author in her right mind would deliberately try to put off large numbers of potential readers? Well, I don't want any old readers. I want readers who are in tune with the spirit of the book, not ones who just sit around expecting it to be good.

Who's still with me? I think those of you who have persevered this far can be separated out into a few simple categories:

*Category A*: The genuinely in love;
*Category B*: Those who aren't in love but, in order to avoid admitting to the boredom/failure of their relationships, feel the need to pretend to be in love and are therefore reading on defensively. If they read this book they must be in love, they tell themselves;
*Category C*: People who are confusing the state of being in love with the state of loving someone. This category will no doubt include a few long-term marrieds who love their spouses but are not in love with them.

3

NB I don't really mind Categories B and C hanging around; it's not their fault, it's a misunderstanding. And then we have the deliberate cheat categories:

*Category D*: Those who are clever and realise that I won't actually know whether they're cheating or not. This lot also believe I do not have total power around here and that they can read whatever they want. Category D contains the true rebels, determined to think for themselves;

*Category E*: The mitigating circumstances category, people who believe that if they could only explain their mitigating circumstances to me I'd make an exception for them. The mitigating factor will almost invariably be that, while not technically in love at the moment, they were once so in love and they remember the state so well that they reckon they still fit the profile of my ideal reader.

NB I've got quite a lot of time for Category E folk, actually. I suppose I was a bit rigid at first with my reader elimination policy. Not all people who aren't in love are the same, after all. It's like the difference between born-again, pain-in-the-arse ex-smokers, who cough and open windows a lot, and those ex-smokers who remember the pleasure of smoking and don't resent those who still enjoy it even though they no longer can. As for Category D – well, it could go either way. I have great respect for free-thinkers, but I don't feel I can rely on this lot. Love is not their primary motivating force; independence is.

And finally:

*Category F*: Bad category. People who are against love, for themselves and for others, either (i) because they have had one bad experience that has made them bitter and twisted, for example Miss Havisham

4

from *Great Expectations*, (ii) because they are natural miseries who resent happiness and excitement of any kind, (iii) because they are control freaks and cannot bear the idea of their emotions behaving in a wild and unpredictable manner, or (iv) because they believe they are sensible, moral and principled, and that all this is more important than love.

I'm not naïve. I know that some Category F readers are still hanging around. Oh yes you are. Why? You've got no excuse, unless you're a publisher or reviewer upon whose desk this book has landed. Anyway, I'm ignoring you from now on.

Do most writers care if they get bad reviews? In my life so far I have written three plays and one short story, and I cared deeply what people thought of them. With this book I feel I've been set free. You Category A-ers will understand. Now I'm in love, so who cares about literary merit? Not me. I haven't got time to worry about that. Love takes up my every waking and sleeping thought.

By my own standards, this will be the best book ever written. It will be the only book that contains Tony Lamb. The presence of Tony Lamb's name in this first chapter makes it the best first chapter of all time. At least I'm assuming no other books have Tony Lamb in them. I don't see how they could. Tony Lamb is a twenty-one-year-old bloke from Slough who doesn't know any writers except me (although technically I'm a teacher, not a writer – I mean, that's how I earn my living) so it's unlikely that he would crop up in anyone else's book.

If Martin Amis or Iris Murdoch or Jonathan Coe wrote a book that featured Tony Lamb, it would undoubtedly be better than mine. But they haven't and they won't, which makes mine the best.

This method of assessment does not apply only to

books. For example, what is the best county in Britain? Berkshire, obviously, because that's where Tony Lamb lives.

By now you're hopefully beginning to get a sense of my priorities. I'm wondering where to begin, not in a linear-versus-circular-narrative literary kind of way, but in a madly-in-love-person way. A madly-in-love person hasn't got the emotional energy to consider whether to start in the present and use flashbacks, or whether to start at the beginning, or what. So, to be blunt, if you don't like my chosen manner of narration, get over it. You're missing the point. This isn't about great literature, it's about Tony Lamb.

# Chapter Two

## The Tony Lamb GLOW

This may be my favourite chapter in the book. You Category A readers know why: because its title contains the name Tony Lamb. But even if no more chapters are named after him, even if his name is only mentioned once more on page 102 (this is purely hypothetical – his name will be mentioned much more often than that, probably on almost every page, in fact), it is still worth reading on because the whole novel is about him. He is its driving force.

I wouldn't have met Tony if it weren't for my job, so I'd better tell you about that first. After nearly eight years of working as a secretary for a gruesome succession of paper-clip counters and itemised-phone-bill obsessives, and fitting my writing in on the side, I somehow managed to get myself a job teaching Creative Writing at the Seth Beasley School of Performance and Creative Arts. I couldn't believe how beautiful the place was when I first saw it. A three-storey neo-classical building with a porticoed front, set in the lush Berkshire countryside near Windsor, it looked more like a stately home than a school and, as I sat in the gleaming reception area waiting for my interview three months ago, I bitterly envied the twenty-five teachers and three-hundred-odd students who were privileged enough to belong here.

I had no idea places like this existed until I read the

advertisement for the job I subsequently got. I thought all schools were pretty much like mine and now I know they aren't I'm a bit pissed off about the one I went to. Could all that Aim, Apparatus, Method, Results, Conclusion tedium have been avoided? Could someone have given me a Bunsen bypass? To be fair, the Seth Beasley School only takes post-GCSE students, aged sixteen and above. But it isn't fixated on GCSE results. It holds auditions, asks to see stories and poems; its admissions system is altogether more civilised. While normal schools have grotty gymnasia and canteens with peeling wallpaper, the Seth Beasley School has bars, restaurants, a plush theatre-in-the-round with velvet seats and an elegant circular gravel car-park with a view of green rolling hills that would put most five-star hotels to shame.

I got the job on the strength of my three plays, which had been broadcast on Radio Four, and my short story 'All the Dead Lie Down' which, to my amazement, had won the first prize of £5000 in the 1996 Shell Petrochemicals Short Story Competition. The latter was a fairly prestigious prize and led to my being interviewed for the *Daily Telegraph* and *The Times*, without which press assistance I would almost definitely still be a secretary.

I think Seth Beasley liked me at the interview. He seemed to respond favourably to everything I said, as though it was exactly what he'd hoped I'd say. I took this as a good sign. His opinion had to be fairly important if the school was named after him. Now, of course, I know exactly how prestigious a person he is, having read his theatre reviews in the *Telegraph* and the *TLS*. There were other people on the interview panel, people after whom the school had not been named. Some of them clearly thought I should be kept in my clerical place, but Seth Beasley later told me that he was a firm believer in real life, which made me wonder about people who don't believe in real life. Where do they live?

I felt incredibly lucky to have this job at Beasley (as the school is known to those on the inside). I couldn't get over the fact that my office door had 'Ms Belinda Nield' painted on its white wood in neat black capital letters. Not because it wasn't my name – it was and indeed is – but because never before had an employer deemed me worthy of door-painting.

I'm almost scared to start writing about Tony. It isn't he who scares me, it's the impact of my feelings for him. Or maybe it's a bit of both.

I met him at the beginning of *Lions*. Every August the school puts on a Youth Theatre play, and *Lions* – or *Lions After Slumber*, to give it its full name – was this year's production. Beasley students are so obsessed with becoming the next Alan Rickman or Miranda Richardson that they are more than willing, it seems, to give up a whole month of their summer holiday every year. Most of them come from privileged families who don't mind paying extortionate fees in the hope that their little darlings might get to play the Dane before the age of nineteen.

*Lions* was what you might call a team effort: written by me, starring Beasley School students and directed by Seth. Darryl Abrahams, the Head of Music and by far my favourite colleague at Beasley, was in charge of the sound-track. Darryl is about thirty-five, but looks a lot younger in the way that spherical, fleshy people often do. He's not really as wide as he is high, but he gives that impression sometimes. He comes from Barnsley and has a faint Yorkshire accent which he seems quite comfortable with, unlike Carmel-Marie White, the formidable Head of Dance at Beasley and *Lions*' choreographer. Carmel-Marie was born and grew up in Birmingham, but according to school rumours she paid

9

vast amounts of money for elocution lessons as a teenager and she now has an accent that makes most of the royal family sound like poor white trash. This wasn't my objection to her, however. What annoyed me about Carmel-Marie was her self-righteous attitude to almost any topic that came up, as though she, at some stage, had been the sole recipient of countless commandments direct from God himself. Spending time with her was like being locked in a Radio Four studio for a *Moral Maze* recording marathon. Hayley Douglas, Seth's long-suffering PA, was *Lions*' Assistant Director, which was Seth's euphemism for general slave. Seth is the sort of person who thinks that making a cup of coffee for him is 'a great way into the world of theatre, for a beginner'.

Normally the Youth Theatre is made up entirely of Beasley students. Tony is the exception. He isn't a student. He's only here to do *Lions* and I have to admit that I don't know why exactly or what he did before because when I first heard his name mentioned – before I'd seen him, before I knew I should pay close attention to every detail that related to him – I was hardly listening.

It was at the very first meeting of *Lions*' Creative Team – such was our collective name – on 3 July, just a few weeks after I'd started working at Beasley. I was feeling super-conscientious, keen to make the most of the first committee event at which I would be a real person rather than a minute-taking servant. Hayley Douglas was the one giving off dogsbody vibes on this occasion, sighing and staggering into the room laden with heavy bundles of paper. Despite her temporary title of Assistant Director, Seth still treated her as his slave, expecting her to arrange the coffees, take notes and do everything he didn't want to do himself. I liked Hayley, but I suspected her of wallowing a bit too enthusiastically in her martyrdom. She was a frail, tiny person with stringy almost white-blonde hair in the most boring style imaginable – a shoulder-length bob. I often wondered whether there was any link between the way she dressed and the way Seth treated her. Her cut-off grey denim shorts and grey vest top reminded me of a Victorian chimney-sweep.

I tried not to think too many disparaging thoughts about her, though, because if it weren't for her I would never have got my job at Beasley. Hayley's husband Phil works with my partner Alistair at Spartaco Systems, a computer programming consultancy in Bracknell, and if Phil hadn't mentioned the job vacancy to Alistair, I would probably still be an office skivvy at Piper Whalley Rooney.

I call Alistair my partner even though I hate the word, because 'boyfriend' makes it sound as though I met him outside the kebab shop last week, whereas in fact we've been living together for five years.

Anyway, there we all were at our first *Lions* meeting, or Storyboarding Session as Seth preferred to call it: Carmel-Marie, Seth, Darryl, Hayley, Rosie, Duane and me. Rosie and Duane were the Technical People and, as if to prove their hi-tech credentials, they were both extensively pierced. Rosie had elaborate metal structures through her ears, nose, eyebrow and lower lip, and Duane seemed to have undergone multiple drillings of the tongue. Every time he opened his mouth you saw flashes of gold and silver. On particularly hot days, as 3 July was, Duane wandered around bare-chested, looking like an ear-ring display board in a jeweller's shop window. Large gold rings dangled from both his nipples and he fiddled with them absent-mindedly in a way that made me feel faint.

As far as I was concerned, we'd met to discuss a few basics about the play so that I could go off and write the damn thing. Most of us were just about to go on holiday and rehearsals were due to start on 4 August. All I wanted was for the Creative Team to approve my plot idea so that I could make a start. Writing this play was the first major task of my new job and it meant a lot to me to do it well.

So when Hayley started the proceedings with a letter from Tony's social worker, I switched off, impatient that an irrelevance was getting in the way. It was too humid to concentrate on anything inessential. We'd opened the french windows in the imaginatively entitled French Window Room above Beasley's theatre to let some air in, but it didn't help much.

Filling in the blanks now, I assume what had happened was this: the school had received a letter from Tony's social worker some time ago, asking if he could participate in this year's Youth Theatre, probably saying it would be beneficial to integrate him into the community or some equivalent caring-profession phrase. Hayley had shown the letter to Seth, who had reminded her of the rule that only Beasley students could take part. The school sent a letter saying no, which prompted the social worker to write back and beg Seth to reconsider.

I'm so annoyed that I didn't listen more carefully. If I had, I might have learned a lot: why Tony had a social worker for one thing. I suppose at the time I didn't care, which shows how much can change in a couple of months. To think I willingly opted out of a conversation about Tony Lamb. Now I feel it's a bit of a cheek when any dialogue dares not to be about him. I feel affronted when Scottish Devolution is discussed on *Newsnight* and he isn't mentioned. If the Middle East Peace Process is debated on *World in Action* and Tony's name is omitted in favour of Yasser Arafat's, it strikes me as a monstrous injustice.

When I switched back on, the Creative Team were discussing sound engineering.

'If he wants to be a sound engineer, there are courses

he can do, aren't there?' asked Seth in his usual beseeching, please-give-me-the-answer-I-crave way. His squeaky voice made it hard to take him seriously.

'I don't think it'd be practical to have him hanging arind,' said Carmel-Marie. 'I mean, I feel sorry for him, but I just think it might do him more harm than good. He might feel left ite.' So successful had Carmel-Marie's elocution lessons been that she now sounded exactly like Celia Johnson in *Brief Encounter*.

'He lives in Slough,' said Rosie. 'How would he get here every day?'

'He could get a train, or maybe some days he could get a lift,' said Darryl. 'Lots of our students live near Slough, and they've mostly got cars.'

'Mm.' Seth nodded encouragingly. 'Except . . . I can't see them wanting to go and pick him up. It's a bit much to ask when they've got the show on their minds.' Seth had obviously been on a course called 'How to Disagree with Tact and Diplomacy'.

'Since when have you minded asking a bit much of people?' Hayley quipped. Seth looked at her blankly, then guffawed heartily to undermine the seriousness of her point. He often laughed uproariously when he didn't know what to say or do. It made him look faintly deformed; his whole face folded itself away behind an enormous, gaping mouth with rather too many teeth in it.

'Well, look,' said Darryl, 'I really don't mind. I mean, I'm doing all the music, so I'd be the one supervising him. I can show him a few things, give him a bit of an introduction to sound engineering. I mean, I'll probably be too busy to do loads with him . . .'

'You'll have enough to do writing the music,' said Seth.

'I don't mind, honestly. He can twiddle a few knobs on the amp – I can find stuff for him to do, show him how all my equipment works.'

13

'Arf, arf!' Seth chortled, elbowing Darryl in the ribs.

'Still, it's hardly going to lead to a career in sined engineering for him, is it?' said Carmel-Marie.

'From this letter' – Hayley waved it in the air as if to remind us of its existence, not to mention her own – 'I get the impression that the social worker just wants him to be involved in something he might enjoy. I don't think she's expecting it to lead directly to a career.'

'It's fine by me.' Darryl shrugged. One of his best qualities is that he's a pacifier rather than an agitator; not a drip like Hayley, but genuinely laid-back.

'Are you sure, Darryl?' Seth asked portentously. 'I mean, you're the one who counts most here. If you're for it, that's good enough for me.'

'Oh, thank you very much!' Carmel-Marie snapped enthusiastically, never happier than when she had something to object to.

'Well, he's the one who'll have to deal with this . . . what's his name?' Seth snatched the letter from Hayley's hand. '. . . Tony Lamb.'

If it hadn't been for Darryl, whose good nature eventually triumphed over Seth's and Carmel-Marie's protests, I would never have met Tony. No wonder I like Darryl so much. I more than like him; I regard him as a Bearer of Extreme GLOW. What I mean by this, Cat As, Es and any discerning Ds who have decided, after a free and independent thought process, to join our little posse, is that when you're madly in love with someone, anyone who is connected to them, or, even better, who links you to them, acquires a special GLOW. Unless that person is an obstacle to your love; obstacles take on an Anti-GLOW.

Okay, think of the person you love (loved, Cat Es. Cat Ds, improvise). How stupid of me to say 'think of them'. You think about them all the time, naturally. Now, how did you meet that person? Was there a particular mutual acquaintance who introduced you or brought you together, like Darryl in the case of me and Tony? If so, they have the biggest GLOW of all, the kind that can be described as Linking or Introductory GLOW.

I should define GLOW, in case anyone is confused. Perhaps I should call it the Tony Lamb GLOW, since it was Tony who inspired me to invent the term, or just the Lamb GLOW.

It is an aura, a positive energy field, that someone with whom you are not in love acquires by virtue of their connection with someone with whom you are in love, or occasions on which you felt love very strongly.

How do you know when someone's got the GLOW? I know Darryl's got it because when I think about him or speak to him, I feel a fraction – maybe a thousandth – of the total Tony Lamb feeling. People with GLOW have a sort of orangeness about them, or at least that's how it seems to me. Maybe your GLOW is pink or blue or gold.

Places can have the GLOW. The Seth Beasley School, *Lions* and its entire cast and technical crew (except those obstacles with Anti-GLOW to whom I'll introduce you in due course), Slough, Berkshire – all these things have it.

I've just realised what I meant when I said in chapter one that this will be the best novel ever written. It will be, because it has the Tony Lamb GLOW. I'm calling it a novel which, strictly speaking, is inaccurate when the story I'm telling is true. I read an article in the *TLS* last week about how fiction is out these days and faction, fact recounted in the manner of fiction, is in. The writer of the article regretted this development and lamented the inability of contemporary writers to make things up. I could make things up if I wanted to, write about characters who don't exist outside my imagination, but the world needs a book about Tony Lamb. It's crying out for one. You know when it rains? Well, what do you think that means?

The woman who wrote the *TLS* article (I only

discovered it by accident after reading one of Seth's theatre reviews which, as usual, was more about him than the play he had seen) has never met Tony Lamb. If she had, she would understand my insistence upon fact.

This GLOW business raises an interesting point about the hypothetical Martin Amis/Iris Murdoch/Jonathan Coe situation. If they each wrote a book about Tony but weren't in love with him then their books would contain Tony but not the Tony GLOW. In which case, mine would probably still be the best, unless their good writing upstaged my GLOW factor. But, you see, this is my whole point: however great literature is, love is better. Good books are good books, but the GLOW is transcendent. The GLOW is power.

# Chapter Three

## The First Day of Rehearsals

I first saw Tony on Monday 4 August, the first day of *Lions* rehearsals. We were in the drama studio in the basement beneath the theatre, working right under the space where the play would eventually be performed.

The drama studio made up for its lack of light and windows by having an efficient air-conditioning system, without which the whole company would undoubtedly have melted to death. It was a large, almost circular room with a dusty wooden floor, various chairs and tables scattered around, and one wall that was made up entirely of mirrors.

I arrived late, although not as late as Darryl, who seemed congenitally incapable of getting out of bed before 10 a.m. I am a naturally punctual person and my lateness was a protest rather than an accident. I wasn't at all happy on the morning of Monday 4 August because we had neither a script nor a plot. Don't worry, I'll explain later. You're probably thinking how can rehearsals for a play start without the play itself? That was exactly what I was thinking but, trust me, it can and did happen.

I walked into the drama studio tentatively, nervous of wading into a sea of thirty-odd strange faces. This was the first time I'd seen any students since the beginning of the summer holidays and, as I had only started at Beasley two weeks before the end of the

17

previous term, I hadn't really had a chance to get to know any of them properly.

Everyone was in skimpy shorts and T-shirts. It was too hot to worry about what sort of clothes suited you; in weather like this comfort triumphed over vanity. I remember being vaguely aware that one person only was wearing a long-sleeved shirt and jeans, and wondering whether he had bad circulation.

Seth's plan, although he didn't quite put it like this, was to distract the Youth Theatre members with various pretentious and pointless ice-breaking activities for as long as it took the Creative Team to come up with the play, which is why at 10 a.m. the entire company – with the exception of Darryl who had yet to arrive – was standing in a big circle, about to play the 'Name Game'.

'This is a great way to get to know each other.' Seth beamed, folding his face up behind his teeth in what he thought was his best reassuring smile.

The game involved looking at someone, saying their name loudly so that everyone could hear, and then swapping places with them in the circle. It sounded like this:

'Phoebe!'
'Yes! Carmel-Marie!'
'Yes! Oliver!'
'Yes! Ed!'
'Yes! Stella!'
'Yes! Seth!'

And it looked like people exchanging positions in a large ring, two at a time. After we'd played for almost half an hour, I still couldn't remember any names except for Phoebe's. Phoebe was quite unusually attractive, tall and leggy with short blonde curly hair, bright-blue eyes and an angelic smile, which is probably why she stuck in my mind.

I know it sounds strange, but I didn't notice Tony then. When I describe him you'll see why it's so

18

unbelievable that I failed to register the face that topped the jeans and long-sleeved shirt. The only possible explanation I can offer is that I was worried about the lack-of-play crisis we were all facing and my apparent inability to learn the names of the people with whom I'd be working for the next four weeks.

Carmel-Marie White, her small pointy breasts poking out of a mauve lycra boob-tube, barked her way through the game, shouting a name and marching towards the relevant person like a sergeant major on barracks duty. Having worked at Beasley for nearly four years, she knew exactly what to bark and where to march, whereas I kept having to change direction mid-crossing, realising that the person I was walking optimistically towards was not the owner of the name I'd shouted. The students must have thought I was geometrically dyslexic.

Further humiliation followed in the form of another barrier-breaking game which Seth called 'Person to Person'.

'Ankle to knee.' He grinned toothily and everybody would have to rush up to someone nearby and put their ankle on that person's knee. 'Good. Now, keeping that contact . . . keeping that contact . . . wrist to shoulder. Good.' Seth nodded significantly, as if he could see barriers tumbling down in their thousands. In fact, what he could see was thirty or so highly embarrassed people, each desperately trying not to fall over in a clumsy heap or look too ridiculous with their feet on somebody else's back and their ears resting on strange shins. The tension increased as Seth started to get experimental, but thankfully he went no further than buttock to abdomen.

I didn't touch Tony, but somebody must have done, must have put his or her neck on Tony's hip or elbow on his knee. It'll be hands to throat if I ever find out who it was.

19

I first noticed Tony on the next day, the Tuesday, when we still had no play. The Creative Team had had a huge argument on the Monday evening about (a) the plot, (b) the characters and (c) how to deal with our disagreements in areas (a) and (b). Nothing had been resolved, so at ten o'clock on Tuesday morning the company in its entirety was lying on the dusty studio floor while Seth told us to pretend that our bodies were filled with a multicoloured liquid. We were instructed to imagine the liquid draining in and out of each limb. This was supposed to relax us. A few people hinted that they'd rather remain tense than get their clothes filthy, but the folly of this attitude was revealed to them when Seth said, with a dismissive flourish of his hand, 'This is just the way I direct, okay?'

At lunch-time the Creative Team went to the Wheatsheaf pub in Windsor to eat and hold yet another *Lions* summit. The Wheatsheaf is a characterless place that has only extreme proximity to Beasley in its favour. It always seems to be empty and the food is okay, but would be considerably more appetising if it were ever hot.

Much tension was aired as we ate our lukewarm roast beef and Yorkshire pudding, except for Carmel-Marie who ate lukewarm vegetarian lasagne in a manner that conveyed high ethical sensitivity. Carmel-Marie was not only against meat, she was against some vegetables too. Ever since the *Guardian* had reported a link between Peaker Frozen Foods and the deaths of thousands of Guatemalan babies – although Carmel-Marie couldn't remember precisely what the alleged link was – she had boycotted Peaker carrots and Peaker peas with a vengeance. 'Are you quite sure there are no Peaker products in this dish?' she interrogated the Wheatsheaf waitress. 'Because if there are I'd rather go withite food altogether.'

We were all feeling snappy and argumentative. We

knew we had to mention the play soon, otherwise the Youth Theatre members would get suspicious. Seth suggested that we divide them into small groups, tell them what we'd got so far and let them improvise the rest. One Creative Team person would be assigned to each group and at the end of the day we would reassemble to compare notes (in other words yell at each other dismissively), pick what we liked best from the day's improvisations and cobble a plot/script out of it.

'But we haven't got anything so far,' I protested. 'We haven't even got anything for them to improvise about.'

'We should have started with a script.' Carmel-Marie pursed her lips, luxuriating in a further opportunity for disapproval. 'Putting a show on is hard enough even with a script. Withite one it's impossible!'

I nodded, as this was my precise feeling on the matter, although agreeing with Carmel-Marie always made me feel slightly uneasy, as if I had just joined a sinister moral majority and was about to go off on an expedition to a local prison, to bash the sides of vans coming in and out that might contain paedophiles.

'We've got the title.' Seth beamed in a feeble attempt to boost morale. He was like a little boy; he hated the thought that anyone might dislike him or be annoyed with him. Fortunately for his ego, he was rarely aware of anyone's feelings except his own. '*Lions After Slumber*, great title. And it's going to be a great show.'

We did indeed have the title. The copy for the school's glossy theatre brochure had had to be in by 4 June, before I even started at Beasley. Seth, who was reading Shelley at the time, made the unilateral decision to call the play *Lions After Slumber*, a quote from 'The Masque of Anarchy'. This had been the cause of some tension, in that nobody but Seth liked it as a title. All this was forgotten by the time rehearsals started, however. There was so much new tension to accommodate that we had to let go of our earlier grievances.

'We've also got the blurb in the brochure,' Seth went on. You've guessed it – same deadline.

'But that's so little for them to go on.' Hayley sighed deeply, as if to assert that she was the main sufferer here and none of us could hope to understand.

'We could tell them all our individual ideas and see which ones they prefer,' Seth suggested.

'What, sort of like Pick Your Favourite Plot?' Darryl chuckled. Less of a worrier than the rest of us, he was thoroughly enjoying the absurdity of our predicament.

'We can't tell them we're unable to agree on anything,' said Carmel-Marie impatiently. 'It's so unprofessional.' And so it went on until we left the Wheatsheaf, having decided to divide the students up, but not what to do with them after that.

By miraculous coincidence I was assigned to the group that contained Tony. It also contained Ed Fewster, Stella Nettleton, Oliver Wild and Trudi Hicks, but I only saw Tony. Obviously I saw the others eventually and I'll describe them in a minute, but that was how it felt at the time.

Tony was sitting directly opposite me in our little circle. And, as they say, that was it. I didn't know it was it, because at that stage I was in severe denial, but now, looking back, I can identify that moment as being the beginning of my love for Tony. My immediate thought was, 'Why does somebody so beautiful need a social worker?' I know; it doesn't stand up to close scrutiny.

He didn't say a word all afternoon. While the others were plotting and characterising away, he sat in shy silence, smiling his cardiac-arresting smile whenever anyone said anything funny, but not speaking even once.

Often when people are very quiet you assume they're boring, don't you? Tony wasn't boring. Speech simply

22

wasn't his chosen medium, his accessory of preference. In fact, now that I come to think of it, a lot of people rely far too heavily on words. I'm guiltier than most in that department. I don't know what Tony relied on – possibly being the most beautiful person ever to walk the earth. It's hard to know things about non-word people.

Stella and Trudi, the two girls in my group, kept staring at Tony, then looking away again quickly, as if to check he was still there, that he wasn't some heavenly mirage, liable to vanish at any minute. Even at that stage I was subconsciously assessing the competition. Not much from either of these two, I thought. Stella was fat, with tightly curled brown hair that fell around her face in clumps. She wore thick-lensed glasses that plagiarised those of Buddy Holly and Dame Edna Everage in equal measures. Her sensible shorts and T-shirt made her look as if she were about to undertake some fieldwork for a Duke of Edinburgh Award. Trudi gave the impression of being colourless and shapeless, and had so much gel on her hair that she looked as if she'd been dipped in an oil-slick.

Oblivious to Tony-temptation, Ed and Oliver did most of the talking. Ed had the body of a rugby player, but spoke with all the melodrama of a would-be actor. 'We must free our imaginations!' he declared earnestly, flicking back his wavy shoulder-length hair. 'We need to create a whole new world.'

'Yes, but . . .' Oliver looked at me hopefully '. . . we need some guidance, you know, something to go on.' Apart from Tony, Oliver was probably the most attractive male Youth Theatre member. His confident personality contributed to this as much as his looks, and that was leaving aside his immensely wealthy family and the swimming-pool in his back garden. He reminded me of the Fonz from the television programme *Happy Days*.

23

I hardly heard him speak as I stared with barely concealed lust at Tony's legs, arms, face, hair, smile, eyes, finger-nails.

I need to describe all these, don't I? Eyes, finger-nails, etc. I'm reluctant to do it now, though, because this chapter has already gone on for seven pages and I'm aware that there's this annoying concept of pace.

Earlier on I said I didn't care about writing well in the literary sense, only about love, but I must admit I've started to want this book to be good. Otherwise it won't get published, unless there's a publisher enlightened enough to publish it solely for its Tony Lamb content.

So to pacify the Pace God I'm going to move on with some action and come back to the various facets of Tony later.

A bit ago I said that when you're madly in love with someone you think about them all the time. That's only half true. They're always part of your consciousness, yes, circling and colouring your awareness, but direct, channelled thought – you've got to go easy on that, haven't you? Cat As?

If I bring Tony to the front of my mind and send my beams of concentration straight at him for more than about five minutes, I risk ending up attached to a saline drip or gibbering in a strait-jacket.

# Chapter Four

## The Darryl–Seth–Natasha Situation

My Tony-denial ended on Thursday 21 August, the day Darryl burst into my office in a state of great alarm. His unexpected tumbling in, and what followed indirectly and contingently from it, brought home to me the full extent of my adoration for Tony. Now it seems unlikely – almost impossible, in fact – that it took so long for me to realise that I worshipped Tony. I had spent nearly three weeks rehearsing with him, seeing him every day. I knew I felt something for him, but I had somehow avoided defining it and therefore managed to dodge it. Perhaps my subconscious had been keeping my emotions under control, knowing that, as I lived with Alistair, any awareness of extreme feelings of love for someone else was bound to be a touch problematic.

The twenty-first of August was a much-needed day off from *Lions* rehearsals. I was in my office on Beasley's ground-floor west corridor, shuffling a handful of BUPA forms on my leather-topped desk and admiring my luxurious surroundings as I often do. As there were no rehearsals today I could have stayed at home, but the novelty of having a room all to myself still hadn't worn off. I was determined to spend as much time there as I could, admiring the pale yellow wallpaper, using my new Power Paq computer and laser printer, sitting in one of my three beige Parker knoll armchairs drinking coffee beside my round teak coffee table. This was my

25

idea of heaven. It isn't any more – I now have a revised idea of heaven – but at the time it was. I had escaped from the sort of environment where people put name tags on their hole-punchers to make sure other people don't use them illicitly to a place where hole-punchers are used primarily as props in plays.

Shortly before Darryl burst in looking like a persecuted tomato, I was considering whether to join the School's BUPA Premier Plus Scheme and looking guiltily at the framed photo of Alistair on my mahogany bookshelf. After five years of living with him, I knew only too well what Alistair thought about private health and it was because of this that the BUPA leaflets had been lying around on my desk since I started working here in June. Every time I convinced myself that it would be sheer insanity not to take advantage of the school's generous offer of free BUPA cover for its staff, I would catch a glimpse of Alistair's trusting blue eyes behind his tortoise-shell glasses and doubt would paralyse me once again.

I was reading about the virtues of BUPA for probably the fiftieth time when Darryl came crashing through my door. His round face was bright red and beaded with sweat, and the lenses of his round wire-rimmed glasses were steamed up so severely that I couldn't see his eyes. Even his scalp seemed to be sweating through its crew-cut. My bookshelf, desk and coffee table shook with the impact of his entry. I automatically reached over to my small tape player and pressed the off switch. Darryl had been known to make disparaging comments about my taste in music and I didn't want him to hear that I was listening to *Women in Country II*.

'Lock the door,' he barked at me. His plump body and flushed face reminded me of the Spacehopper I used to have when I was little. Today he was wearing red baggy shorts, which made his legs look particularly stubby. As well as being Head of Music at Beasley he owns a record label called The Best Don't Mess and plays drums for Qua, an ambient house band. I have no idea what that means. Their music sounds tuneless to me, but I have never told Darryl this.

'What's wrong?' I asked, locking the door as instructed.

'Just about everything!' he panted, taking off his glasses to wipe them with the edge of his creased cotton T-shirt. His Yorkshire accent sounded more pronounced than usual today. 'I don't know what to do, you probably won't even believe me, and no one else would, that's if I even . . .'

'Hang on!' I stopped him. 'Sit down. Calm down. Have a drink. Coffee?'

'I don't want anything.'

'What's going on? Tell me slowly.' I had never seen him so worked up before. Normally he exudes an atmosphere of reassuring jollity.

He fell into one of my armchairs, which creaked in protest. 'Close the window,' he ordered. I was about to object, since this August was the hottest I could remember and I was keen to get as much air as possible, but Darryl looked so petrified that I did as I was told without arguing. While he finished cleaning his glasses and caught his breath I looked at his eyes. They were swollen and bloodshot, as if he had hardly slept.

'I went round to Seth and Natasha's the night before last, right?' he wheezed. I nodded. Natasha Leaf was Seth Beasley's ginger-haired and almost anorexic wife, who kept her own name and had vast amounts of inherited money. I had heard rumours that Natasha had bought Seth the school as a wedding present, but I didn't know whether they were true. She was always hosting lavish dinner parties at which, according to school legend, she never ate anything. I had been preparing Alistair for the inevitable invitation. Our turn hadn't come yet, but I knew it would. Alistair

27

needs to be prepared for encounters with people he doesn't know. He loves socialising with people he knows and likes, but he hates to meet anyone new. I try to point out that the people he now knows and likes were once new people he met, but strangely this doesn't work.

Seth and Natasha seemed to invite Darryl more frequently than anyone else, perhaps because he was single and they felt he needed looking after.

'I knew something was wrong as soon as I got there.' Darryl winced at the memory. 'They were both . . . dressed oddly.'

'Oddly how?' I asked. I always want to know every little detail. I am like my mother in this respect. She insists on knowing what people were wearing, what their hair was like, what food was eaten. My dad's the opposite. So reluctant is he to hear unnecessary words that even close family members don't get to talk freely to him any more. If you want to say something to my dad, you have first to submit a proposal for speaking. You have to say, 'Dad, can I tell you about my first day at the Seth Beasley School?' He then says, 'Yes, but I want the short version not the long version, and stick to the essentials, please.'

'Natasha had her hair all coiled up in a big pile on her head,' Darryl went on. 'She was wearing a clingy black dress, you know, sort of strappy and revealing.' Now I winced too, imagining her bare shoulders jutting sharply into mid-air like isosceles triangles. 'And Seth was wearing a horrible maroon and white pin-striped suit. He looked ridiculous, like a public schoolboy on a day trip.' Darryl shook his head suddenly in an attempt to banish the image. 'I couldn't understand it,' he said. 'I've been round to their house loads of times and they've never dressed so formally before. The lights were . . . dimmer than usual as well, as if they were trying to create an atmosphere.'

'Yeah?' I leaned forward with interest, still uncertain as to why Darryl had got into such a state. It had to be more than Natasha's jutting bones and Seth's silly suit, surely.

'All through dinner they both sort of . . . leered at me. That's the only word that describes what they did. They leered. I nearly asked them what was going on a few times, but I stopped myself. I mean, it would have sounded stupid and I had no proof. Nothing had really happened. Yet.'

'Go on,' I urged.

'When we'd finished dinner Seth piled up the dirty plates and took them into the kitchen. The minute he left the room . . .' Darryl tailed off and sighed heavily. 'Oh God! I still can't believe this happened. Natasha, without saying anything, walks around to my side of the table and comes and stands right in front of me. I'm just sitting there thinking what the fuck's going on. I mean, her pelvis is right in front of my chin.' He grimaced, running his hands over his lower jaw. 'Suddenly she unhooks the straps from her shoulders and her dress falls to the floor!'

'She what?' I gawped at him in amazement.

'So she's standing in front of me,' Darryl went on in a low monotone, like a patient under hypnosis forced to recall a repressed trauma, 'wearing nothing but a lacy black . . . sort of G-string. She looked hideous, like a hunger-striker turned prostitute. It turned my stomach. Then she pulled the lacy contraption down and put her . . . put her . . .' His mouth opened and closed desperately, but no sound came out.

I nodded understandingly, keen for him to continue. If he waited until an embarrassment-free word came to mind we'd be here for ever.

'She put her . . . you know . . . right in front of my face, like, balanced on the end of my nose!' Darryl's glasses began to steam up again and he rubbed his nose frantically. 'It was a nightmare!'

'What did you do?' I asked.

'Nothing! I just sat there for what seemed like a decade, although it was probably only about five seconds, and all the time, there it was, on the end of my nose . . . all . . . orange! I know I should have moved or pushed her away but I was so scared.'

'I'm not surprised,' I said, imagining how I would feel if I were attacked by a naked flame-haired anorexic. 'I've always found Natasha a bit intimidating.'

'Yeah, well, this went way beyond intimidating. Anyway, then, out of the corner of my eye – and I can see this now, I remember it like a cinematic moment – I saw the door slowly edging open and I knew Seth was coming in. Even then I didn't move. It was like I was paralysed by fear. I remember thinking oh fuck, now Seth'll think I've agreed to this and I'll get the sack. His head appeared at the side of the door and . . . sort of lolled there like a huge, prickly wart.' I couldn't help laughing at this, keen as I was to hear the rest of the story. Each strand of Seth's coarse black hair seemed to stick out vertically from his scalp as if he'd recently had an electric shock and his head was several sizes too big for his short, slender body. Darryl's description of it as a huge prickly wart wasn't too far from the mark.

'Don't laugh.' His voice quivered. 'It was awful! Do you know what he did? He smiled, as though he had expected this all along. No, more than that, as if he'd planned it. I tell you, my blood went cold, it turned to fucking ice. It was sinister. It was gruesome. And then Natasha moved even closer. I felt really sick. I thought, I'm going to throw up all over this woman's private parts.'

'I can't . . . Darryl, I can't believe it!' I murmured. Why do we say this precisely when we do believe what we have been told?

'I pushed my head as far back as I could, to get away

30

from her. I was practically suffocating. Some of her . . . hair had got into my mouth.'

'Oh, Jesus!' I felt nauseous. So did Darryl, by the look of him. His round face had turned from red to pale yellow, matching my office wallpaper.

'It gets worse.' He lowered his voice to a whisper. 'Seth began to walk slowly towards me, undoing his belt and fly. His stupid pin-striped trousers fell down and underneath . . . underneath . . . can I have a glass of water?'

I ran over to the little basin in the corner of my room and filled one of my two mugs with lukewarm water. 'Here you are.' I thrust it at Darryl. 'Underneath?' I prompted.

'He was wearing a gold spandex posing pouch, like some sort of . . . stripper.'

'Oh my God!' I gasped. I was really shocked now. I had always suspected Natasha was a bit strange, although I had underestimated the extent of her irregularity, but Seth Beasley, the director of a nationally renowned school, Seth Beasley who had once been described in the *Windsor Gazette* as a genius . . . Geniuses surely were not supposed to brandish their knobs at the dinner-table.

'Anyway, that was as much as I could take,' poor Darryl went on breathlessly in between gulps of water. 'I leaped out of my chair and ran away. Seth lurched over to try and stop me but his feet got tangled up in his trousers and he fell over. He knocked the table over and Natasha started wailing and shrieking. I think she may even have kicked him. For a second it seemed as though they'd forgotten I was there. Seth's thigh was bleeding and Natasha was sort of . . . stroking the broken table. I legged it out the door and into my car.'

'So you got away?' I nodded eagerly.

'I was too nervous to drive!' Darryl almost sobbed. 'I couldn't even get the key in the ignition, my fingers

31

were shaking so much. By the time I'd got it in, Seth and Natasha had followed me outside. They were banging on the car windows, shouting about how it was all a misunderstanding. And Seth's knob was hanging out . . .'

'No! In the street?'

'It was dark, wasn't it? It was out, I'm telling you, it was flapping against my car window like a raw sausage! Natasha was in a heap on the pavement behind him . . . wailing, wearing nothing but the G-string.'

'Oh my God,' I said. Gold posing pouches, black lacy G-strings – had Seth and Natasha been on a day trip to a sex shop? I felt a sudden rush of protective sympathy for Darryl. He was my closest friend among the Beasley staff and I hated to see him so miserable. I wished I could press a button and transform him back to his jokey and jovial former self.

'What happened next was even worse in a way,' he said quietly.

'You mean there's more?' My mind snapped back into focus.

'As soon as I got home, they started phoning me. I kept telling them to get lost and leave me alone but they just rang and rang. Twenty, thirty times. I took the phone off the hook eventually. Then they started ringing me on my mobile, so I switched that off too. I couldn't sleep, I was too freaked out. At about four in the morning I got up to get a glass of water and put the phone back on the hook and that minute, that very minute, the fucker started ringing!'

'Not them again?'

'Yes! They'd been trying all night! The two of them had sat up all night dialling my engaged tone until 4 a.m. when they finally struck lucky! I just slammed the phone down and left it off the hook all night after that. When I drew my curtains the next morning, Natasha was standing on the pavement opposite my house, looking up at my bedroom window. As soon as she saw me she started waving and gesturing for me to open the door. I drew the curtains again and made sure all the windows and doors were locked. It was ridiculous. I was like a prisoner in my own house. The bitch stayed there all fucking day, and Seth joined her in the evening. They stayed there till after midnight, knocking on the door, shouting through the letter-box. I didn't know what to do. At about quarter past midnight they went home and started ringing me again. All night, every time I replaced the receiver.'

'You should phone the police,' I said firmly. 'That's harassment. Not to mention the earlier sexual assault.' Darryl's anger was contagious. A slow rage was taking possession of my body. How dare anyone do this to one of my friends?

At that moment there was a knock at my door that sounded like a tap-dance from a Broadway musical: da-da, da-da-da, DA! There was only one person who knocked like that. Darryl's face turned even paler and assumed an expression of cartoon-like exaggeration which, if I had translated correctly, meant 'Say nothing and on no account open the door.'

'Belinda? Are you in there?' Seth's slightly squeaky West-Country accent wafted feebly under the door. Darryl and I sat in silence until we heard his departing footsteps.

'See what I mean?' said Darryl grimly. 'He's never going to leave me alone.'

'We don't know what he wanted,' I pointed out.

'I know what he wanted. He wanted to ask you if you'd seen me. I'm telling you, he's after me and he's not going to let it go.'

'They probably want to make sure you won't say anything. You know how image-conscious they are.'

'They should have thought of that before!'

'Go to the police, Darryl,' I urged.

'I've done better than that.' He smiled for the first time that morning, although it was a bitter, calculated smile, not the spontaneous Spacehopper smile I was used to. 'I've made an appointment with my solicitor. I'm seeing him at eleven.' He looked at his watch.

I nodded, frowning. I was trying to remould my image of Seth and Natasha. To think I had once admired them both so much. Natasha was a Doctor of Philosophy, as she never tired of announcing to the world. When I was a secretary, I used to think people with PhDs were in a class above the rest of us. I never considered the possibility that maladjusted perverts might be eligible for doctorates.

'We'll laugh about it one day.' I grinned, pleased to be able to bury a long-standing inferiority complex.

'You're laughing about it now,' Darryl pointed out.

'What about *Lions*?' I asked, suddenly realising that the peculiar tale I'd just heard had certain practical implications. 'The tech run's on Monday and the dress rehearsal's on Tuesday,' I said. 'Can you work with Seth after this?' I knew how infuriating it could be to work with people you disliked. I was having my own problems at the moment with Carmel-Marie. Four days earlier she had caught me perusing my BUPA leaflets and accused me of being an élitist queue-jumper. She had treated me frostily at rehearsals ever since. I couldn't believe someone who had had years of elocution lessons to obliterate all traces of her natural Brummie accent had the nerve to accuse other people of élitism.

'I haven't got much choice.' Darryl sighed. 'I can put up with him at work as long as my solicitor can persuade him to keep away the rest of the time.'

'Do you think I should join the school's BUPA scheme?' I asked, thinking a change of subject might help Darryl to put his problem into perspective.

34

'What?' he said distractedly, wiping the lenses of his glasses again. I repeated the question.

'It's what you think that matters,' said Darryl, looking over his shoulder towards the door as though he were expecting to hear Seth's Broadway knock again.

'Alistair is dead against it,' I said. 'Which is a shame because you can also get free BUPA cover for your spouse. Alistair probably wouldn't count, though, since we're not married.'

'So it doesn't affect him,' said Darryl impatiently. 'Do what you want and don't tell him. Or tell him, and he'll just have to accept that your principles are different from his.'

Aha! Darryl had hit upon what I see as the main problem with people who have principles. They often don't accept that other people have different opinions. In my experience they dismiss those opinions as wrong and sometimes get cross rather than simply agreeing to differ. Alistair would certainly do this in a BUPA argument situation, just as Carmel-Marie had. Carmel-Marie has more principles than me, as well as more Christian names. I didn't go into this with Darryl though, because his keenness to exit the building was becoming more evident by the second. A tide of redness was seeping upwards from his chin to his forehead.

'Go on then, make your escape,' I said.

'Could you just check Seth isn't lurking?' Darryl bit his lip anxiously.

I turned the key, opening the door as quietly as I could, and gradually inched my head out. Darryl's office was three along from mine on the ground-floor corridor and Seth was right outside it. Fortunately he had his back to me. He was slumped diagonally against the wall as if he had collapsed into it, as if without it he would have tumbled to the ground. His large prickle-covered head lolled to and fro, like the heads of people who fall asleep on trains.

I was on the point of retreating into my office and breaking the bad news to Darryl when, a few feet to my left, Carmel-Marie's door opened. I forgot to say that my office has one drawback: it is right next to hers. The noise seemed to rouse Seth from his catatonic state and he scuttled off down the corridor.

Then something awful happened. A fraction of a second later Tony Lamb emerged from Carmel-Marie's room and looked around guiltily, as if to make sure no one had seen him. He saw me before I had a chance to duck back into my office and his incredibly beautiful face turned rose-pink. There we were, face to face, like the weather man and woman from *Bagpuss*, popping out of our little holes at exactly the same time. I staggered back into my room, slamming the door after me. My heart was doing some major pole-vaulting activities. It usually got a bit acrobatic when Tony Lamb was around, but nothing so severe as the Olympic feats it was now performing. What had he been doing with Carmel-Marie? Why had he blushed so pinkly? There could only be one reason. That bitch! That hyphenated bitch. At that moment, Carmel-Marie became Chief Obstacle with Anti-GLOW as far as I was concerned.

'Well?' said Darryl. 'What's wrong? Is he there?'

'No,' I moaned. 'He was, but he's gone. You should go now. He may well come back in a minute.' Darryl didn't seem to notice how distracted I was, which was understandable given his own situation.

'Open your window, I'll climb out,' he said. 'I can't risk corridors. What was I thinking of? Seth's probably rigged up a few covered manholes for me to fall into.'

I heaved up the bottom half of my sash window. Darryl squeezed his rotund form through the small rectangle of space and tumbled out the other side, bouncing away determinedly in true Spacehopper fashion. He wasn't someone who moved quickly by choice and his little legs looked as if they were on fast-forward.

I sat down in the warm dent he had made in my armchair and thought about my Tony Lamb problem. Until now I hadn't admitted to myself that I had a Tony Lamb problem. There was no avoiding it now, though. The fact that I suddenly wanted to beat Carmel-Marie White to a pulp had to mean something, didn't it? Clearly my feelings for Tony were not under control as I had naïvely hoped. Thank God Darryl didn't notice anything, I thought. If he'd asked, it would all have come pouring out and I didn't want that. I needed to sit down and think this through, decide what Tony Lamb attitude I wanted to project to the public.

# Chapter Five

## The Seth–Natasha–Darryl Situation Side Two

Shortly after Darryl squeezed himself inelegantly through my window, there was another da-da, da-da-da, DA! knock on my door. I nearly didn't hear it because I was too busy marching around my office in agitation, trying to come to terms with the horror – there was no other way of describing it – I had witnessed. I felt as if I were about to choke, as if Anti-GLOW were crushing my windpipe. After several follow-up knocks, I approached the door tentatively, praying it might be Tony, come to explain how what I had just seen was all a big misunderstanding, even though I knew it wasn't.

I opened the door and found Seth outside in the corridor, wearing last year's Youth Theatre T-shirt which sported the words '*Bladerunner* directed by Seth Beasley'. He was looking up at the ceiling and whistling, as though he just happened to be standing there. Seth is so image-conscious that he is reluctant ever to give the impression that he has stooped so low as to seek you out deliberately. He takes great pains to imply that his contact with other people is purely accidental.

After going through the usual rigmarole of pretending suddenly to notice I was there, he asked me, as Darryl had predicted he would, whether I had seen Darryl. I could have said no but I didn't. I decided in a

38

millisecond of psychological insight that it would be more interesting to see Seth's reaction to the news that I had seen Darryl rather than to the lie that I hadn't. I felt suddenly grateful for Seth's arrival because it forced me to think about something other than Tony and Carmel-Marie. 'He popped into my office briefly this morning,' I said casually. Seth made a strange choking noise, which he tried to disguise by clearing his throat. His hair looked more shocked than usual and his eyes darted around my office, reluctant to settle. Seth has the most fickle eyeballs of anyone I have ever known. He is unable to look in any one direction for more than a few seconds and, as a result, talking to him can be very disconcerting. You get to the third word of your sentence and all of a sudden he's looking over your shoulder or past your left thigh and you wonder whether he's spotted someone far more fascinating in the distance. Today he was worse than usual, shifting focus more often than the average kaleidoscope.

'Is something wrong?' I asked. I'd better admit it now – I was rather enjoying this. I knew the whole thing was awful for Darryl, but for myself I was glad to have such a dramatic distraction from my Tony-and-Carmel-Marie (up a tree, K–I–S–S–I–N–G) misery-cum-rage. They had to be having an affair; there was no other explanation for what I'd seen, which made Carmel-Marie the biggest hypocrite of all time. I'll explain why later.

'I, er, just wanted a word with him. The thing is, there's been a bit of a misunderstanding.' Seth plonked his little body down on one of my comfy chairs and put his oversized head in his hands, groaning slightly. I settled in for Side Two of the Darryl–Seth–Natasha story. I love hearing Side Two of a story after I've heard Side One, don't you? The suspense is great, like in the days before CDs when you bought a new album.

39

However good Side One is, Side Two may be better.

'Darryl came round to our house for dinner the other night,' Seth began, transferring his troubled gaze from me to my bookshelf when he got to the word 'dinner'. 'Natasha ... flirted with him a bit. You know what she's like, she always flirts.' At this point he seemed to be addressing my telephone. I felt like waving and shouting, 'I'm over here!'

'Does she?' I asked. I wouldn't have described what Natasha always did as flirting. I would have described it as telling you how important and wonderful she is at every opportunity while trying to make this behaviour look natural rather than contrived. I'd only met her three or four times at Beasley-related events, but on each occasion she had emphasised how successful and clever she was, that she was one of only two female lecturers in Reading University's Philosophy Department. Natasha knew she couldn't say straight out, 'I'm incredibly bright with an amazing career.' That would appear boastful. Instead, she cunningly related other people's comments in which her all-round brilliance was mentioned, telling me how attractive her postman found her and about the visitor to one of her seminars who had foolishly mistaken her for a secretary, only to be told by the Head of Department that 'Dr Leaf is an eminent scholar in her field'.

I didn't join in her laughter at the foolish dolt who had so heinously erred. I told her stiffly that I had been a secretary for eight years and walked away, leaving her alone under the spotlight of her own ego.

Remembering this made me suddenly sure that Side Two of the story was going to be considerably less engaging than Side One.

'Perhaps she doesn't flirt with you.' Seth's eyes landed on me briefly before flitting off in search of a better view. 'But with men she always flirts. And she's always had a soft spot for Darryl, we both have.'

'I'm sure Darryl can handle a bit of flirting,' I said. 'What was the misunderstanding?'

'Well, half-way through dinner, Darryl just got up and left without saying a word to either of us. I was about to serve up the Creme Brulée and he just . . . left!'

'Why? What happened to make him do that?'

'Absolutely nothing!' Seth's eyeballs lurched evasively. 'I swear, nothing!'

'But a minute ago you said Natasha was flirting with him,' I reminded him. I was clearly going to have to provide the continuity in this dialogue. Seth is not a believer in consistency. He says whatever is least likely to get him into trouble at any given time and feels no loyalty to his own words after they exit his mouth. He is like a parent who believes his responsibility for his children ends when they leave home, adopting a 'They're on their own now' attitude to all·previous statements. 'Not really,' he said defensively.

'Seth, you said Natasha flirted with Darryl. Why did you bring that up if it's irrelevant?'

'Okay, she was flirting with him.' His head lolled in defeat. 'But she's just like that.'

'And was it her flirting that inspired Darryl to leave?'

'Why, what's he said?' Seth went bright red. Veins throbbed beneath his hedgehog hairstyle. 'Has he been talking to you about this?'

I ransacked my head for a diplomatic answer. If I admitted to two-sided knowledge, would Seth resent me, sack me even? Or would he immediately appoint me Official Go-Between? 'Yes,' I said.

'He has? He has?' Seth leaped out of his chair and started to pace the room like an angry gremlin. He clutched his T-shirt in apparent torment, scrunching up the letters of his own name. 'What's he been saying? I hope you didn't believe him. He's lying!'

'Seth, I can't tell you what Darryl said. That's not fair to him.'

41

'I want you to tell him something from me.' He turned on me desperately, keeping his eyes steady for once. 'It's good that he's spoken to you, now you can sort it out. You've got to tell him it was all a mis-understanding.'

Normally I would object to such blatant passing of the buck, but I recognised this for what it was: a good distraction from Tony-feelings. 'So what exactly happened?' I asked.

'Natasha just got a bit out of line, that's all. She was pissed.'

'Out of line how?' I persisted.

'She sort of . . . went over to him and tried to sit on his lap, maybe tried to kiss him, I don't know.'

'Anything else?'

'No!' Seth squeaked indignantly. 'I bet Darryl's exaggerated what actually happened to justify his over-reaction, hasn't he? I bet that's what he's done.'

'So Natasha sat on Darryl's knee, tried to kiss him, and Darryl got up and left. Is that what happened?'

'Yes.' Seth blinked furiously, still pacing.

'Well, that's understandable, isn't it? I mean, you're his boss, you're in the house and your wife is trying to kiss him. What did you expect him to do?'

'I know, I know, I can understand why he left. But then later when we tried to ring him and apologise he wouldn't even speak to us. He kept slamming the phone down. We even went round there to say sorry and he wouldn't let us in. I mean, I'm talking serious over-reaction.'

'Maybe you should have just left it a while, given him a chance to calm down instead of hassling him straight away,' I suggested.

'Hassling him!' Seth exclaimed in a tone of severe outrage. 'Well, it's clear whose side you're on!' His head seemed to fall into his shoulders as if his neck had collapsed under the weight of such a grave injustice.

'Sorry, I didn't mean hassling, I meant ... er ... trying to sort it out with him,' I mumbled feebly.

'We didn't hassle him. We phoned him a couple of times, popped round once – God, I can't imagine what he's been telling you!'

You don't have to imagine it, I thought; you know exactly what he told me. Natasha sat on his lap indeed. The way I heard it, she sat on his nose.

'So what do you want me to tell Darryl?' I asked.

'Tell him we're sorry,' Seth pleaded alternately to my tape-player and the William Morris coaster on my desk. 'We just want him to forget it and for things to go back to normal.'

'Okay,' I said in my capacity as Official Go-Between.

# Chapter Six

## Pace

What does pace mean? Does it mean Seth pacing up and down my office? When I was a secretary, even though I loved writing and reflected on literary matters as much as my nine-to-five hard-labour regime would allow, I never considered pace. All secretaries know about pace is that their tyrannical bosses want their pointlessly tabbed, indented, tabled and columned waffle typed up at an unreasonably fast one.

The whole *Lions* process has made me an expert. According to Seth and Hayley, the directorial component of our Creative Team, there are certain edicts of pace and action pertaining to all plays. Here are the Seth Beasley Seven Golden Rules of Drama:

1. Scenes should be short.

NB The above is not one of the pointless indents I mentioned earlier. A page looks pacier if the eye has forever to adjust to new margins. You see, this is what I love about being a professional creative person. I can get away with saying stuff like that at the Seth Beasley School. If I'd said it to my boss at the building design and construction firm of Piper Whalley Rooney, he would have replied, 'Yoo fackin' woh?' Besides, as I am typing this myself, I'm not inflicting my indents on a secretary.

2. Conversations should be short. A conversation should never be long, however interesting or crucial it is.

3. If a conversation absolutely has to be longer than bomb-explodingly short, it must be intercut with shootings, chases and general carnage. That way it won't be a long conversation but rather several short conversation segments.

4. Audiences are alarmed by too many words. The blow of excessive words must be softened by frequent scenes of extreme and loud violence.

5. Nobody on stage must sit or stand still for any longer than strictly necessary. Even during important and fascinating conversations (short ones, obviously) people should ideally leap about and run around the stage. This will catch the audience's attention in a way that the acting/plot/dialogue cannot hope to do.

6. People should yell, whine, growl and wail rather than speak wherever possible. The audience should not be allowed to have bored ears.

7. The mood of the piece must change as often as possible. If there's a (short) scene in which the main characters are dreamy and romantic, it must be followed by a (short) scene in which the mood is gun-toting lunacy. Otherwise the audience will get bored.

This is because, according to Seth, people have shorter attention spans now than they used to. I found this hard to believe at first. I could listen to a conversation, if I cared about its subject, for ages without feeling any need for a car chase in the middle of it. Perhaps mine is the sole survivor of the old long-span era.

What about *Twelve Angry Men*, I asked Seth. That's my favourite play – and film – of all time, and it consists of twelve men sitting round a table, talking.

Seth said I obviously hadn't noticed that the twelve men got up from the table and moved about a lot, thereby proving him right, and that he didn't like *Twelve Angry Men* anyway because there wasn't enough action in it. 'The script's good,' he grudgingly conceded, 'the acting's okay, but cinematically, dramatically, it's too static.'

The acting's okay? The acting in *Twelve Angry Men* is *okay*? Readers in all categories, I hope this is something on which we can all agree, whatever we may think about love. Does Henry Fonda need to smash someone's head in with a hammer in order to sustain a viewer's interest? Must Lee J Cobb fall out of a window and land in the arms of a brightly-coloured alien in order to keep us hooked?

You can understand my concern, can't you? I need to describe Tony Lamb's checked shirt, his jeans, his other sort-of-veloury top. I can't skimp on those bits; I'd be selling out on everything I believe in, namely that every detail about Tony's person and clothing is miraculous, crucial and must be celebrated in art form. But if what Seth says about pace is right, I'm going to have to do the checked shirt, then insert a random gruesome murder, then do the jeans. Is that what you short-attention-spanned bunch want from me?

Fine. I'll restrict myself, for the time being, to giving you a mere aperitif, a small taste of the delights to come. I shall describe Tony's grin and his trainers, in that order.

The former is higher on one side of his face than on the other. Also, the higher it rises on the right, the lower it falls on the left. It reminds me of the pirate-ship ride at Alton Towers and produces, in me at any rate, the same lurching, gravity-disturbing sensation. It's totally spontaneous as well, unlike the grins you see on the faces of middle-class people in theatres. It isn't an 'I'm on Shakespeare's wavelength and appreci-

46

ate all his witty quips' grin, more a 'Who the fuck's Shakespeare? I'm a God in mortal form' sort of affair.

His trainers, which he wears every day, are well-worn navy-and-white Nikes. If they belonged to someone else I might describe them as battered, but on Tony Lamb they look tired but happy, and what trainer in its right mind wouldn't be? If I were a trainer belonging to Tony Lamb I would be ecstatic. I would go around singing 'I have often clung to these feet before/but a sweaty sock has never smelled so sweet before' to all the Reeboks and Adidases I passed. Clearly, we're dealing with remarkable footwear here. I know I'm hardly objective about this, but objectively, how many shoes have ever inspired anyone to adapt some *My Fair Lady* lyrics in their honour? Exactly.

Anyway, pace dictates that that must be all for now. This must be a recent development. If Pace Laws existed in the old days, why didn't someone tell Herman Melville when he was writing *Moby Dick*?

# Chapter Seven

## Alistair and I Go to Dinner at Seth and Natasha's

Seth and Natasha are Mr and Mrs Ulterior Motive. Sorry, they are Mr and Dr Ulterior Motive. They only invited Alistair and me to dinner because of the Darryl situation. Between my promising Seth that I'd convey his apology to Darryl and this dinner three days later, the following things had happened:

1. I had passed on the apology to Darryl as promised and he had rejected it, pointing out, fairly, in my opinion, that an apology is worthless if you apologise for something that didn't happen while still lying about what did happen.

2. Seth and Natasha had received a letter from Darryl's solicitor, which clearly stated that if they wished to avoid legal proceedings they should not phone, visit or impose their presence upon Darryl in any way, especially not by balancing their genitals on his nose. Okay, I made that last bit up. People who are in love can have a sense of humour, you know. Why does anyone think they can't?

3. Seth and Natasha, on receiving this letter, embarked upon a sort of publicity campaign, which involved bad-mouthing Darryl, discussing his 'over-reaction' with anyone who would listen and inviting everybody from the school to

sumptuous feasts at their house, the assumption almost definitely being that if enough expensive wine and vintage port were poured down one's throat, one would have no alternative but to side with the pourers.

I'm saying things like 'almost definitely'. The danger of writing in the first person is that the narrator's opinion is presented as fact. As a Creative Writing teacher I know that more balance can be achieved, not to mention changes of tone, by third-person narration. Well, I've invented a new category: I'm writing in the madly-in-love person.

It was easier than I'd expected to persuade Alistair to come. Spartaco Systems had just signed up an important new client thanks to his efforts, so he was in a good mood. As soon as I mentioned that the food and wine would probably be the best we'd tasted this decade, he was thoroughly convinced and ready to go. Alistair has three passions in life, not including me: food, football and computers. He tends to talk at length about all three whether I'm listening or not.

It was only a short drive from our perfectly adequate red-brick semi in Langley to Seth and Natasha's luxurious mansion in Windsor. I had never been there before, but I assumed, as Alistair drove us there, that it would turn out to be a luxurious mansion. As soon as we set off he launched into a detailed attack on Bill Gates of Microsoft and his attempts at market domination.

I love Alistair, although he isn't a passion for me in the way that I seem still to be for him after five years. I am not madly in love with him. I fancy him, but I don't feel as though a boulder has rolled through my stomach when I think about his eyes/shirt. This is partly because I'm so used to him being around that I suppose I now take him for granted. When I first met him, at a friend's party in 1990, I remember thinking he was gorgeous and lusting after him desperately all night. He looked like a young Marlon Brando, except blond. He still does, in fact, but I've lived with him for so long that I can't see him properly any more. A large proportion of being madly in love with someone, in my opinion, is yearning and craving for them, and it's hard to maintain that intensity of feeling when you know that person is yours. One can only crave the out of reach, the inaccessible.

I would, of course, be distraught if anything bad happened to him; I want him to be happy, which is why I'm glad he doesn't know about Tony.

Carmel-Marie White once said, with reference to a possible infidelity sub-plot in *Lions*, 'I think people who are unfaithful are crap.' If she ever gets cold at night, she can tuck herself up cosily in one of her blanket statements.

I was thinking about Carmel-Marie as we drove to Seth and Natasha's, convinced she and Tony were having an affair or teetering on the brink of one. I felt a sort of double disappointment. My Tony-lack was exacerbated by the knowledge that he had chosen to bless someone as ordinary as me, but not me, with his love. Losing him to Madonna would be painful, but seem fair; losing him to Carmel-Marie White went entirely against the natural order of things.

Whatever was going on, they had obviously decided to keep it secret because at rehearsals they always ignored each other. Tony rarely spoke to anyone. All he had said to me so far was 'Do you want a chair?' once when I was sitting on the floor. Actually, it was pretty good when he said that. I was ecstatically happy for days. I sat on the floor at rehearsals more often afterwards in the hope that it would prompt him to say it again.

I wondered what Richard White, Carmel-Marie's husband, would do if he found out Carmel-Marie and

Tony were sleeping together. Richard was an estate agent and had always struck me as being conventional to the point of smugness. He and Carmel-Marie made frequent public assertions of how happy they were together. Still, this didn't preclude Richard's being as hypocritical as Carmel-Marie was.

Never mind Richard White, what was I going to do? I needed to make a plan before unrequited love and jealousy ruined my life. If I couldn't have Tony I was going to need a hell of a lot of home comforts to soften the blow.

'Belinda, we're here,' Alistair, my primary home comfort, informed me.

I roused myself from my daze and looked out of the car window. Seth and Natasha's house was semi-detached like ours but, where ours was squat and boxy, theirs was tall and elegant, on the corner of a wide, tree-lined street. Most of the houses here had two cars parked outside them and there were several conspicuous Neighbourhood Watch signs on lamp-posts. The residents of Ferndale Road presumably had a lot worth stealing.

I pulled a mirror out of my handbag and put on some lipstick. Lipstick is the only make-up I bother with these days. I've yet to discover a brand of cosmetics that could, for example, elevate me to Tony Lamb's looks league.

'What's wrong?' Alistair asked me. 'You look really odd. Did you hear what I said about Bill Gates?'

Alistair isn't a very observant person so my moods usually go undetected. On days when his work has gone badly I'm sure I could sit right in front of him with a razor poised above my wrist and he wouldn't notice. Occasionally, however, he surprises me by detecting a barely concealed mood of mine and demanding to know the cause of it. More often than not Alistair can be fobbed off, which is why I can sense immediately

51

when fobbing will not work. Somebody once said that the best way to lie is to make 'skilful use of the truth' and this was what I did. 'It's Darryl,' I said. 'You know Darryl Abrahams, the Head of Music at school?'

'Mm?'

'Well, he's fallen out with Seth and Natasha – I haven't got time to go into detail now, I'll tell you on the way home – anyway, I'm just a bit worried that they'll try to involve me in it all and . . . I don't know, I just think maybe coming here is a bit disloyal to Darryl.'

'Oh.' Alistair frowned. 'Well, what's . . . why didn't you tell me any of this before? What did they fall out about?'

'Look, there isn't time, honestly. It's a long story,' I said evasively. Alistair likes his social acquaintances to be well-adjusted; I had no intention of telling him we were dining chez major sexual screw-ups.

Natasha flung open the door just as I was about to ring the bell. Mercifully her shoulder-blades were covered on this occasion by a red silk shirt that looked extremely expensive and clashed horribly with her orange hair. I wondered whether she was making a deliberate I-will-not-bow-to-the-tyranny-of-colour-co-ordination statement.

'Belinda! Alistair!' she gushed, looking thinner than I had ever seen her. There were dark hollows under her eyes and her lips were chapped and peeling. I nudged Alistair, who was staring a bit too conspicuously at her matchstick legs, which made her black leggings look like baggy jogging pants.

I handed our wine contribution to Natasha, hearing the worrying sound of too many voices. Do you know that feeling? You arrive at the abode of your hosts and are immediately assaulted by the unwelcome realis-ation that there are other guests, people you weren't expecting and may not like.

I have read several articles in women's magazines about dinner party dos and don'ts, but not one of them has ever mentioned the Other Guests Peril. My first dinner party rule would be as follows: make sure when you invite your guests that you let them know who else is going to be there. That way they know what they're letting themselves in for and if you've invited anyone they loathe, they can opt out tactfully.

'Who else is here?' Alistair hissed at me as we followed Natasha down the long, narrow hall. I shrugged in a way that I hoped suggested I was as surprised as he was that it wasn't just the four of us. The unknown quantity of Other Guests is one of Alistair's great fears in life. He finds it hard enough to deal with scheduled new people, those he's agreed to meet, without having to worry about the scheduled hoodwinking him into spending time with the unscheduled.

I couldn't help being impressed by the house. The ceilings were high and all the walls were painted deep shades of plum or apricot. There were prints everywhere by Jackson Pollock, Mark Rothko and other artists similarly defeated by the challenge of drawing actual things. But then actual things have their disadvantages.

'What can I get you to drink?' Natasha asked brightly. 'You've got some catching up to do, the others are pissed already!' She ushered us through to the dining-room at the back of the house.

The others were – I am definitely not one of God's chosen people – Carmel-Marie and Richard White. I would have preferred to have Norman Bates and his mother's skeleton as dining companions. Richard was wearing the sort of drab grey suit that is inextricably linked in my mind with estate agency and Carmel-Marie's perky, upturned breasts were jutting out of a blue, underwired tubelike shift. I felt distinctly underdressed in my white jeans and sweat-shirt.

53

I surveyed the room in which the attack on Darryl took place, noting the large crack in the table that Seth had broken, falling over his lowered trousers. He was wearing the same maroon and white pin-striped suit this evening. Like Natasha, he looked as if he had lost weight, from his body at any rate; his head was its usual bulbous self.

Introductions were made and Alistair struggled valiantly with the concept of four new people. Natasha asked him what he did and he was allowed to talk about computer programming for about four seconds before she interrupted him: 'I've got a fab new computer at work,' she enthused. 'I still haven't worked out how to use all its ... are they called packages?' Without giving Alistair a chance to answer she went on, 'I can't make any sense of the instruction booklet and I've got a PhD, so I don't know how they expect normal people to manage.'

'What do you do?' Alistair asked, which foolhardiness resulted in his having to endure a succession of slice-of-life tales from the Philosophy Department of Reading University. It's lucky my dad wasn't there, with his preference for the Penguin Passnotes to a conversation rather than the conversation itself. I was sure Alistair was bored, but he didn't snore, which would have been my dad's reaction, so I was quite proud of him.

Seth wasn't listening. He looked distracted and unhappy. The usual 'Tee hee I've got a successful wife' spark was absent from his eyes, which were darting all over the place, looking far more waterlogged than usual. Could he be holding back tears, I wondered.

'I'm sure Alistair doesn't need this level of in-depth knowledge,' said Carmel-Marie, just as Natasha was about to describe a fourth member of Reading's Philosophy Department in great physical, psychological and behavioural detail.

'Oh . . . well!' said Natasha with a mixture of anger and embarrassment. 'I suppose philosophy can be a bit much for some people.' She left the room abruptly. My loyalties were battling away, or, to be more precise, my disloyalties. Normally I would have been cheering for anyone who had the guts to call Natasha boring to her face, but the mood I was in I would have sided with Jack the Ripper against Carmel-Marie. I looked at her and Richard, the supposedly happily married and exclusively faithful couple. They seemed to belong together, sitting straight-backed, side by side at the dinner-table like the embodiment of wedding vows. They were both dark-haired and olive-skinned, and both thirty-six. Richard was one of those muscly men whose torsos appear triangular. Carmel-Marie had a figure most women would kill for: not only the gravity-defying bosom I've already mentioned, but also a minuscule waist, making her look very much like an hourglass, although since I now detest her I prefer to call her an egg timer. They would have been a gorgeous couple, were it not for the fact that Richard looked a fraction too much like a duck and Carmel-Marie's face was a bit froggy, with slightly bulging wide-set eyes and an oddly curved upper lip.

They were in each other's league, as surely as Carmel-Marie could never hope to be in Tony's league or age-bracket. Neither could I, but that wasn't the point. At least I was only twenty-seven. A six-year age gap was far better than a fifteen-year one.

What did he see in her? Was it all those revealing, underwired tops that thrust her breasts skywards? In the rare event of her wearing a T-shirt, it was guaranteed to have something emblazoned across it at tit level, forcing one's eye to follow the letters over the bouncy-nippled peaks. By the time you'd finished reading you felt like an exhausted skier. Was Tony a tit-man? Or was it the moral rectitude that turned him on, like when Sky Masterson falls for Sister Sarah in *Guys and Dolls*? Maybe Tony liked that special Mr-Brocklehurst-from-*Jane-Eyre* quality in his women.

'Why are you staring at my bosom, Belinda?' Carmel-Marie asked me.

'Oh, I . . . wasn't,' I muttered. I was going to have to hone my lying skills.

'Everyone should stare at you, my love,' said Richard. 'You're so beautiful.' He leaned over and rubbed his nose against Carmel-Marie's. Alistair watched with barely concealed horror. I looked at Seth, whose evident misery enabled me to refrain from bursting into loud laughter. I couldn't take Richard White seriously in the role of Romeo. If he turned up under my balcony I'd empty my washing-up bowl over his head.

'You see, that's just it!' Seth suddenly burst out. A tear rolled down his wide cheek. 'Just an innocent misunderstanding! I mean, are you going to see a solicitor about this, Carmel-Marie?'

'Abite what?'

'You thought Belinda was staring at your tits. Are you going to see a solicitor about it?' His weepy eyes seemed to throw this question to the Howard Hodgkin print that was minding its own business on the dining-room wall.

'There's no need to be crude.' Richard frowned.

'Don't be ridiculous!' Carmel-Marie snapped. I had a bad feeling about where this conversation was heading. Natasha, alert to the warning signal, rushed back into the room carrying a plate of stuffed vine leaves that looked as if it weighed more than she did.

'No, you're not, because you're not a nutter!'

'Seth . . .' Natasha murmured.

Seth's head lunged backwards and he laughed a macabre laugh. 'What? There's no point trying to keep it a secret, Natasha. I'm sure everyone knows that

Darryl saw fit to send us a solicitor's letter!' He practically spat out the last two words.

'What are you talking abite?' Carmel-Marie demanded.

'What, you mean he hasn't told you?' Seth launched into his rather scanty version of events, prowling lugubriously around the table as he did so. He reminded me of Lee J Cobb in one of his angrier *Twelve Angry Men* moments. Carmel-Marie and Richard listened with a sort of stern attention. Alistair also listened, shooting the occasional the-food-had-better-be-*Masterchef*-standard-to-compensate-for-this glance in my direction.

'I mean, Darryl's one of my closest friends,' Seth wailed. 'I just can't believe he's acting like this.'

'So what does the letter say?' Carmel-Marie asked briskly. Soon she would be in possession of the full facts and able to wallow in the wrongness of one or other party.

'Oh, just that we have to leave Darryl alone or we'll be hung, drawn and quartered!'

'High can you leave him alone? You work together,' said Carmel-Marie. 'What abite *Lions*? The tech run's tomorrow and you both have to be there.'

'That's all right, apparently. That doesn't count as harassment, according to . . .' Seth pulled the letter out of his pocket, 'Mr C P Thickbroom. Necessary work-related communication is permitted, but that's about all that is. Fucking great, isn't it? How can I direct a show in the presence of someone who wants me thrown in jail?'

'Seth, language, please!' said Richard. 'There are ladies present.' That was what he said; what do you want me to do?

'Let's see the letter,' said Carmel-Marie.

'No!' Seth clutched it to his chest protectively and staggered a few paces back. He looked ludicrous, like a character from a Dickens novel who has been set upon by footpads. Natasha hovered beside him, still holding the vine leaves with one hand and alternately stroking the cracked table and picking at her peeling lips with the other.

'Darryl does *not* want you thrown in jail, Seth,' I clarified. 'He felt a bit threatened by your . . . by the other night and he found your subsequent efforts to . . . sort things out a bit oppressive. He only took things this far because he couldn't think of any other way of getting you to give him some space.'

'Why didn't he just say? What does he think I am, a monster?'

'He's a big boy now.' Natasha pouted censoriously. 'He should be able to sort things out like a grown-up. I'm not being nasty, but this sort of pettiness is typical of Animal Laborens.'

'Of who?' Alistair asked.

'Animal Laborens. Hannah Arendt, the German philosopher, coined the phrase. It means, you know, the masses. Its literal translation is "labouring animal".'

'You snobby twat!' Carmel-Marie yelled, with suspiciously Brummie-like vowels. I sat forward attentively. Didn't elocution lessons cover extreme anger?

'Carmel-Marie!' Richard gasped in horror. 'What sort of way is . . .'

'I'm sorry, but that is an unacceptable way to talk!' Carmel-Marie blushed, swiftly reinstating her Celia Johnson voice. 'I've never heard anything so blatantly . . . anti-working class!'

'And Darryl isn't working class anyway,' I interjected. I couldn't have hoped for a better distraction from Tony-pain. 'He's a musician. He owns a record label . . .'

'His origins are working class,' said Seth, 'and

58

Natasha is, sadly, right. It is unfortunately true that the working classes are particularly susceptible to herd morality.'

'I was a secretary for eight years,' I said indignantly, 'and I haven't got herd morality.' I hoped I was right in saying this. I wasn't certain I had any morality at all, but if I did I was sure it wasn't of the herd variety.

'You can't be serious,' said Alistair to Seth, in a tone which only I recognised to be the one he reserves for people he despises. 'If by herd morality you mean prudishness, bigotry, narrow-mindedness . . .'

'That's exactly what I mean,' said Natasha, tensing her neck muscles under her translucent skin so that she looked like a badly knotted rope.

'. . . I think those are qualities someone from any social background could have.'

'Yes!' said Carmel-Marie angrily. 'Bigots in glass hises shouldn't throw stones.'

'Perhaps we should all calm down and eat.' Richard tried to shrug affably and succeeded only in looking like a very nervous man who had developed a tic in his shoulders.

'I'm not eating here,' said Carmel-Marie. 'Not unless they apologise for what they've said.' She turned to Seth. 'I suspected that you were someone with . . . file views.'

'Foul views!' Natasha echoed ominously. 'And I suppose you're a great friend of the workers, with your elocution lessons!' She slammed the stuffed vine leaves down on the table. Alistair, instantly losing all interest in the seething chaos that had broken out, smiled appreciatively at the plump green parcels and popped one into his mouth.

Carmel-Marie's lip curled dangerously. I almost regretted the fact that I was consumed by overpowering jealousy because otherwise I would definitely have been on her side. 'I had elocution lessons,' she stammered, '*not* that it's any of your business, because when I was younger I wanted to be a newsreader and . . .'

'Look, there's no need for all this,' Seth groaned, massaging his immense forehead. 'Let's just all simmer down.'

'Don't tell me, tell her,' Carmel-Marie pointed a painted talon at Natasha, who backed away, as if afraid that Carmel-Marie's nail would go straight through her.

'Oh dear . . . oh dear,' Richard gabbled in terror.

'You're just jealous . . .' Natasha's chapped lips trembled '. . . because I'm a Doctor of Philosophy and you're just a . . . a failed newsreader!'

'If you're going to carry on in this vein we'd better take it iteside.' Carmel-Marie glowered.

'Carmel-Marie!' Richard shrieked. 'Stop it! Come on . . . everybody! Everything has got totally out of hand.' 'Why don't we all apologise and eat?'

'The starter has disappeared,' said Natasha, looking at the now empty plate she had deposited on the table earlier.

'Oh, I, er, ate all that,' Alistair said helpfully.

'You *what*?'

'Well, everyone was yelling,' he explained. 'No one else seemed to want them.'

Natasha burst into tears and ran out of the room.

# Chapter Eight

## I Get Told Off for Having Unhinged Colleagues

'Never again, never a-fucking-gain, am I setting foot in that house! Never!'

'Okay, Alistair.'

'Those people are psychos, they are raving psychos, they need psychiatric help! I mean, no sooner does one argument end than another one begins! Every course was cold by the time we ate it. While that social-class brawl was going on I thought things couldn't get any worse and then that whole BUPA thing started. World War fucking Three or what!'

'Mm.'

'If that long-name woman . . .'

'Carmel-Marie.'

'. . . is so against BUPA, how come she isn't against working in an over-privileged fee-paying school for talentless toffs?'

'That's not fair. I love that school and you know it.'

'Okay, I'm sorry. I'm sorry. I'm not knocking the school . . .'

'Yes, you were.'

'Yes, I was, but I didn't mean it. Look, I'm not particularly keen on private health or private education, but I think there are exceptional cases. Like you taking this job; okay, you hated being a secretary. You're really happy now and you weren't then – fair enough. I think private health insurance undermines the NHS, but if I had a life-threatening disease, I'd obviously use it. But that woman . . .'

'Carmel-Marie.'

'. . . had the cheek to say that it was wrong, even in the case of critical illness! So if she's so black-and-white, how can she work for a fee-paying school? That's not élitist, I suppose! What a fucking hypocrite.'

'Mm. In more ways than one.'

'Hey?'

'Nothing. Why didn't you say any of this to her?'

'You're joking, aren't you? She'd have strung me up! Is everyone at your work as mad as that?'

'Well, you know Hayley. And Darryl's sane.'

'I tell you, even without hearing his side of the story, I'm well on his side. In fact, if either of those Beasleys ever comes near me again, never mind a solicitor's letter, I'm going to get myself a fucking Kalashnikov.'

'Natasha's not a Beasley. She's a Leaf.'

'She's a gargoyle. Why didn't you stick up for yourself?'

'Against Natasha?'

'No, Carmel-Marie. When she was accusing you of being a BUPA sympathiser.'

'I am a BUPA sympathiser.'

'What? You're against BUPA.'

'No, *you're* against BUPA. So you assume I am.'

'Well, aren't you?'

'I'd never thought about it until I started at Beasley, but no, I'm not.'

'You're not going to sign up, are you?'

'I thought you thought it was okay, in certain situations?'

'Yeah, fatal diseases.'

'Well, I think I've got circumstances that justify it.'

'What circumstances?'

'Isn't it a bit late for a heavy discussion? I was hoping

I might shake off that *Question Time* feeling before I went to sleep.'

'Oh, go on.'

'Only if you promise that, whatever happens, you'll stay calm and, however much you disagree with me, you won't start yelling.'

'Promise.'

'Okay, well, this free BUPA cover is a perk of the job, right?'

'Mm.'

'It's something that not a lot of jobs offer, only ... only really good jobs. It's a luxury. It's like the new computer and printer, the free lunches, the book allowance, the parking space ...'

'Loads of people have parking spaces at their work. That's not a luxury.'

'Loads of people don't have it, though! I never had a parking space in any of my other jobs. This is my whole point. I've had loads of shit secretarial jobs where I was basically a skivvy and where the biggest perk was if a day went by when my boss's breath didn't actively stink. So now I've got the job of my dreams ...'

'Despite sharing the building with a load of lunatics.'

'... I want every luxury that's on offer. I want the full experience.'

'I can understand that.'

'And also, as you said, what's the point of not doing the BUPA thing on principle when you work in a private school? There's no point having principles unless you're going to be consistent. You either have to do nothing wrong ever or forget it.'

'That's rubbish.'

'No, it's not. It's like Carmel-Marie boycotting Peaker Frozen Vegetables. What about all the other vegetables?'

'What about them?'

'Who says they're moral? Name a product.'

'Uuh . . . wine. Ernest and Julio Gallo Sauvignon Blanc.'

'Okay, good example. Nobody boycotts that, do they? I mean, there are no documentaries on telly about how immoral it is, no articles in the *Guardian*, no crusties picketing off-licences . . .'

'No, there aren't.'

'But can anyone actually guarantee that Ernest and Julio Gallo are nice people?'

'What?'

'Do you know them?'

'Do I know Ernest and Julio Gallo?'

'Yes.'

'No.'

'Right. So you don't know, therefore, that they aren't the two most immoral people on the planet. You just continue to buy their wine, assuming they're good because you haven't heard that they're bad.'

'I don't assume they're good. I don't assume Ernest and Julio Gallo are good! I never think about them.'

'But they might be evil. So might Mr Jacob's Creek, or Mrs Shiraz Cabernet. So what do you do, give up all wine?'

'So what exactly are you saying? I can't remember how this conversation began.'

'I'm saying there's no point having principles unless you're consistent. Going to Reclaim the Streets demos is fine as long as you never get in a car again. Being a vegetarian is fine as long as you don't wear leather. Being a socialist is fine as long as you don't enjoy luxuries the poor can't have and so on. I don't want to boycott everything, deprive myself of every pleasure in life . . .'

'Who's asking you to?'

'. . . and I don't want to be a total hypocrite, so I've gone for the third option.'

'Which is?'

'No principles. I've boycotted principles. Now I don't need to boycott anything else and I can do exactly what I want.'

'You're mad! You've been at that school too long. Just because you can't be perfect doesn't mean you have to be totally immoral. And anyway, of course you've got principles.'

'No, I haven't.'

'Of course you have.'

'Go on then, what would I never do? People who have principles have to be able to say "I'd never do that" about certain things.'

'Kill? Steal?'

'I would. There are circumstances in which I would. I'm telling you, I really don't think I've got very many principles. The closest I get to principles is when I buy clothes there.'

# Chapter Nine

## The Carl Sillery Plan

I delivered. I came up with the goods. I'm quite proud of myself. When it matters, when things are really hanging in the balance, I always do. Alistair is bad in a crisis. His reaction to a minor difficulty can range from excessive swearing to the demolition of an essential item of furniture. Me, though, I'm the Crisis Queen.

I'd needed an effective safeguard against unhappiness about Tony and now I had one. I had formulated, overnight, the Carl Sillery Plan. I had drafted it, revised it, examined it from all angles and it looked watertight to me.

Carl Sillery was a seventeen-year-old Beasley student and Youth Theatre member. He was *Lions'* leading man, playing the part of Ian Chaddock, the play's romantic hero. The Creative Team had argued long into the night about the feasibility of calling a romantic hero Ian Chaddock. I had argued strongly in favour and won through in the end as I usually do, being a day-saver. Do you know what I mean by that? Tom Cruise is a day-saver in almost all his films: at first he's not the best, then he gets to be the best, then he experiences a major setback, then at the end he's the best again.

Can or cannot a romantic hero be called Ian Chaddock? This argument occurred half-way through the first week of rehearsals, long before I conceived the brilliant Carl Sillery Plan, when, in the absence of a plot and script, we decided we really ought at least to think of some possible names for characters. That way when our protagonists eventually materialised, their names would be ready and waiting.

We invited suggestions from the Youth Theatre members. I keep calling them that to avoid saying 'the kids', because I want to play down the age-gap factor. You'll see why very shortly. I'll call them YTMs from now on.

'Lopelia,' suggested Ed Fewster. 'The heroine should have a long, sumptuous name.' He waved his hand evocatively, a gesture that looked bizarre coming from someone with his hulking physique.

'Oh, that's beautiful.' Phoebe closed her blue eyes and inhaled deeply. With her blonde angelic looks she was clearly main-part material and I sensed she was trying on heroines' names like hats.

'I think we should keep the names short and straight-forward,' said the disapproving Stella, whose sensible suggestions were resolutely ignored by the rest of the company. 'It's got to be realistic. What about Sarah?'

It was thanks to Oliver Wild that we ended up with a heroine called Wristine Vella. He proposed it with his usual air of handsome, rich confidence and no one felt sophisticated enough to disagree. Oliver also named Vilk Vella, Wristine's husband. Now, I know what you must be thinking – how can Vilk and Wristine Vella inhabit the same dramatic oeuvre as Ian Chaddock? Easy: some of the play is set in the present and some in the future.

'I don't see why the hero can't be called Ian Chaddock,' said Carl Sillery. We were sitting in our usual circle on the drama studio floor. 'If there was a really fit bird called Ian Chaddock, I'd shag her. I wouldn't care what she was called.'

'You mad bastard!' said Oliver, who was Carl's best

67

mate. 'Anyway, you would say that, given what your mum's called.'

Everyone laughed, but I didn't get the joke. 'What's your mum called?' I asked Carl.

'Hilary Sillery.' He chuckled.

'Seriously?'

'Yeah. Well, she was called Hilary Chapman until she married my dad.'

'She must have loved him a lot to change her name to Hilary Sillery,' said Oliver.

'I dunno.' Carl shrugged.

'Love!' Ed tossed his hair dismissively. 'All sorts of silliness is done in its name.'

'While this was going on I looked at Tony probably about every five seconds. He was having what I later dubbed 'a glazed day'; his eyes were glazed over, his normally perfect olive complexion was pale and sallow, and he didn't laugh at such ridiculous name suggestions as Worm Dross and Proac Bendy. The day before he had been alert and smiled his heavenly smile at me. The divine statement 'Do you want a chair?' had issued from his lips.

Carl Sillery didn't have glazed days, hidden depths, social workers, or enigmatic silences, which was why he was perfect for my plan. Carl was a typical lad. His priorities were getting drunk, smoking cigarettes and sleeping with as many pretty girls as possible.

He wasn't unattractive. He was incredibly tall, about six foot four, broad-shouldered, with long hair that was shaved at the sides and tied in a pony-tail at the back. He was blond in a green way. Do you know what I mean by that? Some people are just blond. Others are blond, but when you think about them you imagine them to have a sort of green tinge, even though they're not really green at all. His personality and attitude considerably increased his sex appeal. He and Oliver were the most in-demand male YTMs, apart from Tony, of course, who was in a different league.

All he had to do was appear in the drama studio and about twelve girls would shriek, 'Tony! Tony! Come here, Tony!' Perhaps his glazed look was a sort of defence mechanism. As rehearsals progressed and the girls lost their inhibitions, they began to pull, poke, prod and grab Tony on a regular basis. No wonder he hid behind Darryl's music system; he couldn't appear in public without being mobbed. Four girls would grab a limb each and try to drag him off in four different directions.

I didn't blame them. I could see their point. This was why it was crucial for me to formulate and stick to the Carl Sillery Plan. If I didn't distract myself in a major way, I would soon join the grabbers and the pokers.

My plan was to have an affair with Carl Sillery. Would that be the seventeen-year-old Carl Sillery? Yes, it would. The only way to distract yourself from a large and painful case of love/lust/obsession/infatuation is to take up with somebody else.

Now you may well have heard some people advising precisely the opposite course of action. If you wrote in to the Problem Page of *Just Seventeen* (how appropriate), your response would be a letter almost identical to this:

Dear Confused from Windsor

I understand your frustration at not being able to get the man of your dreams. However, I would strongly advise against rushing into another relationship on the rebound. It wouldn't be fair to you or the person you got involved with. You need to give yourself time and space to heal. Once you have found yourself then you can start thinking about relationships again.

Yours sincerely
Sensible-Agony-Aunt-with-Minimal-Life-Experience

I don't need to find myself. I've got myself already. What I don't have is Tony Lamb. Agony aunts encourage you to distract yourself in other ways; they advocate hobbies, friends, family, even work. So why not a new relationship?

Novelty was essential. Alistair was lovely, but he fell into the home-comfort category.

Carl's towering height made him look older than he was. On top of that, there was the Ian Chaddock factor. If you've never written a play you may not understand this but there is nothing sexier than the living embodiment of a character you've created. I hadn't known Carl at all before rehearsals started, but I liked most of what I'd heard him say since, possibly because I wrote it.

The danger of sleeping with a Beasley student and the associated risk of losing my job would provide the necessary adrenalin. I would have to be vigilant in ensuring Carl kept his mouth shut. Obviously, I'd still think about Tony quite a lot and still love him, but Carl-excitement and Carl-fear would enable me to bypass the less dignified aspects of all-consuming passion: the grabbing, the pulling, the sobbing in public places, the removal of brake fluid from Carmel-Marie's car.

I didn't consider the possibility that Carl wouldn't co-operate. In the end it all comes down to leagues. When you lay eyes on a couple for the first time, if you don't think anything in particular, this means they're in the same league. If, on the other hand, your instant reaction is, 'What's she doing with him?' or 'What's he doing with her?' this means there's some serious league incompatibility going on.

I am in a higher league than Carl because of his age and slightly peculiar hairstyle. I'm in the same league as Alistair. Alistair is blond, blue-eyed and handsome in a sort of regular-featured way. He is slightly overweight and wears glasses. I am about five foot six, with a very good figure and particularly impressive legs. I've got long, thick, shiny dark hair, a bit like Sandra Bullock's or Demi Moore's, although in her latest film Demi Moore is totally bald so perhaps that's not a good example. My facial features aren't that great, though. My eyes and chin are slightly too small and my lips are a bit thin. On a bad day I think I resemble a ferret. But my skin's excellent and overall I'd say I'm on the more attractive side of average. If I put it in terms of marks out of ten, Tony Lamb would be an eleven, Tom Cruise and Sandra Bullock would be tens. Well, maybe nine-and-a-halfs. Alistair and I would be sevens. Phoebe Procter, the prettiest YTM, would be a nine. Carmel-Marie White would be a six; despite her frogginess she is quite attractive. Carl would be a six.

I didn't feel guilty about corrupting Carl. If I had opted for honesty and said to him, 'Carl, I would like to use you as a sexual distraction in an attempt to block out my agonising love for Tony Lamb,' he would have said, 'Nice one, I never say no to a shag.' It was an Everybody Wins situation: I would have my diversion and Carl would be getting laid, which he had failed to do during his three-month involvement with the stodgy and prudish Stella Nettleton. I had heard this on the Youth Theatre grapevine.

Although on one level I recognised it to be utter insanity, the Carl Sillery Plan was ruthlessly rational. It had to be, to protect me from misery. I've never been frightened of physical pain but I am almost phobic about emotional suffering. I couldn't bear another night of tossing and turning with the sort of mind-fever that attacks unhappy people in their sleep. Mornings were no better; every day within seconds of waking I was wiped out by my returning Tony-and-Carmel-Marie consciousness. I was getting desperate, and out of my desperation I forged a cool, calculating higher self, a

71

persona that was able to administrate the seduction of one of my students without even blinking.

Have I alienated you, Cat As, with my willingness to sleep with someone other than the love object? Is that something you'd never do? I'm a practical person, an emotional survivalist. When I was at school, I had a Reserve Squad, a list of back-up boyfriends so that if things went wrong with my man of the moment I would have a few solid substitutes to fall back on.

But it's not just you As I need to worry about. There will be deserters from every category. Falling for one man while living with another is par for the romantic course, but a deliberate plot to ensnare a seventeen-year-old boy who is a student at the school where one teaches — now that's really something else. A coach-load of morally outraged readers is leaving from the depot of this book right now, I bet. You see, it's true what I said to Alistair. I have no principles. I know the difference between right and wrong, but if it suits me to do wrong, I will. Which is worse, to do wrong and know you're doing it or to do wrong and believe it's right? I'm not trying to wriggle out of anything; I'm just interested.

Are you condemning me right now? Fair enough. You've already heard my only justification: I believe love is the most important consideration. And while you sit there and slag me off, sipping a glass of Ernest and Julio Gallo wine, just remember that you might be a hypocrite. Who knows what your good mates Ern and Jules get up to in their spare time? They too might be planning to bed Carl Sillery even as we speak (the bastards! He's mine! He's mine!).

# Chapter Ten

## The Devising Process

Do you know what a devised play is? Neither did I, before *Lions*. I bet you thought, as I did, that a play had to be written by a person, as in *Julius Caesar* by William Shakespeare. With devised plays, which are the in thing according to Seth, everything is decided by committee.

Allow me to flash back just once more, in an attempt to explain *Lions'* peculiar origins and what exactly happened between 3 July and now, 25 August, official launch date of the Carl Sillery Plan and the day before the dress rehearsal.

Back in July, at our first *Lions* meeting in the French Window Room, after it had been agreed that Tony could join in, I had presented my plot idea to the Creative Team. It was ruled out immediately. It wasn't my idea that the others didn't like, it was the fact that I'd had a unilateral thought.

Seth wanted Rosie and Duane, the Technical People, to contribute to discussions on narrative thrust. He wanted me to help decide whether the music should be funky garage or hip-hop jungle, something about which I neither knew nor cared. I noticed Darryl looking unhappy when Seth consulted me on matters musical. I knew he was thinking, 'Hang on a minute, she listens to *Women in Country II*. She likes songs about truckers accidentally running over children with leukaemia and then saving their lives.' And he was right, not to condemn my taste in music, but to think that it was a big mistake for everybody to be involved in everything. Why couldn't each of us preside in our particular area of expertise, or at least get the casting vote in a Hilary Sillery – formerly known as an Even Stevens – situation?

But no, Seth had his heart set on the devising process and it was easy to see why. When putting on a devised play it is apparently fine to start with the merest hint of an idea and allow the script to come naturally out of improvisations during the rehearsal period. That way the whole cast gets to contribute to the creative process. This suited Seth down to the ground, allowing him to absolve himself of all responsibility in the name of teamwork.

As Chairman of the Creative Team, he started the negotiations. 'Right, we know it has to be a futuristic thriller, because the blurb in the brochure says it is. The blurb also implies that there's a conflict between present and future society. So I think the first question we need to address is, where is it going to be set? The present? The future? Both, maybe?' Hayley, on Seth's right-hand side, made notes dutifully and didn't say another word for the rest of the meeting. 'I've done my bit with the social worker's letter,' her martyred expression seemed to say, 'and no one cares what I think anyway.'

'It would be easier for me and Duane if it was set in the future,' said Rosie, running her tongue around the stainless steel rod in her lower lip. 'We've still got all those costumes from *Bladerunner* last year.'

'Yeah, and some scenery,' said Duane, his metallic tongue glinting in the sunlight. 'It'd save us a lot of trouble.'

'But surely it has to be set in the present,' said Carmel-Marie. 'People can travel back from the future to the present, because we can assume that in the future there'll be the technology for time travel, but that doesn't work in reverse. If it's set in the future, high will the people from the present get there?'

'Yes.' Seth nodded. 'Unless . . . we have part of it in the future and part in the present.' I was convinced that at some stage in his professional life Seth had been told by a management guru that if you say yes and nod, people won't realise you're disagreeing with them. 'Well?' His eyes darted eagerly around the room. No one responded. Darryl swallowed a yawn.

'Yes . . . urm, okay.' Seth blushed. 'Perhaps we'll leave that decision until later.'

After four days of similar Creative Team meetings, which resulted in total failure to agree on anything, Seth decided that negotiations had been going on far too long and gave us an hour to decide on the world/plot/characters of the play.

What we cobbled together in haste was as follows: the action starts in the year 2197. In this future society, all human beings are hedonistic and see pleasure as the only point to life. Technology is so advanced that robots can do everything, from street sweeping to arts administration, so they do all the work, while humans swan around enjoying themselves.

'We need to stick in a bit of history, bit of background,' said Seth. 'How did the world get to be like this, between 1997 and 2197?'

Ah, easy. In the year 2000 scientists did some research, as scientists are wont to do, and found that work was bad for people's health. They publicised their discovery, invented robots who could do all the work and precipitated a revolution. Central motif of said revolution was Shelley's poem 'The Masque of Anarchy', host to the quote 'Rise like lions after slumber/In unvanquishable number'. The revolutionaries were successful and created an idyllic world

75

in which everyone had fun all the time.

'Shelley wasn't against work altogether,' Carmel-Marie protested, 'only in a capitalist society.'

'Oh. Are you sure?' asked Seth.

'He spent most of his life sailing around on boats, getting pissed and bonking,' said Darryl, whose own hedonistic sympathies explained the trace of envy in his voice.

'So he must have been against work,' Seth concluded.

'I'm sure he wasn't,' said Carmel-Marie. 'I think "Song to the Men of England" makes it clear that he was in favour of work, so long as the workers got a fair share of the profits.'

'Well, the title can't be changed now, it's in the brochure,' said Seth.

To continue with the action, then. Hedonistic future society appears to be ticking along nicely with everyone having a whale of a time. *But* there is an underground movement afoot to overthrow this Utopia. Somehow, a small group of people has survived since 1997 who have the work ethic in their blood. They are anti-self-indulgence and believe work is character-building.

'How can they have survived since 1997? Are they two hundred years old, or what?' I asked.

'We can't have two-hundred-year-olds being played by eighteen-year-olds,' said Duane.

'Um . . . well, we can let the kids work that out themselves,' said Seth. 'It can come out of improvisations.'

Okay, so, the rebels want to overthrow the hedonists, but cannot agree on the best way to do this. Some are in favour of trying to win the masses over to their point of view with reasoned arguments and effect the change democratically. Others feel people will be reluctant to give up their life-style of total pleasure, that the masses don't know what's good for them anyway and that the change should be autocratically enforced.

'That's clever,' said Seth. 'That's a theme. Is it right to make someone do something that's good for them against their will? Always good to stick a theme in, fleshes it out.'

So the rebels divide into two factions. The revolutionary faction prepares to attack the hedonist leaders, when what should happen? The main revolutionary (male) falls in love with the main hedonist (female). Their great love convinces them that both their outlooks are wrong. Too much pleasure is bad, but so is too much hard work. All they want is to give up politics and live happily ever after. They are about to run off together when they are discovered. Both sides now regard them as traitors and they are executed. The two armies then turn against each other and have a battle to decide on the future organisation of society. Nobody wins, everybody is killed and the world descends into chaos. The end.

'Don't be ridiculous. We need a better ending than that,' said Carmel-Marie.

'I like that ending,' said Seth defensively. 'I think we can afford to take it dark.'

'It's a bit . . . hazy,' I ventured.

'It's hazy as a bastard,' Darryl agreed.

'Well, a lot of things can be resolved in the improvisation process,' Seth explained to the open french window, cannily anticipating that it would raise fewer objections than we would.

Alistair and I were setting off to Menorca the next day for a fortnight's holiday and other people had longer trips planned, so there was no more time to argue. We agreed on the hazy-as-a-bastard plot and I arranged to have a meeting with Seth as soon as I got back to confirm the Haze and sort out a scene-by-scene breakdown before I started working on the script.

On 22 July, just over two weeks later, I arrived at Seth's office, happy and tanned, prepared to carry on where we had left off.

'There have been a few slight changes while you were away,' he said. I knew instantly that he felt either worried or guilty, because his eyeballs were indulging in more vigorous aerobic exercises than usual.

'Fine,' I said easily. I had a suntan and, let's face it, any changes to the Haze had to be a good thing. 'Has there been a meeting while I was away?' I shifted a mound of dog-eared papers from an armchair and sat down. Seth didn't seem to appreciate the fact that he had the biggest office in the building with the best view. To say he is messy doesn't quite convey the full horror. Darryl is messy, in a relaxed and harmless way. Every time I go into Seth's room I have to fight back the urge to say, 'Oh no, the FBI have been here, searching for vital evidence!' What distresses me most is the way he treats his students' and prospective students' work. There was a pile of manuscripts beside my feet that had long since given up the struggle to remain rectangular. They were covered with coffee spills and looked as if they had been kicked down the road by unruly drunks.

'Well, no.' Seth sat down and then stood up again immediately, ruffling his prickly hair in agitation. 'But Natasha's had some excellent ideas.'

'Natasha? Your wife Natasha?'

'Yes. It was very good of her, I mean, she's got enough on her plate at the University, but she actually found the time to sit down and replot the entire play.'

'How kind.'

'I think it's a lot stronger now. See what you think.' He handed me a plastic wallet. Inside there was a sheet of paper headed '*Lions After Slumber* – New Synopsis by Dr Natasha Leaf'. It read as follows:

The action is set in 1997 in the philosophy department of a university. Everybody in the department works really hard, too hard (especially some people who have to do more than their fair share to cover for imbecile colleagues!!!). One woman is sent back from the future, from the year 2197, by futuristic world leaders. Her task is to cause (?) provoke (?) initiate (?) the revolution that brings about the new hedonistic world order (à la *Terminator*, basic idea of someone being sent back from future to present to ensure things happen in present that make future possible. But don't mention *Terminator* to anyone, obviously, or they'll think you've stolen the idea.) Woman is trained in philosophy. She becomes an expert on Kant and the categorical imperative, so that she fits in and can impersonate present-day philosophy lecturer without anyone suspecting her. Once there, however, she enjoys her work more than she thought (in her futuristic life she's never done work, robots did it all, so it's a new experience). She gets really into her research on Kant and realises that future world order is bad. She becomes a Kantian and realises that the greater moral good is more important than the pleasure of the individual. With the help of her philosophy department pals (to whom she confesses the truth about her situation) she turns her back on her futuristic roots and sets about ensuring that society continues in its present form. Her supervisors from the future get wind of her betrayal and send some hedonistic heavies to the present to sort her out. The heavies, despite being large and macho, are defeated by the powerful philosophical arguments of the Woman and her colleagues and the present world set-up is safe.

'Well?' Seth looked at me tentatively. 'I like it. I like it a lot. Do you like it?' His eyes were ready to scarper if I said anything negative.

'Has Carmel-Marie seen it?'

'No, not yet. I thought I'd bounce it off you first.'

'Darryl? Rosie? Duane? Hayley?'

'Not yet, no. But I'm sure they'll love it. I mean, it's hardly different from the version we agreed. A few minor changes, that's all.'

'Show it to the others. I'll go along with the majority verdict,' I said. I was gambling for support, like Henry Fonda does in *Twelve Angry Men*. You know, the bit where he suggests another vote and says that he won't stand alone. If everyone else votes guilty, he will too. But if anyone votes not guilty, they all have to stay and talk it out.

In my case it was less of a gamble because I knew for an absolute certainty that Carmel-Marie, Darryl, Rosie, Duane, Hayley – and indeed anybody with any sense – would veto Natasha's synopsis as soon as they read the words 'philosophy department'. According to the Beasley Theatre brochure, *Lions* was a futuristic thriller, so imagine the audience's surprise when the curtain rises to reveal a seminar room full of elbow-patched academics.

Seth didn't show Natasha's synopsis to the rest of the Creative Team straight away. Instead, he waited until 4 August, the first day of rehearsals, and called an emergency Creative Team meeting. The seven of us met under a tree outside the theatre to discuss Natasha's idea. The heat was almost unbearable and we lolled lazily on the grass. Everyone except me was wondering what the emergency was.

The Youth Theatre members, meanwhile, had been abandoned in the drama studio and told to keep themselves busy by hugging each other and creating a positive atmosphere. I've just had a horrible thought: Tony-hugging undoubtedly took place and I missed out on it.

Everybody but Seth poured scorn on Natasha's plot

idea and Rosie pointed out that it was hard enough for the seven of us to make decisions without involving all our partners as well.

'Oh, I've got no time for egos,' said Seth dismissively. 'A good idea is a good idea, whoever it comes from.'

'But this isn't one,' I said, confident of my Fonda-esque majority. There was a minor mutiny, after which Seth had a tantrum and told everyone to go away and come up with a better idea if we didn't like Natasha's. We pointed out that our original Haze had been a better idea, albeit only slightly. But Seth, perhaps out of loyalty to Natasha, said he was no longer especially keen on it. The rest of us exchanged surprised glances. He'd been keen? That was more than could be said for any of us. Still, we would all happily have reinstated the Haze rather than think of anything new. This was getting ridiculous. Rehearsals had started and there was nothing to rehearse.

Days one, two, three and four went by before an agreement was reached. The Creative Team argued every day from 9 to 10 a.m., from 1 to 2 p.m. and from 4.30 p.m. onwards. The Youth Theatre members did lots of improvisations based around what the word lions meant to them, as that word was the only definite thing we had so far. They pretended to be lions, they knocked up a few nice little Daniel-in-den-of numbers, they did the whole three-on-a-shirt routine. Some of the more assertive and intelligent YTMs, particularly Oliver, Ed and Stella, were asking sensitive questions like 'What's the play actually about?' and 'When will we get our scripts?'.

On Friday 8 August, the fifth day of rehearsals, Seth turned purple in the face, produced a ground-breaking and inspired synopsis that he had come up with all on his own without any help from us, and told us that if we didn't like it he would simply cancel this year's Youth Theatre altogether.

His synopsis, he claimed, blended the best aspects of the Haze and Natasha's Kant-rant. It was as follows:

The action is set in a local government office in 1997. Wristine Vella (Seth didn't have names in his synopsis, but I'll insert them as they are now known) is sent back to the past by World Supervisor Ingra Savoy. Her mission is to effect the transition from present work-based world to future pleasure-based world. On no account should *Terminator* be mentioned as an influence. Wristine doesn't want to do this because she will have to leave her husband, Vilk Vella, with whom she is happy. Supervisor Ingra Savoy forces her to go, however, so there she is in 1997 in the Legal Department of Berkshire County Council, working as a secretary. She has never had to work before and she hates it, but she falls in love with a dashing young legal executive, Ian Chaddock, and seeing him every day makes her life bearable. Ian falls in love with her as well and they have an affair. Wristine doesn't want to go back to her future life with Vilk any more because she prefers Ian, but Ingra Savoy will not let her stay in the present or give up on her mission, so Wristine doesn't know what to do. Ian asks her to marry him, and she bursts into floods of tears and confesses all – Vilk, mission, everything. Ian doesn't care and says he still loves her more than ever. Meanwhile Ingra Savoy, suspecting that all is not proceeding according to plan, travels to 1997 herself, taking Vilk Vella with her. Ingra and Vilk are beamed down into the offices of Berkshire County Council's Legal Department, where they confront Wristine. Ian leaps to her defence, telling Vilk and Ingra to get lost. Ingra murders Ian with a futuristic weapon. Wristine, distraught at the loss of her true love, grabs futuristic weapon and kills Ingra. Vilk then murders Wristine in a jealous rage, and commits suicide because without Wristine he has nothing to live for. All killings done with same futuristic weapon. Dark, bleak ending.

Darryl, Carmel-Marie, Hayley, Rosie, Duane and I read the synopsis in horror and, with the fear of cancellation hanging over our heads, said it was fine. The students would be heart-broken if we let them down like that. The tears that would fill the drama studio would be enough to drown us all.

'Just one thing,' said Carmel-Marie tentatively. Just one? I thought. 'There are only four main characters.'

'So?' Seth drummed his fingers on the table. His head's resemblance to a plump aubergine signified that he was still feeling stressed.

'There are thirty kids in there.' Carmel-Marie gestured towards the drama studio, in which improvisations around the theme of slumber were taking place while we argued. 'What are the other twenty-six going to do?'

'Well . . . they can be robots. They can be the robots who do all the work,' said Seth.

'That's what I feel like,' Hayley whinged. Seth had been referring all queries about the apparent lack of play to her, as well as putting her in charge of Keeping Everyone Happy.

'There are no robots,' I said. 'It's set in 1997.'

'Yes, but there'll be the odd scene set in the future. Where the woman's given her brief, where she says goodbye to her husband before going to 1997.'

'We still won't need twenty-six robots.' Darryl chuckled.

'Okay, then, some of them can be people at Berkshire County Council. Legal executives, secretaries. We can easily throw in a few bit parts. Can't we, Belinda?'

'Yes, but . . .'

'I think we should have a chorus,' said Carmel-Marie.

'A what?' I asked.

'You know, a chorus, like in Greek tragedies.'

'Won't it be a bit strange to have the Legal Department of Berkshire County Council with a Greek chorus in the background?' asked Duane, struggling to stretch his perforated tongue around so many words.

'We won't make them look Greek,' said Seth, keen to agree on any solution to the spare-twenty-six-people problem. 'Choruses don't have to be Greek, do they?'

'Of course not,' said Carmel-Marie. 'They just have to make comments abite the action and themes as the play progresses. They often speak in verse. It might be nice to have some poetry in there.'

'Can you do poetry, Belinda?' asked Hayley, ready to be resentful of my versatility if I said yes and disappointed at my limitations if I said no.

'No,' I said.

'Oh, don't sell yourself short,' said Seth. 'Course you can.'

And that was that. I was given four days to write the script, which I just about managed by giving up sleep for the weekend. The following Wednesday morning I gave it to Seth, complete with poetic chorus bits. He cut out all the humour ('I think we can afford to take it even darker'), added more violence and edited out about half the dialogue from every scene including some crucial linking lines without which meaning was lost. Normally my creative vanity would have felt severely affronted by such blatant script-tampering, particularly coming from someone with as hackneyed an artistic vision as Seth's, but the endless hours of directionless arguing by committee had worn me down to the point where I would have agreed to anything. I felt like juror number seven in *Twelve Angry Men*, who changes his vote to not guilty because he's sick of 'all this yakkin'.

Hayley photocopied the script and distributed it to the YTMs, who greeted it with unanimous enthusiasm.

84

They were so desperate to see a reassuring bundle of white A4 paper that we could have given them anything and they would have been happy.

Seth did the casting in about five seconds ('Oliver – Vilk, Phoebe – Wristine, Stella – Ingra, Carl – Ian. Ed, you can be Barry Pilsworth, Ian's boss, the Principal Legal Executive. Trudi, Sinead, Megan – you can be the secretaries Karen, Debby and Chelsea respectively. The rest of you are either robots or chorus, we'll decide as we go along.') and things rattled on at a hassled pace thenceforth, with Darryl churning out music as if his life depended on it, Carmel-Marie frantically making up dance steps and the YTMs manically trying to learn lines.

'We've all got a lot of work to do, a *hell* of a lot of work to do,' Seth yelled bitterly every so often. 'We've only got two weeks – *two weeks* – before opening night!' It wasn't clear which unknown force he held responsible for this state of affairs.

# Chapter Eleven

## The Dress Rehearsal

Tuesday 26 August was the day of the dress rehearsal. We had moved from the drama studio into the much grander three-tiered theatre. As Seth had said at the beginning of rehearsals, in one of our many seminars about how best to use the space available, 'Remember, the audience will be in tiers.' I bet they bloody will, I thought to myself.

I was amazed to see how well things had come together at the last minute; despite the unpromising start we now had a script, costumes, a set, props – all the things real plays had. Even I had to admit that my earlier pessimism might not have been entirely justified. Although I had wanted to push Seth off a steep cliff every time he said 'Trust me, I've done this before', it seemed he had been right and I had been overly neurotic.

A large gold outline of a lion had been painted on the stage and the cast, in silver zip-up boiler suits, were practising the opening dance sequence to Darryl's experimental electronic music, which consisted of loud beeps, throbbing bass-lines and peculiar echoes. If I hadn't known it was Darryl's *Lions* sound-track I would have thought it was a gang of thugs smashing up an answerphone shop.

The opening fifteen minutes of the play were crucial. If the audience didn't understand them, the chances were they wouldn't understand any of it. Seth, because he was terrified of Carmel-Marie and wanted (a) to get her off his back and (b) to make her feel important, had decided that the first part of the story, where the scene is set and the background is provided, should be communicated in the form of a dance. If Carmel-Marie had been a pastry chef Seth would have advocated the use of apple pies as a narrative device.

I sat in the grand tier and watched thirty silver figures move in highly synchronised formation around the huge gold lion at their feet. I thought they were doing rather well.

Carmel-Marie didn't seem to agree. 'Stop. *Stop*!' she barked, in full Mr-Brocklehurst-from-*Jane-Eyre* mode. The theatre didn't have the same strong air-conditioning that the drama studio had had, so anyone who wasn't compelled to wear a sweltering boiler suit was as scantily clad as possible, except Tony, who seemed determined to cover his arms and legs no matter how high the temperature rose. Carmel-Marie, dressed in minuscule black hotpants that went half-way up her bum and a top that looked as if it yearned to be a bra, resembled an egg timer more closely than usual. Her waist looked only slightly thicker than my wrist. 'Listen, this isn't hard you know.' She sighed. 'You should *all* be able to do it by nigh. Trudi, I don't know what you were doing, but you were completely ite of time with the rest of the group.'

'I'm just not a very good dancer,' said Trudi defensively, toying idly with her over-gelled hair.

'You don't need to be a good dancer to do this routine,' said Carmel-Marie impatiently. 'You only need a memory and the ability to cighnt. Nigh, from the top, one, two, three, *four*!'

Darryl had set up his musical equipment behind some of the seats in the circle. He, Tony and Rhys – *Lions*' other wannabe sound engineer who was allegedly eighteen but looked about two – were installed behind big black boxes, twiddling amplifier knobs. Darryl and Seth ignored each other comprehensively. Whenever Seth needed to make a comment that related to the music, he spoke into mid-air, making sure to keep his wandering eyes far away from Darryl.

'The opening music needs more echo,' he now announced to the grand tier, which was empty except for me. I could see even from my great height that Seth's insecurity had started to affect his wardrobe in a serious way. He was wearing a vest top emblazoned with the slogan 'Cinderella Sucks – a Seth Beasley Production'.

Darryl said nothing, but within seconds his answerphone-shop raid sounded as though it was coming from beyond the grave.

'Hold it right there!' Carmel-Marie marched towards Carl and Phoebe, who were huddled in a corner of the stage going over some of their key scenes. 'You're supposed to be in love, Carl. Try to sined less like a bored teenager and more like a man.' She rounded on Seth furiously. 'And that's your job to say that, not mine!'

'Er, yes.' Seth attempted a toothy grin, but Carmel-Marie was not yet ready to let go of her resentment. Everyone knew she felt Seth was skimping on his duties as director and forcing her to take on more than her fair share. I didn't feel Seth could be held entirely responsible; the fact was that Carmel-Marie loved ordering people around and Seth didn't. He was too busy trying to be popular. He wanted the status bestowed upon him by his 'director' title, without the unpleasant burden of having to make any important decisions.

'Let's take it from the top, but with more feeling this time,' he now said earnestly.

'I'm putting lots of feeling into it already,' Phoebe

protested, her big blue eyes filling with tears. 'If I feel any more, I'll collapse!'

'Yes, you're fine as you are, Phoebe, in fact you're so good that you're making Carl look worse,' said Carmel-Marie.

'Cheers,' Carl muttered, chewing gum apathetically. His boiler suit was unzipped to the waist. Underneath he wore a T-shirt that said 'Fuck you, I won't do what you tell me'. My self-brainwashing was working; I was beginning to fancy him.

'From the top, then,' said Seth. 'And,' – he turned his back on Darryl deliberately – 'there's too much static coming out of these mikes.'

Darryl emerged from the shadows with Tony limping behind him and they fiddled around with wires that were sellotaped to the floor. Well, it would be more precise to say that Darryl fiddled with the wires, all the time explaining to Tony what he was doing. Good old Darryl, I thought. He hadn't forgotten that Tony was here to learn about sound engineering. I wondered if he had sprained his ankle, but didn't ask because he looked exceptionally glazed today. He hadn't had a good, alert, do-you-want-a-chair sort of day for ages.

As soon as he emerged from behind the sound system he was accosted by girls shrieking his name and tugging at his limbs. Sinead Riley and Megan Cartledge, two of the more giggly and moronic YTMs, were particularly aggressive Tony-pursuers, I noticed. They were the ringleaders, the ones who shrieked loudest and tugged hardest. But Tony didn't seem angry with them. He just shook them off impatiently, without even looking in their direction, as though his mind were somewhere altogether different.

I looked at Carmel-Marie, who was wandering around the theatre giving people individual tickings-off for their dramatic inadequacies. She and Tony seemed unaware of each other's presence.

A wonderful possibility flooded my mind. Maybe they'd split up!

'What's wrong, Wristine?' Carl whined on stage. 'You can tell me. Don't you trust me?'

'Hold it!' Carmel-Marie hissed. 'It's "you can tell *me*" Carl, not "you can *tell* me", emphasis on the "me". You've got to understand the lines to say them properly.'

'I do understand them!' said Carl defiantly. He turned back to Phoebe. 'What's wrong, Wristine? You can tell *me*.' He overstressed the last word deliberately, making the line sound ridiculous. Carmel-Marie pursed her lips and folded her arms threateningly. Seth, aware that he had missed yet another opportunity to direct, rolled his enormous head around idly, trying to look important and creative.

'I'm scared to tell you,' said Phoebe/Wristine, looking as though she was genuinely on the brink of tears. Her bright-blonde hair was a fuzzy halo under the spotlight.

'But I love you, Wristine. Nothing . . .'

'Carl!' Carmel-Marie barked.

'But I *love* you, Wristine. Nothing you tell me could make me stop loving you.'

'I'm married,' Wristine whispered. This was the adultery sub-plot that Carmel-Marie had tried to veto, using the argument, 'I think people who are unfaithful are crap.' Carmel-Marie thought Wristine would lose the audience's sympathy if she was unfaithful to Vilk Vella, her devoted husband.

'You're . . . you're what?' Carl was getting into it now, I could tell. He was beginning to realise what it meant to be Ian Chaddock. The more feeling he put into the lines I'd written, the more I was able to think lustfully about him.

'Married . . . but, oh, it's not what you think.'

'Leave him, Wristine, we can run away together.'

'I have left him,' said Wristine. 'I've left him in the future. Two hundred years in the future.'

As Carl and Phoebe held hands and stared meaningfully into each other's eyes, fifteen chorus members walked on from the wings, formed a circle around Ian and Wristine and began to chant:

Two hundred years divide,
Two hundred years apart,
So let the present hide
And guard her cheating heart.
She never meant to cheat.
Her husband is estranged.
Never admit defeat.
The future can be changed.
Never admit defeat.
The future can be . . . *CHANGED*!

'And . . . cut,' said Seth, as though he had just made a momentous directorial decision.

# Chapter Twelve

## Flirting with Carl

It was three o'clock and I was sitting on a wall outside the theatre with Carl Sillery. We were both smoking cigarettes. I don't actually smoke, but asking him for a cigarette was the first item on my flirting agenda. The second was sitting very close to him and looking at him in an adoring way. My campaign was working well already because Carl looked flustered but flattered, which is the ideal way for a bloke one is chasing to look.

I had got him away from the dress rehearsal and out from under Seth's hyperactive eye on the premise that I wanted to go through some of his key scenes with him in private. Seth agreed to this at once because he was concerned about Carl's apparent inability to learn the poem he had to recite, Shelley's 'Song to the Men of England'. Carl knew all his other lines, it was just the poem he couldn't seem to grasp.

'Okay, let's do it verse by verse,' I said. 'Start with the first line.'

'Men of, er, England, wherefore . . .'

'Plough.'

'Yeah, wherefore plough. For the Lords who lay you low.'

'Lay *ye* low.'

'Oh, right, lay ye low. Wherefore weave with toil and care, The rich robes your tyrants wear?'

'Good.' I smiled seductively. This is mad, I thought, what I'm doing is mad. Yet the Rational Emotional Administrator in me proceeded according to plan.

'Wherefore . . . erm, wherefore . . .'

'. . . feed and clothe and save.'

'Oh, From the cradle to the grave, Those ungrateful souls who would, Drain your sweat, no, drink your blood.'

'*Nay*, drink your blood.'

'Do I have to say "nay"? I'll feel daft saying "nay".'

'That's what Shelley wrote.'

'I just don't think I can say it.'

'Ask Seth, then.'

'I have. He said "no" was just as good, and no one would notice.'

'Well, he's the director. Okay, next verse.'

'Wherefore, Bees of England, forge, Many a weapon . . . erm . . .'

'Chain and scourge.'

'That these stingless, er, drones may spoil, The forced product of your toil.'

'Produce, not product.'

'Ey? Oh, right, the forced produce of your toil.'

'That's better. I think we should leave at least a few of Shelley's words in there.' I fluttered my eyelashes at him. 'Also, I know you're only learning lines at the moment, but try not to mumble. Remember there's going to be music in the background.' Seth, anxious that the audience shouldn't nod off during the poem and not trusting either Shelley's words or Carl's delivery to keep them awake, had instructed Darryl, in those heady pre-solicitor's-letter days, to knock up some kind of jungle-garage-grunge backing track.

'I'll have to fuckin' yell it, then,' said Carl. 'Have you heard how loud that music is?'

'If it's too loud just ask Darryl to turn it down. Or Tony or Rhys.' That was a bit risky, saying Tony's name out in the open like that, but I think I said it neutrally enough so that Carl didn't realise I was in love with Tony.

'Is it true what I've heard, then?' asked Carl.

Oh my God. My heart flipped over like a tossed pancake. He knew I was in love with Tony! But how, *how*? 'What have you heard?' I stammered.

'About Darryl threatening to sue Seth.' Oh, praise the Lord!

'How do you know that?'

'Everyone knows.'

'How?'

'I think Seth mentioned it to Ed, and Ed told me. Seth's really upset about it. All he wants is to sort it out, but Darryl isn't having any of it.'

'Carl, that's only one side of the story. And Seth had no right to involve ... you lot, or anyone else. It's ... unprofessional.' Inspired by this last word, I pouted and tucked my hair coyly behind my ear.

'Seth's a decent bloke,' said Carl. 'I feel sorry for him. I think Darryl's well out of order. I mean, getting lawyers involved, that's low, that is. There's no need for that.'

'Where were we up to in the poem?' I changed the subject. This wasn't the time for me and Carl to have our first row, before our relationship had even got off the ground.

'Oh, right, erm, Have you leisure, comfort, calm, Shelter, food, love's gentle balm ... Do I have to say "love's gentle balm"?'

'Carl ...' I moaned under my breath, half irritated, half enraptured.

'I wish I didn't have to recite a fuckin' poem.' He kicked the wall with his heel.

'Why?'

'It's embarrassing. It's soppy, innit?'

'What, poetry or this poem in particular?'

'Both.'

'This poem's not soppy. It's rebellious and . . . tough.'

'I just don't think Ian Chaddock would read a whole poem out loud like that, in the middle of the office, with all his mates hanging around. I don't think it's consistent with his character.' Carl looked at me hopefully.

'He's trying to persuade them that work is bad for them,' I said. 'He's in love with Wristine and she's told him all about future society where no one has to be a wage slave. He's trying to win over his colleagues, who are all workaholics. He reads them the poem and that makes them question their boring nine-to-five lives.'

'Well, I don't reckon he'd win them over by reading a poem. In real life, I mean. They'd just take the piss, wouldn't they? Bunch of lawyers and secretaries? They're not going to hang around while he prattles on about looms and tombs, are they?'

'Well, you never know . . .'

'Course they're not,' Carl said with certainty.

'Maybe not, but you have to read the poem, Carl. Seth wants lots of Shelley in the play, to make the title relevant. Anyway, read it really well and you'll be accosted by groupies after the show.'

'Oh, that'll be good.' He blushed.

'Yeah, well, just remember who helped you learn your lines.'

'I will.'

'Yes, well, make sure you do. I don't want you to forget about me when you're carried off by adoring fans. Unless I'm one of them, of course.'

'Oh . . . er . . . right . . . Huhn.'

# Chapter Thirteen

## Snooping Around Hayley's Desk

After my Shelley-and-flirting session with Carl I raced
upstairs to Hayley's office to rifle through her files. I
wanted to find the letter from Tony's social worker. I
still intended to proceed with the Carl Sillery Plan, but
I couldn't stand the thought that there were facts about
Tony that other people knew and I didn't.

It was his limp that set me off. He had hobbled into
the dress rehearsal hoping no one would notice. Darryl
spotted it immediately and asked him what was wrong.
'Nothing,' he said blankly. I was standing next to
Hayley at the time and we exchanged a look.

'Nothing my eye,' she muttered. 'He's been up to no
good again.'

'Again?' I tried to sound innocent and impartial.

'Yeah, like when he came in that day with his wrist
all bandaged up, remember?' How could I forget? Tony
Lamb's bandaged wrist was considerably more attractive than most people's faces.

'So? Maybe he's just accident prone.'

'Come off it.' Hayley laughed. 'He obviously spends
a large proportion of his leisure time kicking people's
heads in.'

I was about to ask how she could possibly make such
a claim without hard evidence when it occurred to me
that maybe she knew something I didn't, something
from the social worker's letter.

96

Nothing could put me off him, that went without saying. I loved Tony for better or worse, richer or poorer, to love, honour and gawp at behind obtrusive musical equipment till the last night of *Lions* did us part – oh God, what a soul-destroying thought. Never mind, the Carl Sillery Plan should have kicked in and anaesthetised me by then.

I couldn't ask Hayley straight out because not only was Alistair her husband's colleague, he was also her landlord.

When Alistair and I first met I was living with my parents and he had his own house in Ascot, which he was keen to move out of. He'd got it really cheap because it was in appalling condition. Alistair is attracted to knackered houses that allow him to fantasise about how stunningly he can do them up, but he underestimates how long and hard the doing-up process will be.

When the two of us decided to buy a house together, Alistair put his Ascot house on the market and, surprise surprise, no one wanted to buy it because it needed thousands of pounds' worth of work doing to it. An estate agent told Alistair that, with the market being what it was, he would get less than he'd paid four years earlier. A better option would be to rent it out until he had made more money from the house than he'd spent on it and perhaps sell it later.

Phil Douglas, strangely anxious to avoid bringing up children on a rough estate in Slough – strangely because he had none – suggested that he and Hayley move into the house and, in exchange for an extremely cheap rent, do it up. Phil is another of these nutters who sees a potential chateau in every heap of rubble, but unlike Alistair he actually owns a toolcase.

It was an Everybody Wins situation, a bit like the Carl Sillery Plan, but it meant that I couldn't risk showing an unnatural interest in Tony when Hayley was around. The Douglases, Alistair and I were far too interconnected.

Hayley's office is at the very top of the building, a fact she is forever bemoaning and attributing to Seth's deliberate persecution of her, so I had to run up three flights of stairs. I gasped as I pushed open the unlocked door and walked in, feeling the temperature increase by several degrees. It was like a sauna in there. Thank God my office is on the ground floor, I thought, with a big window.

As Beasley's only secretary, Hayley has all the school files in her office, including the Youth Theatre ones. Panting and sweating profusely, I hopped around her desk, picking things up and throwing them down again when I saw they weren't what I wanted. I hoped Seth was keeping her as busy as usual in the dress rehearsal; all I needed was to be caught in the act of raiding her filing cabinet.

The Youth Theatre paperwork was in the bottom drawer. Behind the files for *Cinderella Sucks* and *Bladerunner* I found a big grey folder with 'Youth Theatre – *Lions*' written on it in thick black marker. I flipped hurriedly through the pages. What was all this? Oh, right, the application forms. Everyone who wants to take part in the Youth Theatre has to fill one in and send a photo. A wonderful thought occurred to me: there might be a photo of Tony in here. I started to flick more quickly in search of this holiest of grails and stopped when my finger got to Carl's form.

There was a photograph of him wearing his best 'I'm a dude with attitude' expression, jutting his chin out. I read his name, age (he was definitely seventeen, here it was, written in black and white), address. He lived on Cavendish Road in Windsor, near Seth and Natasha's house. I guessed that he made quite an effort to disguise his privileged origins. Unlike Oliver Wild and Ed Fewster, who came across as unashamedly bourgeois,

Carl went to great lengths to present himself as a working-class scally.

There was nothing in the file about Tony. I swore under my breath. Perhaps because of his problems all the information about him was treated as confidential and locked away somewhere.

Suddenly I noticed a pile of papers on the window-sill. I tiptoed tentatively towards it, feeling the GLOW shine out as I approached, and – oh joy – found Tony's application form and social worker's letter buried under a pile of *Lions* posters, leaflets and programmes.

There was a passport-sized photo of him stapled to the top right-hand corner of his application form. This was almost what I had been looking forward to most, but now that it was in front of me, I found it strangely disappointing. It was a photo of Tony and therefore innately superior to all photos that weren't of Tony, but it was lifeless, immobile and totally failed to capture any sense of his inner mystery, his mood swings or the sound of his voice when he said 'Do you want a chair?' I ripped it off the form and stuck it in my pocket none the less. If Hayley was as overworked as she claimed she would never notice a missing photo.

Deciding to leave the social worker's letter until last, I read through Tony's application form eagerly. His full name was Anthony Paul Lamb and his address was Room 4, Sandlea Court, Sandlea Road, Slough. His age was twenty-one and his date of birth was 14 July 1976. This was brilliant: all these new facts about Tony neatly laid out on one sheet of paper. I stroked his address with my forefinger. I kissed his date of birth. I lifted my T-shirt and pressed his 'Reasons for wanting to take part' paragraph against my heart, almost bruising my rib-cage in the process.

His reasons for wanting to take part were as follows:

I am interested in Sound Engineering and would like

to pursue a career in that area. I think that taking part in the Seth Beasley School Youth Theatre would be a valuable experience for me as it would enable me to learn essential skills and help me to get a place on a Sound Engineering course. I have had some experience of theatre work before, as my parents used to run a community theatre in Devon and I helped them sometimes. I love the theatre and regularly go to see shows.

Hmm. That didn't sound like Tony's voice to me. Had someone helped him, perhaps his social worker? Still, how did I know what Tony's voice sounded like, apart from when it said 'Do you want a chair?' I sighed with frustration, realising how little I knew about him, how remote he was from me. I resolved to try and push all thoughts of him out of my mind and instead concentrate on the machinations of the Carl Sillery Plan. But first I had to look at the social worker's letter.

Dear Mr Beasley [it began]
Beasley School Youth Theatre 1997 – Anthony Paul Lamb
 I am writing to urge you to reconsider your decision with regard to Anthony Lamb. While I understand that it is not the school's normal practice to allow non-students to take part in Youth Theatre productions, I feel that Anthony would benefit enormously from such an experience. It would boost his confidence and morale considerably and hopefully help him to get a place on a degree-level course in Sound Engineering.
 I understand your concerns with regard to Anthony's problems and history, as laid out in your letter of 15 June, but I can assure you that, in my professional opinion and in the opinion of his doctor, he would pose no danger to your students or

100

to anyone involved in the production. I therefore sincerely hope you will reconsider your decision.

Yours sincerely

M J Ross (Mrs), Berkshire Social Services East Team

I wanted to kill Seth when I read that. He had dared to say no to Tony. Thank God Mrs M J Ross had written back, and thank God Hayley and Darryl had stuck up for Tony at that meeting, or I would never have met him. My whole life would have passed by without one single Tony-enhanced day. Even Tony-pain, I decided, was better than a Tony-void, a Tony-abyss.

A lot of questions were buzzing around my mind. Tony had parents, which surprised me. I realised I had stupidly assumed he was an orphan. Many people have parents and a social worker, especially when their parents are deficient in some respect. But how could Tony's parents be anything other than GLOWsome, if they produced him? Could they have died, I wondered, between the 'community theatre in Devon' era and now? No, the way he wrote about them made them sound alive. It was all very confusing.

And why had Seth thought that Tony might present a danger to Beasley students? Or had he just made that up for Mrs M J Ross's benefit when the real reason he didn't want Tony around was simply because he was an outsider? Seth knew who and where he was at the Seth Beasley School of Performance and Creative Arts, surrounded by Seth Beasley students. Maybe he wasn't as keen on the real world as he claimed.

One look at all this information wasn't enough. How naïve of me to imagine it would be. I should have known that I would need to scrutinise every punctuation mark, scour each paragraph for possible meanings, analyse the ramifications of every sentence.

You know what's it's like, don't you, Category As —

don't worry, I haven't forgotten you – when you get your hands on a document with GLOW, intimately related to your loved one. It can be anything from a letter in which he or she is mentioned to an article about him or her in the local paper, any related paperwork whatsoever. You can't just pass through it like a tourist, can you? You have to set up house there, get to know it like a native. You have to burrow underneath its commas and curl up in its semicolons.

I stuffed the application form, photo and social worker's letter in my pocket and was about to tiptoe out of the office when Hayley walked in.

She saw me and immediately pretended to be more out of breath than she was, wiping perspiration from her forehead in an exaggerated motion. 'What are you doing here?' she asked.

'I . . . er . . . thought I'd left something in here the other day,' I lied feebly, 'but it's not here. What are you doing? Is the dress rehearsal finished?'

'I wish.' She sighed. 'Seth just told us to take five so I thought I'd pop up and phone Phil. Do you want to stay and talk to Alistair?'

'Erm . . . no, I think I'll go back down.'

'That's probably a good idea. Carmel-Marie's nipped out to Tesco's and I'm not sure it's safe to leave Seth and Darryl down there unsupervised. They may kill each other.'

'So you've heard, then.'

'Yes. I must say, I feel sorry for poor old Seth, I mean, despite the way he treats me. I do think Darryl's been unnecessarily harsh with this solicitor's letter thing. Couldn't he have spoken to Seth, tried to resolve things more amicably?'

I gritted my teeth, seeing exactly what was happening. Seth was making great headway with his bad-mouthing Darryl campaign, while Darryl, decent chap that he was, was saying nothing. As a result, everyone was taking Seth's side and Darryl was too sensitive to correct the misapprehension by telling them the truth. I was going to have to do something about this, I decided. Did Darryl know what Seth was up to? Should I tell him, or should I just tell Seth to stop his muck-spreading? 'I wouldn't take Seth's word as gospel,' I said to Hayley. 'You've not heard Darryl's version of events.'

'Have you? Ooh, tell me.'

'I can't, really, not without asking Darryl. Listen, I'd better get back to the theatre and try to protect my script from further mutilation. Can I take a programme?'

'Course,' said Hayley. 'Take them all, I'm sick of the sight of them. They remind me of all the hours I put in with no help from . . .'

I tuned out, knowing exactly how her comment would end. I lifted a programme from the top of the pile and left the office, stopping on the narrow staircase outside to fondle my latest acquisition.

The programme was a pale-blue sheet of A3 card, folded in half. There was a bad sketch of a lion on the front, above the words '*Lions After Slumber* – a play by Seth Beasley'. Typical, I thought, wondering if I could be bothered to dispute whether Seth, as director, had the right to claim that *Lions* was 'by' him. I decided I probably couldn't, not after my creative pride had been so comprehensively trampled by the devising process. It was hard to feel proprietorial when even the idea for the story hadn't been mine.

I quickly forgot all such trivialities when I saw my name near Tony's on the second page. 'Writer: Belinda Nield', it said, and then, a few lines below, 'Sound Engineers: Rhys Davies, Tony Lamb'.

Oh, GLOW, GLOW, GLOW!

# Chapter Fourteen

## The First Night of *Lions*

### Scene One – Wristine's Mission

*World Management Headquarters, 2197.* INGRA SAVOY, *the World Supervisor, sits at her desk shuffling papers. A robot opens the door and ushers in* WRISTINE VELLA.

ROBOT (*in monotone*)   Mrs Vella is here, Madam.

INGRA (*looking up*)   Thank you. You may go. (*To Wristine*) Take a seat.

WRISTINE   Thank you.

INGRA   Do you know why you're here?

WRISTINE   No, I . . . I've no idea.

INGRA   You have been selected for a special mission.

WRISTINE   Oh.

INGRA   'Oh'. Is that all you can say? Aren't you honoured?

WRISTINE   I don't know. I suppose that depends what the mission is.

INGRA   A wise answer. You have heard of time travel?

WRISTINE   Of course.

INGRA   Your mission is to travel back in time, to the year 1997 to be precise. What do you know about history, about the past?

WRISTINE   Well, nothing really. Only what I learned at school.

INGRA   What you learned was a lie, a glossing over of the real facts. The truth is depressing and thoroughly bad for one. You see, Wristine, we want everyone to be happy. So we try to prevent unpleasant facts from becoming public knowledge. The past was considerably worse than you think.

WRISTINE   Then I don't want to go there!

INGRA (*produces a huge dusty book from a drawer in her desk and hands it to Wristine*)   Turn to page 357, second paragraph.

WRISTINE (*finds the page and starts to read aloud*) 'Most people in 1997 Britain had to work in order to purchase food and other necessities. Humans performed all the tasks which, in a civilised society, are performed by robots, from cleaning to cooking to driving public transport. The average working day started at nine in the morning and did not end until five in the afternoon. During that time, people, or "employees" as they were called, only got an hour's break to eat their lunch. Very few people enjoyed their work; many hated it, but had no alternative but to continue if they wanted to enjoy a comfortable and affluent life. Those who protested were labelled "skivers" and punished.' (*She looks at Ingra in horror*) This can't be true!

INGRA   It can and it is. Now, turn to page 389.

WRISTINE   Which bit . . . oh! Oh, it's me! (*She looks at Ingra*) I don't understand. Why is there a photograph of me in this book? I wasn't around in 1997.

INGRA   Read paragraph three aloud, please.

WRISTINE   'The collapse of the wage-slave regime, in November 1997, had its humble origins in the Legal Department of Berkshire County Council. A temporary secretary called Christine Mellor . . .' Oh! That sounds like my name.

INGRA   Exactly. It sounds like you and looks like you because it is you, Wristine. Christine Mellor is you.

WRISTINE   What? I don't understand.

INGRA   We have to send you back, don't you see? Because you're already there in the past. As an undercover agent with a false name, you bring about the downfall of wage-slavery. The book proves that. So if we don't send you back . . .

WRISTINE . . . the past will be altered and the present . . .

INGRA . . . may turn out differently. Worse, perhaps much worse. We can't risk that.

WRISTINE But I don't want to leave Vilk.

INGRA In a different present, you and Vilk may well end up spending most of your lives apart, him working in a factory, you in a canteen . . .

WRISTINE *Okay*! Okay. Enough. I'll do it.

INGRA I knew you'd see sense. The welfare of the world is in your hands.

# Chapter Fifteen

## The First Night of *Lions*

### Scene Two – The Interval

'What have you done to my idea?' Natasha wailed at Seth as we huddled round the theatre bar sipping our clichéd gin and tonics. We had to shout to make ourselves heard over the enthusiastic din. The audience seemed to like the play so far and were now knocking each other over in a frenzied attempt to get their interval drinks. The room was as crowded as a tube carriage in rush hour and everyone was sweating heavily.

'What do you mean?' Seth's eyelids flickered nervously. 'I hardly changed it at all.'

'Hardly changed it? Where's the philosophy department?' Natasha had donned vast quantities of make-up for the occasion and a glittery black dress. She looked like a corpse awaiting burial.

'Oh, well, er . . .'

'What's happened to Kant?'

'Brian Cant?' asked Mark Ryder, an estate agent colleague of Richard White's, with a florid snub nose and a roadmap of broken veins across his cheeks. I had tried to conceal my surprise when we were introduced. Alistair wasn't even here, let alone any of his colleagues (apart from Phil who was here with Hayley). He would have liked to see the show, but had made it clear that he would only come if 'all those loons' weren't going to be there.

'So, how do you think it's going so far?' Hayley asked me, like a cancer patient desperate for news of a remission.

'Pretty well, actually. The acting's excellent. I think they've done brilliantly in such a short time.'

'Well, Phil's enjoying it. Hasn't even mentioned the fact that he's missing his pub quiz.'

'Oh, well, it must be a great success then!' I grinned.

'Great success!' Carmel-Marie spat aggressively, her breasts wobbling with suppressed rage. Everyone stared at her. 'You've obviously got extremely low standards, Belinda.'

'I'm thoroughly enjoying it,' said Mark Ryder. 'And it's obviously earning its keep, so to speak. Sold out, isn't it?'

'Yes, every night.' Seth folded his arms smugly, momentarily covering the part of his T-shirt which proclaimed, 'Seth Beasley's *Cabaret*, 4–7 November 1988'. Obviously he was in a nostalgic mood tonight.

'Most shows that Seth directs sell out before opening night,' said Natasha.

'That doesn't mean it's good,' said Carmel-Marie.

'I like it,' said Richard encouragingly, looking first to his wife and then Mark Ryder for reassurance.

'It would be okay if any of them bothered to act,' Carmel-Marie snapped. 'But they're all just coasting along on automatic pilot. I can't believe high unprofessional they are.'

'Talking of unprofessional,' Rosie whispered in my ear, 'where's Darryl?'

'Having a drink somewhere far away from Seth, I'd imagine,' I said bluntly. 'And who can blame him?'

'Poor Seth, though,' said Rosie. 'Having to direct a play and deal with all that as well. Darryl must be seriously paranoid if you ask me.'

'You haven't heard his side of the story,' I pointed out.

'I know, but poor Seth's distraught. He was almost in

tears when he was telling me about it the other day.'

'What are we talking about?' Duane strolled over wearing nothing but a pair of cycling shorts. A droplet of sweat dangled from one of his nipple rings and I moved my arm away instinctively.

'Seth and Darryl,' Rosie filled him in.

'Oh, right. Well, I think Darryl must be gay.'

'Of course he's not gay!' I snapped. Behind me, Carmel-Marie was still ranting at Phil, Hayley, Seth, Natasha, Mark and Richard.

'If they want to succeed as actors they need to learn to look immaculate, not so much as a hair ite of place, full make-up at all times! Someone needs to drum it into them that one person looking scruffy makes the whole show look scruffy.'

'Who looks scruffy?' Phil asked.

'Who doesn't!' Carmel-Marie shrieked. 'Phoebe's hair . . .'

'Wristine,' Hayley explained to Phil, who didn't know any of the actors' names.

'. . . is half falling ite of its hairband, Stella's mascara is smudged . . .'

'Ingra Savoy,' Hayley told Phil.

'. . . the idiot Carl Sillery is *still* missing the "g" sined off all his "ing"words.'

I whirled around angrily. 'Carl is playing a normal bloke.' I hurled myself towards the bosom of bigotry. 'A lot of normal blokes, particularly working-class ones, pronounce their "ings" like that. It wouldn't be realistic to have a present-day County Council office where everyone spoke like . . . Trevor Howard in *Brief Encounter*.' I thought it best not to mention Celia Johnson, in case Carmel-Marie telepathically intuited that this was my name for her post-elocution-lessons persona.

'Oh, dear, Carmel-Marie.' Natasha's scarlet mouth cracked into a smirk. 'Haven't turned against the workers, have you?'

'Oh, just fuck off, all you anally retentive wankers!' Carmel-Marie hissed and marched out of the bar.

'Oh, dear,' said Richard. 'I do wish she wouldn't use language.'

'Me too,' I agreed. 'Have you tried Sellotaping her mouth closed?'

'She's changed her tune,' Mark Ryder wittered cheerfully, sniffing and wiggling his red nostrils, oblivious to the tense atmosphere. 'When I arrived tonight she told me how brilliant the play was, said I had a treat in store. Those were her very words, a treat in store.'

Hmm. I suspected he was indulging in a spot of paraphrasing now. To the best of my knowledge, Carmel-Marie's opinion of *Lions* had never left the extremely negative bracket.

'Nobody ever said theatre was safe,' Seth pronounced solemnly. 'It's only a pity about the music.'

'Yes, let's face it,' Natasha sniggered, 'Darryl is hardly Mozart, is he?'

'I like the music,' said Phil.

'So do I.' I looked sharply at Seth and Natasha.

'I'm afraid Darryl hasn't done himself any favours with this lawyer business,' said Seth. 'Sadly, I think some of his colleagues may have adjusted their opinion of him somewhat, in the light of all this.'

'Well, this colleague hasn't!' I said as scathingly as possible. It was at times like this that I could have done with some of Carmel-Marie's inner venom. 'I'm going to go and find him right now and congratulate him.'

I wandered off and took a few deep breaths. I couldn't see Darryl in the bar or in the foyer. It suddenly became desperately important for me to speak to him before the second half started. What with my Tony obsession, the Carl Sillery Plan and the hectic run-up to opening night, I hadn't had a proper conversation with Darryl for days. I wanted to make sure he knew I was on his side.

Just as I was on the point of giving up and going back to the auditorium I saw him at the other end of the foyer, holding some wires, leads and other items whose functions were beyond me. 'Darryl!' I yelled. 'Come here!'

He hurried over. 'Can't be too long,' he said. 'Tony's up there on his own, probably breaking my equipment.'

'Why do you say that?'

'Oh God.' Darryl laughed. 'He's a real case! You know what he told me tonight, just before the show started? That he's deaf in one ear! I've been wondering why he never does anything I tell him to do over the headphones. Well, now I know. I mean, you'd think he might have mentioned that a bit earlier.'

I laughed. 'What's he like apart from being deaf in one ear?'

'Oh, he's a nice lad. Well, I think he is, I mean, he never really speaks. He just sits there and, whatever I say, he grins at me.' Oh, lucky, lucky Darryl to be the recipient of Tony-grins. 'I don't think he's God's gift to sound engineering, if you want my honest opinion. He's too much of a zombie half the time. I reckon he quite often comes in stoned. Either that or he's practising to be a Trappist monk. Anyway, tonight he's in zombie-mode so I don't want to leave him alone for too long.'

You won't believe what I did next, Cat As. I changed the subject, despite the high GLOW factor of the conversation so far. I needed to talk to Darryl about Seth and now was the perfect time to do it, when I was fired up from the GLOW of our Tony-talk. 'Darryl, I just wanted to say, I'm sorry I haven't had a chance to tell you this before, but . . . I'm on your side over this whole Seth thing.'

'Oh . . . thanks. You're in the minority.'

'I know. I can't believe people are taking Seth's side so . . . easily.'

'I can,' said Darryl. 'He's putting a lot of time and energy into talking them round.'

'Have you told anyone what really happened?'

'No. Apart from you.'

'Don't you think you should? I'm sure people would believe you if you just told them.'

'I'm not. If they're so ready to believe Seth and condemn me, why should I tell them? If I go round contradicting him, it keeps it alive. If I say nothing it'll die down a lot sooner.

'Not with Seth stirring like mad, it won't,' I said doubtfully.

'He'll get fed up of it eventually. Or at least I bloody hope he will. It's not very pleasant, you know, to be disapproved of by the vast majority of your colleagues.'

'But if they're wrong . . . I mean, who are they to judge you, anyway? You only need one person's approval and that's your own.'

'"This above all, to thine own self be true"?'

'Exactly.'

'I'm doing well, then, because I've got not one but three people on my side. Me, you and Carmel-Marie.'

'Carmel-Marie?' I wrinkled my nose.

'Yeah, she was really good about it. She said I didn't have to tell her what had gone on if I didn't want to, but she just wanted me to know that she wasn't taken in by Seth's whitewash.'

'Oh . . . well, good on her.' I tried to look enthusiastic.

'What's up?'

'Oh, I'm a bit pissed off with her, that's all. She's in a right strop tonight. She just yelled at everyone in the bar and called us all anally retentive.'

Darryl laughed. 'Yes, she's not in the best of moods, is she? Probably just first-night nerves.'

'Hm. I'm not convinced.'

'She can be a bit aggressive, but I think she's basically a good egg,' said Darryl. 'I'd better go and check on Tony. I don't want him to drift off into another dimension before the second half starts.'

I took my seat grimly in the auditorium. Carmel-Marie a good egg? That hypocritical, Tony-pilfering, tit-thrusting tyrant? I couldn't remember how I'd felt about her before the Day of Despondency, when I saw Tony sneaking out of her office. Had I liked her? It's hard to recall old feelings once they have been overlaid with new ones.

Could Tony and Carmel-Marie have split up, I asked myself for the billionth time since the dress rehearsal. They had been on-stage together for ages and not exchanged even one glance. Was that why Carmel-Marie was in such a foul mood tonight, because Tony had dumped her? I banished that particular glimmer of hope before it had a chance to make itself at home in my consciousness. Resigned gloom was infinitely preferable to hope followed by disappointment.

Another point that had been nagging at the back of my mind, but hadn't surfaced until my GLOW-conversation with Darryl was the question of how Tony, a virtually silent and frequently glazed loner, could manage to have a relationship at all. Hard as I tried, I simply couldn't imagine him interacting with anyone to an extent that would make an affair possible.

Don't be naïve, I scolded myself. He wouldn't have had to do any work at all. Carmel-Marie probably frogmarched him into the bedroom . . . which bedroom? Where? Not, presumably, the one that contained Richard White. Perhaps the bedroom of Room 4, Sandlea Court, Sandlea Road, Slough, then. Or perhaps they just did it on the carpet in Carmel-Marie's office. I couldn't continue with this line of thought, not without giving myself a heart tremor.

It's funny how asking one question can answer another, isn't it? The thing I had found hardest to comprehend was why Tony had chosen Carmel-Marie instead of, say, the stunning Phoebe Procter, or Lisa, a robot/chorus member who looked like a younger Whitney Houston.

The answer was staring me in the face. With any of the YTMs he would have had to take some positive action. Even if he'd fancied a liaison with one of the grabber-shriekers, he would somehow have had to move things on from the grabbing-and-shrieking stage which, given his reluctance to speak, would have been difficult for him.

Someone with Carmel-Marie's maturity and Brocklehurstian efficiency, on the other hand, would have been able to see to it that an affair was had, even if Tony's sole contribution was continued breathing.

There was no proof, though, that a full-blown affair had occurred. I didn't know what had gone on in Carmel-Marie's office immediately prior to Tony's guilty and rosy-cheeked exit. What if Carmel-Marie had tried to sweep him up into a passionate clinch and he had run away in terror?

I replayed the scene in my mind – the door inching open, Tony sliding out, blushing furtively – and was convinced that leaving Carmel-Marie's office un-observed was his priority, not simply leaving.

On with the Carl Sillery Plan, then. Come on Carl, I thought as the bell rang for the second half, work your magic. Do your stuff.

# Chapter Sixteen

## The First Night of *Lions*

### Scene Three – Ian and Wristine

*Berkshire County Council Legal Department.* IAN
CHADDOCK *is standing beside* WRISTINE VELLA*'s desk, or
Christine Mellor, as she is known in 1997.*

IAN   Christine, have you done those letters for me yet?
WRISTINE (*turning away from him*)   No.
IAN   Christine, we need to talk. I know there's
   something wrong.
WRISTINE   You don't know anything. You don't even
   know my real name.
IAN   Your name's Christine Mellor.
WRISTINE   No it's not. It's Wristine Vella.
IAN   What? Wristine Vella? What sort of a name is
   that?
WRISTINE   Oh, that's right, just go ahead and mock me.
IAN   I'm not mocking you, Chris . . . er, Wristine. I just
   don't understand what's happening. I thought we
   had something going. I thought you loved me.
WRISTINE (*crying*)   I do.
IAN   So why are you shutting me out like this? It's like
   you've just switched off. Have I done something
   wrong?
WRISTINE   It's for your own good. You should keep
   away from me. If you knew the truth . . . you
   wouldn't want to have anything to do with me.
IAN   That's not true. There's nothing you could tell me

115

that would make me stop loving you. Is it because we work together? Has Barry Pilsworth said something about keeping private life and work separate?

WRISTINE (*indignantly*)  No, he has not! Why, has he said something to you?

IAN  Well . . .

WRISTINE  He has, hasn't he? I can't believe it! I expected better from you Ian, I really did. Your love for me can't be very strong if you let Barry Pilsworth turn you against me! Who is he to tell us what to do anyway? I don't recognise his authority. I don't recognise anyone's authority except my own!

CHORUS  There's no authority she'll recognise,
No individual, no church or court
Whose will trumps hers, whose petty rule applies,
No one to whom she's programmed to report,
No one whose good opinion is worth more
To her than doing what she wants to do,
No one whose word could ever pass for law
Or ever could dictate her point of view.
Whether the world approves or disapproves,
No disapproval is too a high a cost
To pay. Don't cage her, don't constrain her moves
Or else your friendship will be better lost,
And Barry Pilsworth, that presumptuous, fat
Legal executive can't change all that.

IAN  Now, just a minute! What right do you have to talk to me like that, to make those accusations? You claim to love me, but you're very quick to assume the worst! Of course I didn't listen to Barry Pilsworth. As if I would! I told him straight out to mind his own business.

WRISTINE (*guiltily*)  Oh.

IAN  You know what your problem is? You're a

116

coward. You're too scared to make this relationship work, so you're pushing me away, freezing me out.

WRISTINE    I'm not! Oh, you just don't understand. It's not as simple as that.

IAN    I don't expect it to be simple. I don't care if it's simple or not. All I care about is you, about us being together. I thought you did too.

WRISTINE    I do, but . . .

IAN    Then it is simple, don't you see! Stuff everyone else, stuff everything – this office, Barry Pilsworth, the world. We're more powerful than them, our love makes us invincible. We could crush the whole world with the strength of our love.

WRISTINE    But Ian, I can't stay here. I have to leave soon.

IAN    So? You can get another temp job. We can still see each other. Love makes everything possible.

CHORUS    Shake off the fears that ail you.
　　　　　Pray to the Lord above
　　　　　Not that love won't fail you
　　　　　But that you won't fail love.

# Chapter Seventeen

## The First Night of *Lions*

### Scene Four – After the Show

'Belinda Nield?' A tall, angular woman in a blue-and-white boating dress tapped me on the shoulder.

'Yes, that's right.' I turned round, giggling slightly. Post-show euphoria had broken out in the bar and everyone was giving each other sweaty hugs.

'Hilary Sillery. I'm Carl's mother.' That figures, I thought, noticing that, like her son, Hilary was blonde in a green way. We shook hands. 'What a wonderful play! Congratulations.'

'Thank you.' I blushed, partly in response to the compliment and partly from a fear that she could read my thoughts. If she had had any idea of my intentions with regard to her son, she wouldn't have been nearly so pleasant. 'Carl was brilliant,' I said truthfully. He had surpassed all expectation. Some of us, including me, had doubted whether he was main-part material. The Ian Chaddock role required lashings of emotional gravitas, and Carl had seemed too cynical and frivolous at the beginning of rehearsals.

I'd been amazed at his performance tonight. He was the Ian Chaddock of my dreams, the ideal, platonic Ian Chaddock. Watching him hold Wristine masterfully in his arms, it was easy to fancy him. A little bit of will-power, a little bit of transference of Tony-feeling and pretty soon I'd be a bona fide Carl groupie.

'This is my husband, John,' Hilary Sillery went on.

118

'John, this is Belinda Nield who wrote the play.' John Sillery shook my hand energetically. He was a dark hefty man with hairy hands. Carl took after his mother physically.

'Pleasure to meet you, my dear. We've heard a lot about you.'

'You have?'

'Oh yes,' Hilary Sillery enthused. 'Carl's always talking about you. He admires you very much.'

'Oh . . . er, right.'

'You helped him learn that poem, didn't you?' said John Sillery. 'He said he wouldn't have been able to learn it without your help. Poetry's not really his thing.'

'It's not really my thing,' I said. 'I was a bit worried when I found out I had to write all those chorus bits.'

'Oh, they were *wonderful*,' Hilary gushed.

'Mum. Mum! Dad!' We all turned to see Carl waving from the other side of the bar. We waved back, watching him body-surf the teeming crowd in an attempt to reach us.

Hilary enveloped him in a motherly hug, clucking and cooing about how proud she was. Carl blushed and tried to wriggle free. 'Buy us a drink, Dad,' he said.

'It had better be orange juice, darling,' his mother cautioned.

'Oh, come on,' I said. 'He deserves a proper drink.' I don't know what I thought I was doing, interfering in Sillery family politics like that, but somehow I managed to get away with it and Carl gave me a quite fanciable look of conspiratorial gratitude. John Sillery went off to the bar.

'You were brill,' I said. 'Honestly, I was really impressed. I can't believe how much you've improved since rehearsals started.'

'Carl's very good once he gets going,' said Hilary. 'He's always been a slow starter, haven't you dear, but once he gets involved there's no stopping him.'

119

'Mum!' Carl protested.

'Oh, I don't know! I'm not allowed to say anything! Honestly, I thought it was children who were supposed to be seen and not heard, not parents! Do you have any children, Belinda?'

'No, I'm too young. Well, I mean, not biologically too young but . . . mentally too young. Or that's how I feel.' Great! Now Hilary Sillery would think I was calling her an old bat.

'Oh, I quite agree, no need to suffer until you have to. This one' – she tweaked Carl's ear – 'insists that I walk ten paces behind him whenever we go out together.'

'Only when you're wearing your ridiculous bobble hat,' said Carl and I laughed my best flirtatious laugh. I was about to ask him for a cigarette when I realised there was a high chance his parents didn't know he smoked.

The cast were starting to drift into the bar, congratulating each other and giggling about the performance's few minor mishaps. At least six audience members approached Carl and told him how talented he was and that Ian Chaddock was their favourite character in the show.

'I told you you'd get mobbed by groupies,' I whispered in his ear and he grinned.

'I know! I thought you were just trying to make me feel better, so's I'd learn the poem.'

'So, how does it feel to be a star?' I asked. For a second, I saw myself through my own mother's eyes and I looked ridiculous. What the hell are you doing? I asked my cool, administrative alter-ego. What I have to, it replied.

'Brilliant!' said Carl. 'All I need now's a big cigar.'

'Do you want me to buy you one?'

'Nah! My parents'd kill me. I'm hoping they'll piss off home soon so I can get off my face and have a few fags.'

'Carl! Here's your lager,' John Sillery returned from the bar. His own drink looked distinctly non-alcoholic. He enunciated 'lager' as though it were an exotic word he didn't feel quite comfortable with.

'Bye!' said a voice from behind me. I turned around and Mark Ryder grabbed my hand and shook it enthusiastically. 'I loved the show,' he said, his nostrils twitching rhythmically. 'You could be a playwright full-time, no question about it. Some of it tonight . . . well, it was worthy of Shakespeare.'

I smiled. The fact that he was quite staggeringly wrong didn't prevent me from enjoying the compliment.

'I'm serious, you could get rich writing plays like that.'

'I doubt it,' I said. 'Not nearly as rich as if I were an estate agent.'

'Us?' he said incredulously. 'You've got to be kidding. What the likes of me and Richard get, that's pin money, that. I've got to look elsewhere for the real money, I tell you.' He settled easily into boasting mode. I hoped he wasn't trying to chat me up.

'Oh? Where do you look, then?' I saw blue and white squares out of the corner of my eye and turned round instinctively. Most of the shirts Tony wore were checked, so I was on permanent check-alert.

Tony was standing on the large concrete patio just outside the foyer with two blokes I didn't recognise. One was very short and stocky with a face like a bull-dog. The other was nondescript, with metal braces on his teeth. The three of them were talking and lighting cigarettes.

In front of me Mark Ryder was doing his best to appear mysterious and alluring. 'Oh, now that'd be telling.' He guffawed. 'Let's just say I've got . . . fingers in some very lucrative pies.' I suppose I can't stop you from saying that if you can't think of anything better, I thought. My mind was suddenly swamped with Tony-opportunity.

121

I looked around to see where Carmel-Marie was. She was engrossed in conversation with Richard and two old ladies, and seemed totally unaware of Tony and his companions.

I mumbled something incoherent to Mark Ryder, pushed my way out of the bar and ran across the foyer towards the patio, ignoring Carl's efforts to attract my attention. Bulldog Face and Brace Man had gone but Tony was still there, smoking a cigarette in the darkness.

I came to a breathless halt just in front of him. 'Hi!' I said.

'Hi.'

'Aren't you coming for a drink?'

'No. I've got to go.' Tony was doing the Seth Beasley eye trick, refusing to look at me. He seemed almost annoyed that I was speaking to him.

'Go on, come for a quick drink,' I said in my best cajoling voice.

'I can't. A friend of mine's having a party.'

'Oh, right. Well, can't you have a drink and then go to the party?'

'No. I've got to go now. Bye.' He dropped his half-smoked cigarette on the floor, crushed it with his ravishing Nike trainer and walked away quickly and purposefully.

I picked up the half-extinguished cigarette and inhaled deeply. Tony's mouth has touched this, I thought, and nearly keeled over with passion.

One of his mates was having a party indeed! That was an excuse if ever I'd heard one. Everyone knows that parties don't require punctuality. Couldn't he have made up something a bit more convincing, like a train he had to catch? He wasn't interested in me, that much was clear. He hadn't smiled or used his nice do-you-want-a-chair voice. Maybe by rushing up to him eagerly, all sweaty and out of breath, I had revealed

122

myself to be a grabber-shrieker, as immature and pathetic as all the others.

I finished the cigarette and went back to the bar. There was no sign of Carl. I asked Oliver Wild where he was and was told that he'd left a few minutes earlier with some unspecified mates. Damn! I felt this latest mishap land on the large pile of Tony-disappointment in the pit of my stomach.

'He was looking for you before he left,' Oliver said. 'Don't know what he wanted.'

Good old Carl, I thought. I knew what he wanted – for me to continue flirting with him. My resolve hardened. I may not be able to get Tony, I thought, but then who could? I mean, let's face it, he *did* act like a zombie a lot of the time, Darryl was right. Maybe no one had ever had him and no one ever would. The explanation for his presence in Carmel-Marie's office needn't have been romantic. She might not have been in there with him. Perhaps he was robbing her. Members of staff were supposed to ensure that their doors were kept locked but I often popped out briefly without bothering to lock mine. Carmel-Marie could have done the same.

Bugger. If only Carl hadn't gone off. Predictable, hassle-free Carl. Why hadn't he waited? I could really have given him a passionate seeing-to, fired up as I was with Tony-rejection, brimming with rebound motivation.

Despite Tony's indifference and Carl's unfortunate departure, I managed to cheer myself up by planning what I'd say to Carl the next day and imagining how things might progress. The Carl Sillery Plan, I felt, verged on altruism. Our affair would be a well-deserved treat for him, a reward for his impressive performance on stage.

You often hear people saying 'I can't make myself fancy him!' when their friends try to matchmake on their behalf. I must have a lot of will-power because I've trained myself to fancy some quite revolting specimens in my time, sometimes for rebound reasons and sometimes to alleviate the boredom of my everyday secretarial life.

I drove home, imagining myself and Carl as Tevye and Golde in *Fiddler on the Roof*, singing our version of their song: 'For three and a half weeks I've worked with him, rehearsed with him, smoked with him. For three and a half weeks, my lines are his. If that's not love, what is?'

*Fiddler on the Roof* is a flawed musical in my opinion. Tevye ruins it at the end by becoming an obstacle with Anti-GLOW and forbidding Chava to marry Fyedka.

I gave Alistair an abridged account of the evening's events when I got home and asked him half-heartedly whether he fancied coming to see *Lions* on one of its three remaining nights.

'I'm not sure.' He looked worried. 'I might get molested.' I'd told him Darryl's side of the story and he had been most alarmed to discover that he had unwittingly dined with *aficionados* of pornographic underwear.

I didn't really mind Alistair not coming to *Lions*. It would make it considerably easier for me to ensnare Carl. One of the ways in which I justify my infidelity is by believing that my extra-curricular activities exist in a different world. Everybody's happy, I say to myself, no one's getting hurt and this thing has nothing to do with that thing.

I could love Alistair, be madly in love with Tony, fancy and sleep with Carl, and keep all three completely separate. I've got room for all that and more in the seething vortex of my consciousness. Sometimes I think that anything could get in there, absolutely anything.

# Chapter Eighteen

## Mark Ryder

My hopes of a late lie-in the next morning were dashed; the phone beside our bed rang shrilly at 7.30 a.m. I swore loudly and picked it up, making a mental note to shout at Alistair later. We only ever received calls at uncivilised hours from Spartaco Systems. Ever since they promoted Alistair to Database Administrator – I really should know exactly what that means but I'm afraid I don't – they have felt free to ring him at all hours with queries about malfunctioning software.

'. . . yeah . . . yeah . . . anywhere'll do. Cheers. Belinda? Seth here.' I stifled a groan. Seth liked to make his phone calls seem as accidental as his visits to my office. He would ring me, then make me feel as though I were interrupting a far more important conversation he was having with someone else.

'It's seven thirty,' I protested. 'Surely it's not just lions who are entitled to their slumber?'

'Belinda, something awful's happened.'

'What?' I sat up poker-straight in bed. Please not Tony, I prayed.

'It's Mark Ryder, Richard White's colleague. Apparently he was attacked last night on his way home.'

'What? Where? Is he okay?'

'Well, he's still alive, but . . . he's not great. He's . . . well, he's critical.'

'Where did this happen?' I demanded. 'When?'

125

'I don't know the details. Look, the police are coming to school and they want to interview everyone. I'm phoning round the whole company. Can you get in for nine?'

'Yeah,' I said, wide awake. I shivered in spite of the rays of sunshine streaming through the bedroom curtains.

I arrived to find that the police had taken over the smaller of the theatre's two dressing-rooms. They wanted to talk to us all, one by one. Even the silent Tony had to speak to them. I couldn't help feeling a bit jealous, when he stayed in there for fifteen minutes, of the police's ability to have a private conversation with him. He couldn't stroll away from them apathetically and I, perhaps unfairly – no, definitely unfairly – resented them for this.

Still, thinking about cute Carl enabled me to rise above my petty grudge and I answered Inspector Francis's and Sergeant Drury's questions as fully as possible. I told them every single word that had passed between Mark Ryder and myself, as well as what I'd heard him say to other people. I gave them my impression of his mood and character, even described his flaring red nostrils. Sergeant Drury looked as if he was beginning to wish I'd shut up at this point but I ignored him, directing my information exclusively to Inspector Francis. I wasn't going to let some sidekick intimidate me; I'd read countless detective novels and I knew that any detail, however small, might be crucial.

I couldn't persuade either officer to tell me whether Mark Ryder was likely to survive. I was sure he would, for some reason. I mean, if he was alive now, things were looking good, weren't they?

In the larger dressing-room several people were crying, especially Phoebe Procter, who I'd always thought was the sensitive type. Oliver had his arm round her and was trying to comfort her, telling her he was sure Mark Ryder would be all right. I couldn't help wondering whether he had an ulterior motive. I would have comforted Tony like a shot, but he had a real 'everybody keep away' look on his face, an expression he wore with increasing frequency. I couldn't comfort Carl either because he was too busy trying to look cool by reassuring scared and miserable girls. Good old Carl. I like transparency of motives in a person; you save so much wondering-time.

Seth, the King of Transparency, spent the whole day wringing his hands in anguish and pacing the floor, saying loudly how he felt *Lions* was responsible, how, as director, he felt personally responsible, but that the show must go on none the less. Carmel-Marie sat in silence, looking subdued. Apparently she and Richard hadn't known Mark Ryder very well at all. Richard didn't socialise with colleagues much and had only invited Mark to see *Lions* because his wife was away for a week and he'd been complaining about how bored he was on his own.

Once the interviews were over, Seth got everyone together and gave them a pep talk. He told them tonight was going to be the hardest night of their careers, that they had to give it all they'd got for Mark Ryder's sake – is there no shot too cheap for this man, I wondered – and that perhaps it would be a good idea if everyone hugged each other a lot. We went through the motions but it didn't seem to have its usual effect. Even though nobody really knew Mark Ryder, most of the students had never encountered extreme violence at such close range before and its sudden forcible entry into their cosy world had shocked them deeply.

Tony remained in his seat, refusing to participate. If Seth noticed, he evidently decided not to say anything. Sinead the grabber and Megan the shrieker dawdled uncertainly beside Tony's chair, but in the end decided not to attempt to drag him up on to the floor for a hug.

127

Maybe he'd exuded hostile, off-putting vibes for so long that people were starting to want to leave him alone.

Everyone except me, that is. He could have had fangs, scars and a broken bottle in his hand and I wouldn't have wanted to leave him alone. I did, though. This was the new purposeful and gripful me. I smiled at Carl and later, when I could talk to him without anyone overhearing, suggested we went outside for a fag. Being the object of my attentions was costing poor Carl a lot of cigarettes, I realised, making a mental note to buy him some Marlboro Lights and give them to him in a winsome and coquettish manner.

'Pretty bad, hey?' he said, as soon as we got outside. The baking sun seemed inappropriate given what had happened.

'Terrible.' I nodded. 'I hope he's all right.'

'Doesn't sound like he is.'

'No, I mean, I hope he lives.'

'Do you reckon he will?'

'I don't know. Yes, I mean, if he's survived this long.'

I wondered if Mark Ryder had BUPA cover, suddenly feeling very glad I had ignored Alistair's disapproval and joined the school's Premier Plus scheme.

'Do you think the police'll catch whoever did it?' asked Carl.

'I don't know. I hope so.'

'I don't feel like doing *Lions* tonight,' he said. 'I know the show must go on and all that, but I'm just not in the mood. I don't think anyone is.'

'I know. Well, I'm saying I know but I don't suppose I do really. It's not me that has to go on stage and perform. All I have to do is sit in the audience and watch.'

'So . . . you're definitely coming, then?'

'Course I am. I wouldn't miss a night, would I?'

'Suppose. Where did you get to last night?'

'Where did *you* get to? 'I introduced a flirtatious tone in an attempt to lighten the atmosphere. I wanted to try and cheer Carl up, poor sod. It wasn't long before he had to don his legal executive's suit and become Ian Chaddock again. 'Whisked away by adoring fans, were you?'

'Something like that.'

'I told you, didn't I?'

'Yeah.' He shrugged. 'I'd rather have been whisked away by you.' For a second my whole body tensed with something that felt a bit like fear. I looked at Carl, to check he'd said what I thought he'd said. He was blushing furiously. 'Sorry,' he said, sort of slinking away. 'I probably shouldn't have said that, but . . . oh well, fuck it. Nothing ventured, nothing gained.'

'True,' I said. 'Tell you what, why don't we go for a curry after the show tonight?'

'What, just us?'

'Yeah.'

'Yeah, that'd be . . . but I mean, will we say we're going for a curry?' Carl was obviously thinking more clearly than I was. Of course we couldn't just go off together in full view of the whole company.

'I don't think so, no. I think they might think that was . . . odd,' I said, and with that one sentence I had committed myself. Despite the fact that I fancied Carl even more now that I knew he fancied me, the transitional moment when theory turns to practice is always pretty scary.

'So what will we do, then?' Carl asked, half grinning, half frowning.

'Um . . . I don't know. I'll think about it. Don't worry, it'll be fine.' My stomach was starting to whir and gyrate.

'Okay then,' he said. 'Fucking hell. I can't believe it!'

'What?'

'That you want to go for a curry with me!' He looked

happier than I'd ever seen him look. At that moment I found him intensely attractive. I even forgot Tony for a millisecond. Inwardly, I congratulated myself on the brilliant concept of the Carl Sillery Plan. Apart from anything else, it would be good for the show; instead of thinking about Mark Ryder's uncertain future Carl would be thinking about getting laid, which would surely add to Ian Chaddock's on-stage magnetism.

Carl nodded over my shoulder. I turned and saw Rosie walking towards us.

'I'll join you if you've got a spare cig,' she said. 'I don't smoke, but . . . all this is just so horrible!'

It's amazing how a real crisis reveals the pettiness of our niggly, everyday crises. I hadn't heard a single person bad-mouth Darryl today, not even Seth. I'd noticed people who had avoided him for the past few days talking to him in a friendly, normal way. Let's hope it lasts, I thought. It seemed Seth was right about most people's attention spans being short.

'I'd better go and get ready,' Carl said. 'So . . . I'll see you later, yeah?'

'Yeah. All the best for tonight. I'm sure you'll be as wonderful as you were last night.' He walked back inside, turning around every few seconds to grin at me. Rosie, looking faintly puzzled, put out her cigarette and followed him.

I got into my car and drove home to change. Just because Carl was only seventeen and desperately lucky to get me in any outfit didn't mean I shouldn't make an effort.

# Chapter Nineteen

## The Second Night

### Scene One – Vilk Takes Action

INGRA SAVOY *is in her office.* VILK VELLA *storms in angrily.*

VILK   I want a word with you!

INGRA   Sit down, please.

VILK   It's about Wristine. I'm worried. I want you to bring her back.

INGRA   I'm afraid I can't do that. She has not yet done what she was sent there to do.

VILK   But it's been three months. You said it would be two at the most that we'd be apart.

INGRA   That's true, I did. But things do not always go according to plan.

VILK   So when will she be back?

INGRA   I'm afraid I don't know.

VILK   I just miss her so much. Why won't you let her communicate with me any more?

INGRA   What do you mean? Wristine is free to make contact with you whenever she likes.

VILK   But she said you wouldn't allow it. She said that you said it would endanger the whole project.

INGRA   (*leans forward with interest*) When, exactly, did she say this?

VILK   Oh, I don't know, whenever I last spoke to her. A month, month and a half ago.

INGRA   (*incredulous*) You mean to tell me you

haven't spoken to your wife for a month?

VILK   No . . . but, how can you not know that? She said you had ordered her to break off contact.

INGRA   I did no such thing.

VILK   But you must have done. Wristine wouldn't lie to me.

INGRA   What exactly did she tell you? Try to remember.

VILK   I don't know, it was weeks ago. I didn't take it all in. Something to do with the phones in that office where she's being a robot. She said that you said the office phone bills were all itemised and that she couldn't phone me any more in case someone saw the number and traced it to . . . here.

INGRA   She said I said that? And you believed her?

VILK   Well . . .

INGRA   If there was a problem with using the phone at work, didn't you suggest she phoned you from her lodgings? From a phone box?

VILK   Of course I did, I suggested everything I could think of. But she just kept going on about itemised phone bills and how risky it was, how people at the Telephone Exchange might get suspicious and . . . she said you said not to risk blowing her cover.

INGRA   (*really angry*)   Why didn't you come and see me about this sooner?

VILK   Wristine made me promise not to. She said she'd get in trouble if I made a fuss, that you'd take it out on her. I only came today because I was getting desperate for some news of her.

INGRA   You fool! Can't you see what she's doing? She's trying to deceive us both. And for a month and a half you've allowed her to get away with it! If the plan goes wrong now, it will be entirely your fault.

VILK   But how was I supposed to know?

INGRA   I can't believe how gullible you are. Office phones and itemised bills! Do you really think 1997 society had – has – the technology to trace a number two hundred years in the future?

VILK  So it's not true, then? About the itemised bills?

INGRA  (*sighs*)  Did your telephone number exist in 1997?

VILK  No.

INGRA  So how can a number that doesn't yet exist show up on a phone bill?

VILK  I see what you mean. But if it's not true, what's the real explanation for why Wristine isn't making contact?

INGRA  There's only one way to find out. We must go to 1997 immediately.

*Cut to Berkshire County Council Legal Department office, where* IAN *and* WRISTINE *are alone.*

IAN  You know, the way I see it, you're not being unfaithful to Vilk. You're not even married to him.

WRISTINE  What do you mean? Of course I'm married to Vilk.

IAN  Not yet you're not. What year did you marry him?

WRISTINE  Twenty-one ninety-three. August the twenty-second.

IAN  Exactly! That date hasn't happened yet. Which means that, at the moment, you're single. Vilk doesn't even exist.

WRISTINE  Yes he does, he exists in the future. He only doesn't exist in 1997.

IAN  But we're *in* 1997. There is only 1997 at the moment.

WRISTINE  Stop it! I won't deny my roots, Ian, not even for you.

IAN  Look, I don't care if you're married or not. You're the one who feels guilty. I was just trying to make you feel better.

WRISTINE  What's the point of feeling better? I'd only be kidding myself. You know it can't last, Ian. Ingra Savoy knows there's something wrong, so does Vilk. They're going to turn up here sooner or later, I just know they are.

IAN  You're such a defeatist. You give up so easily.
What do you think Shelley would say if he could see
you now?

WRISTINE  Don't you dare use Shelley as a weapon
against me! You'd never even heard of him. Until I
told you about him. You thought he was a shoe shop!

IAN  But I've heard of him now, Wristine. I'm not
surprised your society worships him. You know
why? Because he's got guts, he's got spirit! (*Picks up
Shelley's* Collected Poems, *which is lying on
Wristine's desk beside her hole-puncher, and starts
to read*) 'Rise, like lions after slumber / In
unvanquishable number! / Shake your chains to
earth like dew / Which in sleep had fallen on you: /
Ye are many – they are few!' Do you see what I'm
saying, Wristine, what Shelley's saying?

WRISTINE  Don't put your words into Shelley's mouth,
Ian. Shelley's dead.

IAN  How can you say that? Your whole society, your
whole belief system is based on Shelley. I thought he
was like a God to your people.

WRISTINE  I don't know what I believe in any more.
Maybe nothing. (*Turns to him*) Who exactly are my
people, Ian? Have you got any idea what it's like to
be torn between two time zones? No, of course you
haven't. How could you?

IAN  So you don't believe in Shelley any more?
(*Wristine shrugs*) Well, I do. I believe in him. He's
dead in 1997, sure, but as you said, 1997 is not the
only place, is it? Shelley is still alive, somewhere,
some time.

WRISTINE  Oh, Ian, I just wish I had your faith, your
confidence. You're so strong. I do love you, you
know.

IAN  I know.

*They kiss. Suddenly the door flies open and* INGRA

SAVOY *enters, followed by* VILK VELLA.

INGRA   I knew it!

WRISTINE   Ingra, wait, let me explain.

VILK   Who's he? Get your hands off my wife, you Southey!

IAN (*to Wristine*)   What's a Southey?

WRISTINE   It's an insult from the future. Southey was an evil man who turned against Shelley . . .

INGRA   Don't bother! You don't honestly expect him to understand, do you? Our way of life, our language, our ideas? A man from 1997!

IAN   I understand more than you think.

INGRA   Rubbish. Wristine, you're coming back with us. I'm very disappointed in you. You've let me down badly.

VILK   Do you love this man, Wristine?

WRISTINE   I . . . yes, I do.

VILK   How disgusting! He's two hundred years younger than you!

# Chapter Twenty

## The Second Night

### Scene Two – Carmel-Marie, Carl and Curry

'Any news of Mark Ryder?' I asked Carmel-Marie after the show. We were in the bar which was, mercifully, not nearly as packed as it had been the previous night.

'No. He's still unconscious.' She eyed me defiantly, as if challenging me to say something that hadn't yet occurred to me. The more time I spent with Carmel-Marie, the less I understood her.

'How's his wife?'

'I've no idea. We don't know them very well. No dite you'd prefer me to sob and wail like the students did,' she said impatiently. 'They seem all right nigh, don't they?' I followed her gaze to a huddle of cast members who were gossiping eagerly. 'I love the way people can switch their caring on and off,' Carmel-Marie sneered.

'I think that's a really negative attitude,' I said, looking around for someone less depressing to talk to. 'They were genuinely upset.'

Carl, as always, was in the centre of the huddle. When he saw me trying to catch his eye, he disentangled himself and started to approach me, stopping when he saw I wasn't alone.

'I think Carl wants a word with you,' said Carmel-Marie in a tone I didn't like.

'Oh, yeah.' I did my best to sound innocent.

'I hope you've got the sense to put a stop to it,' she hectored, evidently forgetting I already had a mother.

'He's obviously got it bad, poor boy. And the way you've been leading him on, I don't blame him.'

'What?' I couldn't believe this. I thought I'd been really subtle about flirting with Carl. 'Have you gone mad or something?'

'You're the one that's mad, risking your job for a spotty seventeen-year-old.'

'I'm not . . . I'm not! I like Carl, but that's all.'

'Hmm, well. I just think women who flirt and lead men on are crap.'

'Oh, do you?' It wasn't so much what she said as her tone that made me want to smash her face in. I'd heard of Papal Infallibility but never Choreographical Infallibility. 'So how do you justify what you're doing with Tony?' The words were out of my mouth before I could do anything about it.

I expected her to laugh her usual harsh laugh and come out with a suitably crushing put-down, but to my amazement all the colour drained from her face like the multicoloured liquid Seth had told us to imagine as we lay on the drama studio floor. She gawped at me in horror, her froggy eyes bulging menacingly. 'What's that retard been saying?' she demanded.

'Nothing,' I said. My hands were shaking so much that I nearly spilled my drink.

'Can't you just mind your own business?' Carmel-Marie hissed at me, her face contorted with rage. Carl was still hovering nearby.

'I was minding my own business,' I began feebly. 'You were the one . . .'

Carmel-Marie gave me a voodoo-curse-laden stare and walked away without letting me finish.

Carl was at my side the second she'd gone. 'What was all that about? ' he asked eagerly.

'Nothing, really.' I forced myself to breathe deeply. 'Just Carmel-Marie being her usual pleasant self.'

'Are you all right?'

137

'Yes, I'm fine. Shall we go? Are you ready?'

'Yeah.' He nodded. His T-shirt, which declared 'Bad Boy', belied the obedient expression on his face.

'Okay, meet me outside by my car in about two minutes,' I said.

'Okay.' Carl went off to tell his mates he was going home and I headed in the opposite direction towards Darryl, who was on the other side of the bar, chatting and laughing with Rosie. I started walking towards them, intending to say goodbye to Darryl in a loud and ostentatious manner so that lots of people would see me leaving on my own. As I got closer I saw that Tony was also there, listening to the conversation and even smiling quite a bit in his unique and heart-wrenching way. It was so long since I'd seen him unglazed that his smile and the twinkle in his alert eye hit me as powerfully as it had when I'd first met him. I wanted to fall down in a heap on the floor and sob at his feet. I wanted to murder him for getting involved with Carmel-Marie rather than me. Instead, I smiled casually and said to Darryl, 'I'm off now, Darryl. See you tomorrow night.'

'See you, Belinda. Good tonight, wasn't it? All things considered.'

'Yes, very good. Well, bye then.' I started to walk away and stopped when I felt a tap on my shoulder. I turned round and saw that Tony was right behind me. It was all I could do to remain upright. Blasphemy though it was, I wished he would just go away. I had to go for a curry and maybe more with Carl Sillery; it wasn't fair for Tony to choose this moment to remind me of his irresistibility.

'I'm having a drink now,' he mumbled earnestly.

'What?' His voice was so quiet that I had to lip-read.

'I couldn't come for a drink last night, but I'm having a drink now.'

'Oh. How was the party?'

'What party?' he muttered. He really is a weird bloke, I thought. Why doesn't he speak with his whole mouth?

'Last night,' I reminded him.

'Oh. Crap.' We stood there for a few seconds in awkward silence.

'I have to go,' I said. Tony shrugged and turned away as if to say, 'I don't care what you do.' Stuff him, I thought. Did he expect me to go down on my knees and praise the Lord because he was having a drink tonight? I probably would have done if Carmel-Marie hadn't just killed off my very last hope. Why didn't he tap her on the shoulder? Did he realise that she referred to him as a retard? Or perhaps she'd only said that to put me off the scent.

The party Tony had so conveniently forgotten was clearly an excuse. He must have been meeting Carmel-Marie after she had somehow broken free of Richard.

I went outside feeling depressed and unsettled, but I perked up as soon as I saw Carl's shadowy figure towering above my Vauxhall Nova, making it look even smaller than it was. He was smoking and tapping his feet impatiently. What excellent insulation against Tony-pain that boy is, I thought to myself fondly.

'I thought you'd changed your mind,' he said.

'No, I was just saying goodbye to Darryl and Rosie.'

We got into the car and I drove us to the Jewel in the Crown restaurant in Slough. I wanted to get out of Windsor for superstitious reasons. Crossing a border into another town made me feel symbolically safer. On the A332 a white BMW passed us that looked very similar to Carmel-Marie's. 'Look!' I blurted out in panic. 'It's Carmel-Marie's car. She must have been following us!'

'Why would she do that?' Carl asked. He had pushed the passenger seat as far back as it would go, but there still wasn't enough room for his long legs.

'Oh, I don't know, she probably wouldn't,' I said. 'I'm being neurotic. We have to be careful, though.'

'I know. Just chill.'

'Okay,' I said and tried to. Carl was displaying remarkable composure and maturity for someone of his age.

The Jewel in the Crown is in the middle of a small row of shops on Imperial Road in Slough, between a hairdresser and a newsagent. It has several diagonal parking spaces in a lay-by in front of it. 'Here we are,' I said, pulling into a tight diamond-shaped vacancy between a Renault Espace and a VW Golf GTi. Carl looked at me. He didn't make any move to get out of the car.

'Do you really fancy a curry?' he asked me.

I realised I was starving. First Mark Ryder and then the Carl–Tony–Carmel-Marie developments had pushed all thoughts of eating from my mind. I hadn't had anything all day apart from coffee. 'Yeah,' I said. 'Don't you?'

'I really fancy you.' Carl put his hand on my thigh. 'Why don't we just forget the curry and . . . you know.' I didn't know what to say. I was impressed by Carl's bedside – well, roadside – manner. He'd obviously been around a bit and was well used to making sexual advances. The idea that I might corrupt him seemed laughable.

He leaned over and kissed me with surprising proficiency. His kiss had structure, it had form, but it wasn't pedantic. There was a lot of feeling in it, which impressed me. I had expected Carl to be the sort of bloke who regarded kissing as a necessary but tedious prelude to penetration.

He began to unbutton my blouse and I suddenly remembered we were parked right outside the restaurant. I disentangled myself quickly. 'Hang on a minute. We can't do this here.'

'Why not? There's no one around.'

'Not now, but anyone could walk past.'

'Come on then.' Carl opened the passenger door.

'Where?' I asked, bewildered. Was he going to forget all about what we'd just been doing, stroll into the restaurant and order a chicken vindaloo? I watched him walk straight towards the alleyway that ran alongside the newsagent's shop at the end of the row.

He turned round and beckoned to me urgently. I considered protesting, but somehow it didn't seem fair to Carl or to alleyways which, after all, are only places and no less valid than bedrooms.

I nearly laughed when his hand popped out of the darkness to beckon me again. It struck me as hilarious that his solution to the problem of my not wanting to have sex in a car on a main road was to lure me into a back alley. I giggled and followed him into the shadows.

He grabbed me by the blouse and dragged me towards him, his unbuttoning hands carrying on where they'd left off. He was keen, but not in too much of a hurry. His fingers crept over my breasts in a way that suggested they knew what they were doing. 'He's good at this,' I thought to myself, then, 'Oh no, I haven't got any condoms,' then, 'Isn't this great, I'm not thinking about Tony at all, apart from just now, but that doesn't count.' The alleyway smelled of curry and wet cardboard.

Carl eased my skirt up over my thighs, pressing himself against me at the same time, kissing me heavily one minute and breaking off suddenly the next to breathe hard into my left ear. I know this is no time to mention my mum, but she used to say how important it is for schoolteachers to be passionate about their subjects because enthusiasm is contagious. She was right, it is. My knees felt all fizzy, the way they usually only did when I looked at Tony for too long or got too

141

close to him. I wanted to lie down, but the sight of old chip papers, fag ends and bricks deterred me.

Carl completed my underwear's press-stud challenge in under three seconds. I can't believe this, I thought. I can't tackle an all-in-one that quickly and I'm a girl.

Just as I was beginning to wonder what was keeping him, he put one hand in his pocket and produced a condom. A few deft moves, a few sleights of hand later and the plastic was off, the condom was on and he was in, slamming me roughly against the wall with the rhythm of his body.

He's really good at this, I thought, and then, as Carl built up the pace, I stopped thinking altogether, which is really rare for me.

Afterwards we stood with our arms around each other for a while without saying anything. Then Carl got out his Marlboro packet and lit a cigarette before offering me one. He smoked in an I'm-a-hero-I-deserve-a-smoke sort of way, which was fair enough. He had done very well indeed. Briefly, I wondered whether Tony was that good in bed, or rather in alleyway, but the whole idea seemed so far beyond the realm of possibility that I couldn't begin to hazard a guess.

'Shall we go for a curry?' Carl asked suddenly.

'Yeah, I'm starving,' I said. 'Just don't go out there too obviously. Check there's no one about.'

'I don't care if there is,' Carl said defiantly.

'Carl! We've got to be careful, remember.'

'Yeah, yeah. Being careful's boring though, isn't it?'

'I suppose so, but . . .'

'Come on, let's go and eat. There's no one out there. If we stay here too long I'll forget all about curry again.' He grinned.

'Okay,' I said and we slid out of the alleyway on to the pavement. As we approached the Jewel in the Crown, a waiter saw us and held the door open. I smiled at him and was about to walk in when Carl grabbed me, put his arms around me and started kissing me with a vengeance. I fought him off and looked anxiously at the waiter, who was still smiling, but in a slightly alarmed way. Was the age-gap between us obvious, I wondered. Carl's height had to count in our favour and most people said I looked younger than twenty-seven.

I dashed inside, keen to escape the waiter's puzzled stare, and Carl strutted after me, laughing at my embarrassment.

'Are you ashamed of me or what?' he said as we sat down at a table for two in a private wooden alcove. We were the only customers apart from a middle-aged couple who chomped their food in silence, looking as though they hadn't spoken to each other in years.

'No, of course I'm not,' I said. 'But you're just being stupid, taking a risk like that. What if Seth had driven past at that moment?' The alarmed waiter brought over some popadoms and relishes. Was it my imagination or did he lean away from the table as he deposited them?

'Would you really lose your job?' Carl asked.

'Of course I would. I'm one of your teachers, Carl.'

'So you're risking all that . . . just for me?'

'Which is precisely why I don't want you increasing the risk!'

'All right, all right. I'm sorry. Look, honestly, I won't do it again. I was just . . . in a good mood, that's all. You're not going to finish with me, are you?'

'No,' I said, feeling slightly uneasy. 'Look Carl, you do know I'm not . . . well . . . that we can't . . . have a proper relationship, don't you?'

'Why not?' He munched a popadom casually.

'Because I'm your teacher, because you're seventeen . . .'

'So? It's not illegal or anything.'

'And because I live with someone.' I really should have mentioned this sooner, I know, but what with

143

everything else that was going on I just forgot. I sort of assumed that because I knew I lived with Alistair, Carl would too.

Far from being upset, he brushed this consideration aside with a wave of his popadom. 'Don't mind about that. I knew you lived with someone. That doesn't bother me.'

'Oh. Good.'

'I don't believe in possessivenes.' He nodded sagely. A new, unalarmed waiter appeared at our side and we ordered some food: a Prawn Madras for me and a Lamb Tikka Masala for Carl. For some reason I couldn't relax.

'Have you cheated on him before?' Carl asked.

'Why?'

'Just wondered. You don't have to tell me. I've cheated on most of my girlfriends.'

'Stella?' I asked.

'Especially Stella. She was well frigid. I only went out with her in the first place because I thought she's such a minger she's bound to be an easy shag. I wouldn't normally go out with someone so ugly.'

'Oh, right. Have you had a lot of girlfriends?'

'Thousands.'

'That many?' I grinned, suspecting it was a slight exaggeration. 'Am I the oldest person you've ever . . . been involved with?' I asked.

'I don't know how old you are.'

'Twenty-seven,' I said.

'Are you? You don't look it. You don't act it either.'

'I know,' I said. 'I'm very immature.'

'I think that's good,' said Carl. 'Most people are really boring by the time they're your age, but you're just like . . . one of us really. I knew you fancied me, you know.'

'Did you? How?'

'Body language,' he said. "I'm really good at reading body language.'

I ate my Prawn Madras without noticing its taste. By

144

the time we'd finished and paid the bill I was ready to call it a night. I wasn't bored of talking to Carl, but I was keen to get home to Alistair. Intrigue has this effect on me. I enjoy it, but in small doses. I need some normality in between earth-shattering events, so that I can digest what's happened and sort it out in my head before moving on to further emotional agitation.

'Do you want a lift home?' I asked Carl. 'I can't take you right to your house, obviously, but I can drop you on the next street or something.'

'Okay,' said Carl. 'Cheers.'

He crammed his gangly legs into my Nova again and we set off back to Windsor.

'Take the next left,' said Carl as we got near his house.

I turned into a small cul-de-sac called Cartwright Gardens and pulled in at the kerb. 'Is this near enough?' I asked. 'Will you be okay walking from here?'

'Yeah, fine.' He leaned over to kiss me, which was reasonable in the circumstances, but I just wanted to get out of there and safely away. I was having visions of John or Hilary Sillery knocking on my car window, demanding to know what I was doing to their son.

'Carl, this isn't a good . . .' I tried to say, but he wouldn't let me have my mouth back for long enough to complete the sentence. I could feel his fingers at my neck and descending, starting to undo my blouse buttons again.

'Carl!' I said indignantly into his mouth.

'I want to do it again,' he muttered, 'now.'

'Now? We can't, not here.'

'Yes, we can. Please. Please.'

'But Carl . . .'

'Look, just get in the back seat. It'll be okay, no one will see us.'

I didn't have the heart to say no to him. I knew, even as I climbed into the back seat, that this surpassed all

145

previous levels of stupidity, that I was breaking my own personal lunacy record, but I would have felt too mean saying no. This was all my fault. I had deliberately got Carl into the state he was now in and I would have to take the consequences.

He climbed on top of me and we did it again. A woman walked past at one point and Carl looked up briefly. 'It's all right,' he panted. 'I don't know her.' I heard her footsteps rattle off into the distance in her hurry to get away. Could have been worse, I thought, could have been Hilary Sillery. I couldn't help feeling touched by Carl's keenness. Screwing him by the side of the road very near to his parents' house was a truly selfless act, I thought, given the possible horrific consequences. And the sweetest thing of all was that when it was over he said thank you. Hilary Sillery had brought her son up well, obviously.

It took me a while to persuade Carl to get out of the car and go home. He kept saying he was going and then kissing me goodbye again. Eventually I pushed him out on to the pavement, starting up the engine at the same time to prove I meant business. 'I'll see you tomorrow,' I said. 'And Carl, you mustn't, you really *must not* act suspiciously in any way in front of the rest of the company.'

'Would I do that?' He laughed.

'Yes, you would. But don't. If I lose my job because of you, well . . . you know.'

'No more sex,' he summed up gravely.

'I don't want to sound like I'm threatening you, I just want you to understand how important it is.'

'I do!' he protested indignantly. 'I'm not stupid.'

I waved at him and drove off, feeling slightly annoyed with myself for ending the night on a down note. Perhaps I should have credited him with more sense. I'd only wanted to make sure he knew the correct procedure. But now I felt as though I'd been unduly strict. I hadn't really threatened him, had I? Well, I hadn't meant to. I resolved to make it up to him at the earliest available opportunity.

# Chapter Twenty-One

## The Third Night

### Scene One – Office Politics

*Berkshire County Council Legal Department.* BARRY
PILSWORTH *and* IAN CHADDOCK *are working in their
office along with a couple of other legal executives. The
secretaries* KAREN, DEBBY, CHELSEA *and* CHRISTINE
MELLOR, *the new temp, are in an adjacent office on the
other side of the stage.*

BARRY  What are you doing, Ian?

IAN  I'm, er, colouring in this plan.

BARRY  We have secretaries to do that.

IAN (*blushing*)  Oh, well, I just thought I'd make
Christine's life a bit easier.

BARRY (*sitting down on the edge of Ian's desk*)
Supposed to be the other way round, mate. She's
supposed to make your life a bit easier. (*Other legal
execs snigger*)

IAN  Well, she's only a temp, she's still quite new. I
didn't want to bombard her with too much work.

BARRY (*leering and winking*)  But you wouldn't mind
bombarding her with something else, am I right?

IAN  Um . . . no . . . well . . . oh, give over.

BARRY  No need to be shy, old son. She's a bit of a
looker, that Christine. Wouldn't mind giving her one
myself. But I sure as shit would mind doing her work
for her! You must be mental. It's people like you
make these lazy secretaries think they can get away

with sitting around on their arses all day filing their nails. You're a soft touch, you are.

IAN   Christine's different. She . . .

BARRY   What?

IAN   You'd just take the piss if I told you.

BARRY   Go on, I'm all ears.

IAN   She doesn't seem cut out for work. I've watched her typing, doing things the other secretaries do and she looks . . . wrong somehow. As though it doesn't come naturally to her, as though she's forcing herself.

BARRY   A skiver, hey? I'll have a word with the agency, see if we can't swap her for a better one.

ISAN   *No*! No, please don't do that.

BARRY   You really have got it bad, haven't you?

IAN   It's not that. I mean, yes I like her, I'm not denying that, but . . . it's more than that. She's different. Like the other day, I came in early and she was the only person in. She was sitting completely still, not doing anything.

BARRY   Fucking hell! I'm not wasting council money on a lazy bitch like that!

IAN   But it isn't laziness. I asked her why she was . . . just sitting there and we got talking. You're going to think this sounds mad, but . . . she doesn't believe in work. She thinks it's bad for people.

BARRY   Does she now, does she indeed?

IAN   Yes! Oh, I can't put it as well as she did, but what she said made sense, it really did. She said that we – that working people – spend our whole lives just acquiring the means to life.

CHORUS   Cleaners get tired of cleaning.
Teachers get tired of classes.
Philosophers tire of meaning.
Opticians get tired of glasses.
Whether you slum it or toff it,
It's the same at the bottom and top.
The boss is a slave to his profit

149

Like the cleaner's a slave to the mop.
Whatever your job, work is tiring
And stress and resentment are rife
For we spend our whole lives acquiring
The means to a decent life.

BARRY (*patting Ian on the shoulder*)   Ian, old son, she's pulled the wool over your eyes good and proper. She doesn't want to work, so you're doing her work for her. She's got you right where she wants you. I'm going to have to get rid of her. I can't have a secretary in my department who won't do any fucking work.

IAN   No, please Barry. Please let her stay. She does work, I mean, you've seen her working, haven't you?

BARRY   Well, I thought I had, but after what you've told me . . .

IAN   She meant in an ideal world. She accepts that she has to work because that's the system . . .

BARRY (*sarcastically*)   How good of her!

IAN   . . . but in an ideal world, she says, people would spend their lives actually living, not just being wage-slaves.

BARRY   She's not a fucking commie is she? Or some kind of weird hippy or dopehead?

IAN   You wouldn't think that if you spoke to her about it. She explains it all so much better than I can.

BARRY   Yeah, well, I just hope she's not explaining it to the other girls. One idle bitch of a secretary's bad enough, I don't want her talking all the others round to her commie point of view. Listen, Ian, I'm a sensitive bloke. If it was up to me I'd sack her, but you don't want that and she's your secretary so fair enough. I can tell you like her, so I'll let her stay, give you a chance to get your leg over. But I'm telling you, as soon as you've had your oats she's history. Lazy bitch!

*Cut to secretaries' conversation in next room.*

KAREN   Haven't you got any work to do, Christine?

CHRISTINE   No, not at the moment.

DEBBY   Huh! All right for some!

CHRISTINE   I did have a plan to colour in, but Ian's doing that for me.

DEBBY (*crossly*)   Huh! All right for bleeding some!

CHRISTINE   You just said that. Is it working every day that makes you use the same phrases over and over again?

DEBBY (*under her breath to Karen*)   Cheeky bitch!

CHELSEA (*snappily*)   You can have some of my work to do if you're bored.

CHRISTINE   No, I'm not bored. Why would I be? I'm only bored when I work. Otherwise I'm quite happy.

CHELSEA (*nastily*)   Well, aren't you the lucky one!

CHRISTINE (*thoughtfully*)   Can I ask you a question, all of you?

KAREN   Make it quick. We can't sit around all day chatting, we've got work to do.

CHRISTINE   How terrible, not to be able to sit around all day chatting. How can you bear it?

DEBBY   You're a right divvy cow, you are.

CHRISTINE   Why? This is my question: why are you all so horrible to me when I don't work? When I'm working like you, you talk to me normally, politely. But when I stop you all become aggressive. Why? Is it because you think work is a good thing?

KAREN   No, we just don't see why we should have to do it if you don't. It's all right for you! Ian Chaddock lets you sit around all day twiddling your thumbs.

CHRISTINE   But . . . you should be pleased for me.

DEBBY (*incredulously*)   Pleased for you? We're the mugs who have to do all the work while you're skiving.

CHRISTINE   So, what you're saying is you'd rather not work, but you have to?

KAREN   Are you dense or just taking the piss? No, we don't *want* to, but we've got no choice. God, you're a divvy. You're mental, you are.

WRISTINE   And because work makes you unhappy, you want everyone else to be unhappy as well, is that right?

CHELSEA   It's just not fair, that's all. Why should you enjoy yourself if we can't?

WRISTINE   Well, because for one person out of four to be happy is better than for all four to be miserable. That seems obvious to me.

DEBBY (*under her breath*)   Miss-Bleeding-High-and-Mighty. Who does she think she is?

WRISTINE   Listen, I can help you, all of you.

KAREN   Now you're talking. Here, you can type these Local Government Review memos. (*She tries to hand Wristine a bundle of papers*)

WRISTINE   No, I don't mean help with your work. I mean I can help you to be like me, a proper, happy person with a fulfilled life. Look at yourselves, you're all so . . . so dull and narrow-minded, trying to stamp out pleasure and happiness wherever you find them. But it's not your fault, you don't have to be like that. It's society, it's 1997 that's done this to you. Your lives are so awful! How can you be anything but grudging, mean-spirited slaves?

DEBBY   Listen, you cheeky cow, I've had about enough of your attitude. Think you're so much better than us, do you?

WRISTINE   Of course I'm better. You must be able to see that. That's why I can help you. Oh, if you'd only listen to me.

CHORUS   She cannot force them to be free
When slaves is all they want to be.
She cannot teach them how to smile
When all they do is type and file.
She cannot show them their true needs

When all they do is schedule deeds.
But don't give up, not while you've breath
To tell them office life means . . . DEATH!

# Chapter Twenty-Two

## The Third Night

### Scene Two – Confiding in Darryl

I was sitting in my office in the dark, hiding from Carl, when there was a knock on the door. 'Come in,' I shouted wearily. I was so relieved when Darryl walked in that I nearly jumped out of my chair and hugged him. His round face looked particularly reassuring and I wanted to laugh uproariously. 'Thank God it's you,' I said, getting up to lock the door. 'Oh, I love your face!' I chortled hysterically.

'You what?' Darryl looked embarrassed. 'What are you doing in here with the light off? Why aren't you in the bar?'

'I just couldn't face the after-show drinks, not tonight.'

'It's getting better every night, isn't it? There was a tear in my eye in the final scene . . . hello? Belinda, are you listening? What's wrong?'

'Oh, I'm sorry, Darryl. I've got a lot on my mind, that's all.'

'Like what?'

'If I told you, you'd run away screaming.'

'Wow! Now I really want to know.'

So we sat there in the dark and I told him, fervently hoping that Carl wasn't at that very moment confiding similarly in one of his chums. To tell Darryl was safe; to tell Oliver Wild or Ed Fewster could be disastrous.

I told Darryl everything I felt was relevant, which

was quite a lot. It was lucky I wasn't talking to my dad. His ideal rendition of the story would be as follows: 'I'm in love with a bloke called Tony. I'm sleeping with a bloke called Carl.' Or perhaps on this one occasion he would have preferred a slightly longer version that went something like this: 'I *was* in love with a bloke called Tony, I *was* sleeping with a bloke called Carl, but now I've pulled myself together, stopped all that nonsense and will behave sensibly from now on.' What a fairy-tale.

Darryl listened in silence. The only interruption to my story came in the form of a knock on my office door and Carl's voice shouting my name in forlorn desperation. Darryl and I held our breath, just as we had the previous Thursday when it had been Seth outside. We had extensive experience of cowering in locked rooms.

It took me an hour and a half to get to the turbulent and unresolved present. By the time I finished my throat ached and my voice sounded gravelly.

Darryl's reaction was a pleasant surprise; he started to laugh. His amusement was infectious and pretty soon tears were streaming down both our faces and we were clutching our chairs and groaning. I couldn't remember the last time I'd laughed like that. Not since before I met Tony, unless you counted my inner reaction to Natasha's *Lions* synopsis.

When we'd both calmed down, Darryl said, 'That's the weirdest thing I've ever heard! You couldn't make that up, could you?'

'I wouldn't want to,' I said.

'Oh, come on, it's not that bad, is it? You've got your distraction, Carl's getting laid, Alistair doesn't know and Tony . . . well, Tony's just Tony. This thing with Carmel-Marie, though, something about it doesn't gel. Tony's so . . . distant. I can't imagine him with anyone.'

'Not that bad!' I was heartened but not convinced by

155

Darryl's use of the phrase in connection with my situation. 'What about Carl's desire to have sex every five seconds? In my original plan I made no provision for hiding in a darkened room to avoid shagging him for the fourth time in twenty-four hours!'

I wasn't exaggerating. We'd already done it three times that day: my office this lunch-time, the gents' toilet backstage before the show and a patch of waste ground behind the theatre building during the interval. It was too much for me, as well as far too risky. Every time I gave in to Carl my feeling of panic grew. He was trying to seize control of the Carl Sillery Plan and depose me, its rightful leader. I was getting the intrigue I wanted, but not my much-needed normality intervals.

'He is a seventeen-year-old lad,' Darryl pointed out. 'He's at his sexual peak. Just let him know that this . . . affair has to be on your terms. That's if you want it to carry on. You don't seem that keen.'

'I am,' I whined. 'I just wish he was a bit more . . . controllable.'

'But I mean . . .' Darryl hesitated. 'You'd never consider leaving Alistair for him?'

'Of course I wouldn't!' I was shocked. 'What a horrific thought! He's seventeen.' I realised this made it sound as though I didn't like Carl very much.

'Would you leave Alistair for Tony?' Darryl asked.

'I don't know. I wouldn't want to leave Alistair. He'd be really upset and so would I. I mean, I think we're quite well suited. I don't think me and Tony are well suited at all,' I concluded miserably. 'But I'd risk it if I could have Tony. I'd do anything.'

'I've never met anyone I'd risk everything for.' Darryl stretched his arms philosophically. 'I can't imagine ever wanting any woman more than I want to produce albums.'

'I can't picture me and Tony living together.' I had hardly heard Darryl's last comment. 'He and everyday life just seem so . . . far removed from each other that it would seem unnatural somehow. Do you know what I mean?'

'I think so.' Darryl frowned.

'Darryl, do you think I'm depraved?' I leaned forward seriously. 'I mean, I haven't got any principles, but from an objective point of view, as someone who's a sort of . . . moral entity, what's your honest opinion?'

'If I tell you you'll think I'm being judgemental,' he said.

'I won't. You've got my best interests at heart. I'm not sure I trust myself in that department any more. Is it possible to be bad for yourself?'

'No, you're not depraved. In the grand scheme of things, what you're doing is nothing compared with, say, what Seth and Natasha did to me. Or what happened to Mark Ryder. But I do think you should put a stop to this thing with Carl. Sounds as though it's already getting out of hand and, distraction or no distraction, is it really worth risking losing your job?'

'Unemployment would be another diversion from Tony-pain,' I pointed out.

'You'd hate it, Belinda. The way you moan about what it was like to be a secretary! Look, if you're really madly in love with Tony, tell him how you feel.'

'Are you mad? Darryl, Tony's hardly the sort of person you confide your feelings to.'

'Well, personally, I think he's not the sort of person you fall in love with either. I mean, he seems a bit thick and boring to me,' Darryl suggested apologetically.

'But you don't love him.'

'Are you sure you do? Are you sure it's not just lust? I mean, even I can see that he's unusually good-looking. Mightn't it just be that you're . . . dazzled?'

'I don't know what it is,' I said. 'I just know how it feels. Yes, his looks may have something to do with it, but it's not just that, it's everything about him: his

157

shirts, his jeans, the bandage on his wrist, his mood swings, his vulnerability, even his zombieishness.'

'Hmm. Well, if you feel that strongly, tell him.'

'I'm too much of a coward,' I admitted gloomily. 'I really couldn't take the knock-back. It would feel as though I'd . . . I don't know, been rejected by God or something.'

'Well, I don't know what else to suggest.' Darryl shrugged. 'You can't tell him the truth, you can't forget him . . .'

'Precisely. Now you see how I've been driven into the arms of Carl Sillery.'

The phone on my desk rang suddenly, reminding us that there was a world outside.

'That's probably Alistair wondering where I am,' I said. After my late arrival home the night before I'd promised to be a bit earlier this evening. Talking to Darryl had made me forget the time completely. I glanced at my watch as I picked up the phone and saw that it was after midnight.

'Belinda?' Alistair's voice was dull and stony. A wave of fear hit me. What if he'd found out, somehow, about Carl?

'What is it?' I stammered.

'It's Mark Ryder,' said Alistair. 'He's dead.'

# Chapter Twenty-Three

## The Last Night

### Scene One – The Interval

Seth had called an emergency Creative Team meeting for the interval. The seven of us met backstage, grumbling vaguely about missing out on our usual half-hour in the bar when what was really on our minds was Mark Ryder. I was still having difficulty coming to terms with the fact that he had died after having survived for forty-eight hours. If the doctors could keep him alive that long then why not longer?

Seth looked dreadful. His eyes were red-rimmed and bloodshot, as if he had a bad case of conjunctivitis. Dirty-looking stubble had broken out over the wide plain of his lower jaw and he smelled stale, as if he hadn't washed properly for days. I couldn't believe this was the same man who normally doused himself liberally with Monsieur Givenchy. He had even forgotten to wear a self-promoting T-shirt.

Despite my gnawing fear that tonight might be the last time I would ever see Tony, I had managed to cobble together a reasonable last-night outfit – a long black skirt and russet velvet shirt that already felt a bit damp. The heat was intense and the hundreds of bodies in the theatre didn't help matters. Hayley and Carmel-Marie were visibly sweating in their almost identical short, tight black velvet dresses. Darryl had defied theatrical convention by wearing his usual summer uniform – red baggy shorts and a Fun Loving

Criminals T-shirt. Rosie and Duane both seemed to have made an effort, but their attire was too irregular to be transcribed. My mum would have described them as 'alternative goths'.

Carmel-Marie and I were very definitely not talking to each other; we made Seth and Darryl look like old pals. At least their eyes occasionally met. Carmel-Marie and I were still at the each-pretending-the-other-didn't-exist stage of our dispute.

'I've called this meeting,' said Seth miserably, 'to arrange a party.'

'A party?' said Hayley. 'When someone's just died?'

'Exactly,' said Seth. 'This whole Mark Ryder thing's been a ghastly business for all of us . . .'

'Particulary Mark Ryder,' said Duane.

'Well, yes,' said Seth, 'but for all of us, really. I mean, putting a show on is hard enough at the best of times, but with police interviews and deaths to contend with as well, it's been pretty gruelling for the kids, I think.'

'Yes, it has,' I agreed. 'They've been really professional about it as well. Despite being upset and shocked, they just got on with it.'

'So I think they deserve a party. I've arranged it already . . .'

'With a little help from your friends,' muttered Hayley.

'. . . straight after the show in the staff-room.'

'In the *staff-room*?' said Carmel-Marie, in a tone that suggested she had heard some appalling ideas, but none quite so contemptible as this. 'We're going to let a lot of drunken teenagers sweat, spill beer and vomit all over our staff-room?'

'It's the only room big enough that isn't a lecture theatre.' Seth's lip began to tremble.

'They're all house-trained, you know. They're not animals,' I snapped, speaking to Carmel-Marie but looking at a point in the middle distance. I was damned if I was going to be the first to break the Treaty of No Eye Contact.

'Carmel-Marie, do you mind if there's a party?' asked Hayley.

'No, but I mind if I have to spend the next two years sitting on beer- and vomit-stained furniture.'

'Give them a break,' said Darryl. 'They're a decent bunch.'

'I meant, you know, with Mark Ryder being a friend of yours,' Hayley persevered. 'I just thought you might feel a party was . . . inappropriate.'

'Don't any of you listen?' Carmel-Marie yelled. 'Mark Ryder wasn't a friend of mine! I hardly knew the man!' She tossed her hair over her shoulder and marched out into the foyer, slamming the door loudly.

'Methinks the lady doth protest too much.' Rosie raised a pierced eyebrow.

'What do you mean?' I asked.

'Well, maybe she and Mark Ryder were . . . I don't know. It was just a thought. She does seem to get annoyed whenever people mention him.'

'Maybe that's just her way of expressing grief,' said Hayley.

'Giving us grief, more like,' I muttered, wondering whether there was anything in Rosie's idea. It would be a bit rich, I thought, if Carmel-Marie, self-professed warrior against all things adulterous, had not one but two bits on the side. If she had been seeing Mark Ryder, though, that would explain why he was there on the first night – to admire his mistress's choreography. Perhaps Carmel-Marie and Tony were no more to each other than the virtual strangers they appeared to be.

'I think a party's a great idea!' I beamed enthusiastically around the room. 'I can't wait.'

'Oh, good.' Seth rubbed his swollen eyelids desperately. 'At least someone's happy.'

I saw Darryl looking at me in a slightly worried way

and I knew he knew why my mood had improved so suddenly. I think he was afraid I might get my hopes up about Tony and then be disappointed, but he didn't understand. I knew I'd never get Tony. I accepted that, basically, Tony-disappointment was my lot in life, but I also knew that I might as well enjoy the few small crumbs of consolation that were available.

# Chapter Twenty-Four

## The Last Night

### Scene Two – The Denouement

*Berkshire County Council Legal Department.* INGRA
SAVOY *and* VILK VELLA *face* IAN CHADDOCK *and* WRISTINE
VELLA *across a large wooden desk.*

INGRA  So you want to stay in a place where you'll
  have to work like a robot every day until you're an
  old woman?

WRISTINE  Ian is all that matters to me. I'd work for
  Berkshire County Council for the rest of my life
  rather than lose him.

VILK  You don't mean that, Wristine. You don't really
  love him, it's just an infatuation. Come back with me
  where you belong. I'll forgive you.

WRISTINE  I know you mean well, Vilk, but I don't want
  to be forgiven. I've done nothing wrong.

IAN  There's another alternative. To us staying here, I
  mean. If you would allow me to travel forward in
  time with Wristine, with all of you, I would be happy
  to give up my 1997 life.

VILK  Ingra, I'm *not* having this man in my time zone.
  It's bad enough that he . . .

INGRA  Oh, calm down, Vilk. He's not going anywhere.
  Neither is your wife. Wristine still has a mission to
  accomplish here and she will not be allowed to
  return home until I am satisfied that she has
  completed her task. (*To Ian and Wristine*) I'm afraid

you don't have a choice. From now on you will have nothing to do with each other except as colleagues. I will be monitoring you closely, much more closely than before since you've proved to be so unreliable.

IAN (*takes a defiant step forward*)  No way. You can forget it. We don't agree.

INGRA  You don't agree?

IAN  We love each other. That's all we care about.

INGRA  This sort of selfishness is just what I'd expect from a 1997 man. Wristine was not sent here for your benefit, nor for her own amusement. She was sent here to further the greater good of mankind. You are a distraction, a hindrance.

IAN  And you're a hypocrite!

INGRA  I am no such thing. How dare you speak to me like that?

IAN  I thought your society was supposed to believe in freedom, in pleasure?

INGRA  Don't tell me about my society! You're not qualified . . .

IAN  I am qualified! Wristine has educated me. (*He picks up Shelley's* Collected Poems *which is on Wristine's desk and waves it in the air.*) I've read this from cover to cover! I think I understand your society better than you do. And I'll tell you one thing for sure: I've got Shelley on my side.

VILK  Ingra! Are we really going to listen to this blasphemous nonsense?

INGRA  (*looking angry but uncertain*)  What do you mean? That's rubbish.

IAN  Really? What would Shelley have said if someone had told him he and Mary had to split up? Mary's father tried to, in fact, and Shelley ignored him. He eloped with Mary.

INGRA  But . . . I . . .

IAN  'Love withers under constraint; its very essence is liberty; it is compatible neither with obedience, jealousy nor fear.' Shelley said that.

INGRA   Sometimes the freedom and pleasure of one person has to be sacrificed for the greater good.

IAN   There is no higher good than love. Why don't you leave us alone? Just go, we don't want you here. Go on, get out of my office before I call security.

INGRA   (*pulls big silver gun from her pocket and aims it at Ian*)   Don't say I didn't give you a chance.

WRISTINE   No! Don't kill him! Ian, say you'll do what she says. (*To Ingra*) We'll do whatever you want, just don't kill him.

VILK   Keep out of it, Wristine. Wristine, look at me. I'm your husband. Forget him.

IAN   Just shoot me dead, so I can rise above
This earthly hell. Death's better for the heart
And ten times more compatible with love
Than any life where lovers are apart.

CHORUS   Death, death is better for the heart
Than lovers who are torn apart.

INGRA *shoots him dead.*

WRISTINE   No! (*grabs the gun out of Ingra's hand and points it at her.*)
You fool! Your precious freedom is a lie.
I can't break free from love. There's no escape.
I had no choice, not since the day that I
First heard his voice, dictating on to tape.
You care so much about the greater good
That you'd do anything, so you should know
Why I must kill you. Any lover would.
Ian is dead, and you're the next to go.
You killed my love. I'll kill your big ideals.
Now we both know how desperation feels.

*She shoots* INGRA *dead.*

CHORUS   One lost her love, one lost her big ideals.
Now they both know how desperation feels.

165

VILK (*grabs gun from Wristine and points it at her*)   We
   can still go back together.
WRISTINE   Haven't you heard a word I've said?
VILK   I'll kill you, then. I can't stand the thought of you
   being alive if I can't have you.
WRISTINE   Well go on, kill me. Shoot me in the head,
                    Fill the whole room with blood and brains
                       and gore.
                    Let the police arrive and find a red
                    River has drowned the Legal Office floor.
                    Slit both my wrists and tear me limb from
                       limb.
                    Take this hole-puncher – punch me full of
                       holes.
                    Nothing could cause more pain than losing
                       him.
                    Kill me, so death can reunite our souls!
CHORUS   Her heart is full of holes.
                    Death, reunite their souls.
VILK   (*shooting Wristine dead*)
                    Some people live and love. Their love's
                       requited.
                    They and the loved one form a blissful pair.
                    Some love and die, but these are reunited
                    With both eternal life and love to share.
                    But I, who know love's power and love's glory
                    And love someone who didn't love me back,
                    I'm the narrator of the saddest story:
                    Dead or alive, my universe is black.
   *He shoots himself.*
CHORUS   Here the sleeping lions lie.
                    This is not a game.
                    One by one they fall and die
                    All in love's good name.
                    Love is God and love is free.
                    True love never dies.
                    Love means immortality.

166

Sleeping lions, rise.
Sleeping lions . . . RISE!

**THE END**

# Chapter Twenty-Five

## The Last-Night Party

Everyone crowded into the bar straight after the show. It took me nearly half an hour to get served. I was in a surprisingly good mood. It had gone brilliantly, with all the cast giving their best performances to date. Carl had really excelled himself as Ian Chaddock, as I told him when he approached me discreetly.

'It's okay, you know,' I said, seeing him hovering hesitantly nearby. 'You can speak to me.'

'I know,' he said. 'I just thought you might have been getting a bit sick of me. Look, I know I've been a pillock, hassling you and stuff. I'm sorry.'

'Forget it,' I said.

'You're not going to finish with me?'

'No.' I smiled, trying to push aside the unease that this question made me feel.

'Can I have everybody's attention please!' Seth yelled, wobbling precariously on a rickety bar stool. The success of the show had done nothing to improve his ghastly appearance. Natasha stood beside him, smiling bravely in a red chiffon trouser suit and white scoop-necked top that clung dutifully to her protruding rib-cage.

'Thank you,' Seth declared mournfully as the noise died down, 'cast and audience, for making *Lions* such a brilliant success.' There was a general cheer and some clapping. 'I'd like to announce that there's going to be a party starting shortly in the staff common-room. Now I'm afraid there will be no bar facilities in there . . .'

'Boo!' Oliver Wild protested, looking suitably last nightish in a blue linen shirt and spotless white chinos.

'. . . but you're welcome to buy takeouts from here and bring them along. And we've managed to rig up a music system. The only thing is we have to be out by midnight, because the security staff won't stay any later than that to lock up the building.'

'We can go to the lake at midnight,' Oliver said to Ed Fewster and a few other cast members, who nodded enthusiastically. I noticed Stella Nettleton tighten her lips disapprovingly.

'What lake?' Richard White asked Carmel-Marie. He and Phil Douglas were standing side by side in dark grey suits that were as similar as Hayley's and Carmel-Marie's black dresses. I wondered if the Whites and the Douglases went shopping together.

'It's abite five minutes from here,' said Carmel-Marie. 'I don't think I fancy that. It'll be freezing by the lake at midnight. Raining too, no dite.'

'Well, the kids can go if they want to carry on partying,' said Hayley. 'I'll probably be ready to go home by then.' She sounded so weary that I half expected her to add 'if not ready for the glue factory'.

I followed the Whites, the Douglases and Seth and Natasha to the staff common-room, leaving Carl, Oliver, Ed and most of the others buying takeouts at the bar. Ed's white ruffled shirt and cravat made him look like a pirate of Penzance.

There was no sign of Tony. It would be typical of him to vanish right after the show without saying goodbye to anyone, I thought. I resigned myself to never seeing him again and realised, as I traipsed glumly towards the staff-room, how little I knew about him. What did he do when he wasn't doing *Lions*? Did he have a job? My heart was pounding painfully, struggling to accommodate the GLOW of finality.

A rush of intense joy pulsed through me when I got to the staff-room and saw Tony and Rhys plugging wires into big black boxes. So that was where he'd been! I caught his eye briefly and he smiled a whole-hearted, alert smile. I wanted to go and talk to him but I was trapped in a circle of married people and I thought it would look too obvious.

Cast members were starting to arrive and Sinead and Megan, clearly as pleased as I was to see that Tony was still around, headed straight for him with a sort of last-night urgency. I knew they were thinking, as I was, that after tonight there would be no more chances. It's strange how you can think that at the same time as knowing you never had a chance.

'Oh, it was a terrible shock,' Richard White said to Natasha in response to a comment of hers that I, in my Tony-day-dream, had missed. 'Poor man. Absolutely terrible. The police have been in and out of the office all week. They won't tell us much but I don't think they've got very far.'

'Bloody police,' said Phil, and at that moment I loathed him for daring to be there. He might have thought he was just getting on with the business of being Phil Douglas as usual, but to me he had lost his identity altogether and was merely a representative of Alistair and real life, an obstacle with Anti-GLOW. If he hadn't been there I would have joined the growing crowd around the hi-fi equipment and grabbed and shrieked with the multitude. Carl was leaping around the room with Oliver, shouting and spilling lager all over himself, so he wouldn't have noticed.

Oh well, I thought, I should probably be grateful to Phil for sparing me a humiliating ordeal. I wouldn't have got a look in, not with my dowdy blouse and long skirt. There were six girls, including Megan and Sinead, queuing up next to the sound system in a

170

jostling row of hot-pants and skimpy halter-necked tops. Occasionally an arm would shoot out and a hand grab at thin air. Cleverly, Tony had arranged the equipment in a little barricade around him so that he couldn't be reached. He was standing with his back to the wall, looking at the outstretched hands in glazed horror. Normally the grabber-shriekers gave up after a while and wandered off, but, this being the last night, they were particularly persistent. Their grimly set mouths were testimony to the fact that they were prepared to wait there as long as it took for Tony to emerge from behind the black boxes. He had to come out some time – to go to the toilet, to go home at the end of the night – and when he did they'd be ready for him.

'Look at Tony.' Hayley nudged me. 'Those girls won't leave him alone. I wonder why he doesn't . . . do anything.' I deliberately didn't look at Carmel-Marie.

'Maybe he's gay,' said Natasha abruptly. She quickly tired of any conversation that didn't revolve around her.

'I don't think he is,' I said quietly. 'I think he's just shy.'

'He must be mad,' said Phil. 'That one with the long blonde hair's a bit of all right.'

'Megan,' said Carmel-Marie. 'Yes, she's a walking erogenous zone, isn't she?' She sounded quite relaxed. Did she really feel so tolerant about the masses marauding her man? Unless, as Rosie had suggested, Mark Ryder had been her extra-curricular activity. Richard White displayed none of his wife's defensive oddness when the subject of his late colleague came up, which was consistent with the affair theory.

'I think Tony's a bit too thick to know what to do with a woman.' Carmel-Marie laughed snidely. 'I can't see why else he'd ignore advances from nubile nymphomaniacs.'

I decided that, as this was a conversation I was

interested in, I would break the Treaty of No Eye Contact and No Conversation. 'Maybe he's just very fussy,' I said. 'I mean, he's so attractive. He's out of their league.'

'Don't be ridiculous,' said Carmel-Marie. 'He's just a pretty face. There's nothing going on in there. That puts him in a low league as far as I'm concerned. I can't find a man attractive unless he's intelligent.' She smiled lovingly at Richard, which was a bit of a shock. I didn't know loving smiles were in Carmel-Marie's repertoire.

'Stupid men are a nightmare, from an intelligent woman's point of view,' Natasha leaped in eagerly. 'They can't handle the fact that a woman might be their intellectual superior. Before I met Seth I was beginning to worry that I'd never find a man who didn't resent the fact that I had three degrees on my CV rather than in my record collection.'

All the chairs had been moved out of the way to create a dance-floor area and those of the Youth Theatre members who weren't participating in the Tony vigil were dancing. 'Don't Let Go' by En Vogue came on and I dragged Hayley up to dance with me. I had liked that song anyway, but now it really meant something to me. The lyrics came closer than those of any other current chart-topping hit to defining my exact feelings for Tony. Art of any genre is always enhanced by Relevance GLOW.

Carl and Oliver kept staggering on and off the dance floor. Mercifully, Carl was too busy getting drunk to pester me. I turned round so that I couldn't see Tony from my dancing position.

'All right!' Darryl bounced sweatily up to me, holding a can of Stella Artois in his hand.

'Hi!' I yelled over the music. 'How are you?'

'Natasha and Seth are avoiding me, so I'm fine.' Hayley gave him a dubious look and retreated.

'Just ignore her,' I said.

172

'Oh, I don't give a shit,' said Darryl. 'What about you? Tony's surrounded, I see.'

'Yep. Last-night desperation,' I explained. 'I would have joined the queue, except fucking Phil's here.'

'I know. The old married couples are out in full force.' Darryl grinned. 'Don't they look out of place?'

I looked over at the spouse ghetto in the corner. 'They look like they got lost on their way to a dinner party,' I said.

'Why don't they dance? Why don't they get pissed?' Darryl winced in disgust. 'I'm never getting married if it means being sensible and well-behaved all the time.'

'If Alistair were here, he and I would get pissed and dance. Not all couples are old before their time.'

'Yes, but you and Alistair aren't married.'

'As good as,' I said.

'What, with you falling in love with other men and . . . well, you know.'

'I'd feel and do exactly the same if I was married, though,' I said.

'No, you wouldn't.' Darryl shook his can of Stella at me. 'I think it makes a difference, psychologically. It's like a way of saying you're resigned to your fate which, in effect, makes you old before your time. Reckon you'll ever do it?

'Marry Alistair?'

'Yeah.'

'Nah. I've been with him for ages and things are fine. Marriage wouldn't change anything, so what's the point?'

'Would you marry Tony?' Darryl asked.

'In my dreams!' I said. 'Don't ask me questions like that, not unless you've got a life support system on standby.'

Darryl laughed. 'I never know when you're kidding.'

'I never joke about Tony,' I said gravely.

'So would you? Marry Tony?'

173

'Darryl, of course I would! I can't believe you have to ask. Didn't you take in what I told you last night?'

'You said you couldn't imagine living with him,' Darryl reminded me.

'That's different,' I explained. 'Marriage is about romance and being madly in love. Living with someone's about . . . real life.'

'But when you marry someone, you live with them.'

'Not necessarily,' I laughed. 'I could live with Alistair and marry Tony – that'd be great.'

'Aren't you forgetting someone?' Darryl pointed his lager at Carl, who at that moment was lying on the floor while Oliver poured vodka into his mouth.

'He could be the gardener or something,' I giggled. I heard a loud cheer behind me and turned around to see Rhys and Lottie, a chorus member, kissing passionately with their arms around each other while everyone watched and clapped.

'First cop of the night!' Oliver shouted. 'Cop alert, cop alert!'

'Cop . . . lert,' Carl mumbled. He looked a bit the worse for wear, far greener than usual. I felt slightly guilty for joking about him being the gardener.

There was another loud shriek, right next to my ear this time. Darryl and I both stepped back instinctively.

'Are you all right?' Darryl asked Trudi, the source of the appalling noise, who was standing beside us with her mouth open, waving her hands above her head. 'Is something wrong?' Trudi shrieked again, even louder than before. In honour of the last-night party she had broken all previous styling gel records. Her hair was submerged beneath at least two tubs' worth of Boots Extra Firm Hold.

'He's so gorgeous! He's so gorgeous!' she wailed.

'Who?' My ears pricked up competitively. If she meant Tony I might have to drag her away from the party and lock her in Hayley's stationery cupboard. I

174

knew by now that Tony didn't respond well to grabber-shrieker tactics, but Trudi's approach was far more direct. It shared its base element – shrieking – with the hi-fi vigilantes' strategy, but its top note, as perfumers say, namely loud proclamations of gorgeousness, was an innovative departure from the Tony-chasing norm. All I needed was to see Tony and Trudi form a sealed unit of lust the way Rhys and Lottie had.

'Who?' Trudi repeated in a tone that implied it should have been obvious. 'Ed! Ed Fewster! He's so gorgeous.'

'Oh!' I beamed at her in relief. 'I didn't know you fancied Ed.'

'He's lovely.' She sighed and emitted another loud shriek.

'Will you pack it in?' Darryl shouted. 'You're giving me a headache.'

'Does he know you like him?' I asked.

'I don't know.'

'Well why don't you go and chat to him?'

This suggestion provoked further shrieks. 'Oh, I couldn't. I couldn't. Will you talk to him for me, Belinda?'

'No, she won't,' said Darryl. 'Now go away and find someone else to mither.'

'What would I say?' I asked. Now that I knew it wasn't Tony she was after, I was feeling all magnanimous and public-spirited.

'I don't know. Ask him if he likes me. No, no, just tell him he's got a secret admirer.'

'For fuck's sake,' Darryl muttered.

'Okay, I'll have a go,' I said. 'But what if I ask him and he's not interested? I don't want to be the bearer of bad news.'

'It's okay, I'd rather know either way,' said Trudi. 'Thanks, Belinda, I really appreciate it. I'd never be able to pluck up the courage to say anything myself.'

She ran off, giggling and squealing.

'You fool,' said Darryl. 'You utter fool!'

'I'm only doing her a favour,' I said. 'I don't mind.'

'You will when Ed tells you he thinks she's a Slough slapper and you have to think of a way to break it to her gently. God, I'd forgotten what parties are like when you're that age. Oh well, this is what we get for hanging around with a bunch of seventeen-year-olds. Oh ... sorry. I didn't mean ...' His voice tailed off uncertainly.

'It's all right,' I reassured him impatiently. 'You are allowed to say "seventeen-year-olds", you know. You're even allowed to suggest they're a bit immature.'

'Sorry.' He smiled sheepishly. There was another loud cheer from behind us and we turned round. 'What now?' said Darryl. This time the applause was for Carl, who was on all fours in front of the hi-fi vigilantes, vomiting on to the floor.

'See!' Carmel-Marie announced triumphantly. 'I knew someone would throw up. Well, I'm not clearing it up.'

'Ugh!' Sinead backed away from the grey-brown slushy pool, visibly gagging. 'It's gone all over my shoes!'

'Hayley,' said Seth imploringly, 'you couldn't just ... could you?'

'Clear it up, you mean?' said Hayley.

'Well ... I'd really appreciate it.'

Hayley trudged off to get some cleaning implements, sighing loudly.

'Can't your wife say "no"?' Carmel-Marie spat at Phil, who grinned.

'Would you if you were married to me?' He winked, ogling Carmel-Marie's upturned nipples.

Carl was lying on the floor, groaning. 'Somebody should take him home,' I said to Darryl. 'He looks terrible. I would, but ... well, you know.'

'We should phone his parents,' said Stella Nettleton, whose outfit, I noticed, was more suited to a Salvation Army meeting than a cast party. 'They'll have to come and pick him up.'

'Are you mad?' said Oliver. 'His mum'd freak if she saw him in this state. He wouldn't be allowed out for about a year!'

'I'll take the reprobate home,' said Ed. 'Come on, Carl, let's go. Yes, an upright position we like. No, don't fall in that, you won't smell very nice.' I heard a stifled shriek and turned to see Trudi gnashing her teeth and making forceful pushing gestures with her hands.

I leaped into action immediately. 'Ed,' I said, strolling over to him casually. 'Could I just have a quick word before you take Carl home?'

'Oh dear,' he said. 'Whatever it is, I'd rather not know. That is, I already know. Trudi, right?'

I nodded.

'I'm not interested. Much as her hair sculptures fascinate me . . . she's not my type.'

'Oh,' I sighed. Darryl was right. Telling Trudi wasn't going to be much fun. 'Could you be persuaded, or is it a definite no?'

'As definite as a no can be. Sorry.' Ed smiled and walked off. Trudi zoomed in on me as soon as he had dragged the staggering, groaning Carl out of the room.

'Why did you let him go?' Her lower lip trembled.

'I couldn't stop him,' I said, slightly perplexed. 'He offered to take Carl home. Trudi . . .'

'It's all right, I know. He doesn't like me, does he?'

'He likes you,' I said, 'but not in that way. Sorry.'

'Did you try to persuade him?' She began to cry, mascara running down her face in black, fluid lines.

'Well . . . no.'

'You should have done!' she wailed. 'I bet you could have talked him round.'

'Trudi, you can't force someone to like you,' I said gently.

'No, but that doesn't mean you have to give up straight away. I'm going after him. I'm going to talk to him myself.' She bared her teeth in a terrifying grin and ran after Ed and Carl.

I watched with embarrassment, for her and for myself. I knew how she felt. I must have looked equally stupid when I ran out of the theatre to talk to Tony after the first night. I also wasn't very good at giving up.

It was nearly midnight. I had been planning to go to the lake, but I suddenly didn't feel like it. Phil Douglas and Richard White had each produced a set of car keys in spousal synchronicity; the moment had come for the grown-ups to go home and leave the kids to it. Maybe it was time I faced the fact that I was as much an Old Married as the people Darryl and I had been mocking earlier. I wasn't seventeen any more. I was silly and immature, trying to recapture my youth. The real teenagers were probably praying I'd go home with the rest of the dinosaurs so that they could get out their cocaine wraps and hard-core porn.

Caroline Helm, a robot/chorus member, came out of the toilet and stopped when she saw me. 'Are you okay?' she asked.

'Fine,' I said. 'I was just thinking about leaving.'

'Don't go!' she said. 'Come to the lake. There's plenty of beer left. Or are you . . .' Her voice faltered and she blushed furiously.

'What?'

'Nothing.'

'What were you going to say? Caroline, tell me. I won't be annoyed,' I reassured her hastily.

'I was just going to say . . . are you going to see Carl?'

'Why would I be?' I held my breath. The extent to which I didn't want to lose my job hit me and I nearly gasped from the impact. Why hadn't I thought about this, really thought about it, before?

'Well, there's a rumour – I'm not saying I believe it – that you and Carl are . . .'

I adopted an expression of concerned outrage that could have won me an Oscar. Even without my recent theatrical experience my performance would probably have been flawless. People like me who have no principles but like an easy life have to learn to lie convincingly at an early age. I started practising at junior school and by the time I left secondary school I was world champion standard. Occasionally I meet people who claim never to lie. Carmel-Marie once told me that she had never lied to her parents as a teenager and I wondered how she'd made it through to adulthood.

Personally, I only ever consider honesty as an option if I'm sure it will have no unpleasant consequences, like someone trying to stop me from doing exactly what I want. Dishonesty is often the best policy, if it leads to more happiness all round. For example, I don't believe in God. My parents are both atheists and brought me up to be one, but if I were to have children I'd tell them there was a God and a heaven where they'd go after they died. I'd say that hell and all the bad stuff was a load of rubbish, of course, and that all the silly rules people attribute to God are man-made. I don't want my kids to think they have to spend their whole lives carrying lepers around on stretchers for fear of burning for ever, but why shouldn't they enjoy all the perks of faith?

I remember how I felt when I understood for the first time that I was going to die at some point. I resented, and still resent, having to contend with such an unpleasant reality. I wish my parents had spared me the truth for once and told me instead that I'd spend eternity in Paradise being asked by Tony Lamb if I wanted a chair.

179

Actually, the existence of Tony Lamb forces me to question my atheism. It's hard to believe his ancestors were apes and amoebas. There must have been some pretty damn sexy amoebas knocking around.

That's it, I thought. Carl is history. Next time I saw him I'd tell him it was over. I hoped and prayed that the fact that Seth hadn't yet given me my notice meant he didn't know.

'I can't believe Carl would say that.' I shook my head. 'Doesn't he know how dangerous it is? I could lose my job if he goes around saying things like that.'

'Oh, no one would say anything to any of the teachers or to Seth,' said Caroline. 'I mean, we tell each other things, but we'd never tell one of them.'

'But it's not true,' I said indignantly, seeing checks out of the corner of my left eye. I turned just in time to see Tony disappearing into the toilet. I waited for his pursuers to go bursting in after him and began to get a bit suspicious when they didn't arrive.

'Hang on a sec,' I said to Caroline and went off in search of an explanation. I soon found it. Sinead and Megan were crying and circling each other, like hens preparing for a pecking contest.

'I'm not going home now,' Megan sobbed. 'I'm going to the lake.'

'But you promised you'd share a taxi back with me!' Sinead wept. 'I'm not going if you're staying here!' The wet mascara was flowing freely.

'Don't go then. Let's both stay.'

'I *can't*! You know I have to be home by half-twelve.'

'Well, that's your problem. Why should I go just because you have to?'

'Because we agreed! Because you promised! I know what you're doing, you just want to get me out of the way so that you can have him all to yourself!'

I dashed back to my alcove, where Caroline was still waiting for me. Tony should be making his exit from the toilet any minute now, I thought. I didn't want to miss what would probably be my last opportunity to talk to him.

The toilet door edged open after a few seconds and he emerged surreptitiously, wary of the potential hazard of a grabber-shrieker entourage. It reminded me of his exit from Carmel-Marie's office, except that now he looked hunted rather than guilty.

'Hi!' I said cheerfully. 'I think you're safe. They're busy fighting.'

'Oh. Right.' Tony leaned against the wall next to me. He isn't going, I realised with excitement that no Richter scale could hope to accommodate, he's staying put. Quick, quick, think of something to say.

'So, what do you think of it then, all this theatrical stuff?' was the best I could manage.

'Brilliant,' he said, looking me alertly in the eye. Can you imagine, Cat As, the splendour of that moment? The wondrous spectacle of Tony both saying and being brilliant at the same time?

'Yeah?' I said casually. 'I wasn't sure you liked it that much. I thought you might have found it all a bit luvvyish.'

'I want to be a sound engineer,' Tony mumbled.

'You really are incredibly good-looking,' said Caroline suddenly, in a tone that was more analytical than flirtatious. She sounded like a scientist who had just observed a new and amazing species.

Tony shrugged. 'Whatever,' he said, not looking at her.

'Caroline, could you just do me a favour?' I said. 'Could you go and have a look for Trudi? She ran off after Ed and I'm a bit worried about her.'

Caroline looked at me oddly but did as I asked.

Once she was safely out of the way, I turned back to Tony who, miraculously, was still there. 'So you want to be a sound engineer?' I said.

'Yeah.' He smiled. 'I'd really like to work in theatre full-time. Or in television or something.'

'Why don't you, then?'

'You've got to do a degree first,' he said, 'and I can't afford it.'

'Can't you get a grant?'

'Nah. Tried.' I fought back the urge to offer him a four-figure lump sum.

'Who did you apply to?' I asked. 'For a grant, I mean?'

'Dunno.' He shrugged. 'The government?'

'You don't sound sure,' I said.

'Well, the people who run the hostel where I live, they did most of it. They're really good like that.' However commonplace Tony's conversation may seem to you, for me each word held a deep and lasting significance.

'Could you start making your way outside, please,' shouted a large man with a bunch of keys in his hand. 'Some of us have got homes to go to.'

'Are you going to the lake?' I asked Tony.

'Might as well.' He shrugged. 'I've missed my last train home anyway.'

'Oh, right. So how will you get home? Eventually, I mean?'

'Dunno. Walk.'

'How long will that take?'

'Hour, hour and a half.'

'You can't do that!'

'I've done it before,' he muttered.

'You can't!' I said. 'You're not doing that. Don't worry, we'll sort something out.' I had no idea what I meant by this or why I suddenly felt it was within my remit to supervise Tony's nocturnal arrangements. I also had no idea why Tony nodded his acceptance. He's letting me boss him around, I thought joyfully. I was flooded with Possibility GLOW.

Why is it always in crucial, every-second-counts

situations that one has a desperate need to go to the loo? I'd been putting it off all evening and I couldn't postpone it any longer. The pain in my bladder was distracting me to the point where I couldn't concentrate on my Tony-experience as fully as I wanted to. But what if he disappears while I'm in there, I panicked. Just as I was about to resign myself to continued bladder pain, I thought of a solution 'Do us a favour,' I said, thrusting my large shoulder bag into his arms before he could protest. 'Mind this for me while I nip to the loo.' It was only when I was inside the cubicle with the door locked that I realised anyone with any experience of women knew that they always took their handbags to the toilet with them. Tony was bound to see through my ruse.

I washed my hands and looked in the mirror. I was dripping with sweat although luckily it hadn't gone through my blouse. My lips were still too thin and my chin and eyes were still too small. If I could see that, surely Tony could. Why had he engaged me in conversation when I was so obviously his physical inferior?

I fiddled with my hair hastily and nearly fell out of the toilet in my eagerness to get back to him. He was exactly where I had left him, but I no longer had him all to myself. Megan was hovering by his side with two new sidekicks, Sally and Jeanette. Tony appeared to be holding my handbag in front of his face for protection.

'Here she is!' Megan snapped when she saw me. 'Come on,' she said to Tony. 'Give her back her bag and we can go.'

# Chapter Twenty-Six

## The Lake

'Where are you going?' I asked, forcing myself to smile and be calm.

'To the lake,' said Sally.

'Oh, that's where I'm going too,' I said.

'Come on, Tony!'

'Tony, come with us!'

Megan grabbed Tony's left arm and Sally took his right. Jeanette got behind him, put both her hands on his back and between them they dragged and pushed Tony out of the building.

I followed closely behind, seething with rage and muttering, 'I think Tony can manage to walk on his own.'

The five of us staggered out into the darkness. There appeared to be some sort of commotion in the car-park. I could hear a horrible scraping and the sound of bodies thudding against each other. It looked like one of the lower circles of hell: lots of people gurgling, shouting, crying and kicking gravel into the air. It took me a while, in the midnight blackness, to work out who was there and what was going on.

Ed Fewster ran up to me. 'I don't know what to do,' he said shakily. 'She's really upset. She's threatening to kill herself.' His cravat was hanging off and some of the ruffles appeared to have been torn off his white shirt.

'Who?' I was confused. 'I thought you'd gone home with Carl.'

'I took him home and came back for the party,' said Ed. 'I wish I hadn't. I bumped into Trudi and now all this hideousnes . . .'

Trudi was wailing like a burglar alarm, projecting a high-pitched, unpunctuated blare into the night. Caroline was crying and trying to hug her, but Trudi kept breaking free and lunging towards Ed. Hayley and Carmel-Marie were also there, which I wasn't thrilled about. I thought they'd gone ages ago. In their uniform of skimpy black cocktail dresses, wagging their fingers and tutting, they looked as if they were on playground duty in a Salvador Dali painting.

'Trudi!' Carmel-Marie intercepted her mid-lunge. 'Leave Ed alone. You're upsetting him. Pull yourself together.'

'Where are Richard and Phil?' I asked Hayley.

'They've gone,' she said. 'Me and Carmel-Marie had to stay and deal with this! Honestly, why is Seth never here when there's a nightmare situation that needs sorting out?'

'How long has this been going on?' I asked, looking around to see where Tony had got to. I saw the grabber-shriekers transporting him away from me towards the lake. The four of them looked like a giant fork, with Tony sticking up on top and Megan, Sally and Jeanette forming the tines.

'For about half an hour,' said Hayley. 'She keeps throwing herself at Ed. He's tried talking to her and she just won't listen.'

'Ed!' Trudi blared, running towards him with her arms outstretched. Ed grabbed me and pulled me in front of him like a shield. Before I could shake him off, I found myself squashed between him and the distraught Trudi.

'Move!' she yelled at me. 'I want Ed! I want Ed!' Her face looked wet and rubbery.

'I wish I could,' I said. Ed was clinging to me as if his

life depended on it.

'No! No!' he shouted.

Carmel-Marie and Hayley dragged Trudi away and Ed finally let go of me. Caroline ran around the outskirts of our little area of devastation, shouting, 'Oh, it's so awful, it's so awful, what shall we do?'

'Ow!' I muttered, adjusting my clothes. 'That hurt.'

'Sorry.' Ed gasped for breath. 'But what else was I supposed to do? She's all slimy and disgusting. She'll never leave me alone. I'll have to go into hiding.'

Trudi bobbed up and down energetically in between Carmel-Marie and Hayley, who were holding an arm each. She looked like a heavyweight boxer being restrained by her two coaches from laying into the opposition.

'Just calm down,' I said to Ed. 'I'm sure it'll all blow over.' In the distance I could see Tony bobbing along on a human rickshaw comprising Megan, Sally and Jeanette. 'Got to go,' I said, ignoring Ed's pleas and protests. I put my bag over my shoulder and ran across the car-park and over the gentle slope of Beasley's front garden after the disappearing Tony. Sympathetic as I was to Ed's plight, I had other priorities.

When I had almost caught up with the three forktines, I slowed down and took a few deep breaths. If anyone turned round I wanted it to look as though I'd been strolling behind them in a calm and composed manner all along. It had been raining on and off all evening and I could feel the heels of my black suede shoes sinking into the mud as I crossed the soggy field between the school and the woods where the lake was.

I don't know whether Tony sensed I was there, but he kept trying to twist his neck round. He caught sight of me behind him, waved and tried to say something, except I couldn't hear it over the general shrieking.

'Put Tony down,' I said in my best authoritative voice.

'Oh, get lost,' said Megan with her back to me.

'Megan! Have you forgotten who you're speaking to?' You can say things like that when you're a teacher and get away with it. I don't make use of this facility very often because, let's face it, it does sound a bit petty, but it's nice to know the vocabulary of superiority is there when you need it. I couldn't pull rank on anyone when I was a secretary, apart from the abusive bag lady who used to sit on Piper Whalley Rooney's steps wrapped in bin liners, shouting 'The lifts that take you up can take you down' over and over again.

'But I can't put him down,' Megan protested. 'I want him to make my dreams come true!'

'Tony, Tony!' Sally giggled. 'Come into the woods with us and make our dreams come true.' They rotated Tony into an upright position, still clinging to him fiercely.

The lake was kidney-bean shaped and shimmered in the darkness beside us. Everyone called it the lake although technically it was probably only a pond. There were a few benches around its rim and, about a hundred metres away, a dense cluster of trees formed the edge of a wood.

It was too dark and misty to identify people at a distance, but I could hear Oliver, Stella, Phoebe and a few other voices I recognised, as well as the sound of lager cans opening.

I stood in front of the fork-tine girls threateningly. On no account was I going to let them drag Tony off into the woods. Who knew what might happen to the poor boy? I remembered Hayley, at the dress rehearsal, saying that he must spend a lot of his time kicking people's heads in because he seemed always to be sustaining new injuries. I thought it was far more likely that his wounds were inflicted by horny teenage girls.

I don't know how I did what I did next. I walked over to Tony and somehow managed to wedge myself

187

between him and Megan. With a deft elbow movement I pushed her to one side and she staggered back, landing, by the sound of the splash she made, in a nearby puddle. I took advantage of the fact that Sally and Jeanette were momentarily distracted by taking Tony's hand and pulling him towards me, twirling round immediately afterwards so that I was between him and the fork-tines. My eyes met Tony's for a split second and, in a moment of Telepathic GLOW, we came to a wordless understanding. We held hands and ran towards the trees, leaving Megan, Sally and Jeanette staring dumbly after us. I bet they never thought a teacher would pull a stunt like that.

Once we'd got far enough away from them and caught our breath, I said to Tony, 'It must be a bit of a pain, being chased by girls all the time.'

He shuddered. 'It's a fucking nightmare,' he said quietly. I had to stand practically on top of him to hear what he was saying. 'It's been like this all my life. I can't even walk into a room without it happening. I hate it.'

If anyone else had said this I might have thought they were boasting in a Natasha Leaf I-was-so-embarrassed-when-I-got-twelve-Valentine-cards-at-work sort of way. But I sensed immediately that Tony was telling the truth. Well, think about it, you'd hate it too. If you think you wouldn't, that's because it doesn't happen to you. It doesn't happen to me either, or to most people.

I didn't make any jokes about it being all right for some, as no doubt the insensitive Carl would have, because I could imagine exactly what Tony had had to put up with, probably since he was about twelve if his secondary school was anything like mine.

'No one ever talks to me,' Tony went on, his expression alternating between blankness and distress as if it couldn't quite make up its mind. 'I've always known I could have absolutely anyone I wanted, but I'm not interested. They don't even know me, they don't care what I'm like as a person. Everyone thinks I haven't got a brain just because I'm good-looking.'

'I don't think that,' I said. 'It must be awful. I'm sorry.'

'Why are you sorry?' he asked bitterly, lighting a cigarette. 'At least you talk to me. You're different, you're intelligent.'

I would say this was the best moment of my life – it definitely was at the time – but since those words came out of Tony's mouth, instantly knocking do-you-want-a-chair off the top spot in the Tony Lamb Phrase Hierarchy, even better things have happened.

'Well, I'll say sorry anyway,' I said. 'On behalf of my gender. You must be totally sick of the whole female race.'

Now, you are never going to believe, Cat As, Es and anybody else who has followed us out to these drizzly woods, what Tony Lamb said next. You'll think it's as unbelievable as I thought it was when I heard it. The gorgeous, glazed, silent Tony Lamb we all know and love – well, I love him; you'd better not, unless you want me to dedicate my remaining years on earth to bringing about your downfall – said this: 'I don't mind women. It's just girls I'm sick of.'

Out it came, a real chat-up line, the sort of thing you might expect to hear from a slicked-haired, Porsche-driving accountant.

I looked at Tony to make sure I hadn't imagined it. He smiled at me. I mumbled something incoherent and giggled. Precipice GLOW had struck me dumb momentarily, the sense that I was teetering on the brink of more GLOW than I had ever believed it possible to experience.

Now is not the time to be inarticulate, I told myself sternly. Tony had implied that he liked me because I was different from the grabber-shriekers, because I spoke to him. I needed to think of something pretty monumental to say before he lost interest.

'I don't know what to do now,' I said, with an honesty that was unusual for me. 'I think that was a come-on, but I'm reluctant to act on it because of what you've just said. I don't want you to think I'm like all the others, which is what you might think if I . . .'

I never got to finish my sentence. Tony dropped his cigarette on the floor, pulled me towards him and kissed me. He knew all about pace, it seemed, about interrupting dialogue with action. We clung together. I could feel the muscles in his arms tightening around me. I couldn't remember the last time I had been kissed so passionately. It was as if Tony had been deliberately zombie-like for the past four weeks in a carefully planned attempt to reserve all his powers of expression for this moment, which instantly became the best moment of my life.

I had never had so many contenders for Best Moment slot in one evening before. Usually a few years pass between possible best moments and I'd already had two in one night.

I stood there by the lake in the light rain, my heels sinking deeper and deeper into the mud, kissing and being kissed by Tony Lamb. A lynch-mob of teenage girls had formed behind me and many violent verbal attacks were made on both my behaviour and my person.

'That bitch! Why can't she just fuck off?'

'Stop her. Somebody stop her!'

'The slag! She's a right dog, anyway.'

'Tony must be pissed.'

These comments and more formed the backing track to our kiss. Did I care? Did I fuck! I was so ecstatically happy that even insults had GLOW. Insults had GLOW and mud had GLOW and rain had GLOW and even Carl Sillery and his vomit – especially his vomit, since it got

190

him out of the way – had a little bit of GLOW.

'She's got a bloke already!' a high-pitched voice protested. 'She's a right slag.'

Tony must have heard this. It was loud enough to get past his deaf ear and reach his hearing one, but he didn't stop kissing me. He held me even tighter, in fact.

Was I a slag, I wondered ecstatically. Perhaps, but for what I'd done with Carl, not for what I was doing with Tony. And, as Julie Andrews quite rightly pointed out in *The Sound of Music*: 'Nothing comes from nothing / Nothing ever could / So somewhere in my youth or childhood / I must have done something good.'

NB I know why that's relevant to me, but why was it relevant to Julie Andrews? It's hard to imagine her doing anything immoral. She was a nun who never shagged seventeen-year-olds in alleyways.

*Part Two*

# Chapter Twenty-Seven Old Time,
# Chapter One New Time

## The Moment of Supreme GLOW

Part two. Of this book and of my life. I think that calls for
a new typeface, don't you? Actually I don't care what you
think because I've kissed Tony Lamb and you haven't. I'm
different now. I have been lifted on to a higher plane. I
walk down the street radiating GLOW, wondering why
people don't stop me and say, 'You've kissed Tony Lamb,
haven't you?' And there's more. But you're not getting the
rest yet. If I go straight on and tell you what followed from
that lakeside kiss you might assume the kiss was merely a
rung on a ladder, a link in a chain, a means to an end. Too
many images, did I hear you say? I'm sorry, have you
kissed Tony Lamb? Didn't think you had.

Without wishing to detract from the significance of what
happened next, I would like to stress that that first kiss was
a high-significance moment in its own right. It was the
Moment of Supreme GLOW. If I had dropped dead
immediately afterwards, spontaneously or courtesy of the
lynch-mob, it wouldn't have made any difference to an
objective assessment of my life. In that moment my life
went from normal to great.

I'll tell you another thing: kissing Tony Lamb has
made me a better writer. If you read my feeble pre-Tony
radio plays, you would see I'm right. I wouldn't advise it,
though – they're just not that good. They have no GLOW.
This book, on the other hand, has full GLOW. *Lions* had a
bit of GLOW because I'd met Tony and was in love with

him when I wrote it, but even *Lions* pales into insignificance beside what I'm writing now because it was written by the old Me, the pre-lakeside-kiss Me.

I think it's important that the marketing of this book should capture the GLOW factor. The posters should be orange and perhaps a bit shiny. No, on second thoughts, to laminate the GLOW would be to cheapen it. It's more fuzzy and textured. It's furry.

I know where I want the posters to be: in those frames that run diagonally along the sides of escalators on the London Underground. If there's going to be a quote on the front cover, I want Martin Amis. I don't think it's too arrogant of me to ask for that, not with my new status as Tony-kisser. I want him to say, 'This is the first book ever to be about Tony Lamb. It has the Tony Lamb GLOW,' because that's what my book has that others don't and everyone knows that in order to market a product successfully you have to highlight its distinctive qualities. He can paraphrase a bit – Martin, that is – as long as he gets the point across.

If a film is made there's going to be a problem. I can't think of any actors who are even half as beautiful as Tony. I could be played by Demi Moore, if she screwed her eyes up, pressed her lips together and tucked her chin in. And if she wasn't bald at the time, obviously. But nobody could capture Tony's essence apart from Tony, and I couldn't risk introducing him to Demi Moore and allowing them to perform love scenes together.

You can see how changed I am, can't you? I used to worry about Megan Cartledge and Sinead Riley. Now I worry about Demi Moore. For the first time in my life, I'm a Communal Worry Object. Tony chose me over everyone else and now all the female Youth Theatre members are worrying their little heads off on my account. Long may I continue to distress them.

I'm going to carry on with the story in a minute. It's important that you remember, however, that no matter what events follow – moral or immoral, happy or sad, tempestuous or peaceful, funny or serious – I kissed Tony Lamb and Tony Lamb kissed me. So from now on, no calling me a cradle-snatching slut, no thinking it, even. I want a bit of respect around here.

# Chapter Twenty-Eight Old Time
# Chapter Two New Time

## The Click

I pulled away from Tony's kiss after a few minutes and said, 'Shall we move a bit further away? I may get stabbed if we stay here.' Our kiss had stopped the rain, it seemed, but increased the mist.

'Like where?' said Tony.

'Further into the woods,' I suggested. 'I mean, at least we wouldn't be right next to the grabber . . .'

'Who?'

'Oh. The grabber-shriekers. That's what I call the girls who try to grab you all the time and shriek whenever you appear.'

'Good name for them.'

We walked hand in hand through the trees. My hand felt small and weak in Tony's firm grip.

'Where are they going ?' somebody moaned pitifully and further assassination of my character blew towards us on the night wind. Tony and I walked until we couldn't hear the voices any more, until the mist swallowed the figures that lurked in the distance. Once we were safely ensconced in woodland we stopped and kissed again.

This time it was Tony who pulled away. 'Oh no,' he mumbled, casting his eyes up towards the sky. 'I'm worried. I'm worried.'

'What about?' I asked.

'I don't know. You're a writer.'

'So?' Surely he hadn't heard one of my plays on Radio

Four and taken against it to such an extent that it was now going to ruin our relationship.

'I'm not as intelligent as you,' he said.

'Don't be silly,' I said. 'Course you are.' I tried to kiss him again, but he seemed distracted. His eyes were darting all over the place, not purposefully like Seth's, but aimlessly, as though he were in some kind of trance.

'But you're a writer,' he said again.

'Yes . . . but . . . look, shall we sit down? I mean, it's a bit wet, but . . .' Tony shrugged. I took the initiative and lowered myself on to some damp grass by a tree, mentally writing off my entire outfit. At this stage I must have looked as if I'd jumped fully dressed into a mud bath. 'Come and sit down,' I said, hoping we wouldn't both catch pneumonia. I wondered whether Carmel-Marie was still hanging around. I hadn't heard her voice for a while, but I half expected her to swoop down from a branch and whisk Tony away.

He sat down next to me and kissed me again. I was just beginning to think that his worried phase had passed when he pulled away and said, 'Oh no, this is bad. This is bad.' He hugged his knees and began to rock back and forth.

'What's bad?' I asked.

'This. We'll probably never see each other again after tonight. *Lions* has finished. That's it, isn't it? I'll probably never see anyone here again, so what's the point?' He rocked faster.

'Of course you'll see me again,' I said. 'If you want to.' He didn't seem to hear me. He had gone into glazed mode and was rambling incoherently. I thought I could make out odd words, including 'naked' and 'biddable' but I had no idea what he was trying to say.

I was concerned but not particularly surprised by Tony's sudden change of mood. It seemed appropriate, predictable almost, that kissing him should lead to strangeness of some description.

'You live with someone,' he declared with sudden

clarity, his upper torso still swaying rhythmically.

'Yes, but . . . that doesn't matter,' I heard myself saying. 'Look Tony, I don't know exactly what you're worried about, but if it's just that . . . I mean, circumstances change. I really like you.' Enough to leave Alistair, I added silently. Enough to do anything. The fact that I was willing to kiss him passionately in front of the entire company proved that.

'But it's not going anywhere.' He shook his head ominously. 'You don't know me. You live with someone.'

'Tony,' I said sternly, putting my arms around him. 'Look at me.' He turned to face me and I kissed him in what I hoped was a reassuring way. He wasn't too worried to kiss me back, I noticed, for which I offered up profuse thanks to the heavens. I could feel him beginning to relax. After a while I pulled away gently. 'See? There's nothing to worry about,' I said. 'I may not know you very well yet, but I'd like to get to know you. I really like you Tony . . . a lot.'

'But it's just tonight, isn't it?' He started rocking again and biting his nails. 'I'll never see you again.'

I sighed, wondering why he felt it necessary to say the same thing over and over. A limited vocabulary was one possible explanation. Perhaps he relied on a few tried and tested phrases because speech, otherwise, would be too daunting a prospect. 'You will if you want to,' I said. 'I mean, I'll do whatever you want. If you want to see me again, you can, whenever you like, as much as you like.' I didn't see the point in playing hard to get. 'But if you don't, you don't have to.'

'But I really like you!' he said with sudden vehemence, rocking energetically with his arms crossed over his chest as if he were in a strait-jacket. 'I really like you, but I'll never see you again. I mean, I could have sex with you, right . . .'

'Right,' I confirmed.

'. . . but then that would be it. And I could have sex with anyone. I really like you, you're different.'

'Tony, I don't understand,' I said patiently. It was as though we were taking part in two different conversations.

'If you knew me you wouldn't like me,' he muttered into cupped hands. 'You've got no idea.'

'About what? What an awful person you are?' I wasn't mocking him; I had a feeling this was what he was getting at.

'Something like that.'

'Tony, however bad you think you are – however bad you are, even – will not make me like you even a tiny bit less.' He looked at me hopefully for a minute, then his eyes glazed over defensively, but that instant of breakthrough was enough to spur me on. I put my arms around him and we kissed again. I heard the sound of a sudden brief downpour, spattering the leaves above our heads.

'You wouldn't say that if you knew.' He pulled away.

'Yes I would,' I said. 'I'd still like you as much as I do now, even if you'd . . . murdered a hundred people.'

'I clicked with you straight away,' he said, lighting another cigarette nervously. 'That first day when you sat opposite me in the circle.' He smiled at the memory. 'And when you sat on the floor and I asked you if you wanted a chair.'

'You remember that?' I asked, amazed. 'You remember those two times?'

'Course.' He nodded. 'I clicked with you straight away. We definitely clicked.'

This was one phrase I didn't mind him repeating. I was overwhelmed with joy. 'I knew I'd . . . clicked,' I stammered, 'but I had no idea the clicking was mutual. I wish you'd said something sooner.' The reason why he perhaps hadn't been able to occurred to me suddenly. 'Tony,' I began gently. 'Is it . . . was Carmel-Marie . . . were you . . . involved with Carmel-Marie?'

He inhaled deeply on his cigarette. 'Do you mind if I go for a walk, clear my head?' he asked, ignoring my question.

I decided not to press the point. He was with me now and that was all that mattered. 'No, I . . . no.'

'Okay. Thanks,' he said, standing up. I sat cross-legged on the wet, muddy grass and watched with mixed feelings as he strolled further into the mist-wrapped woods. I was glad of the normality interval, but what if Tony disappeared for ever? Was his sudden departure my fault, for mentioning Carmel-Marie?

Still, so confident was I of the click factor that I didn't seriously worry that he was trying to escape or suspect him of dashing off to meet a gorgeous supermodel on the other side of the woods.

I indulged in a bit of instant nostalgia, replaying in my head the words 'I clicked with you straight away'. Another life-changing moment to add to the night's inventory.

I heard a colossal splash followed by loud exclamations in the distance. I was weighing my curiosity about recent lakeside developments against the fear that Tony would return and find me momentarily absent when I heard muddy footsteps squelching in my direction. The substantial figure of Ed Fewster lumbered towards me, groaning. 'Oliver's such an imbecile!' he grunted in disgust. His shirt was now totally ruffle-free and had several large tears down the front. There was a long, diagonal scratch mark across his left cheek.

'Why?' I asked. 'What's going on over there?'

'Some bint claiming to be Oliver's girlfriend turned up. Trouble is, he's snogging Phoebe. He's such a . . . rampant womaniser. There was a huge fuss and the alleged girlfriend, who Oliver claims is no such thing, fell in the lake! And now everyone's talking about going back to Phoebe's, undeterred by the catalogue of horrors that have plagued the evening so far!'

Everyone going back to Phoebe's? Didn't these children ever get tired, I wondered generation-gappishly.

'So now everyone's drenched and wittering about love,' Ed continued. 'I detest love!'

'Do you? I asked. 'Is that why you don't want to get involved with Trudi?'

'I don't want to get involved with anyone. Ever.'

'You don't mean that,' I said firmly.

'Yes I do. It's all so . . . undignified! Look at everyone tonight. You and Tony, Oliver and Phoebe, Lottie and Rhys, Robbie and Bev . . .'

'Robbie and Bev! God, I'd never have predicted that!'

'. . . and Megan crying and the wet girlfriend crying! It's all so moist and horribly biological. It's because it's the last night, everyone's just lost it, everyone's running around leaking bodily fluids in a state of . . .'

'Griplessness?' I suggested.

'As in not having a grip?'

'Yeah.'

'Well, then yeah, griplessness is a good word for it.'

'I can see what you mean,' I said. 'But sometimes you just have to let yourself go.'

'Ugh! I don't have to and I won't. Not if it means behaving like a demented person.'

I laughed. 'Do you think me and Tony are demented?' I felt a twinge of fear, thinking of Tony alone in the woods. What if he got depressed in there and decided never to come out? I resolved to reassure him of his wonderfulness even more convincingly as soon as he reappeared and never to mention Carmel-Marie again.

'Tony's certainly demented,' said Ed, 'and you are for getting involved with him.'

'But it's not just a last-night thing,' I explained. 'I really love Tony.'

'Ugh! I hate that! That means you've lost control of your brain and you're a teacher! I fear for the education system of this country, I really do.'

I couldn't help laughing. Ed was too witty and charming to be an Obstacle with Anti-GLOW.

'What about Carl?' he asked, just as I was getting ready to enjoy a Tony-conversation.

'That's utter bollocks,' I said with confidence. 'All in his mind, I'm afraid.' Ed nodded grimly, as if the derangement of yet another of his close friends was no surprise to him.

I thought I'd pulled off the Carl indignation with aplomb. From now on I wasn't going to let that bother me. I would simply deny everything. It was my word against his and, let's face it, it's not as if people always, or even usually, believe the truth, is it? Look at the Darryl and Seth débâcle. The truth was right there for everyone to see and yet the majority of people chose to believe the lie. So I ask you, folks, if this is the reception honesty gets, I for one think we should all start lying a bit more. Why expose our blameless, vulnerable true stories to the scorn and disbelief of bigoted bandwagon-jumpers? Our lies, on the other hand, are fair game, legitimate targets. They're tough, mean and cynical. They can hack it out there in the tarring, feathering and stoning world.

'Anyway, it's all too horrible.' Ed threw up his hands in despair. 'I shall have to go and live on a mountain somewhere with no other people, that's the only thing for it.'

'Don't be silly.' I smiled. 'You'd hate that. No one to talk to. I thought you wanted to be a writer.'

'I do.'

'Well, writers need conversation. They need other people.'

'I don't need the sort of conversations I'm forced to endure on a daily basis, sordid little snippets about who's done what with whom. I certainly wouldn't want that to be the main influence on my writing. I'd end up writing books called *Bodily Function* and *Bodily Function II*, the sequel. No, I shall have to live alone on a mountain and write about an imaginary civilisation where people's minds are not permanently fixed on their genitals. Ugh, what a horrible word, genitals.' He shook his head sorrowfully and stomped off in the direction of the lake.

I heard the sound of moving branches and saw something tall approaching from behind me. It was Tony, I realised with intense joy. He'd come back!

# Chapter Three

## Out of the Woods

'Drugs,' Tony said quietly when he reached my side.

'What?' I'd been hoping to carry on the conversation where we'd left off; I didn't feel our respective thoughts and feelings on the matter of our mutual Clicking had been adequately covered, but Tony obviously did. 'What about drugs?' I asked.

'Forget it.' He shook his head, sitting down next to me.

'Oh! You mean . . . you take them? Deal them?' I almost giggled as I said this. As if anything could put me off him now. Drugs, kidnap, fraud – everything paled into insignificance beside the Click, whose presence I felt as strongly as if it had been physically there, a big cuddly creature sitting on the grass beside us like one of those cute monsters from *Where the Wild Things Are*.

'I used to be an addict,' he said, rocking again. 'I was really bad. You can't imagine how bad I was.'

'What sort of drugs?' I asked. 'Heroin?'

'Everything,' he whispered. 'I nearly died.'

'But you're off them now?'

'Yeah,' he said.

'So you've done really well!' I enthused. 'You should be proud of that.'

'You don't know how much,' he said, rather cryptically.

'You keep saying I don't know, I can't imagine,' I said. 'I'm not that naïve, you know. I mean, I've known a few drug addicts in my time. When I was twelve I had a boyfriend who used to make me buy him canisters of gas, which he'd then inhale in an alleyway behind some shops.'

This was true. My life in alleyways did not start with Carl Sillery. I was being depraved in alleyways before he was born. Makes you think, doesn't it? Makes you think, do we really want to be narrated to by this low-life? Must we continue to suffer this scummy authorial voice?

'I heard, a few years later, that he'd become a rent boy to finance his drug habit and then he died from a heroin overdose,' I continued. 'Then, when I was seventeen, I went out with a drug user and dealer. One of my best friends lived with a bloke who had to wear gloves all the time, even in summer, because he had no veins – he'd knackered them all by injecting heroin. So you see, I do know a bit.'

Tony didn't seem impressed. 'You just don't know,' he said, shaking his head. I'm sorry if you're getting fed up of Tony's repetition of the same phrases, Cat As, but how do you think I felt?

He was looking particularly glazed now, I noticed, double-glazed even, like the windows in my Auntie Eileen's house – however desperate you are for fresh air you simply can't get the buggers to open. Maybe my little trip down memory lane had gone on a bit too long.

'I'm bad,' said Tony. 'You shouldn't have anything to do with me. You're good. You should stay with your man that you live with. He's better than me.' He smiled a sinister smile. 'He couldn't be worse.'

'Why, because you were an addict? You're not one any more.'

'I'm schizophrenic,' he mumbled to his knees, 'and psychotic.'

'Oh.' I nodded understandingly. 'Both?'

'Apparently.' He shrugged.

'What do you mean, apparently? Did someone say you were?' He nodded. 'Who?' I asked.

'Doctors. Psychologists.' He pronounced this last word

206

slowly and deliberately, loading each syllable with sarcasm.

'Oh. That's not very nice of them to say that,' I said sympathetically.

'Well, that's what they say. That's what they all say.' He refused to look at me.

'Tony, I don't care!' I pleaded with him. 'I mean, I care, obviously, I care about you, but I don't care what you've done or what you are. I love you.'

'Why?' He stared at me oddly. 'What's there to love about me?'

'Absolutely everything.' I reached for his hand and he didn't stop me. We kissed again and Tony squeezed me tightly against his chest. I was beginning to think he found it easier to express emotion physically rather than verbally.

'I used to be different you know,' he said, when we had reluctantly disentangled our mouths. 'I wasn't always like this. I used to be the life and soul of the party, real extrovert. I was like . . . who's the most outgoing person in *Lions*?'

'Oliver?' I suggested.

'Yeah, I was like Oliver.'

'So what happened?'

'Bad times,' he said. 'Bad times. Nobody knows. Nobody can understand.'

'Don't be so defeatist,' I said briskly. 'I'm a very understanding person. You're so bogged down in your own problems that you're making all these assumptions. I bet you think I'm too good for you, don't you?'

'Yeah.' He laughed, as if I were stating the obvious.

'Well, you're wrong. I can be really bad. I wouldn't be to you, but I can be to other people. I have been, often. I wouldn't regard myself as a good person.'

'I think you are,' said Tony.

'Well, I think *you* are! Look, come here.' I kissed him again, aware that we were beginning to sound like a misunderstanding scene from a Marx Brothers movie.

207

'Nobody has ever gone right down into the depths of me and come back out,' Tony said when we separated, curling his body into a ball.

'Well, I'm not just anybody,' I said. 'I can do it. I can do anything as long as I've got you.' Sorry if you're cringing, but that was what I said. Luckily, I don't think Tony realised it was a cliché. I didn't care anyway; it was true. Well, half true. I was indeed keen to go down into the depths of Tony Lamb, but as for coming back out – why would I, or anyone in their right mind, want to do that? I intended to stay in Tony's depths for as long as I could.

I suddenly realised that the implication of what he'd just said was that some people had gone into his depths and not come back out. I wondered where they were now. Swimming around in his stomach? Banging on his eardrum? That might explain his deafness in one ear.

In the hope that a change of subject might lighten the atmosphere, I said, 'Everyone's going back to Phoebe's in a bit, to carry on partying. Shall we go?' Tony shrugged. 'I'll go and ask her if it's okay, shall I?' I said, trying to provoke a reaction. 'I mean, we need somewhere to stay tonight.'

'Okay,' he said distractedly, as though he was only half listening.

'Wait here,' I instructed and set off towards the lake.

When I got there I realised that a lot of people had gone home. Instead of the thirty or so shadowy figures from whom Tony and I had fled earlier, there were now no more than about seven. Lightweights, I thought, not feeling even remotely tired despite the fact that it was nearly two in the morning. I felt like Eliza Doolittle did when she sang 'I Could Have Danced All Night', although Tony and I weren't dancing types. We were more sitting-on-wet-grass-talking-about-sordid-pasts types.

I heard giggling, sucking and squelching as a big dark blob approached. I prodded it with my finger and discovered that it was an entanglement of Phoebe and Oliver.

'Oliver, have you got a mobile phone?' I asked, realising I ought to phone Alistair. I'd said I'd be late, but not this late. Getting no response, I yelled, 'Hey, stop kissing Phoebe for a minute, this is important. Have you got a mobile phone?'

'Yeah,' Oliver slurred pissedly. 'In my pockeh.'

'Can I have it? Oliver!' He and Phoebe were back in full blob formation. I inserted my hand into the pocket of Oliver's chinos and removed his phone. He was so drunk that he didn't notice. I dialled my number and Alistair answered after one ring.

'Where the fuck are you?' he asked impatiently.

'I'm at a party with all the kids,' I said. 'By a lake near school. Listen, I think it's going to go on all night.'

'All night? Outside? Isn't it raining there?'

'Yes, but . . . you know what it's like,' I said. 'Last night and all that.'

'Hmm, well. Mad, if you ask me. So when will you be back?'

'Tomorrow morning some time, probably. Is that okay?'

'Yeah. I'm glad you phoned, though, I was getting worried. Are you having a good time?'

'Brilliant,' I said.

'How was the show?'

'Brilliant,' I said again, although I could hardly re-member it now. It seemed like so long ago, as if it existed in another time zone, as far removed from the present as Ingra Savoy's world was from Ian Chaddock's.

'See you later, then,' said Alistair drowsily. Now that he knew I was safe he was already falling asleep.

'Bye,' I said. I won't insult your intelligence by whingeing on about how guilty I felt. Not enough to stop doing what I was doing, evidently. And that, in my view, is what counts. People who go on about how guilty they feel are usually total hypocrites, who want to do wrong but look good at the same time. 'Oh I feel so awful about sending my children to a private school,' they say, but they still do it.

Alistair is happy, I thought to myself in a moment of stark clarity, while Phoebe and Oliver groped each other beside me. I just won't tell him about Tony, simple as that. Phil Douglas didn't know anything; he had gone home before the Moment of Supreme GLOW. Hayley was bound to hear on the Beasley grapevine, but I was sure my powers of intimidating persuasion would be sufficient to stop her telling Phil.

'Phoebe,' I said. 'Phoebe!'

'Yeah?' She turned to face me, keeping her arms locked around Oliver's neck.

'Is everyone going back to yours tonight?'

'Yeah, well, a few people.'

'Yeah!' Oliver cheered. 'We're going back to Phoebe's! We're going back to Phoebe's!'

'Have you got room for two more?'

'Who?' Phoebe asked.

'Me and Tony,' I said, hoping this was a phrase I'd be using a lot in the future.

'Tony the sound engineer?'

'Yeah.'

'Are you and he . . . together?' she asked coyly. I nodded frenetically, keen to make our coupledom official. 'Aah, that's really sweet!' Phoebe smiled. 'How romantic! You and Tony!'

'How romantic,' Oliver echoed, grinning drunkly. 'Tony and Belinda. How romantic.'

'So can we come back? Is there room?'

'Course there is,' said Phoebe. 'We'll make room. You and Tony can have my bed. We'll sleep on the floor.'

I wished that I had a special prize I could give out, an official Belinda Nield Award for Excellence in the Field – we were in a field, as it happened, but that's not all I mean – of Romance Facilitation. It's not all bad news, Cat As. Just when you are steeling yourself to brace the onslaught of all those obstacles with Anti-GLOW, a Romance Facilitator will come along unexpectedly and,

210

with Enabling GLOW, offer you and your loved one a bed for the night. I looked into Phoebe's eyes, which seemed to say, 'May the GLOW be with you.'

At that moment it was clear to me that Phoebe Procter was the Good Fairy of Love. I'd been a bit slow on the uptake not realising this sooner. Of course she was. Blonde curly hair, blue eyes; she looked like an angel because she was one. I wondered if Oliver Wild knew how lucky he was.

'Here's Tony now.' Phoebe pointed over my shoulder. 'Aah, how lovely that you two . . . hello Tony!'

Tony grinned at her, putting his arms round my waist.

'Tony, we can go back to Phoebe's tonight,' I said.

'I'm too drunk to drive!' Oliver suddenly yelled. 'I'm too drunk to drive to Phoebe's.'

'You're not going to Phoebe's!' I heard a sudden harsh voice shout. I whirled round and found myself face to face with Stella Nettleton, the wide black night spread out behind her like a cape.

# Chapter Four

## The Good Fairy of Love and the Wicked Witch of Anti-GLOW

'Yes he is,' I said, thinking this had to be a misunderstanding. 'Oliver is coming back.'

'Belinda, *shut up*!' barked the Wicked Witch of Anti-GLOW with a ferocity that I found uncommonly rude, given that we barely knew each other.

'But Oliver is staying at Phoebe's,' I said. 'So are me and Tony. It's all been arranged.'

'You and Tony?' Stella sounded horrified. 'Tony the sound engineer?'

'Yes, Tony!' I said huffily. 'This Tony.' I pointed to him in a show-and-tell sort of way, since he was right next to me. Exhibit A: Tony Lamb.

'Phoebe, can I have a word with you in private?' Stella yanked Phoebe away from Oliver with unnecessary violence. I was sure I heard the sound of a snapping bone as she dragged her into a cluster of trees.

'What's going on?' Oliver looked at me in ruffled confusion. 'What's Stella doing?'

'I don't know,' I said, 'but don't worry, you are coming back to Phoebe's. Phoebe wants you to come back. I know she does.'

'She does, doesn't she?' Oliver sounded as if he was trying to reassure himself.

'Yes. And it's got nothing to do with Stella.'

Oliver nodded, burped and staggered away.

About a minute later Phoebe returned, looking tearful

212

and persecuted. It hadn't taken Stella long to cast her misery spell. 'Stella says Oliver can't come back.' Phoebe started to cry, her wide, long-lashed eyes glinting in the darkness.

'I don't understand,' I said truthfully. 'Does Stella live in your house?'

'No, but she's staying tonight.'

'So?' I said angrily. 'It's up to you who stays, not her.'

'She says he's just using me.' Phoebe sobbed. 'And that if I let him come back, I'll regret it.'

'What utter bollocks!' I said. 'Oliver really likes you.' I looked around, seeking confirmation from the man himself, but Oliver and Tony had wandered over to a nearby bench where they were now sitting side by side, smoking in silence.

'I know Stella means well.' Phoebe wiped her eyes. 'She's only saying it because she cares about me and doesn't want me to get hurt.'

'Rubbish,' I said. Is frog-marching someone into the woods and reducing them to tears what you do when you don't want them to get hurt? Of course it isn't. The cruel-to-be-kind myth is the public face of Anti-GLOW. 'Can't you just tell her to get lost, Phoebe?'

'I don't want to piss her off, I mean, she is my best friend. And Oliver has got a bit of a reputation.'

'So what? I'm telling you, you regret the things you don't do more than the things you do. Look, Oliver's wondering what's wrong.' I gestured towards the bench. 'He really likes you, Phoebe, I know he does. Don't let Stella stand in your way. If she was a true friend, she'd give you a bit of space to make your own decisions.'

'She doesn't want you and Tony to come back either. She said I shouldn't be an ... accessory to deceit. You know, because you live with someone.'

'Oh, really!' I resolved to defeat the Wicked Witch of Anti-GLOW if it was the last thing I did. If I had my way, a pair of dark red Kickers protruding from beneath Phoebe's house would be all that remained of Stella Nettleton tomorrow morning. 'Look, Phoebe, Tony and I are coming back. Oliver's coming back. You want us to, don't you?'

'Yes, but . . .'

'But nothing,' I said. 'Let me deal with Stella.'

'Stella's a freak,' Tony said cutely behind me. He and Oliver had wandered back over to us. Oliver tried to grope Phoebe, but she pushed him away uncertainly.

I kissed Tony, feeling that the bond between us had been strengthened by our joint stand against Anti-GLOW. 'Back in a sec,' I said and trudged off through the wet grass yelling 'Stell-a-a-ah!', like Marlon Brando in *A Streetcar Named Desire*. *A Streetcar Named Frigidity*, more like, in the case of this particular Stella.

'What?' she said curtly as I stumbled towards her.

'Oliver *is* staying at Phoebe's and don't dare to try and put any more obstacles in their way.'

'You're so fucking stupid,' said Stella. It was odd to hear a swear-word emerge from the lips of someone who looked as if she was dressed for a Salvation Army singalong.

'I'm sorry?' I pretended to be puzzled. 'Did you say what I think you said?'

'Yes, I did. You think you know everything but you're . . . Can't you see the harm you're doing?'

'To whom, exactly?'

'To Tony, to yourself, your partner, Phoebe, Carl . . .' The moonlight bounced off the lenses of her glasses.

'I think you've omitted to mention a few rice paddy workers in Malaysia,' I said.

'That's right, just make a joke out of it. You don't know Phoebe like I do, you don't know Oliver . . .'

'*Lions* is finished,' I reminded her. 'You don't have to play Ingra Savoy any more.'

'. . . You don't know what will happen and I do! They'll have sex, Oliver will get up tomorrow morning and sod off, and Phoebe will be distraught, and I'll be the one who has to pick up the pieces as usual. Phoebe's very sensitive, you know.'

'So, what, you thoughtfully protect her from nasty men? Oh, come on, at least be honest with yourself. You're not doing this for Phoebe, you're doing it for you! You thrive on ruining other people's relationships! You're an obstacle with Anti-GLOW!'

'I'm a what?' Stella demanded curiously.

'It doesn't matter, just take my word for it, you are one.'

'And you're a sad, immature, cradle-snatching slag!' Do you think I was surprised to hear myself thus described by the Wicked Witch of Anti-GLOW? Of course I wasn't. No one has ever managed to insult me in a surprising way. That was why I had the advantage over Stella; I could have written her lines in this particular dialogue, whereas she could never have written mine. Obstacles with Anti-GLOW have no imagination. They just go around limiting and forbidding things. They are the human equivalent of parking tickets.

'Fine,' I said. 'We've both had our say. Now let's agree to differ. We're going back to Phoebe's together so we need to resolve this somehow.'

'We are not!' Stella spat venom at me. 'If you think I'm coming back with . . . you lot there . . . I'm going home. The rest of you can all be stupid together.' She turned and walked away.

Thank God, I thought, she isn't coming to Phoebe's! As I wasn't going to be spending the remainder of the night with her, I no longer needed to be diplomatic so I yelled after her, 'And you can go home and be morally outraged on your own! I hope you have lots of fun disapproving of everything. Carl says you're frigid, anyway!' Satisfied that I had won the argument, I returned to Tony and the happy, slurping blob of Oliver and Phoebe that, in the absence of Stella, seemed to be back to its old jolly self. 'Right, shall we make a move?' I said.

'Is Stella all right?' Phoebe gazed dreamily at Oliver.

'She's fine. We're the ones who are damned for ever, apparently,' I said.

'Freak,' Tony muttered.

'How will we get back?' Phoebe asked.

'I'm too drunk to drive,' said Oliver.

'Phoebe, what about your parents?' I suddenly realised that Stella wasn't the only potential obstacle.

'Don't worry, they're cool,' she said.

'I could proberly drive, actually.' Oliver changed his mind.

'I'm sober,' I said. What with all the excitement, I'd forgotten to drink anything since about ten o'clock. 'I'll drive us home in Oliver's car.'

That was how, at 3 a.m. on Saturday 30 August – well, strictly speaking it was Sunday 31 August – Phoebe, Oliver, Tony and I came to be hurtling through the streets of Windsor in Oliver's red Peugeot 306.

Phoebe sat in the passenger seat next to me and I could tell from the expression on her face that she was feeling all the same things I was feeling, only about Oliver instead of Tony. From time to time we smiled at each other. There was an undeniable bond between me and the Good Fairy of Love. She'd facilitated my romance and in return I'd facilitated hers. That was what friendship was about. It certainly wasn't about being hectored by a puritan in some shrubbery. I was pleased that I had made space in my Tony-worshipping schedule to be a good citizen and do my helpful deed for the day.

# Chapter Five

## The Appearance and Clothes of Tony Lamb

Tony is the most beautiful person I have ever seen, of either gender. He is about six feet tall, with broad shoulders and a body that is athletic but not too muscly. His hair is short, straight and very dark brown, with a centre parting, and he has big brown eyes. His skin is dark with an olive undertone of which no doubt he is unaware; he almost definitely has not read *Colour Me Beautiful* by Carole Jackson.

Describing Tony is depressing because no combination of words could do him justice. Maybe this is why he doesn't speak very much. Looking like he does, he must have become aware of the inadequacy of words at an early age. He must have seen his face in the mirror at some point and thought, 'Well! How the hell can I even begin to comment on this?'

Just as there is an uncrossably wide gulf between Tony's looks and the looks of most people, there is an equally gaping canyon between Tony's clothes and the clothes of most people. I have no idea why this is. Obviously, anything would look better on him than on all other men, but it is more than the combination of the garments and Tony Lamb; it is the garments themselves.

How many checked shirts have you seen? Lots, right? But how many that you could think about, dream about and fantasise about for three hours without getting bored? None, probably.

I could think about Tony's blue and white checked shirt

for any number of hours. I could be ecstatically happy wandering around with nothing but that shirt in my head for days. I love it, not just as a Tony-possession but in its own right. I don't know where he got it, but it can't have been from a shop. If a shirt like that hung from a rail in a high-street shop even for thirty seconds there would be riots, suicides.

Then there are Tony's jeans, which are not merely blue but blue in an excellent way. They are the best shade of blue that a pair of jeans could be. If you put someone I disliked and didn't find attractive in Tony's clothes, I could probably manage to fall in love with them fairly easily. As with the shirt, the jeans cannot possibly have come from a normal retail outlet. Hysteria would surely have broken out in the streets of Slough.

Incidentally, I don't hold a grudge against the poet John Betjeman for writing a poem which starts 'Come friendly bombs and fall on Slough'. I don't think you should, either. He wrote it before Tony Lamb was born, in the days before Slough became the romantic epicentre of the Western hemisphere. Interestingly, the second line of that poem is 'It isn't fit for humans now'. If you look carefully, you may spot the double meaning. Slough isn't fit for humans now because Tony Lamb lives there and he is so god-like that mere humans should not dare show their faces in the same town.

The third transcendent item of clothing is Tony's pale blue veloury top. I don't know what material it is made from, but it looks like a combination of waves from the sea and the tears of angels. He has only worn this top once, but even after just one brief sighting I feel closer to Tony's blue veloury top than I do to most of my friends and relatives.

Phoebe lived on Finch Close in Windsor, part of a new, affluent estate populated primarily by businessmen-commuters and their families. Phoebe, gesturing for us to keep quiet, unlocked the front door and led us through to the kitchen. I noticed under the glaring neon striplight that Tony's heavenly checked shirt and blue-in-an-excellent-way jeans were covered with half-dried mud, as was my own inferior outfit.

'Oh no,' I said, 'we're all muddy.' He just shrugged. Clearly he didn't value his clothes as highly as I did.

Phoebe's parents were, as promised, cool. They didn't march downstairs in censorious dressing-gowns as soon as they heard the front door and demand to know who these strangers were who had turned up on their doorstep in the early hours of the morning. Coolly, they stayed in bed and left us to our own devices.

'Are you tired?' I asked Tony. He nodded. Oliver was half asleep, slumped in a kitchen chair.

Phoebe kept propping him up, yawning every so often. 'I'm exhausted,' she said.

'Where are you and Oliver going to sleep?' I asked her. In the car I had tried to insist that Tony and I should sleep on the floor, but she wouldn't hear of it.

'In the lounge,' she said. 'I'll make us a bed out of the sofa cushions. Come on, I'll show you where my room is.' Tony and I followed her upstairs, both of us covered with streaks of dirt. I hoped Mr and Mrs Procter wouldn't choose this moment to make an appearance. Surely no parent on earth would react with equilibrium to finding two mud-caked degenerates on the landing at four in the morning, heading straight for their daughter's bedroom.

Phoebe's room was small and cosy, with lots of Van Gogh and Monet prints on the walls and a plum-coloured carpet that you could lose your toes in. She also had a double bed, which I hadn't been expecting, with a few cuddly toys perched at the end of it, including Tenderheart Bear from the Care Bear range. I wondered whether Tony had ever had cuddly toys when he was a kid. Somehow he didn't seem the type.

Phoebe gave us whispered instructions about where the bathroom and toilet were, grabbed her pyjamas from

219

under her pillow and went back downstairs to Oliver.

'Isn't this weird?' I whispered to Tony, closing the bedroom door.

'Why?' he asked.

'Well, Phoebe's parents are in the next room. They don't know we're here, they don't even know who we are. What if they come in in the morning, expecting to see Phoebe?'

'So, they'll see us instead.' Tony walked over to the window and stared out into the Procters' back garden. I wanted to ask him about his parents, but I was scared it might bring on some new emotional crisis.

I tried to force myself to think calmly. Were we going to sleep together in Phoebe's double bed? I certainly couldn't imagine Tony taking off his clothes and leaping under the duvet, not when he'd spent the whole of a sweltering August in long sleeves and long trousers. I had a feeling he might be a virgin but, as with many of my areas of uncertainty about him, I was afraid to ask.

'I'll never see you again after tonight,' he said suddenly, still facing the garden.

'What? Tony, of course you will!' I pleaded with him. 'Why do you keep saying things like this? I love you. Don't you believe me?'

'This is all bad,' he said enigmatically, biting his nails nervously. 'We shouldn't have come here. It's too dangerous.'

I walked over to him and tried to kiss him, but he pushed me away roughly. 'Don't,' he yelped. 'I've got a say in this too, you know. You should get away from me. If it wasn't for me he'd still be alive.'

'What?' I felt faint. 'Who? Tony, who would still be alive?'

'Mark Ryder,' he mumbled through clenched teeth, peeling flaking wood from the window-frame. I think I only heard him because I was half expecting him to say that.

'What about him?' I seized Tony by the shoulders and

spun him round to face me. 'What? What about Mark Ryder? Tony, tell me. Did you . . .?'

'I didn't do it,' he said, 'but I was there.'

# Chapter Six

## Prioritising Loveloads

Monday 8 September was the first day of Beasley's autumn term. At 8 a.m. I drove my Vauxhall Nova through the school's big iron gates and along the wide tree-lined gravel drive towards the car-park.

For the first time since I had started working here in June, I didn't think how lucky I was. The word had a different meaning now; my priorities had changed. All I could think about was the hellish week I'd had between the end of *Lions* and today. Never in my life had seven days seemed so agonisingly long. Endless hours passed during which I did nothing but lie on the sofa in tormented silence, oblivious to Alistair's presence and conversation. The days were easier because he was at work, but every evening I had to pretend to listen to him as he laid into Bill Gates and Phil Douglas – who apparently was annoying him at the moment – with his customary wit and as he tried to discuss our financial situation.

I had gone over and over the events of that night at the Procters' house, trying to assess what happened objectively. After making his mysterious comment, 'I didn't do it, but I was there', Tony ran from the room and before I had even registered what he was doing I heard the front door slam.

I spent the rest of the night crying. When I went downstairs the next morning, Oliver, Phoebe and Mrs Procter were already up. They told me that Princess Diana had died in a car crash, along with her lover Dodi Fayed. It took me a while to digest this information. It seemed such a coincidence that two incredibly famous people should die on a date which, as far as I was concerned, was already historic. Now it was doubly legendary.

I was desperately worried about what Tony had told me – although I clung to the reassuring phrase 'I didn't do it' – and his sudden disappearance in the middle of the night. Where had he gone? I hated the thought of him walking all the way from Windsor to Slough in the early hours, alone. I made some excuse to Phoebe about his having had to get up early to visit an uncle, but I don't think, given my swollen eyes, she was convinced.

I got a taxi home at about midday and forced myself to appear normal for Alistair's sake. I had to wait nearly four hours until he went upstairs for a bath, leaving me free to ring Tony.

I kept all my GLOW documents in my office for safety reasons, but I knew his phone number by heart. I dialled it with trembling fingers, after first taking several deep breaths. Conversations with Tony needed to be prepared for. I felt drained after them, as though I needed to stock up on inner resources, do a big shop at the Sainsbury's of Emotion. There was something so discontinuous about him, or maybe there only seemed to be; he had, after all, remembered us clicking well enough to describe it to me nearly four weeks later.

A young male voice answered the phone and said, rather officiously, 'Hello, who is it, please?'

'Er, it's Belinda,' I stammered. 'Is Tony Lamb there?'

'No. He's out. Do you want me to give him a message?' I gave my home number and told him to get Tony to phone me as soon as possible, which was pretty stupid considering Alistair might have answered the phone, but I was too worked up to think clearly. In any case it didn't matter because Tony didn't phone. Every day and every night I sat in, willing him to ring, but he never did. I didn't care what his involvement in the death of Mark Ryder had been. I

223

was just desperate to hear from him. It was without doubt the worst week of my life so far.

Alistair, seeing that I wasn't my usual cheerful self, did his best to entertain me and cheer me up, and his best was, objectively, pretty good. He wanted to take me out for dinner and to the cinema but I was unwilling to leave the phone unattended. He tried to make me laugh and failed.

I remember how attracted I was to Alistair's dry, sharp sense of humour when I first met him. Why isn't he enough for me, I asked myself over and over again. He is witty, interesting, intelligent – everything Tony isn't, I thought disloyally. And yet I was going through conversations with Alistair on automatic pilot, my head full of the far more limited exchanges I'd had with Tony.

I concluded that whether we find people boring or interesting depends far more on our state of mind than on any qualities of theirs. I wasn't bored of Alistair; we weren't one of those sad couples who had run out of things to say to each other. Before Tony had appeared on the scene, Alistair was the person I most enjoyed spending time with, my first choice for company and conversation. Now, however, the only people who didn't bore me were Tony and anyone who was prepared to talk to me about Tony and nothing else. I've become a Tony bore, I realised, and felt totally helpless.

Today was the eighth day, both of September and of no contact. I wondered, as I parked my car in between Carmel-Marie's BMW and a green Renault Clio, if I would always feel as dreadful as I did now.

I was dragged out of my anguished introspection by a sudden loud knock on my car window. I looked up and saw Carl. I opened the door and he backed off a little, pacing back and forth across the gravel, smoking. I groaned inwardly, noticing that he had been crying. All I needed was someone else's misery to contend with in addition to my own. People who are blond in a green way don't look good when they have been crying. Nobody does, but they don't especially. Their skin goes red and puffy, and their eyes turn gooey and translucent.

I realised with a certain amount of guilt that I could hardly be bothered to speak to Carl. I was no longer interested in sleeping with him, and I couldn't even summon the energy to shout at him for being indiscreet and telling all his friends about us. That didn't seem to matter any more. I was still here, wasn't I, at Beasley? The iron gates hadn't swung closed on me. No one had intercepted me on the driveway and told me I had been fired on grounds of moral turpitude. Seth Beasley was so self-obsessed that he probably only registered gossip that involved him.

I wished I could get back a bit of my old Carl-consequences fear. At least then I would have an incentive to talk to him. But I was too full of Tony-loss fear to accommodate Carl on my list of possible worries.

I got out of my car reluctantly. 'Carl,' I said.

'Is it true?' he looked at me accusingly with puffy eyes. 'You and Tony?'

'Carl . . .'

'It is true, isn't it?'

'That depends what you've heard,' I said. I knew he wouldn't have heard anything from Phoebe and Oliver. They had promised not to say a word to anyone, seeming to understand the complexity of my situation without my even having to explain it. I was going to finish with Carl, there was no doubt about that, but I saw no reason to make him unnecessarily miserable.

'Yes, but . . . it was only a drunken kiss,' I said.

'I can't believe you'd do that,' he shouted. A globule of spit flew from the corner of his mouth. 'When I was sick, as well!'

'Carl, I don't understand this. I live with someone. You know that. It's not as though I ever promised you anything.'

'That's different.' His voice was thick from crying. 'You lived with someone before you met me.'

'So?'

'You were cheating on him, with me. I didn't mind that. But now you're cheating on me!'

'That's ridiculous,' I said crossly, although deep down I could see his point. 'Carl, I wasn't cheating on you, I'm not . . . it's over.'

'It's over? What do you mean, it's over?' His face crumpled. I could see him hovering between tears and anger. After struggling for a few seconds, he managed to achieve the latter. 'You can't just say that!' he snarled.

'I can and I am,' I said firmly. 'Even before Tony and I . . . well you know. Even before that happened I had decided.'

'Is that supposed to make me feel better?' He flicked his ash at me bitterly.

'I don't know. I'm just saying it's not because of Tony.'

'So why is it?'

'Because . . . you told all your friends, Carl. You promised you wouldn't and you did.'

'I didn't,' he said indignantly.

'So how come everyone knows about it? Caroline, Ed – everyone. You told Oliver and Ed, didn't you?'

'Well . . . only them, no one else. They're my best mates. I mean, didn't you tell anyone? Not even your close mates?'

'No,' I lied. 'I told you over and over again, telling anyone is just too risky.'

'Well . . . all right, I'm sorry! I'm sorry!' he wailed desperately. 'They won't say anything, anyway. Look, just give me another chance . . .'

'Carl! ' I put both my hands up instinctively in a go-no-further sign. If Carl was as good at reading body language as he claimed, he should have had no problem translating my gesture into English. 'No, okay? No. Look, it's not just that. I was annoyed about that, but it isn't the only reason. I just . . .'

'It is Tony, isn't it?' Carl demanded.

'No, it isn't. It's . . . I don't know, I never meant for it to get serious. I thought it was just supposed to be a bit of fun.'

'It is fun.' His voice shook. 'So why are you trying to end it?'

'It was fun,' I corrected him, 'but, Carl, we just can't carry on. *I* can't carry on. I didn't realise how . . . stressful I'd find it, I suppose.'

'But you can't just ditch me,' he said angrily.

'Why not? What are you going to do, force me to see you? I thought I was a free agent.'

'Don't be clever! I mean . . . well, don't you know how I feel about you?'

'How you feel about me?' I repeated incredulously. 'Carl, to be honest, I didn't think you were the heavy emotional type. I thought you were a good-timer, you know, just in it for sex.'

'That's what you thought?' He looked hurt and I felt a bit guilty.

'Well . . . yes.'

'Well, that just shows how stupid you are!' he croaked tearfully. 'I loved you. In fact, I still do. So if you think you can just push me to one side you've got another think coming!' He threw his cigarette at me and ran away.

I slumped against my Nova and sighed heavily. Where would he run to, I wondered? Straight to Seth's office to tell on me? Isn't that what kids do when they've been hurt, tell teacher? At any minute I could lose my job and perhaps not only that.

What if Carl told Alistair about our sordid affair? As far as I was aware he didn't know Alistair's name or where he worked. Our number was listed in the directory under Alistair's surname, Hardisty, which was different from mine, but if Carl was crafty enough he could follow me home one day; he could do any number of things. I just had to hope his love for me, in which I didn't entirely believe, would be sufficient to deter him from ruining my life.

If he did decide to bring down my adulterous empire, I knew the thing that would irk me most was that I had made it so easy for him. I had failed to include a get-out clause in the Carl Sillery Plan. It hadn't occurred to me that I might want to get out and he might not, which seems in retrospect to be a fairly major oversight. Did you think of it? Did you foresee problems, when I first told you about the Plan? Or did you, as I did, assume Carl would be manageable and user-friendly? That was what he was supposed to be: friendly, however much I used him.

I walked slowly to my office, forgetting Carl in a matter of seconds, hearing only one phrase in my mind over and over again: 'I didn't do it. But I was there.'

# Chapter Seven

## A Hard Life and a Sexy Grin

Later that afternoon there was a knock at my office door. 'Belinda! Belinda, let me in. Look, this is ridiculous!' Impatience brought the Yorkshire element to the forefront of Darryl's accent. 'This isn't like you, you're normally so cheerful. Misery doesn't suit you. And turn off that shite music, it'll only make you feel worse. It certainly makes me feel worse.'

I got up, sighing, and turned off *Women in Country II*.

'That's better,' Darryl yelled. 'Now let me in.'

I opened the door and smiled weakly.

'That's more like it!' He walked in and sat down in one of my armchairs, taking his glasses off to clean them. He was wearing his term-time clothes now, as opposed to his summer-holiday ones. The red shorts had been abandoned in favour of a denim shirt and grey jeans. 'Belinda, this has got to stop. Everyone's talking about you in the staff-room. They all know about Tony.'

'Even Seth?'

'He must do. I don't know, we're not exactly on speaking terms.'

'Sorry, I forgot.'

'You seem to have forgotten everything except . . .'

'Tony. Yes.'

'Can't you just . . . pull yourself together? Act a bit more normally? You know, smile, speak to people?'

'Why should I?' I said resentfully. 'I made an effort all

last week with Alistair. When I come to work, I want to be able to be myself.'

'But this isn't you.' Darryl's puzzlement reminded me of the opening scenes of *Invasion of the Bodysnatchers*, when people start to realise their close friends have changed into altogether more sinister entities.

'It is now, unfortunately. I don't like it any more than you do,' I said grumpily. 'We discussed this at lunch and we agreed there was nothing I could do.'

'You agreed that,' Darryl corrected me. 'I said no such thing. I said, if you remember, that you should ring Tony again.'

'And I said I can't. I've already rung once. If I ring again I'll look desperate. He's obviously gone off me.'

'Maybe he's scared Alistair'll answer the phone,' Darryl suggested.

'Alistair is at work all day,' I said impatiently.

'Well, Tony doesn't know that, does he? Maybe that lad didn't give him the message. Just ring him again, for God's sake.'

I winced. Talking about Tony made my whole body ache.

'Look, I really don't think he's gone off you,' Darryl continued, 'and whether he has or not . . .'

I gasped in terror at the possibility.

'. . . you need to know. I mean, look what a state you're in now, when you don't know. Wouldn't it be better to know?'

'Not if it's bad, no,' I explained. 'You think this is a state? If I phoned Tony and he gave me the brush-off I promise you I'd be far worse. In fact, I'd have to kill myself.'

Darryl sighed. 'Don't be daft,' he said. 'You'd get over it.'

'With anyone else I would,' I said, 'but not Tony. Anyone else who rejected me I'd just think it's their loss if they're stupid enough to dump me and go off them immediately. But Tony . . . I could never make myself believe it was his loss because I'd know full well that it was mine.'

'Why would he have gone off you?' asked Darryl. 'He resisted the advances of all those tasty teenagers, remember. He chose you.'

'Look, don't bother, Darryl. You're wasting your time. There's nothing you could say that I haven't already thought of. I've analysed all the facts scientifically. Yes, he might still be interested, but he might not. I can't risk it. Nothing, nothing in the world, could be worse than hearing Tony say he doesn't want to see me any more. I've got no alternative but to adopt a Maximin strategy.'

'What the fuck's a Maximin strategy?' Darryl slumped into his chair and rubbed his forehead wearily.

'It's where you maximise the worst outcome,' I told him. 'You set out all the possible options and all the possible outcomes, right. Option one: I phone Tony. There are two possible outcomes. One: he loves me and everything's all right. Two: he's lost interest and everything's shit. Option two: I don't phone Tony. Again, two possible outcomes. One: he phones me because he loves me, which already hasn't happened, so let's in fact scrap that as a possible outcome. So Option Two has only one possible outcome: I never hear from or see Tony again.'

'Yeah.' Darryl frowned, concentrating.

'A Maximin strategist chooses the option which has the best possible worst outcome. In this case it's Option Two because never seeing Tony again, however awful it would be, would still be better than being rejected by him.'

'Not much better, the way I see it.' Darryl looked at me as if he thought I'd gone raving mad.

'Yes, much better. Don't you get it? I may never see him again, but I won't know for a fact that it's because he's gone off me. I will always be able to think to myself that maybe he never got my message, maybe he lost my number. I'll be able to hang on to the possibility that he's sitting in Slough pining for me.'

231

'That's the fuckedest logic I've ever heard,' said Darryl in disgust. 'Where does this Maximin shit come from anyway? Nashville?'

'No, Natasha. It's some philosophical thing. One of the more interesting conversations I had with her.'

'Well, I never got the benefit of her philosophical wisdom.' Darryl's eyes clouded over moodily. 'I only got the benefit of her fanny.'

'There's something else,' I said. 'Something I can't tell you.'

'Oh, great!' said Darryl. 'I hate it when people do this. If you can't tell me, why even mention it?'

'Because it's relevant. Tony told me some things about himself, things that were . . . quite personal.'

'Like his drug problem?'

'Not just that. Other things. If you confide in someone and then regret it, it can often put you off them. That might be why Tony ran away. Maybe he couldn't face me because of . . . what I know.'

'But he told you, whatever it is.' Darryl struggled to keep up with my Tony-deductions. 'Why would he regret telling you? Is it something awful?'

'He thinks it is.'

'Oh, Belinda, tell me,' he pleaded.

'I can't,' I said. 'Partly for your own sake.'

'Whatever it was didn't put you off him?'

'No,' I said confidently. I had been startled by Tony's possible connection to a violent death, but my feelings for him were stronger than ever. He could have gunned down an entire village and I would still have wanted him.

'Would it have put most people off him?' Darryl proceeded with the interrogation.

'Probably, yes. Darryl, I'm not playing twenty questions about this. I can't tell you.'

'I'm just a bit worried, that's all. Maybe I shouldn't be persuading you to ring him.'

'You shouldn't, but that's not why. You shouldn't because there's no point. I've rung him once and I can't ring him again.' Darryl shook his head in frustration.

'I've written a song about Tony,' I said. 'Last week, while I was going mad at home waiting for him to ring. Do you want to hear it?'

'Oh, God.' Darryl looked as if there was nothing he wanted less. 'It's not a country song, is it?'

'No. If you get your guitar you can play the tune while I sing it.'

'I don't know the tune,' he protested.

'Yes, you do. It's to the tune of 'Candle in the Wind'. In fact, it's another version of 'Candle in the Wind', but for Tony. I thought since Elton John had written new words for Diana he wouldn't mind if I wrote new words for Tony.'

'Tony isn't dead,' Darryl pointed out.

'I know. I've adapted the words to suit a living person. Well? Are you going to get your guitar?'

'Do I have to?'

'No. I can play you the tape if you like. I made a tape of me singing it. It's got no music, though. Just my voice.'

'Go on, then. Oh, God. I've heard enough of that song in all its many forms to last me a lifetime.'

I got the tape out of my bag and put it in my tape player, putting *Women in Country II* back in its case. I pressed play. Darryl took off his glasses and covered his eyes with his left hand. I could tell he wasn't expecting my version of 'Candle in the Wind' to be very good.

'Goodbye, Tony Lamb,' my unaccompanied voice started,

> though I only knew you one day
> (not including all the times
> you ignored me or ran away),
> even if I never see
> your blue jeans or checked shirt again,
> you will always be for me
> the best of Berkshire's men

and you seemed to me, on *Lions'* last night,
like a candle in the wind,
like a candle with a hard life
and a sexy grin
and I loved you from the beginning –
perhaps you realised
my love was burning long before
the play had been devised.

Gorgeousness was tough.
It was a cross you had to bear.
People thought you had no brain
just because your face was fair
and even when you'd hide,
Megan and Sinead still hounded you.
You must think that mauling men
is all us girls can do

and you seemed to me, on *Lions'* last night,
like a candle in the wind,
like a candle with a hard life
and a sexy grin
and I loved you from the beginning –
perhaps you realised
my love was burning long before
the play had been devised.

Goodbye Tony Lamb,
though I only knew you one day
(not including all the times
you ignored me or ran away).
Goodbye Tony Lamb,
from this writer sitting in the grand tier
who saw you as something more than sexual,
more than just our sound engineer

and you seemed to me, on *Lions'* last night,
like a candle in the wind,
like a candle with a hard life
and a sexy grin
and I loved you from the beginning –
perhaps you realised
my love was burning long before
the play had been devised.
I loved you from the beginning –
perhaps you realised
My love was burning long before
the play had been devised.

'What do you think?' I asked when the recording had finished. 'I want a professional musical opinion.'

'Um.' Darryl coughed and spluttered a bit. His face was beetroot red.

'Is it as good as the other two versions? Elton John's two versions?'

'Well . . . I'm not that keen on the song anyway, but . . . "the best of Berkshire's men"?'

'I know. I was worried about that bit. It implies that there are men outside Berkshire who might be better than him. I really wanted to say "the best of the world's men", but it didn't scan properly.'

'That wasn't what I meant,' said Darryl. 'I meant . . . well, I don't want to hurt your feelings, but don't you think some of the lyrics are a bit cheesy?'

'Like which?'

'Well, like "the best of Berkshire's men". And "a candle with a hard life and a sexy grin".'

'What, because candles don't grin, you mean?'

'Well . . .'

'It's all right, I'm not offended. I did wonder about that. But I like it, just because it's about Tony. Any other bits you think don't work?'

'Well . . . I'm not wildly keen on the "grand tier/sound

235

engineer" rhyme.'

'Oh, that's one of my favourite bits,' I said, disappointed.

'Well, it's your song.' Darryl gave in gracefully. 'Sort of, anyway. Insofar as it isn't Elton John's.'

'Are you taking the piss?' I asked suspiciously.

'Have you written any songs about Carl?'

'Don't.' My mood deteriorated rapidly.

'What? Has he been pestering you again?' Darryl asked.

'You could say that. Read this. He pushed it under my door about an hour ago.' I took a piece of paper out of my top drawer and passed it to Darryl.

'"Dear Belinda,"' Darryl read aloud. '"You can't keep avoiding me like this. I love you and I thought you loved me." Oh fuck! "You've got to realise that you can't just use people and then throw them away . . ."'

'Can't argue with that, can I?'

'"You say you live with someone else and you never promised me anything,"' Darryl read on. '"Well, I don't want any promises. I don't even mind if you see Tony as well, as long as you don't finish with me. I've tried to be as discreet as I can like you said for your sake, but if you're going to treat me like this then maybe I won't bother. I'm really upset and all my mates are asking me what's wrong and so are some teachers. I haven't said anything yet, because I still love you and I don't want to cause trouble, but you shouldn't take me for granted. I want to see you soon. I'm really missing you. Love you with all my heart, Carl." And about a hundred kisses. Fucking hell! He's threatening you.' Darryl gawped at me in amazement.

'He certainly seems to be, doesn't he?'

'What are you going to do?'

'I've no idea. Tell him to fuck off, probably.'

'But Belinda . . .'

'I know, I could lose my job. To be honest, Darryl, I don't much care about anything at the moment.'

'What about Alistair? What are you going to say to him if you get sacked? He'd be sure to find out why.'

'I don't know. I don't want to lose Alistair. If I can't have Tony, I need Alistair. At least he's . . . something good in my life. If he left me . . . well, then I'd really have nothing.'

'But why . . .'

'Why didn't I think of this before? How could I have been so stupid?'

'Well . . . yeah.' Darryl looked vaguely apologetic, as if his wondering this might be construed as disloyal.

'I don't know,' I said honestly. 'Maybe I'm just a stupid person. You know what they say, sometimes the most obvious explanation . . .' The phone rang, interrupting me mid-motto. I picked it up, expecting it to be Carl, hoping it would be Tony.

'Is that Belinda Nield?' a strange, congested voice asked.

'Yes. Who's that?'

'Vinny.'

'Vinny who?'

'Tony Lamb's mate.'

'Tony's mate?' I gestured frantically at Darryl, waving my hands in the air and nearly knocking the phone off my desk in excitement.

'Tony got me to ring you. He would've rung himself but he's been ill. He can't walk.'

'Can't walk? What do you mean?' I yelped. 'What's wrong with him?'

'Keep your voice down,' Darryl hissed.

'Dunno. He's ill. He wants you to come and see him,' replied the faceless nasal twang.

'Of course I will, but . . . is he all right, I mean, what's wrong with him?' I felt faint. The combination of anxiety about Tony's health and excitement that he wanted to see me was too much.

'Dunno. I ain't a doctor.' His friend laughed annoyingly.

'Where is he?'

'Here, in the hostel.'

'Okay, I'm coming now. Tell him I'm coming right now,' I ordered. Vinny said he would. 'Darryl . . .'

'No.' Darryl was already backing off towards the door, shaking his head vigorously. 'No way.'

'You have to come with me. Tony's ill.'

'Belinda, I've got classes this afternoon. Haven't you?'

'Stuff classes. Tony's ill. Come on! You'll have to drive, I'm too worked up.' I started laughing hysterically. 'He phoned! He got his friend to phone! Oh, it's all so wonderful. Thank you, God, thank you Elton John!'

'Elton John?' Darryl scowled. 'There's no need for that.'

'Oh God, what's wrong with him?' I ran in frenzied circles around my desk. 'Oh, why didn't I phone before?'

'Belinda . . .'

'Come on, Darryl, we've got to go.' I grabbed my handbag with one hand and Darryl with the other.

'But I've got . . . oh, sod it.' Darryl allowed himself to be dragged out of my office.

Carl Sillery was lurking in the corridor nearby. He approached me tentatively as I locked my door. 'Did you get my letter?' he asked shakily. His eyes still looked puffy and revolting.

'Yes. Listen, Carl. Darryl and I have to go out urgently. A friend of Darryl's is ill and we need to . . . go there. Could you do me a huge favour?'

'Yeah, course.' Carl straightened his back to demonstrate his competence.

'Could you put a big notice on my door saying I've had to rush off and my classes are cancelled? And could you do the same for Darryl?'

'Yeah, but . . .'

'Thank you.' I kissed him on the forehead. 'You're a star. Listen, I'll be in tomorrow and I promise I'll talk to you properly then. Everything'll be fine. Okay?'

'Okay.' Carl smiled as if he couldn't quite believe his luck.

I ran out of the building to the car-park and Darryl ran after me.

'What did you say that for?' he yelled. 'You're such an

idiot. Now you've gone and got his hopes up. Don't you ever learn?'

'One good turn deserves another,' I said. 'Fate did me a good turn by getting Tony to get Vinny to ring, so it's only fair that I should be nice to Carl in exchange. To prove I'm not ungrateful,' I panted. 'Anyway, I'm so happy I just want everyone else to be happy too.'

'Except me, obviously,' Darryl wheezed, collapsing against his car. 'You clearly want me to be in hospital having suffered a heart attack.'

'Oh, you're so funny.' I giggled, kissing him loudly on the cheek. 'Come on, let's go.'

We got into Darryl's VW Golf and set off to Slough.

# Chapter Eight

## Slough: the Romantic Epicentre of the Western Hemisphere

Darryl and I stopped at the first garage we came to in Slough and bought an *A–Z*. Sandlea Road was a cul-de-sac at the bottom of Gilchrist Street, very near the town centre. As we turned into it I saw a sign that said ' Private Road – Access Only'. How typical of Tony, I thought, to live somewhere that was so labelled.

I'd been far too excited to speak to Darryl on the way there. All I could think about was that, in a matter of minutes, I would see Tony again. I would have to restrain myself from leaping on him and crushing him with enthusiasm. I wondered whether he would mention the Mark Ryder business again and, if he didn't, whether I should.

Since his cryptic statement at Phoebe's I had been listing possible explanations in my mind. If Tony had witnessed the attack, why hadn't he told the police? Maybe he had, but his eyewitness evidence hadn't been detailed enough to lead them to the culprits. Perhaps I was doing him an injustice, but Tony didn't strike me as star witness material.

There were a few houses at one end of Sandlea Road and two larger, more institutional-looking buildings at the other. I wound the car window down as Darryl drove along slowly. 'It's not that one,' I said. 'That's a dental clinic. It must be the one further on.' As we approached the next building I saw a sign that said 'Sandlea Court Car-

Park – Residents, Staff and Visitors Only'. 'This is it!' I squealed ecstatically.

'Do you want me to come in with you?' Darryl asked, swinging the Golf into the car-park that was empty apart from a battered beige Ford Escort. 'I mean, I could wait for you here if you like.'

'No, it'll cheer Tony up to see you,' I said. 'You're his sound engineering mentor.'

'If you say so. What sort of place is this hostel anyway?'

'I've no idea,' I said. 'It's weird, I hardly know anything about Tony.'

'Mm,' said Darryl ominously.

'I must try to find out a bit more about him. I want to know everything: his favourite food, what sort of music he likes. Still, there'll be plenty of time for that, I suppose. The first thing I want to find out is what's wrong with him. Oh God, I'm so nervous.'

We got out of the car and made our way to the main entrance, Darryl walking normally and me creeping as if one miscalculated footstep could ruin everything. Sandlea Court was a large, squat bungalow and reminded me of the part of my old primary school that we used to call the prefab. Through the glass panel in the front door I could see a payphone, an unattended reception desk and a cork notice-board with lots of leaflets pinned to it that were headed 'Sanctuary Housing'. This looked like the outer lobby. There was another glass door beside the payphone that led through to the main part of the hostel, from which emerged a short, stocky young man dressed in jeans and a Benetton sweat-shirt. I recognised him as Bulldog Face, one of the two blokes I'd seen talking to Tony outside the theatre after the first night. He saw me and Darryl peering in and came to open the door.

'You Belinda?' he asked nasally. I nodded, too emotional to speak. 'I'm Vinny. Who's he?' Vinny jerked his thumb towards Darryl.

'I'm Darryl. I'm a friend of Belinda's. And ... er,

Tony's,' Darryl added reluctantly.

'Come on, Tony's up here.'

We followed him through the outer and inner doors, through a big TV room in which two malnourished teenage girls were watching *Knotts Landing* and on to a long, beige-carpeted corridor. The walls were white and looked newly painted. I was impressed by the standard of the décor.

Vinny stopped outside a door with the number four on it and knocked. 'Tone,' he shouted. 'That Belinda's here. And . . .'

'Darryl,' said Darryl.

'And Darren.'

'Come in, it's open,' I heard Tony's faint voice call out. I clutched Darryl's arm in excitement at the rapture of hearing him again.

'Ow.' Darryl shook me off. 'That hurts.'

'Just go in,' said Vinny. 'And by the way, I hope you're for real.'

'What?' I stopped in my tracks. What was he talking about?

'Tony's been through a lot. I hope you're not going to mess him about.'

'I have no intention of messing him about,' I said, smiling persuasively. It wasn't a good idea to alienate Tony's friends. It might cause problems later in our relationship.

Vinny wandered off and Darryl stared after him distastefully. 'What a creep,' he muttered.

I pushed Tony's door open. He was propped up in bed, wearing a thin navy-blue jumper with a red stripe across it and a capital letter F logo in red and blue, which I assumed stood for Fila, the sportswear company. On the navy and green checked duvet in front of him were a packet of Marlboro Lights and a green plastic lighter.

His room was small and there was nothing on the walls apart from a poster, which looked like ex-video shop marketing merchandise, advertising the film *Cool Runnings*, in which the late John Candy coaches the Jamaican bob-sleigh team. Next to the bed there was a small white cabinet on top of which were two books by Dean Koontz, *Sole Survivor* and *Strangers*, and a Classic Soul CD. I was thrilled to see all these items, as they gave me information about my beloved that he himself would probably never give me, on the basis that accessories speak louder than mumbles. Forgetting temporarily that Darryl was behind me, I ran over and threw my arms around Tony.

'Oh my God,' I said. 'I'm so pleased to see you. I've missed you so much.' Tony blushed but he looked happy. 'Look, Darryl's here too,' I said. Tony nodded curtly at Darryl who nodded curtly back. Men! I thought.

'I've got this thing,' said Tony uninformatively.

'What?' I asked.

'Dunno. I can hardly walk.'

'But . . . why? Is it your legs?'

'No. I don't know what it's called. The doctor told me some long weird fucking name. I didn't know what the fuck it was.'

'So you've seen a doctor?' I asked.

'Yeah. I have to have an operation.'

'But . . . Tony, try to describe the thing, if you don't know what it's called,' I pleaded. I couldn't believe this. I had to know what was wrong with him and I'd assumed he would be able to tell me. That's exactly the sort of assumption you can't make about Tony Lamb, that he will know the name of his own illness.

'It's like a big . . . wound. On my co . . . at the bottom of my back.'

'Oh,' said Darryl suddenly. 'On your coccyx. It's not called a pi-something sinus, is it?'

'Yeah.' There was a brief flash of recognition in Tony's eyes. 'Yeah, it was something like that.'

'What's that?' I snapped at Darryl. Everyone seemed to know more about this than I did.

243

'A pilonidal sinus, that's it,' said Darryl. 'My brother had one last year. They're quite common. Really nasty.' He saw my petrified expression and added hastily, 'But not at all dangerous. I mean, it's a simple operation to get rid of it.'

'Yeah, that's it,' said Tony. 'A what's-it sinus, like you said. I think that's it.'

'What is a pilonidal sinus, Darryl?' I asked impatiently.

'It's an ingrowing hair follicle,' he explained. 'Very common among young men with dark hair. It's when a hair follicle at the base of your spine starts growing in instead of out. When my brother first got his he thought it was a boil. It's horrible, like a big sort of wound – all pussy and bloody.'

'You can't walk properly,' Tony added. 'Mine keeps going away and coming back. I ignored it the first few times, it wasn't as bad as this time. One of the care assistants got a doctor for me. I didn't want to see a doctor.'

'No, my brother didn't either,' said Darryl. 'He was too embarrassed, but he had to in the end because he was in so much pain.'

'It started during rehearsals,' said Tony. 'But it wasn't too bad. I could walk, I was just limping a bit.'

'Oh God – I remember,' I said. I'd thought it was a twisted ankle.

'But then it went away. Then it just seemed to come back.'

'My brother had to wait ages for his operation,' said Darryl.

'Doctor said I might have to,' said Tony.

'How long?' I asked.

'Dunno. Could be a year, maybe more. I got some other medicine though. To make it better until I can have the operation. It's getting a bit better already.'

'Tony . . . why did you run away the other night?' I couldn't keep the question in any longer.

'I think I'll, er, go for a wander,' said Darryl, reaching

for the door. 'I'll wait for you in the car, Belinda. See you Tony. Hope you feel better soon.'

When Darryl had gone I repeated my question.

'Dunno.' Tony looked away. He seemed uneasy now that we were alone.

'Tony . . .' Hard as it was, I had to bring it up. I had to know. 'What you said about Mark Ryder . . .' I began.

'I don't want to talk about that,' he muttered. 'Forget it.'

'But Tony.' I fought back tears. 'I've been out of my mind worrying about it. You've got to tell me.'

'Ask Carmel-Marie.'

'Carmel-Marie?' I felt my heart jolt like a crashing train. 'What's she got to do with it?'

'She paid me to do it. Five hundred quid. Me and my mates.' He reached for his cigarette packet and lighter. I searched his face for signs of agitation, but found none. He stared blankly ahead as he lit a cigarette.

'That day when I saw you sneaking out of her office . . .' I said, almost to myself.

'She'd just given me the money.'

'She paid you to kill Mark Ryder? But why?'

'He wasn't supposed to die,' Tony said simply.

'So . . .' I struggled to say something useful, something that would get us a bit further on. 'But you said you didn't do it.'

'I couldn't.' He sucked on his cigarette, turning to face the wall. 'I was supposed to, but when it happened . . .' His voiced tailed off and he shuddered slightly. I wanted to hug him, but I sensed he didn't want to be touched. 'My mates did it.'

'Vinny?' I asked, thinking back to the first night of *Lions*, when Mark Ryder had been attacked.

Tony nodded. 'And Graham,' he said. Graham must have been the one I thought of as Brace Man. 'I watched,' he said. 'It was horrible. They just went mad. He was never supposed to die.'

I put my hand on the cool surface of Tony's bedside

cabinet to steady myself. Probably for the first time in my life I felt real fear. I wished someone would knock me out and only let me wake up when this situation had gone away. 'Why did Carmel-Marie want him beaten up?' I heard myself ask. 'Why did she ask you?' He didn't do it, I thought, Tony didn't do it. That was the most important thing, the one reassuring fact I clung to. My beautiful Tony wasn't a murderer.

'I tried to stop them,' he mumbled, starting to rock back and forth in bed. I was coming to recognise this action as a sign of impending emotional distress. 'I need money, don't I?' said Tony. 'I always fucking need money. For my course. I'm never going to get a grant. I'm not the right sort of person. So I said yeah, I'd do it.' He was really rambling now. 'Police. I should tell the police.'

'No!' I yelled, grabbing his arm. 'You can't. Tony, promise you won't.' I didn't care about protecting Carmel-Marie, but the thought of Tony getting done for conspiracy or manslaughter or whatever it would be made me want to throw up. There was no way I was letting that happen, whatever he'd done. 'Why?' I whimpered. 'Why did Carmel-Marie want him . . . beaten up?'

'I dunno. I never asked.' Tony looked at me apologetically. I smiled reassuringly at him, trying not to let my inner panic show. Carmel-Marie. I repeated her name in my mind, over and over again. It didn't make sense. She was annoying, possibly a bit intimidating, but this . . . people I knew and worked with didn't do things like this.

At the same time, I didn't doubt that Tony was telling the truth. My love for him wasn't so blind that I thought he had the imagination to come up with such an outrageous lie. But how could he have failed to ask why he was being paid to do this . . . this awful thing? Didn't he have any curiosity? It occurred to me that he rarely asked me anything about myself.

If only they'd been having an affair, I thought. That would have been better.

'I'm bad, aren't I?' Tony said with tears in his eyes. 'I should be punished.'

'No, you shouldn't,' I said. 'You made a mistake, that's all. It wasn't your fault.'

'You don't like me any more.'

'Yes I do.' I took his hand and held it firmly. 'Don't worry. Everything will be okay.' I was wondering whether to say anything to Carmel-Marie, whether I was brave enough. Half of me was desperate to confront her, beg for more information, fill in the substantial gaps in Tony's version of events, while the other half wanted to leave the whole mess alone and try to pretend it had never happened.

'It won't be,' Tony contradicted me. 'It's even worse now. I've told you, which makes you a . . . what's it called . . .'

'Accessory. Don't worry about me,' I said. 'I can look after myself.'

'You don't hate me?' His voice trembled.

'Tony, I love you. How many times do I have to tell you before you believe me?'

'I love you too,' he said. 'I wish I'd met you before. Then none of this would have happened.'

I rubbed my temples, trying to pull myself together. Somebody needed to sort out this horror and it looked like it was going to have to be me. I started to think in terms of damage limitation. 'Tony, have you told anyone else about this?' I asked.

'No.'

'So the only people who know are me, you, Carmel-Marie, Vinny and Graham?'

'Yeah.'

'What about Carmel-Marie's husband? He worked with Mark Ryder.'

'Did he? Dunno.' He shook his head.

'Right,' I said. 'Well, don't say anything to anyone else, okay? The police obviously don't know. What did you say to them, when they interviewed you?'

'I don't remember,' he said.

'Well . . . try to think. What did they ask you? Did they seem suspicious?'

'Dunno. Don't remember. Can we talk about something else? This is doing my head in.'

I sighed, trying to picture myself in Inspector Francis's and Sergeant Drury's position. The temptation to get rid of the glazed and uncommunicative Tony and move on to someone with more social skills must surely have been great. I found it hard enough to converse with him and I loved him. They were probably tired and overworked with stamina levels too low for a sustained period of Tony-questioning, for which I thanked God, because if they'd pressed the point, who knew what he might have let slip.

'Of course we can.' I smiled, leaning forward to kiss him. Even amid the terror of this new knowledge, I wasn't too preoccupied to notice that Tony had just said he loved me for the first time.

# Chapter Nine

## Carl, Me and the ANP

'You're crazy,' said Darryl, as he drove us back to Beasley. 'I almost can't let you do it. It's just insanity, Belinda. Even by your standards.'

'What do you mean, you almost can't let me do it?' I asked wearily. I didn't want to get into an argument with Darryl; thoughts of Carmel-Marie paying Tony to beat up Mark Ryder were swimming around my confused brain and I was afraid I might burst into tears if Darryl was too harsh with me. Maybe I shouldn't have told him about my plan.

'I mean,' he said, 'I would like to prevent you from doing it, but . . .'

'But you know you can't. Exactly. It isn't insane, anyway. Tony has just said he loves me, Darryl. Do you realise, can you even begin to understand, how much that means to me?'

'I bet he can't believe his fucking luck,' said Darryl angrily, pulling out on to a roundabout without proper care and attention. 'To get someone like you. Can't you see how far apart the two of you are on the evolutionary scale? Don't you realise he could never make you happy? And what about Carl? Belinda, you've got to tell him it's over.'

'I can't.' We stopped at some traffic lights and I stared out of the window at a downtrodden-looking couple who were trying to persuade a screaming toddler to get into his pushchair. 'I could if it weren't for the ANP.'

'The ANP? Who are the ANP?' Darryl asked, confused.

'The Ace New Plan,' I clarified. 'I make up silly names for things in my head sometimes and I forget no one else knows them.'

'The ANP is far from ace. It's ludicrous, Belinda. It's unthinkable.'

'No, it's not. Don't be so rigid, Darryl. It's not like you. You're usually so easygoing and open-minded.'

'Yeah, well, I'm beginning to wonder how much of this preposterous madness is my fault. Maybe I should have tried harder to make you see sense earlier on, when you first told me about Carl and Tony and everything. Maybe I shouldn't have driven you to Slough. It might do you good to have someone put their foot down for a change.'

'Oh, try not to bore me with pop psychology, Darryl. This isn't some attention-seeking ploy. I'm not seeing how far I can go before someone will stop me. That's what children do whose parents don't give them enough discipline. My parents gave me more than enough, I assure you.'

'What about Alistair?'

'It's not his job to discipline me.'

'No, I mean, what if he finds out?' said Darryl impatiently. 'He's bound to.'

'No, he's not. No one will know except me, you, Tony and Vinny.'

'Vinny! That creep!'

'He's not all bad,' I said, trying not to picture him laying into Mark Ryder. 'He got me and Tony back together.'

'You've not thought this through.' I could hear panic in Darryl's voice. 'You'd have to tell the school. Seth would find out.'

'No, he wouldn't. Seth knows nothing about what goes on at Beasley. I'd have to tell Hayley, but that's okay. I can handle her.'

'Hayley won't want to be involved in something like this,' said Darryl.

'She'll have no choice,' I said, icily calm.

'Do I have a choice?' Darryl looked at me, his forehead creased with anxiety, as we nearly swerved into a lorry in the adjacent lane. Darryl swore and zigzagged back to safety.

'Yes,' I said. 'I'm asking you because you're my friend.'

'Tony doesn't even know about this yet. He's not going to agree.'

'Of course he is. He loves me. What's he got to lose?'

'People don't do things like this, Belinda. It's not an option.'

'Yes, it is. It's an option you don't like, is what you mean.'

'That's exactly what I mean!' Darryl yelled. 'I don't like it. I never will.'

'So you're saying no?' I could hardly believe how mean he was being. 'I'm going to do it anyway, Darryl. I'd feel so much better if you were there. Please. I'd do it for you. I wouldn't even disapprove.'

'Belinda, I could fuck a goat and you probably wouldn't disapprove.'

'Depends who the goat was.' I grinned, feeling a bit of colour returning to my cheeks. There was something intrinsically comforting about Darryl even in this sort of mood.

'What about that thing you couldn't tell me?' he asked and I felt my fear begin to rev up again. My hands instinctively flew to my stomach.

'I still can't tell you,' I said.

'What if I agree to do what you're asking? Will you tell me then?'

'No.' I turned away from him and watched a row of square grey houses fly past the car window.

'Because if I knew whatever it was, I'd be even more against it, right?'

'Probably.' Shut up, shut up, shut up, I thought.

'Oh God, Belinda. Just listen to yourself.'

'Darryl, give me a break,' I groaned. 'There's nothing I can do about any of this. I can see on some remote logical level that what you're saying is sensible and what I'm saying is stupid, I can even agree with you in theory, but I can't make myself act differently.'

'If you can't, who can?' he said sceptically.

'No one,' I said. 'My instincts are so strong. I have to follow them. My heart is telling me . . .'

'Oh, your heart's telling you, is it?' Darryl interrupted sarcastically. 'That *Women in Country* tape has got a lot to answer for.'

'No, it hasn't,' I said patiently. 'I'm responsible for my own irresponsibility. But . . . Darryl, even irresponsible people need friends to stand by them and make allowances for them, however stupid they are. And you're my friend, Darryl.'

'Don't remind me,' he snapped. 'Okay, I'll do it. But only out of a sort of . . . grim fascination, in the same kind of morbid spirit that I look at horrific car crashes on the motorway.'

'Well, if that's the best you can do . . .' I said, hurt.

'Fuck, you don't ask for much, do you?' He glared at me.

'Okay, okay. Well, thanks. You won't regret it. Well, you might, but . . . look, just think of it like Christmas. It's going to happen anyway so you might as well enjoy it instead of carping on about shallow consumerism and the crap jumper you always get off your grandma.'

'Please don't give me analogies,' said Darryl. 'Just . . . let me get used to it, okay?'

'Okay.' I decided to quit while I was ahead. I had known Darryl would agree eventually. People have always made special allowances for me, probably because I'm a good talker. I can make the most bizarre things sound like harmless fun.

When I was at sixth-form college we got a report every term with a bit at the bottom where each of our subject teachers would fill in our possible attendance and our actual attendance. Luckily I cottoned on to this before my first term's report was due to be sent, like an Incitement to Bollock, to my parents. My actual attendance was considerably smaller than my possible attendance. If numbers were people, my actual attendance would have been my possible attendance's grandchild.

I decided to maximise contentment all round by ensuring my parents never saw any of my reports. I was going out with Dale Farrell at the time, the drug dealer I had told Tony about in an attempt to keep up with him in our sordid past contest, and Dale had a friend called Icky, also a drug dealer, who lived on his own in a very dirty house in Wokingham. I asked Icky (whose real name was Iqbal, I think – I don't know whether his nickname was a comment on his unhygienic life-style) whether he would have any objection to receiving my reports once a term and destroying them. He had none. He merely asked, in the stoned slur that was his usual mode of address, how he would recognise them. I told him to look out for envelopes addressed to Mr and Mrs D P Nield with an Aquinas College logo in blue ink next to the postmark. Even Icky could manage that.

The next day at college, I told my form tutor Mrs Perry that me and my whole family were moving in with my grandma, who had been taken ill and could no longer look after herself properly. I gave her Icky's address – 45 Fielding Road, Wokingham – and told her to address any correspondence to my parents care of 'I. Yunis' which was Icky's name and, coincidentally, the name of my fictional gran. If Mrs Perry wondered why I had a grandmother with an Asian name, she didn't say anything. I'm quite dark-skinned, so it was just about feasible that I might be a quarter Asian.

My parents never saw a single report. The only person who did was Icky and he presumably either threw them straight in the rubbish or snorted lines of cocaine through them. My mum asked me about reports once, half-way through my first year, and I said that Aquinas didn't have them. I don't know whether I was imagining it, but I thought she seemed quite relieved. Maybe the biennial laziness-bollocking routine was becoming as tedious for her as it was for me.

The point, and how this relates to the Ace New Plan, is that I know what I can handle, exactly how far I can go without ruining everything. Darryl may have thought I was getting in too deep, but he was wrong. There's a difference between very deep and too deep. For some people the two might be the same, but not for me.

'I'd better find Carl,' I said, as we screeched to a halt outside Beasley's porticoed front. I still hadn't decided whether I could face a confrontation with Carmel-Marie. Carl was more than enough for me to tackle for the time being.

I didn't have to look very far. He was still loitering with blackmailer intent outside my office, even though it was nearly two hours later. His eyes had unpuffed somewhat and he radiated a desperate optimism in my direction that made me cringe.

'You haven't been standing here all afternoon, have you?' I asked. 'Didn't you have classes to go to?'

'Yeah,' he said. 'I've been to them. I just thought I'd see if you were back yet. Where did you go?'

'I told you, to visit one of Darryl's friends.' I tore down the notice that Carl had obediently stuck on my door.

'Is that really where you've been?' he asked. 'Why did you both have to go?'

'Carl.' I took a deep breath. 'I'm trying, I'm really trying, to improve things between us, but you just don't know when to lay off. You'd better come in,' I said, holding my office door open. He traipsed in miserably. He was like a little kid – all smiles when I was nice to him and sulky when I told him off. I know, what did I expect, right?

'You've got to trust me,' I lectured him. 'Stop following

254

me around and interrogating me. I feel swamped. I can't handle it. It's not because I don't like you; I do.' This particular lie almost made me retch. 'But we have to do it my way or not at all.'

'So you're not finishing with me any more?' His eyes lit up.

'No.' I forced a smile.

'Why did you change your mind?' Carl asked.

Because you started fucking blackmailing me, you tosser, I thought. 'Carl, what did I say about interrogating me?'

'I was just asking.' He retreated like a wounded rabbit.

'Well, don't,' I said firmly.

Unexpectedly, Carl burst into tears. 'You're so different,' he said. 'You're always annoyed with me.'

'I'm sorry.' I made myself hug him. 'Don't cry. Look, I'm just under a lot of pressure at the moment.'

'You only liked me when I was Ian Chaddock.' He sobbed. 'You don't like me as me.' This was considerably more perceptive than most of Carl's observations. The great thing about Ian Chaddock was that he said and did what I wanted him to. He didn't have a mind of his own the way Carl did.

'I do like you,' I murmured in his ear. 'I do, Carl, honestly. I'm sorry if I've been ratty. Come on, let's . . . you know.'

'Here? In your office?'

'Yeah. Why not? I'll lock the door.' This was going to be hard, there was no denying it, but I could do it. I had to, for Tony's sake and for the ANP.

I walked over to my window and drew the curtains quickly, first making sure no one was watching from outside.

Carl didn't need much encouragement. It was awful. At first, as he was panting away on top of me, I tried pretending he was Tony, but that seemed like sacrilege and anyway I couldn't entirely shake off the unwelcome fact

255

that he wasn't. Then I tried pretending he was Alistair, but that didn't work either. Eventually I gave up and gritted my teeth, feeling absolutely disgusting. Not many experiences are more unpleasant than having sex with someone you don't at all fancy. You may be lucky enough to have avoided it over the course of your life, but I certainly haven't.

I wish he'd finish, I thought, I wish he'd just hurry up and finish. He never usually takes this long. Usually – listen to me. Anyone would think we were an old married couple. I hoped Carl hadn't been reading any sex manuals in an attempt to impress me, to develop a more mature sexual technique.

Don't you think Good Sex guides and magazines like *Cosmopolitan* are a bit irresponsible, going on about how women like slow sex and lots of foreplay? I do. Women only like copulation to last a long time if they're doing it with someone they actually like, you foolish journalists, you naïve editors. Don't you realise what you're doing? Men all over the world are reading your pernicious articles and thinking, 'Oh – I can't just get my end away and fuck off any more. I've got to do all this other stuff now.' So us women have to endure hours of tweaking, twiddling and mauling.

It's all very well saying no one should be going to bed with people they don't fancy, but this is real life we're talking about. Get your heads out of the sand. I hate to mention real life. As you know, I'm not a big fan, but occasionally it must be taken into account.

Carl didn't just get his end away and fuck off. He tweaked. He twiddled. He mauled. I concluded that he must have purloined a Nancy Friday book from his mother's bedside table. Why couldn't he just read porn mags like other teenagers, I thought crossly. All I had ever wanted was for him to use me for sex. What did I do to deserve blackmail, allegations of love and sensitive screwing?

Finally the horror ended. I would do anything for Tony Lamb, I thought, but I can't do this too often. I wonder whether a similar situation inspired Meatloaf's chart-topping song, the one that went 'I would do anything for love/ but I won't do that / No, I won't do that'? Did Meatloaf suffer an equally gruelling ordeal? .

'I'm so happy,' said Carl, zipping up his fly. 'I thought it was really over.'

'Well, we can't do this too often, you know,' I said quickly. 'It's not that I don't want to. It's just too risky.'

'But . . . sorry. I'm not putting you under any pressure, honest I'm not.' He cowered obediently.

'Good,' I said. 'Now, I'm not trying to get rid of you, but I've got lots of work to do.'

'When can we . . . when can I see you again?' Carl hovered awkwardly next to my desk where I was already sitting, shuffling papers around and trying to look busy. 'Apart from in the Creative Writing class, I mean.'

'I don't know. Not this week. I'll let you know, okay?'

'Okay,' he said. 'You won't change your mind, though?'

'No.' I shuddered inwardly. 'I won't.'

'Okay. Bye, then.' He took as long as a person could take to leave a room. His leaving verged on failing to leave. For a minute or two I wondered whether he would ever reach the door. Mercifully he did. I waited a few minutes and then rushed to the nearest Ladies, where I washed as comprehensively as I could in the pathetically stunted basin. Why, I wondered angrily, did all the toilets in the Seth Beasley School of Performance and Creative Arts have washbasins that were designed for people whose hands had been amputated?

I went back to my office and made a few research phone calls, laying the groundwork for the ANP. The last of my calls was to Darryl's brother, Lee Abrahams. I discussed pilonidal sinuses with him for half an hour. He was very helpful, describing all the gruesome symptoms in detail. If I had had any doubts about my plan, talking to Lee would

have convinced me that it was unquestionably in everybody's best interests.

I took a deep breath and headed for Carmel-Marie's
office.

# Chapter Ten

## Confronting Carmel-Marie

CARMEL-MARIE WHITE *is sitting in her office.* BELINDA NIELD *walks in, white-faced. She seems unable to speak for a few minutes.*

CARMEL-M   Well? Spit it ite.

BELINDA (*shakily*)   Is it true?

CARMEL-M   Is what true?

BELINDA   That you . . . that you paid Tony and his mates to beat up Mark Ryder?

CARMEL-M (*clearly disconcerted*)   What?

BELINDA   Tony told me.

CARMEL-M (*in a Birmingham accent*)   He's mad. He doesn't know what he's talking about. He's making it up.

BELINDA   You'd better hope the police agree with you.

CARMEL-M   He wouldn't go to the police.

BELINDA   He's considering it. He feels really guilty. So, it's true then?

CARMEL-M (*regaining composure slightly*)   I don't believe you. He wouldn't risk it. He'd go straight to jail.

BELINDA   I doubt it. I think he'd get diminished responsibility, or whatever it's called. Besides, he didn't even touch Mark Ryder. It was his mates who did it. He tried to stop them.

CARMEL-M   He would say that, wouldn't he, to get himself off the hook.

BELINDA   He doesn't want to be off the hook. I told you, he wants to go to the police. I'm the only person who can stop him.

CARMEL-M   Oh, you're so close are you, after one drunken grope?

BELINDA   We're in love.

CARMEL-M   Yeah, right.

BELINDA   I don't care whether you believe me or not. Why did you do it? I want to know the whole story. If you tell me, I won't go to the police. And I'll make sure Tony doesn't.

CARMEL-M   I'm not admitting anything but ... why should I trust you?

BELINDA   I don't want Tony to have to go through a court case. And it wouldn't be in my interests to grass you up – you could grass me up right back, couldn't you? You could tell Alistair about me and Tony. I'm surprised you haven't already.

CARMEL-M   He's getting what he deserves.

BELINDA   I'm a very good girlfriend to Alistair, I'll have you know. I make him very happy, which is what counts in my book.

CARMEL-M   Well, I'd hate to be in your book, then.

BELINDA   What have you got against Alistair?

CARMEL-M   I've seen Hayley worrying herself sick about where the next month's rent's going to come from. Do you know that some months Phil and Hayley can't afford to go out more than one evening, they're so skint?

BELINDA   I fail to see how this is Alistair's fault.

CARMEL-M   He's their landlord.

BELINDA (*incredulously*)   He charges them a very reasonable rent. Two-hundred and fifty pounds a month.

CARMEL-M   He's a landlord! Can't you see there's something wrong with being a landlord?

BELINDA   No. Not even remotely. Can't you see there's something wrong with paying people to kill other people?

260

CARMEL-M   He wasn't supposed to die. That was a mistake.

BELINDA   A pretty big one! A pretty fucking serious one, from Mark Ryder's point of view, I'd say! One that wipes out all the good things you've ever done, all the moral stands you've ever taken! What does it matter now that you don't eat Peaker vegetables, or that you stood up for Darryl when everyone was taking Seth's side against him? I can't believe I used to think you were more principled than me. You make my skin crawl, you're such a fraud. And talking Tony into it. You must have known how vulnerable he was. It's not what you did to Ryder that makes me hate you, it's what you did to Tony.

CARMEL-M   That doesn't surprise me. You don't care what people do as long as it doesn't affect your scummy little world.

BELINDA   At least my scummy little world doesn't involve GBH and murder!

CARMEL-M   I can justify every single thing I do. Every. Single. Thing.

BELINDA   Go on then, justify it.

CARMEL-M   Mark Ryder was a drug dealer.

BELINDA   So that means he deserved to die?

CARMEL-M   Are you going to listen or not? Cocaine, heroin, softer stuff, he was into the lot. He ran his drugs business from work. Richard knew something dodgy was going on. He kept hearing Mark on the phone, calls that didn't sound like business, or that sounded like a different sort of business. Richard was Mark's superior in the office, so when he started getting really suspicious, he had a word with him, asked him what was going on. Mark admitted he was dealing. He boasted about it, laughed it off. Richard didn't know what to do. I told him to report Mark to Richard Dancy.

BELINDA   Who's Richard Dancy?

CARMEL-M   Richard Dancy is the big boss, Richard's

boss. So he did and guess what Dancy said? He knew about it already! He said Richard should just forget it, ignore it, pretend it wasn't happening. He said Mark was good at his job and brought a lot of money in so they couldn't afford to lose him. He had a real go at Richard, called him a prig and a goodie-two-shoes.

BELINDA   So? Is that it?

CARMEL-M   You don't think that's enough? I wanted Richard to go straight to the police. Dancy may not have been interested but they certainly would have been. But Richard was scared he'd lose his job. Knowing Dancy and Mark Ryder, they would have found some way to cover it all up and then quietly disposed of Richard somehow. We couldn't afford to risk that, not with our mortgage and everything, but I was buggered if I was going to let Mark Ryder get away with it scot-free.

BELINDA (*after a long pause*)   That's sick! Why is it up to you to see that justice is done? Who gave you the right to decide how to punish people?

CARMEL-M   It's wrong. It's an injustice. I wanted to correct the balance. You know why bad people get away with doing evil? Because good people are too weak to fight them. Good people need to toughen up or else bad people will always win.

BELINDA   That's the sickest and most twisted philosophy I've ever heard. I mean, I might be able to understand if Mark Ryder was some sort of, I don't know, child killer, or had done something to you personally. I mean, I'm not justifying drug dealing but . . . well, he was only a drug dealer. What about people who work in cigarette factories? Do they deserve to be beaten to death as well?

CARMEL-M   That's different. And it's easy for you to say he was only a drug dealer. My mother died of a drug overdose. So did my sister.

BELINDA   What?

CARMEL-M   I know, I've never mentioned it before. That's because it's none of anybody's fucking business. If drugs had devastated your family the way they did mine, you wouldn't be sitting there saying (*puts on stupid voice*) 'he was only a drug dealer'. Tony used to be a druggie, didn't he?

BELINDA   How do you know that?

CARMEL-M   Hayley told me. That social worker of his told her, when they were discussing whether he should be allowed to take part in the Youth Theatre. That's why I was so against him from the start. I hate drugs and everything, anyone, involved in them. But I was out-voted by the bleeding-heart brigade. So I thought, right, how can I turn this to my advantage? All this shit at Richard's work was going on and I saw a way to . . . kill two druggies with one stone. Let one deal with the other, I thought. It was seeing Tony that gave me the idea. One look at him and I knew he'd do anything for money. I saw his friends dropping him off one morning. They looked like just the sort of unsavoury bunch I expected him to associate with. Perfect, I thought.

BELINDA (*crying*)   Tony isn't unsavoury. He may have problems, he may make mistakes, but he's a good person at heart.

CARMEL-M   No drug addict is a good person. It's not possible.

BELINDA   He has nothing to do with drugs now. He's as against them as you are. Doesn't your moral code allow any room for forgiving people?

CARMEL-M   Some people are just evil.

BELINDA   You're the only evil person around here.

CARMEL-M   There's one less drug dealer in the world, that's all I know.

BELINDA   You do anything to Tony and I'll kill you. I really mean that, I would kill you.

CARMEL-M   Why? (*Mockingly*) Is it because you love him so much?

BELINDA   Yes, it is.

CARMEL-M   Don't worry, I won't touch your precious

retard. We've got a deal, haven't we? I have no desire to go to prison. Who would have guessed that the catatonic Tony would suddenly start talking? Oh well, I suppose you can't plan for everything. You don't love Tony. You may think you do, but you're mistaken.

BELINDA   You're wrong.

CARMEL-M   So are you going to leave Alistair?

BELINDA   I don't know.

CARMEL-M   Of course you aren't. Tony's a nice little romantic fantasy for you, but you won't give up your comfortable life for him because deep down you know that Alistair has all the right social credentials and everyday life with Tony Lamb, once the novelty had worn off, would be a pain in the fucking tits!

BELINDA   You don't know anything about the way my mind works.

CARMEL-M   If *Lions* isn't a play written by a romantic fantasist I don't know what is! All that bollocks about love conquering everything and making people immortal. It was embarrassing.

BELINDA   You cheeky bitch! It was sold out every fucking night!

CARMEL-M   I never said you were the only dickhead in the world. There are millions of them out there. You have no idea what real love means.

BELINDA   I suppose you really love Richard, do you?

CARMEL-M   Yes, I do, in the true sense of the word. I live with him day in, day out. I cook his meals, I wash his clothes . . .

BELINDA   And that's your idea of love? Washing and cooking?

CARMEL-M   You can't claim to love someone until you've lived with them in the real world.

BELINDA (*angrily*)   Me and Tony are as real as you and Richard. Does Richard know, by the way?

CARMEL-M   About Mark? Of course he doesn't.

BELINDA   We've got more in common than you think.

Mutual blackmail, for one thing.

CARMEL-M   At least we both know where we stand. Now, can you go?

BELINDA   Don't you feel guilty at all? About Mark Ryder?

CARMEL-M   No. I didn't plan for him to die, but I'm not going to lose any sleep over the fact that he did.

BELINDA   Drug dealers only exist because there are people stupid enough to buy drugs from them. People like your mother and sister. Is the world well rid of them too?

CARMEL-M   Get out! Out!

*Belinda leaves.*

CHORUS   You wash, you cook, you clean.
　　　　　What does a man's life mean?
　　　　　You wash, you cook, you shop.
　　　　　Why does a man's heart stop?
　　　　　Whether you put your trust
　　　　　In justice or in lust
　　　　　Everything turns to dust.
　　　　　Everything turns to dust.

# Chapter Eleven

## I Get a Seconder

'Are you sure?' Tony asked. 'You'd really do that, just for me?'

'Not just for you. For me as well. I want to do it, Tony. But, yes, I would do it just for you. I'd do anything for you, you know that.' It was Thursday 10 September and I was visiting Tony during my lunch-hour. He was no longer bedridden. The antibiotics had begun to clear up his infection and he could move around a bit more easily. We were sitting on his bed, holding hands.

'This can't be right,' he said. 'I can't be feeling relaxed and happy. I'm not used to it.'

'Well, get used to it,' I said.

'I don't deserve to be happy, not after what I've done. I've been having nightmares about it. It's being stuck in here that does it.'

'You've got to try to put it behind you.' I squeezed his hand.

'I was supposed to be starting college this week, but I was too ill,' said Tony. 'Now I'm going to be a week behind everyone else.'

'College? What college?' I tried not to sound angry. How could I possibly not know this already? I knew it was my own fault for not asking the right questions at the right times. Tony was not, and probably never would be, the sort of person who volunteered information.

'This college in Slough. I'm doing an AS level.'

'In what? Sound engineering?'

'Nah. Music for Performance, it's called. It's crap. I'm only doing it because I can't get the money to do the course I really want to do.'

'Well, we'll see about that,' I said.

'What do you mean?'

'I mean, first let's get this pilonidal sinus sorted out and then we can start thinking of ways for you to do your sound engineering course. What's an AS level anyway?' I asked.

'I don't know. Half an A level, something like that. It's crap. Won't do me any good.'

'It might be interesting, though,' I said.

'Yeah, but it won't get me a job as a sound engineer.'

'Getting a job isn't the only reason to do a course, you know.' I rehashed the words of Aquinas College's careers advisor. 'You can do something just because it's interest-ing, just because you like it. You never know what it might lead to. Tony . . .' I changed the subject. 'Will you talk to Vinny? You know him better than I do.'

'Okay,' he said. 'I don't know what to say, though.'

'Just ask him if he'll do it.'

'When?'

'I don't know, exactly. I'm sorting that out today. If he agrees, tell him to ring me at work.'

'Okay.' Tony nodded and giggled. 'You're strange.'

'Why?' I asked. He shrugged. 'Give me three reasons why I'm strange.'

'One: you're here with me. Two: you're a writer. And three . . . dunno.' He grinned.

'Do you think Vinny'll agree?' I asked anxiously.

'Don't see why not. He likes you.'

'Does he? How do you know that?'

'He said, after you'd gone yesterday. He said you were all right.' I wanted to ask how Vinny had reacted to the news of Mark Ryder's death, whether he regretted what he'd done at all or whether he would still do anything for

267

money. He didn't look particularly remorseful to me. I wondered what kind of a life Vinny had had, what had happened to him between birth and becoming a freelance thug who lived in a hostel.

'I'd better go now or I'll be late for school,' I said. Tony put his arms around me and hugged me tightly. 'I don't want to go,' I explained. 'But I need to stay in the school's good books. If I get sacked now, the whole plan's ruined.' I didn't mention the Carl angle. I hated having to sleep with him behind Tony's back, but I couldn't risk telling Tony the truth. How could I expect him to understand that Carl was effectively blackmailing me and that, in order for the Ace New Plan to run smoothly, I had to submit to his demands, at least for the time being?

# Chapter Twelve

## Persuading Hayley

HAYLEY DOUGLAS *is sitting alone at a table in the staff canteen drinking a cup of tea.* BELINDA NIELD *enters, sees* HAYLEY *and sits down opposite her.*

HAYLEY    I thought you were avoiding me.

BELINDA    No.

HAYLEY    Oh, come on. You haven't said a word to me since the last night of *Lions*. Every time I pass you in the corridor you look away.

BELINDA    Sorry. You know why, don't you?

HAYLEY    I think so. But you must have worked out by now that I haven't said anything to Phil about Tony. What you do in your private life is your business. It's not up to me to decide whether it's right or wrong.

BELINDA    Thanks. I'm amazed.

HAYLEY    Why?

BELINDA    Well, let's just say that's not the majority view.

HAYLEY    It's the most sensible view. Some people are probably just jealous. Tony's so attractive and you've got Alistair as well. And . . .

BELINDA    What?

HAYLEY    Well, there was a rumour about Carl . . .

BELINDA    Oh my God! Seth doesn't know, does he?

HAYLEY    I doubt it. You know what he's like, he's in a little world of his own. He hasn't been the same since Darryl fell out with him, you know. Have you noticed

269

how miserable he looks these days?

BELINDA   I haven't really noticed much, to be honest. I've been too preoccupied with my own problems. Hayley, have you ever been unfaithful to Phil?

HAYLEY (*lowering her eyes*)   No. But that doesn't mean I wouldn't.

BELINDA   Would you?

HAYLEY   I might. If the opportunity arose.

BELINDA   Would you feel guilty? About Phil?

HAYLEY   I don't know. A bit maybe. Guilt's better than boredom, though.

BELINDA   Are you bored of Phil?

HAYLEY   Look, can we change the subject? Are you still seeing Carl?

BELINDA   Don't you even disapprove of that? I can't believe it. Even I disapprove of that.

HAYLEY   I think it's funny, to be honest. Carl Sillery. The idea of you and him!

BELINDA   Don't! I'm still seeing him, yes, but I don't want to. I'd give anything to be rid of him.

HAYLEY   So what's the problem?

BELINDA   He's . . . he's blackmailing me. He could get me sacked and he knows it.

HAYLEY   Belinda, that's terrible! Surely there's some way . . .

BELINDA   There's no way, at least not for a while. This is what I wanted to talk to you about. You see, I've got a bit of a problem. It's Tony. He's ill.

HAYLEY   Oh no. What's wrong with him? Is there anything I can do?

BELINDA (*laughing*)   You may regret asking that. There's rather a lot you can do, actually.

HAYLEY   What? What's wrong with him?

BELINDA   He's got what's called a pilonidal sinus.

HAYLEY   A what?

BELINDA   I'd never heard of it either, but apparently they're really common. It's an ingrowing hair follicle at

270

the base of your spine that becomes infected. Darryl's brother Lee had one. The thing is, it's painful but not that serious. It flares up, but then it goes away again. There's no way of knowing how often it'll recur or how bad the pain will be when it does. Tony's has been infected a few times, but usually not that seriously. But this time it's worse. On Monday he couldn't even walk.

HAYLEY  Oh no, that's awful.

BELINDA  The point is, there's a simple operation he can have to get it removed. It just involves cutting it out, I think . . .

HAYLEY  Euch!

BELINDA  . . . or cutting it open, something like that. The trouble is, Tony's doctor said it could take a year or more for him to be able to get into hospital to have it done.

HAYLEY  Can he wait that long?

BELINDA  Well, he could. I mean, he's got antibiotics and pain-killers which get rid of the infection when it appears, but there's no telling how often he'll have to go through the whole rigmarole while he's waiting for his operation. It may not flare up again – he could be lucky. But it could come back every month or something, it's just impossible to predict.

HAYLEY  But . . . why does he have to wait that long?

BELINDA  Because it's not life-threatening. That's how long it takes, with waiting lists and everything. The worrying thing is, though, according to Lee Abrahams, the longer you leave these things, the worse they get, the more regularly they get infected.

HAYLEY  Oh dear.

BELINDA  So this is where you come in.

HAYLEY  What? Where?

BELINDA  Now, don't over-react. I know it sounds mad, but I've thought it through and I know it can work.

HAYLEY  Just tell me, for God's sake.

BELINDA  I'm going to marry Tony.

HAYLEY  *What?*

BELINDA  Ssh! Keep your voice down. I'm going to marry him. Remember that BUPA form I filled in when I first started working here?

HAYLEY  Yes. Oh no.

BELINDA  I remember what that form said. It said, 'The scheme allows for the spouse and any children of the employee to have the cost of private health insurance covered by the school. Please notify . . .'

HAYLEY  'Mrs Hayley Douglas, the school secretary, as soon as you marry or have children.'

BELINDA  Yes. If I marry Tony, he can have his operation done privately, almost straight away. I've already contacted Slough Register Office . . .

HAYLEY (*shocked*)  You haven't?

BELINDA  I have. Tony and I can be married within a week.

HAYLEY  That quickly?

BELINDA  Yes, if you do it by licence instead of certificate.

HAYLEY  Belinda, I'm really not sure . . .

BELINDA  Why not? I am. It wouldn't be dishonest or anything. I mean, we really would be married. All you'd have to do is get the paperwork sorted and not tell anyone. No one ever looks at any of that stuff except you. Seth never looks at it, does he?

HAYLEY  I don't think he even knows where it is.

BELINDA  Right. So no one would need to know about it, except you, me, Tony, Darryl and Tony's friend Vinny. He and Darryl are going to be the witnesses. Well, Vinny hasn't agreed yet, but I'm sure he will.

HAYLEY  Darryl? Darryl has agreed?

BELINDA  Well, he took a bit of persuading.

HAYLEY  I bet he did! And I'm going to take a bit of persuading.

BELINDA  That's ridiculous. You can't stop me marrying Tony and once we're married he's eligible for BUPA cover. That's the school rule.

HAYLEY    But ... I've heard of marriages of convenience so that someone can get British citizenship but not for BUPA cover. I mean, isn't there another way?

BELINDA    I don't want another way! This isn't just a marriage of convenience, Hayley. I want to marry Tony. I mean, yeah, I want him to have his operation quickly and get better as soon as possible, but that's not the main reason I want to do it. The main reason is ... love, basically.

HAYLEY    But ... would you leave Alistair and move in with him?

BELINDA    No. I don't think Tony wants to live with me.

HAYLEY    Why not?

BELINDA    It's complicated. He finds it difficult to ... be around people too much. Having a relationship is an effort for him. He's ... well, you know his history. Which is another good reason to marry him as far as I'm concerned. If BUPA covers psychological health care as well as physical, you never know when he might need that too.

HAYLEY    But if you're not going to live together ... ?

BELINDA    I'll carry on living with Alistair and see Tony as often as he wants to see me.

HAYLEY    Isn't that what's normally known as going out with someone?

BELINDA    Marriage doesn't only mean living together. It usually involves that, but it doesn't have to. Marriage is about true love, a commitment to love someone for ever, for better or for worse ...

HAYLEY    Yeah, yeah, I know. But Belinda, what about Alistair?

BELINDA    What about him? He won't know anything about it.

HAYLEY    He'd find out.

BELINDA    How? I'd take my wedding ring off – assuming Tony remembers to buy me one – before I got home. How would he find out? The only way you find out

273

someone's married is when they tell you, when they invite you to their wedding or whatever. Most people don't want to hide the fact that they're married. I mean, how do you know Seth's married? How do you know (*she pauses momentarily*) Carmel-Marie's married?

HAYLEY   Oh, come on . . .

BELINDA   Because they told you, right? Because they wear wedding rings to advertise the fact. They might only be pretending to be married for all you know.

HAYLEY   I just don't think you could keep a secret that big.

BELINDA   A big secret is no harder to keep than a little secret. It's the same method, just on a larger scale. You just have to make sure you've anticipated and dealt with all the potential pitfalls.

HAYLEY   I don't like it. It scares me. I feel as though I'm being sucked into some kind of . . . whirlwind of insanity. I could lose my job if Seth found out.

BELINDA   How? If I get married, my spouse is entitled to private health insurance. You're not doing anything wrong.

HAYLEY   Of course I am. I'm allowing the school to be party to a major deception.

BELINDA   It's deceiving Alistair, though, not the Inland Revenue. My personal life is none of the school's business. It's not as if I'm committing fraud of any kind. I mean, I really will be married. You won't be lying to BUPA. Tell me one way in which the plan could go wrong.

HAYLEY   Well, this Vinny character. You never know who he might say something to.

BELINDA   I'll make sure he doesn't. Anyway, he doesn't know anyone. What's he going to do, ring Seth out of the blue and say 'Guess what? Belinda Nield married Tony Lamb so that he could have his operation straight away, and by the way, Hayley Douglas knew all about this'? He doesn't even know your name, for a start.

HAYLEY    Good. Oh, you're tiring me out. I'll do it, okay. But I don't like it. I just don't like the whole idea of it.

BELINDA    Just sort the paperwork and forget it ever happened.

HAYLEY    Oh yeah, great. How am I supposed to do that?

BELINDA    Easy. I do it all the time. You just tell yourself something over and over again until eventually you believe it.

HAYLEY    That may work for you, but it wouldn't for me.

BELINDA    How do you know? I bet you've never tried. You can come to the wedding if you want to.

HAYLEY    Of course I don't want to. I think you're seriously deranged.

BELINDA    (*singing*)  'Make of our hands one hand, Make of our hearts one heart, Make of our vows one last vow, (*she gets up to leave*) Even Seth won't part us now.'
*She exits, laughing.* HAYLEY *looks at her cold tea in despair.*

# Chapter Thirteen

## A Love Rhombus

Do you remember rhombuses from your secondary-school days? They have four corners, not three. Love triangles are common. Wristine Vella had a love triangle. Love rhombuses are not common. What I had on my hands was a love rhombus. This is what it looked like:

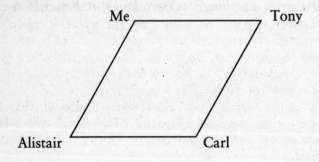

Carl loved me. Alistair loved me. Tony loved me. I loved Alistair. I was madly in love with Tony. I hated Carl. That's why I've allocated him the corner of the rhombus that is furthest from mine.

Love is like religion: responsible for a lot of horrors but also many good things. It has turned Carl into a better writer, for example. He would never have been able to write the poem he wrote in my love poetry class if he hadn't been in love with me. Anyone who would accuse me of corrupting him should bear in mind that without my influence in his life, Carl might still be churning out such appalling monstrosities as 'Childkiller', the poem he brought to my first creative writing class at the end of last term, which contained the immortal stanza:

> If those were your children,
> What would you do?
> You'd want to chop his bollocks off
> And feed them to a kangaroo.

I had planned my classes well in advance, practically as soon as I'd started at Beasley and long before I had formulated the Carl Sillery Plan. I reserved one session specifically for love poetry because it was the only kind I really liked, but seeing it in my diary now I felt like crying and going home. The last thing I wanted to do was read and discuss love poems in the presence of Carl Sillery.

'Change of plan!' I said brightly as the class trooped into the lecture theatre. Carl was predictably at the front of the queue, bursting through the door as soon as the bell rang. 'We're not doing love poetry today. We're doing rhyme and metre instead.'

'Thank God for that,' Ed Fewster muttered. 'Far less scope for patheticness all round.' There was still a faint mark on his cheek, a remnant of Trudi's last-night-party scratch.

'Oh no!' said Phoebe Procter, nearly dropping her bag in dismay. She came up to me quickly. 'Please don't say that. I've been looking forward to it all day. I can't bear not to do it. I feel really . . . inspired. I want to write a poem about Oliver.'

'Okay.' I gave in immediately. Refusing a request from the Good Fairy of Love was totally against my whole code of ethics. 'Sorry, folks, we are doing love poetry after all.' There was a general cheer from most of the girls. Oliver and Carl looked as though they wanted to join in, but stopped themselves just in time.

'Oh typical.' Ed Fewster raised his eyes skywards. 'No doubt I shall be engulfed by hysteria again.'

'Belinda, is it okay if our poems are really sad? Can we write about unrequited love?' asked Trudi, looking pointedly at Ed, whose failure to requite was still a source of much chagrin. She looked as if she had lost about half a stone since *Lions* and there was no gel in her hair.

'Yes, of course it is,' I said. 'You can write about any sort of love.'

'Can we write about love between friends, or family members?' asked Stella Nettleton, primly dressed in a white blouse and grey skirt.

The bitch is trying to catch me out, I thought. 'No,' I said at once. 'It must be romantic love.' I certainly didn't want to have to wade through reams of tedious dog and grandma poems.

I read them a few classic examples of the genre: two Shakespeare sonnets, a couple of Edna St Vincent Millay's, my favourite poet of all time, Yeats's 'No Second Troy' and Padraic Fallon's 'The Poems of Love'. I told them that for some reason that possibly had to do with modernism, the traditional love poem was not as common a form now as it once was. There was a lot of Anti-GLOW floating around the contemporary poetry scene, a lot of critics who seemed to think it was better to write about folding towels or putting nappies on babies than about love and passion.

I asked them to write a love poem in the first person. A few of the boys said they didn't want to, including Ed. I told them that writers were supposed to have imaginations and if they weren't in love they could jolly well pretend they were until 3.15, when the class ended. After they had written their first-person love poems, I told them to start again and write on the same theme but this time in the third person.

'Do you mean write about three in a bed?' Chris Emerson called out and most of the boys laughed.

'No, Chris, I don't mean that. I mean use "he" and

278

"she" instead of "I". The point of the exercise is to look at different techniques for writing love poetry.'

I stared out of the window and day-dreamed about my wedding, while the students wrote in silence. I couldn't believe that I was really going to marry Tony. Was it possible to be so fortunate? If the deal was that I got Tony, but in return I had to suffer sex with Carl, I would accept it without complaint. Just as people who earn enormous salaries have to be prepared to pay a bit more tax than everyone else, I had to expect to pay a fair amount for my privileges. Sleeping with Carl was my emotional national insurance contribution.

How unusual was it, I wondered, to marry someone you've never slept with? It was the norm once, but in this day and age it had to be fairly rare. Tony had made no sexual advances so far; he seemed happy to hug and kiss and hold hands, which I thought was rather sweet. My guess was that he was a virgin. Would we do it once we were married and, if so, would I have to make all the moves? I decided to worry about it once the wedding was out of the way. The highest kind of love, of which mine for Tony was definitely an instance, is more spiritual than physical. This notwithstanding, I was keen to leap into bed with him at the earliest available opportunity.

Despite my rationalisation of my relationship with Carl, I was none too happy when he stayed behind after the class to show me the love poem he had written.

'Just put it on the pile with everyone else's,' I said without looking at him.

'I want you to read it now,' he said. 'Before I go.'

I sighed and took the sheet of lined A4 paper from his outstretched hand, hoping it wouldn't be sexually graphic. I wasn't encouraged by the title: 'To Belinda'. 'Did anyone see you writing this?' I asked. 'What did we agree about being discreet?'

'I know,' he said resentfully. 'I'm not stupid. I only added the title just now, when the others had gone.'

279

'Oh.'

'Well, go on, read it.'

'I'm reading it,' I said. The title turned out to be the least offensive part. No doubt, readers of all categories, you are hoping to be spared the teeth-clenching cringeworthiness of Carl's poetic offering, but I had to read it so I don't see why you should escape. It went like this:

> You are the only person that I live for.
> For you alone I breathe my every breath
> And there is nothing that I wouldn't give for
> The chance to be with you, not just till death
> But after death as well. Don't ever leave me.
> Nobody else could ever take your place.
> Whether you love me back, whether you deceive me
> I am in heaven when I see your face.
> I'd rather have your cruel words that fill me
> With misery than never hear your voice.
> Life without you would definitely kill me
> And so you see, I do not have a choice
> For I will suffer every tortured pain
> If I can see your lovely face again.

Normally I grant my students a certain amount of artistic licence, but the prospect of being with Carl not merely until death but beyond it was so terrifying that I felt it had to be nipped in the bud at once. 'I don't like the "beyond death" bit,' I said as calmly as possible. 'It sounds too archaic. It's the sort of thing the metaphysical poets used to say, people like John Donne, but it doesn't make sense nowadays when people aren't as religious as they used to be. I think you should change that bit.'

'What about the rest of it?' Carl looked upset. 'Do you like the rest? I mean, do you like the poem?'

'There are too many syllables in line seven. And don't you think "every tortured pain" is a bit extreme? You shouldn't do metaphors to death, you know. "Pain" on its

280

own would be more effective than "tortured pain".'

'Yes but . . .'

'And what's all this stuff about deceiving and cruel words? Are you getting at me, or what?'

'Of course I'm not getting at you!' Carl said tearfully. 'It's a love poem.'

'Yes, but you're saying my words are cruel and fill you with misery.'

'Well, they do sometimes.'

'Like when?'

'Like now!' Carl snatched his poem from my hand and ran out of the room. I felt a bit mean. I could at least have told him that it was better than 'Childkiller'. Or that, as a first attempt at the sonnet form, it was pretty impressive. I could have praised his skilful combination of masculine and feminine rhymes or the way his syntax strained across his line-endings, creating rhythmic tension. Why did I find it so hard to be nice to him? I was more than willing, in theory, to pay my emotional national insurance contributions. I told myself over and over again 'Be nice to Carl', but whenever I had an opportunity I blew it. I should have just thanked him and smiled and that would have been the end of it. Now I'd upset him and I'd have to go and find him and sort it out before he decided to tell Seth all about what a dreadful person I was.

# Chapter Fourteen

## The Questioning of Witnesses

'I reckon it'll fit. If not, they said they'd alter it,' a nasal voice whined in my ear. I was on the phone to Vinny, who was making what I regarded as an unnecessary fuss about wedding rings. 'Have you got Tony's ring yet?'

'Yes,' I said impatiently. I'd bought it the day before from Beaverbrooks, a plain fourteen-carat gold band that set me back nearly two hundred quid. I told Alistair I'd taken the money from our joint account to get the Nova serviced. I hoped Tony hadn't spent that much, given his dire financial situation. I would have been happy with a ring-pull from a Coke can as long as it came from him.

It was Wednesday 17 September and the wedding was tomorrow.

'What about the honeymoon?' Vinny proceeded in a businesslike manner. He sounded as if he had a list in front of him and was ticking off items as we dealt with them.

'Vinny.' I took a deep breath. 'I've already told you I can't go on a honeymoon. You know the situation. You know that I live with someone, and Tony and I are only getting married so that he can have his operation. Well, that's not the only reason, I mean, I love him, obviously . . .'

'So you should have a honeymoon,' he insisted. 'Just a short one, like. Why don't you go to a posh hotel for a long weekend or something?'

'And what would I tell Alistair?'

'Who's Alistair?'

'The man I live with.'

'I don't know. Make something up. Look, do you want me to arrange it for you?' Vinny, I had realised after knowing him for only a brief period, was the sort of person whose desire to help verges on hindrance. If he regards you as a friend, he will assist you with or without your consent. He will assault you with altruism.

'Vinny, you're just not listening to me,' I sighed. 'I can't . . .'

'What about just one night, then? You can't not have any kind of honeymoon at all. It's not fair to Tony, that. It's his wedding too.'

'Well, I suppose one night . . .' I began to concede. I had to admit he had a point. I wanted it to feel like a proper wedding. After all, it wasn't really a marriage of convenience, however convenient it was from the point of view of Tony's operation.

'Tell you what, why don't you let me sort it for you?' Vinny prattled on happily, pleased that his excellent advice had at last been taken. 'Go on, it can be my wedding present to you and Tony.'

'You can't spend that sort of money . . .'

'Yes, I can,' said Vinny. 'I got some money, right.'

I didn't like to ask where from. I didn't want to know what other feats of free-lance thuggery Vinny had performed in addition to the one I knew about.

'That's settled then,' he said firmly. 'I'll sort it.'

'Okay then.' I gave in gracefully. 'Thanks.'

Vinny, to give him credit, was being very good about the wedding. He was by far the more compliant of our two witnesses.

'I still can't believe it's tomorrow,' Darryl had spluttered when I phoned him this morning. 'How can something so . . . important happen so quickly?'

I explained again about marriage by licence instead of certificate.

'You can get married almost immediately,' I said patiently, 'and the advantage is that, because there's so little time, the Notice of Marriage doesn't go up on the public noticeboard like it does if you get married by certificate, which means there's absolutely no chance of Alistair finding out.'

'Of course there's a chance!' Darryl grouched. 'Marriages aren't classified information.'

'I know, but you know as well as I do that Alistair is hardly likely to take to leafing through Register Office records.'

'You never know who's going to look at stuff like that. All it would take is for one person who knows Alistair and is doing research into, I don't know, local history or something . . .'

'Darryl, stop it! Come on, you're being silly now.' Ever since our first visit to Sandlea Court he had been trying to talk me out of going through with the ANP and it was beginning to get on my nerves.

'But it could happen!' he protested.

'It could, yes, but I'm sure it won't. Alistair doesn't know anyone who would spend their time looking at Register Office files. Everyone he knows is into computers and football.'

'Well, don't say I didn't warn you,' said Darryl mournfully.

'I won't! I'll say you warned me until I was thoroughly fed up of being warned. Anyway, tomorrow: we're all meeting outside the Register Office at 2 p.m.'

'What about classes?'

'I've invented a chiropodist's appointment. You'll have to do the same,' I said briskly.

'What, a sudden outbreak of verrucas among the staff? You expect people to believe that?'

'No, not a chiropodist's appointment, you fool. Something else. Dentist, I don't know, use your imagination. Tony's going to get the time off college, Vinny's already sorted it with his boss . . .'

'Oh, the bulldog works, does he?'

'And that's another thing, Darryl. Whatever you may think of him, Vinny is Tony's friend and he's been very helpful over this whole wedding business, so please, please try to be civil to him. No, in fact, try to be friendly to him. I don't want you ruining my wedding day by arguing with the only other guest.'

'So what does the bulldog do? Astro-physicist? Marine biologist?'

'Don't be a snob!' I scolded. 'You sound like Natasha. Vinny works part-time at McDonald's. Look, you'd better cheer up by tomorrow. I don't want any long faces in that Register Office. I want it to be a happy occasion.'

'You don't ask for much, do you? It isn't enough that I agree to participate in this madness. Now you want me to be ecstatic about it as well!'

'Good, I'm glad we agree,' I said firmly and slammed the phone down.

After work I went into town and bought my wedding outfit, a clingy dark-blue dress from Warehouse and navy, square-heeled court shoes from Dolcis. I also popped into La Senza and bought a lilac silk night-dress. My usual baggy blue pyjamas were not suitable for a honeymoon, however brief.

I doubted Tony would buy anything new. He would probably arrive at the Register Office in his jeans, trainers and checked shirt, which was fine by me. Unless Vinny intervened, of course, with his definite ideas about how these things should be done. I imagined him dragging a reluctant Tony from shop to shop and laughed out loud. There were so many ordinary things that seemed somehow ridiculous in connection with Tony and shopping was one of them. I could picture him walking on the surface of the moon more easily than I could see him emerging from a changing room cubicle in Stolen From Ivor and saying to Vinny, 'Do you prefer this one or the last one I tried on?'

Although I hated to see Tony in pain, I was secretly

grateful for the pilonidal sinus. I would never have had the courage to propose to him without the back-up of a pragmatic reason and even if I had, I doubt he would have accepted. His inferiority complex and fear of happiness would have scared him off. The pilonidal sinus acted as an anchor, grounding the idea in the sort of unpleasant reality Tony felt comfortable with. Its link to our wedding made marriage, the optimism of which would normally have terrified him, seem feasible.

I got home at half past six and ran upstairs to hide my carrier bags before Alistair saw them. He was very sensitive about money at the moment and the lilac night-dress might have been a bit of a give-away, even for someone of Alistair's obliviousness to detail.

As I came back downstairs, he launched into a rant that he had clearly been saving for my return. 'Do you know he's got a stupid alter ego, for example?' he yelled, stomping moodily across the lounge. 'He calls himself Sonny Brown.' Alistair's cheeks were flushed and he combed his hands through his blond hair furiously, nearly knocking off his glasses, as he often did when he was angry.

'Who, Bill Gates?' I asked wearily.

'And when he's pissed off with someone he says, "They can suck my Sonny Brown"!' Alistair raved on, barely aware of my presence. 'He calls himself and his knob by the same name, can you believe it?'

'How do you know what Bill Gates calls his knob?' I asked, puzzled.

'Not Bill Gates, you fool! I'm talking about Phil Douglas! I'm so fucking sick of his little jokes, which aren't jokes at all . . .'

I switched off, trying not to let my impatience show. Alistair would have to choose the eve of my wedding to make a huge fuss about work. I know: how was he supposed to know it was the eve of my wedding, right? Which is why I smiled and pretended to listen. I am a fair person, whatever else I may be. I re-entered the conversation when

I heard Alistair say, 'Maybe I'll just evict him. Serve the bastard right to be thrown out on the street.'

'Alistair! You can't do that. Hayley's my friend, remember.'

'Yeah, yeah. All right. I'm just angry, that's all.' He exhaled sharply and sat down on the sofa. 'Do you mind missing *Brookside* tonight?' he asked. 'There's a programme on BBC 2 about blizzards I wouldn't mind watching.'

'Fine,' I said, blinking back tears. There was little I minded more than missing *Brookside*. Splitting up with Tony, death – that just about exhausted the list. I couldn't believe my needs were being so callously dismissed on the eve of my wedding and I glowered at poor, unsuspecting Alistair all the way through his blizzard programme.

# Chapter Fifteen

## Not to be Entered into Lightly
## nor Lightly to be Put Aside

Tony, Vinny, Darryl and I met outside Slough Register Office at two o'clock as planned. Tony was wearing his stunning checked shirt and blue-in-an-excellent-way jeans, as I'd predicted he would. Darryl was also dressed casually in brown canvas trousers, a beige T-shirt and a leather jacket. I couldn't help thinking he had dressed down deliberately to spite me.

I was glad I'd bought a blue dress rather than a white one. I wanted to make the point that this wedding was in a category of its own. Tony and I didn't need all the trappings that most people hid behind. We could get married in rags and our wedding would still be better than all weddings that didn't have the Tony Lamb GLOW.

Not including Tony's ring and my new outfit, the whole thing cost almost a hundred pounds: twenty-pounds for giving notice of marriage, a forty-five-pound licence fee, twenty-seven pounds for registration of the marriage and three pounds for the marriage certificate. The amount surprised me. I knew the associated extravagances could be pretty pricey, especially if you went in for all the crap that most of my secretarial ex-colleagues were so keen on – the bells, the choir, the horse-drawn carriage, the sit-down lunch, the stand-up evening buffet, the huge, tasteless marquee in the garden, the photographs, the video, the fancy cars – but I had assumed the ceremony was free. What did really poor people do? Tony couldn't have spared a hundred pounds for a wedding if it weren't for me.

Of the four of us, Vinny was the only one who was properly dressed for the occasion. He was wearing a black pin-striped three-piece suit, the jacket of which sported a prominent Pierre Balmain label, and shiny black lace-up shoes.

'Looks like I'm the only one who's made an effort here,' he said when Darryl and I arrived. 'I said to Tony, you can't get married in jeans.'

'You don't care what I wear, do you?' Tony asked me, frowning anxiously.

'Of course I don't,' I reassured him. 'You look gorgeous. Oh, God, I'm so excited!' Tony smiled. He was happy to be marrying me, there was no doubt about it, and not only because of his operation. 'Aren't you excited, Darryl?'

Darryl ignored me and stared at Vinny with intense loathing. 'Don't talk to me about making an effort. I've had to lie, cancel all my classes, let my students down . . .'

'All right, calm down!' Vinny squealed nasally. 'Fucking hell! Can't you take a joke, man?'

'You two, stop it!' I snapped. 'Shall we go in?' I didn't want to hang around outside the Register Office for too long. Anyone could have driven past and wondered what I was doing there. Once we were inside the building I started to relax a bit.

At 2.30, the Registrar of Marriages, a bald middle-aged man with small round glasses and several strange dents in his skull, asked us to follow him into another room. He introduced us to the Superintendent Registrar, who looked disconcertingly like my dad. There was a lot of hand-shaking, which unfortunately I was unable to avoid. I was so nervous that my palms were horribly sticky. Tony didn't look nearly as nervous as I was. He seemed calm and happy, more so than usual. I had expected it to be the other way round, me in full control and Tony agitated and jittery. Perhaps it was simply that I had a lot more to be excited about. I, after all, was about to marry the great Tony Lamb, which would be enough to reduce anyone to a quivering jelly, whereas he was only marrying me and therefore had far less to get steamed up about.

The Registrar welcomed us and asked if the Best Man wanted to place the ring on a small cushion he was holding. Vinny obediently produced both rings, smiled and put them there without batting an eyelid. He certainly knew his wedding etiquette. There was nothing romantic about the room we were in; it looked like a typical local government office, the sort of place I imagined Ian Chaddock and Barry Pilsworth working in.

'Before we commence the ceremony of marriage,' said the Registrar, 'I have to tell you that this place in which we are now met has been duly sanctioned according to law for the celebration of marriages.' We all nodded solemnly. 'You are here, as you know, to witness the joining in matrimony of Tony and Belinda.' I didn't nod at this bit, since it was addressed specifically to Vinny and Darryl. I heard Darryl sigh quietly behind me. 'If any person here present knows of any lawful impediment why they may not be joined in matrimony, it should be declared now.' The Registrar paused and looked at us all for a few seconds. I shot Darryl a look of sharp warning and he sighed again. I wouldn't have put it past him to come up with some crazy objection, pretend I had a mad husband in the attic or something, just to stop the wedding. He really was against it, it seemed, more so than I'd realised. Still, he had turned up which was the most important thing.

'If you two would like to stand.' The Registrar smiled at me and Tony. I scrambled hastily to my feet. Tony stood up in a more leisurely, relaxed manner and smiled at me. I think he was trying to reassure me, which I was pleased about. It wouldn't do any harm to have a bit of role reversal in our relationship.

'Could you state your full names, please?' said the Registrar.

'Belinda Claire Nield,' I said.

'Anthony Paul Lamb,' said Tony.

'Before you are joined in matrimony,' said the Registrar, 'I have to remind you of the solemn and binding character of the vows you are about to make. Marriage, according to the law of this country, is the union of one man with one woman, voluntarily entered into for life to the exclusion of all others. But further it is a solemn union to provide the love, friendship, help and comfort that each ought to have for the other, both in times of joy and in times of difficulty, not to be entered into lightly nor lightly to be put aside.' I smiled at Tony, then at Darryl and Vinny. That was a good bit, I thought – 'not to be entered into lightly nor lightly to be put aside'. When I had come to give notice of marriage last week the Superintendent Registrar had given me a little leaflet with the wording of the ceremony on it and I had spotted that bit straight away. It sounded almost poetic. I decided I would have to base a future poetry class around those lines. Trudi and Phoebe would like that, even if Ed wouldn't.

'I am going to ask you both in turn to make declarations that you are free to marry one another.' The Registrar turned to Tony. 'Tony, I invite you to repeat your declaration first after me. I do solemnly declare that I know not of any lawful impediment why I, Anthony Paul Lamb, may not be joined in matrimony to Belinda Claire Nield.'

'I do solemnly declare that I know not of any . . . lawful impediment why I, Anthony Paul Lamb . . . why I, Anthony Paul Lamb . . .' Tony frowned and looked at me, hoping for a prompt.

'. . . should not be joined in matrimony to Belinda Claire Nield,' said the Registrar quickly. He was obviously used to people forgetting their lines.

'Should not be joined in matrimony to Belinda Claire Nield.'

'Good.' The Registrar turned to me. 'I invite you to make a similar declaration. I do solemnly declare that I know not of any lawful impediment why I, Belinda Claire Nield, may not be joined in matrimony to Anthony Paul Lamb.'

I repeated the words hastily.

'Tony and Belinda are now going to contract their marriage before you, their witnesses,' the Registrar said to Darryl and Vinny. 'Will you please stand?' Once Vinny and Darryl were on their feet, the Registrar asked me and Tony to turn and face each other.

'You are going to give your bride a ring,' he said to Tony. 'Take the ring and place it upon her finger.' Tony did this without even blinking. I was pleased to find him so alert on our wedding day. 'Now, still holding the ring on her finger I am going to ask you to make your next declaration which is your vow and contract to your marriage. If you could repeat after me, With this ring I thee wed . . .'

'With this ring I thee wed,' said Tony.

'And I call upon these persons here present . . .'

'And I call upon these persons here present . . .'

'. . . to witness that I, Anthony Paul Lamb,'

'. . . to witness that I, Anthony Paul Lamb,'

'. . . do take thee, Belinda Claire Nield,'

'. . . do take thee, Belinda Claire Nield,'

'. . . to be my lawful wedded wife . . .'

'. . . to be my lawful wedded wife . . .'

'. . . and receive this ring as a token of our love and marriage.'

'. . . and receive this ring as a token of our love and marriage.' Tony grinned at me casually. He wasn't nearly as emotional as I was. I nearly collapsed and started sobbing all over the Registrar's feet. Luckily, I managed to remain upright long enough to make my declaration and give Tony his ring.

'Tony and Belinda,' the Registrar continued, pushing his glasses higher up his nose, 'you have both made the declarations prescribed by law and together with the custom of the giving and receiving of rings you have made a solemn vow and binding contract with each other in the presence of the witnesses gathered here today. You are now husband and wife.'

I fell into Tony's arms and we kissed for longer and with more enthusiasm than I think the Registrar expected. Vinny cheered enthusiastically behind us.

We signed the big leather book, got our certificate and that was it. We were married. I was the Wife of GLOW. The Registrar and Superintendent Registrar congratulated us, but I knew they didn't fully appreciate how brilliant it was. To them it was all in a day's work. Only Tony and I knew – or perhaps only I knew – that it was the most momentous event in world history.

Vinny had brought some confetti, which he scattered over our heads as we walked outside, holding hands. I wasn't wildly keen on this. All I needed was for someone who knew Alistair to drive past and see me being pelted with confetti. I didn't say anything, though, because Vinny's heart was in the right place, on this occasion at any rate, and he really was doing his best to make our wedding day special. More than could be said for Darryl, I thought, crossly observing his miserable attempts at smiles.

'Let's all go for a drink to celebrate,' I suggested. It was only 3.15 and Tony and I had plenty of time to spare before dinner and our honeymoon at the Bracknell Hilton.

'Why didn't they say any of that stuff they normally say?' Tony asked suddenly. 'In sickness and in health, for better or worse, till death us do part – all that?'

'Yeah, you didn't have to say you'd love, honour and obey Tony,' Vinny chipped in, anxious that a wedding convention might have been flouted.

'Well, I will,' I said. 'I don't know why, that was just the wording they gave me. But I will love, honour and obey you,' I said to Tony, 'for better or for worse, in sickness and in health, till death us do part!'

'That's sorted, then.' Vinny lit a cigarette. 'Let's go for a drink.'

Darryl and I walked behind Tony and Vinny towards the Boar's Head, the nearest pub to the Register Office.

I kept looking at my ring from every different angle possible. It was a slightly rounded nine-carat gold band, thicker in the middle than at the edges. 'Isn't it gorgeous?' I said to Darryl.

' "To the exclusion of all others",' he muttered. 'That's what you said. Are you sure you haven't just committed fraud? You live with someone else, for Christ's sake. And you're shagging Carl.'

'Ssh!' I hissed. 'Tony doesn't know about that. How can you mention that today of all days? Carl's the last thing I want to think about. Do you want me to be unhappy, or what?'

'No, Belinda, I just don't want you to juggle three men and lead a life of total deceit, which for some strange reason you seem perfectly happy to do.'

'We've been over this,' I whispered. 'As soon as Tony's had his op, I'll be dumping Carl like a hot brick. I couldn't care less about the job any more. I just want Carl out of my life, whatever it takes.'

'The whole thing is just so . . . sordid, Belinda,' Darryl ticked me off. 'I'm sorry, but it is.'

'How can you say that?' I whimpered, offended. 'I love Tony and he loves me. That's all that matters. The sort of marriages I think are sordid are the ones where everything's all posh and fancy and the couple are bored stiff of each other. How many weddings have you been to?'

'Just yours. And I'll be quite happy if I never go to another in my life.'

'Well, I've been to two apart from mine and they were utterly passionless, just polite social events with everyone showing off and eating freaky little snacks off paper plates. There was no . . . love in the air; in fact, I felt as though I was at a town hall reception or a PTA meeting, it was all so impersonal.'

'Belinda, what about that "exclusion of all others"

business?' Darryl sighed.

'Well, the marriage is,' I said. 'I'm not married to anyone else, am I? Okay, I live with Alistair but it doesn't mean that.'

'How do you know?'

'Look, Darryl, could you give it a rest? Can't you try to join in the fun instead of ruining everything and getting me all worked up? I was really happy until you started on me.'

'Okay, okay. I'll join in the fun. The fun!' he repeated sarcastically, traipsing along moodily with his hands in his pockets.

We walked the rest of the way in silence. The Boar's Head is a small pub with a slightly geriatric image, just outside the town centre. It's a homely, quiet pub with dusty books on shelves in various alcoves, the sort of place in which both comfort and conversation are possible, although there wasn't much of the latter from Darryl or Tony. Tony just held my hand and grinned at me, and Darryl stared gloomily into his pint and shuddered from time to time.

I thanked God, with reservations, for Vinny, who wittered on happily, covering a wide range of topics which included his bastard supervisor at McDonald's who did his head in, the car he wanted to buy but couldn't afford and why divorce should be made more difficult. 'It's like I said to Tony, people don't have no respect no more, no respect for the vows they make, like. I said to Tony, if you're going to stand there and make them vows, you better be fucking sure you mean it, or else it's all shit, isn't it? I mean, it's taking the piss, some of these people who get married and then they're divorced a year later. Marriage should be for life.'

'I agree,' I said and then, seeing Darryl's face turn a worrying shade of puce, added, 'but I suppose if people make a mistake and are really unhappy . . .'

'So?' said Vinny. 'They shouldn't have got married, then, if they were going to be unhappy. What's the point of making a commitment and not sticking to it? If I ever get married, it'll be for ever. No messing about.'

'Unless your wife decides to divorce you,' said Darryl, in a tone which implied he would have strong empathy for Vinny's hypothetical wife should such a situation occur.

'Well, I wouldn't marry no one who'd divorce me, would I?' said Vinny cockily. 'I'm not having no one leaving me. I'd go and get her back, I wouldn't mess about. I'd fucking kill her!'

'I'm sure you would,' said Darryl.

'He's joking,' I cut in quickly.

'I mean, like, you live with someone else, yeah.' Vinny turned to me. 'But you still married Tony. That's what I call real love, that.' I smiled at Tony, who giggled timidly, blushing a bit. I don't think he liked being the main focus of attention.

'Oh?' said Darryl. 'It isn't what you'd call ridiculous, then?'

'Ey?' Vinny scratched his nose in confusion.

'I wouldn't have expected you to approve, with your views on marriage,' Darryl clarified.

'It's all about sacrifice, innit? Belinda loves Tony, so she wants to marry him. She won't let nothing stop her, even though it's hard. I think that's sound.'

'Anyway,' I said, 'thanks a lot, you two. You were . . . really good witnesses.'

'No problem,' said Vinny. 'Any time. Well, there isn't going to be another time is there? You can't get married twice!' He guffawed nasally, elbowing Tony in the ribs and launching into a series of highly tasteless wedding-night jokes.

Please don't feel excluded, Cat As, but I want to keep the details of my honeymoon to myself. Writing sex scenes embarrasses me and besides, that night at the Bracknell Hilton I encountered a new kind of GLOW – Untellable GLOW, the kind that you don't talk or write about for fear of it dimming.

What I will say, though, is that the Bracknell Hilton,

directly opposite Sainsbury's on a large, busy roundabout, is, as far as I am concerned, the Mecca of Romance. Bracknell is the World Capital of Love. Some readers in their infinite wisdom may wish to dispute this and suggest what they feel are stronger contenders for such a title, places like Venice or Paris. In my view, a honeymoon in Venice is like a ready-made spinach and ricotta cannelloni from Tesco's – everything is done for you. It's all there already; the newly-weds have no GLOW-bringing responsibility whatsoever.

So from this day forth if you drive past the Bracknell Hilton on your way to Bagshot or Crowthorne, make sure to look at it with a new respect because it evermore shall be the Temple of GLOW.

# Chapter Sixteen

## From Weddings to Funerals

At 10 a.m. on Thursday 16 October I was wandering aimlessly around my office, wishing time would speed up. Tony was in the Princess Margaret hospital in Windsor and his operation was scheduled for 10.30. I knew it was a simple procedure, but I still felt nervous about it.

If everything went according to plan and he was discharged tomorrow needing no further hospital treatment, I would finally be able to get rid of Carl. Although I had kept my encounters with him to a minimum, I was finding it increasingly unbearable. Once Tony was in the clear I could tell Carl to piss off and, if he wanted to try and make trouble for me at school, so be it.

My phone rang suddenly and I hoped it wasn't the hospital ringing to say Tony's operation had had to be postponed. Surely one avoided that sort of thing with BUPA.

It was Darryl, who was off school with an alleged cold that I suspected was a hangover. He had taken to haranguing me every day about what he perceived as my intense stupidity, and the fact that he was off sick wasn't going to make him miss a day. 'It's all going to come out eventually,' he prophesied. 'You can't expect to get away with this deception for ever.'

'Why not?' I asked him, telling him about my Aquinas College reports. 'I've got away with loads of deceptions in my time.' I entered into the argument whole-heartedly, eager to be distracted from thoughts of Tony under the surgeon's knife.

'Not this one,' he said with certainty. 'And even if you could, would you really want to? I mean, just think about it, Belinda. It would mean lying for the rest of your life. What if you die at the age of seventy and Tony and Alistair are both still alive?'

'God, you're a morbid wanker!' I giggled.

'What would happen at the funeral? What would the vicar say, "Beloved Wife of Tony Lamb"? Don't you think Alistair would be a bit suspicious, or are you planning to find some way of keeping him at home that day?'

'You're sick!'

'No, *you're* sick, Belinda!' His self-righteous defensiveness rang in my ear. 'Come on, answer the question. What will you do if that happens?'

'I'll be dead, so I won't have to do anything,' I said, smirking at my witty reply. There was a brief, unimpressed pause. I could imagine the exasperation on Darryl's face.

'So it doesn't bother you, then, if Alistair finds out at the age of seventy-five that the last forty-odd years of his life have been based on a lie?'

'They haven't been based on a lie!' I protested. 'I love Alistair. I won't stop loving him, just because I love Tony as well. God, why can't you understand?'

'Do you think Alistair would understand?' Darryl persisted. 'Do you think that's how he would see it?'

I had to admire his spirit. Most people would have given up by now, but Darryl still struggled tirelessly to make me see sense, laying into my flawed life-style with reformist zeal. I'd had an inkling of this side of his personality before, I realised, remembering his determination to destroy and rebuild my CD collection. But he hadn't succeeded in stopping me listening to Reba McEntire and he wouldn't succeed now.

'There's only one solution, then,' I said. 'You'll have to lead a healthy and abstinent life, make sure to outlive me

299

and find some way of keeping either Tony or Alistair away from my funeral. Or else have a word with the vicar – although, to be honest, I don't see there being a vicar at my funeral. I'll probably just be hurled into a pit full of the bodies of reviled sinners. But if there is a vicar you could tell him not to mention anything about the men in my life. He can confine his speech to my personality and creative achievements. There, that's settled.'

What did Darryl expect me to say? I knew my situation wasn't ideal. I desperately wanted to be with Tony, but leaving Alistair didn't seem an option, somehow. Living with him felt so natural, like gravity or some sort of geological force. I couldn't just tamper with it, could I?

I wondered how other people coped, people who leave their spouses or partners for someone else. Are they much braver than I am? Are they less sensitive to the feelings of others, less worried about hurting people who love them?

'What did that bloke say when you got married?' Darryl nagged on. 'Something about not entering into marriage lightly . . .'

'"Not to be entered into lightly, nor lightly to be put aside." My creative writing class did some good work based on that only last week.'

'It obviously didn't mean much to you, did it? I mean, you seem to be taking it all very lightly indeed.'

'Darryl, believe me, I'm not. I'm just trying to . . . soldier on, that's all. Make the best of things. What do you want me to say? Yes, it would be a problem if I died before Tony and Alistair, but what do you want me to do? I can't think that far ahead.'

'What if Tony decides he wants to live with you? I know he's a weird fucker, but at some stage someone's bound to tell him that's what normal married couples do. And what if Alistair wants to marry you one day? I mean, that could happen. People often decide they want to get married after living together for years.' Had Darryl stayed up all night, I wondered, compiling a list of possible problems?

300

'I'll just say I don't want to get married. Plenty of people don't think it's necessary these days. I can say I'm one of them.'

There was a loud sigh in my ear that signified Darryl had given up for the time being. I told him to get well soon and said goodbye cheerily, but the conversation bothered me more than I would admit. The funeral horror that he had described so evocatively had to be avoided at all costs. Maybe I ought to start going to a gym.

# Chapter Seventeen

## Seth, Darryl, Natasha – The Remix

By the time I'd got rid of Darryl it was nearly 10.30. I was about to phone the Princess Margaret hospital and check that Tony had gone into the operating theatre on time when there was a da-da, da-da-da, DA! knock on my door. I went over to open it wearily and Seth lurched in so violently that our foreheads nearly collided. I was glad they didn't because mine would undoubtedly have been the more damaged.

For the first time ever there was no pretence that Seth had come to see me by accident and one look at him was sufficient to tell me that he was very far from being his usual self. His eyelids flicked manically open and shut, and his brown, prickly hair was streaked with grey. He was wearing a T-shirt that said 'Peter Shaffer's *Amadeus*'. For Seth Beasley to have someone else's name on his chest was a worrying symbol of self-negation.

Without saying anything he sank into one of my armchairs and began to sob loudly. 'It's Darryl.' He wept, not bothering to wipe his tears away. 'I can't . . . seem to . . . get over what's happened.' I rummaged in my bag and handed him a tissue hastily. Unwiped tears frighten me; I am a firm believer in the practice of fighting unhappiness with Kleenex.

'But it was ages ago. I thought everyone had forgotten about it,' I said, meaning, I suppose, that I had.

'It seems . . . like yesterday . . . to me,' he gasped, ripping the tissue I'd given him into strips, which he then scattered on my carpet. 'Oh, I can't . . . bear it. Belinda, you're the only person around here I can talk to.'

'Oh,' I said unenthusiastically. I needed to be Seth's main confidante like I needed the love of Carl Sillery. I sneaked a glance at my watch. It was 10.45. I hoped Seth wouldn't stay too long. I wanted to go and visit Tony in hospital as soon as I could.

'I've got to write him a letter . . . I've got to explain.' Seth wrung his hands, tears dripping pathetically off his sagging cheeks.

'What would be the point?' I asked. 'Wouldn't it be better to leave it alone?'

'But I have to explain,' he wailed. 'I have to apologise . . . for what really happened.'

'So you admit it, then? Darryl was telling the truth all along?' I leaned forward with sudden interest. This was an unexpected twist. For Seth to admit he had been wrong about anything was unheard of.

'Yes, but it wasn't . . . there was no violence in it!' he whimpered defensively.

'There doesn't have to be. Sexual assault doesn't necessarily involve violence. It just involves . . . forcing yourself on someone. That's what Darryl says you did.'

'But . . . I love him!' Seth thumped the arm of my chair. 'What else was I supposed to do?'

'You love him?' I could hardly believe what I was hearing. 'You love Darryl?'

'Yes! Oh, I know he's straight, I'm not stupid. But I can't bear to lose his friendship. Oh, it's such a relief to tell someone.' Finally he embarked upon the task of mopping his drenched face with his hands.

'But, Seth, you're straight as well.' I eyed him sharply. 'You're married.' I wouldn't have put it past him to feign homosexuality to fit in with current theatrical trends.

'I don't know what I am any more.' Seth wept, wiping his eyes on his jacket sleeve. 'All I know is I'm in love with

303

Darryl. Can you imagine, have you got any idea, how awful that is, loving him so much and knowing he'll never feel the same because I'm . . . a man?'

'I suppose so, but . . . well, where does Natasha come into this? Is she in love with him as well?'

'No, no, it was all my fault, my idea. I talked Natasha into it.' He gulped. 'I've never really fancied women. Once a month I force myself to sleep with Natasha but . . .'

'Seth!' I was shocked. Even in my state of heightened revulsion I serviced Carl more frequently than that. Maybe I was being too lenient; it simply hadn't occurred to me that anyone would put up with such infrequent inter-course.

'Well, even that's more than I can bear these days. I think about Darryl, you know.' He smiled bitterly, two stray tears glistening on his cheeks.

'I don't want to know!' I protested. I hadn't yet decided how much if any of this conversation I was going to pass on to Darryl, but that last comment of Seth's was definitely one to leave out. Darryl would have plastic surgery and assume a new identity if I informed him that he was Seth's sexual fantasy.

'I told Natasha our sex life needed spicing up,' he con-tinued, determined to complete his confession. 'I suggested a threesome, you know, with Darryl. She wasn't keen at first, but she's so miserable, Belinda. She'd do anything if she thought it would . . . solve our problem. I thought it would work, I really did. I mean, I knew Darryl wouldn't be interested in . . . in just him and me, but that was where Natasha came in, you see. She was supposed to make things look more normal.'

'Normal!' I blurted out before I could stop myself. 'Inviting a friend round for dinner, and you and your wife both trying to shag him is not what I'd call normal.'

'Look, I know I fucked up, okay,' Seth blinked furiously with embarrassment. 'All I want to do now is put it right. Do you think I should just tell Darryl the truth?'

304

'No!' I yelled, appalled, then tried to tone it down by adding, 'I don't think Darryl's ready to forgive you yet. I mean, it wasn't just what you did, Seth, it was the way you tried to turn everyone against him afterwards.'

'I know that was awful of me.' Seth winced. 'But I . . . had some sort of mental breakdown. I panicked, tried to pretend it had never happened. That's why I have to apologise. I can't let him think I'm this . . . this awful person, this monster. Oh, if only we could be friends again.' His head lolled to one side in anguish.

'Write him a short letter of apology,' I advised, 'but keep it short and don't on any account tell him you're in love with him, not if you want him to be your friend again, although I'm not sure friendship is such a great idea from your point of view. If you feel so strongly about him it won't be enough for you. If I was in love with someone who didn't love me back, I'd rather have nothing to do with him. I couldn't stand to see him every day and be reminded of what I couldn't have.'

'But if we're not even friends, there's no hope!' Seth wailed despondently.

'I understand,' I nodded. 'I know exactly how you feel, believe me, but you're only delaying the inevitable pain. I know it must be awful for you, but Darryl is heterosexual and he always will be.'

'How do you know? People can change.'

'Darryl is not gay, Seth. You've got to face facts. You'll be happier if you do.' I glanced at my watch again.

'I'll never be happy again,' said Seth flatly. 'I'm sorry if I've bored you. No doubt you want to go and visit Tony in hospital.'

I sat rooted to the spot, feeling my heart thud against my rib-cage. 'What?' I stammered eventually.

'Everyone here treats me like a fool.' His eyes slid around deviously.

'Seth, what did you mean? About Tony?' I held my breath until I felt my chest would burst. This cannot be happening, I told myself, this cannot happen.

'I know everything, Belinda. Carl, Tony, your . . . er, peculiar marriage. You know what this place is like for rumours.' I studied his face carefully to gauge his reaction, but he seemed totally uninterested in what he was saying. 'I heard Hayley on the phone to BUPA. She didn't know I was outside . . .' His voice whirred on like air-conditioning, chilling my blood.

'So are you going to sack me or what?' I said when he'd finally finished listing my misdeeds.

'Sack you?' Seth looked as if the thought had never occurred to him. 'Belinda, I admire you.'

'But I screwed a Beasley student,' I reminded him, thinking he must be toying with me in a particularly cruel way, letting me think I was off the hook, only to come down hard later on. 'Don't you care?'

'No,' he said. 'I only care about Darryl. I wish I could be like you.' He gazed at me sycophantically. 'You do exactly what you want, never mind the consequences, while the rest of us scrabble around miserably trying to make the best of our sad, pathetic little lives.' I was beginning to see why I had been selected as prime confidante. Damn, I thought. There were few people whose admiration I wanted less than Seth's. I still had an image in my mind of him prancing around his dining-room in a gold spandex posing pouch.

'Nobody knows I know,' Seth tried to reassure me, mis-interpreting my alarmed expression. 'I can't be seen to condone it.'

'Seth, please just go.' I walked over to him and seized him by the arm. There was something I had to do as a matter of great urgency. It was even more important than visiting Tony.

'Well, I . . .' Seth protested as I propelled him forcibly towards the door and ejected him into the corridor.

As soon as he had gone I ripped a sheet of lined A4 from the notepad on my desk and began to write a letter. I'd got as far as 'Dear Carl' when I realised it would be better to do it on the computer. That way he would know I meant business.

Dear Carl [I typed]
There's no easy way to say this, so I'll just say it as quickly and simply as I can. I don't want to see you any more, at least not for the time being.

It isn't that I don't like you – I care about you a lot – but every time we sleep together I get so scared and I'm starting to feel really stressed because you're one of my students and I'm risking my job.

I know it seems like a lot to ask, but I would like to wait until you leave Beasley. I know it will be hard and it means waiting nearly a year – well, nine months or so – until next summer, but if you really love me I hope you'll agree to do this. Then, if we both still feel the same about each other, there will be nothing to stop us being together.

I'm really sorry to have to end our relationship temporarily, but please try not to be too upset. Nine months can pass very quickly and if we care about each other then I think it's worth waiting.

Please destroy this letter as soon as you've read it.
Love,
Belinda.

I put it in an envelope, sealed it carefully and wrote Carl's name on the front, congratulating myself on my masterly powers of deception.

# Chapter Eighteen

## Sinus of the Lambs

I arrived at the Princess Margaret hospital at 1.15 and parked in the Visitors' Car-Park. The reception area was plusher than the hospitals I was used to, reminding me of the foyer of the BBC building in London, through which I had passed to sit in on the recording of my three radio plays. Nurses were walking back and forth briskly, and I was pleased to see that they didn't look tired or overworked. There was a Kwik-Fit-fitter eagerness about them that I found encouraging.

The receptionist directed me to Tony's room and I went up three floors in a luxurious mirrored lift that actually spoke to me. Admittedly, its conversational powers were limited, phrases such as 'first floor' and 'second floor' being about the height of its linguistic prowess.

Tony's room was on the third floor. I didn't want to see him until I knew everything was all right because I had a feeling he would demand instant reassurance, so I sought out Sister Clary who, according to the literature the hospital had sent Tony a few days before the operation, was the person to whom all queries should be addressed. When I finally found her, I was pleased to see that she looked cheerful and capable.

'Hello, Mrs Lamb,' she said. She was a short, plump, middle-aged woman with iron-grey curly hair. 'Have you come to see Tony?' I revelled in the luxury of being able to wear my wedding ring and identify myself openly as

Tony's wife. Alistair didn't know any nurses or doctors so I figured I was safe.

'Yes, but I wanted to talk to you first,' I said. 'How did the operation go? Were there any problems?'

'None at all.' She smiled. 'He'll be right as rain and ready to leave tomorrow. He won't be able to go to work for a few days, though.'

'That's okay. He's a student,' I explained, thinking he might not be one for much longer. Whenever I asked about his Music for Performance AS level he told me it was shit and that he was expected to learn about notes.

'And he'll have to get his dressing changed every day for at least a week,' Sister Clary went on. 'The District Nurse will come round and do it. But there's nothing to worry about.' I thanked her and ran as fast as I could to Tony's room.

He was sitting up in bed reading *Salem's Lot* by Stephen King which, from its plastic cover, I assumed was a library book. I added possible library membership to my list of facts about Tony. Even in a hospital gown, his beauty made my head spin.

He giggled when he saw me. I walked over to the bed and kissed him gently. I didn't want to get into a passionate clinch in case he was still weak from the operation.

'I've just spoken to the sister,' I said. 'She said everything's fine. The operation was a success and you can go home tomorrow. How are you feeling?'

'Fine. Vinny came to see me before,' said Tony. 'He said the room was well posh.'

'It is,' I agreed, taking in the en-suite bathroom, large colour television and phone. 'It's almost as posh as our room at the Bracknell Hilton. Perhaps we should have come here on our wedding night.'

'I hate hospitals,' said Tony. 'I've spent fucking half my life in them.'

'Have you?'

He looked away, clearly not wishing to discuss it

further. I was, as always, aware of the limitations of Tony's conversation. Any impartial observer might have predicted that I would get bored of him pretty soon, but my sense that Tony would always be in some way remote from me, even now we were married and had had sex, the ultimate demystifying experience, would make my passion for him live longer. He was too unstable ever to be taken for granted. I would always yearn to solve the mysteries his mind contained and I would always fail.

'They're sending some nurse round to change the dressing,' he said, shuffling to get comfortable. 'I wish you could do it. I don't want some nurse fiddling with me.'

'Nurses are used to fiddling with people,' I said. 'It's just a job to them. You'll be fine.'

'Vinny said he'd pretend he'd had an operation as well and shag the nurse when she came round.' Tony laughed at the memory of his mate's witticisms, then his eyes clouded over suddenly. 'I've got to go to the police,' he said. 'I can't handle it any more. I keep . . . seeing it.'

I swallowed uncomfortably. 'Try to forget about it.' I stroked his forehead.

He turned away, shifting on to his side. 'I can't,' he said. 'I remember it all. The blood, the noises . . . his head . . . I'll never forget it.' I prayed he'd stop before I too was stuck with the same gruesome mental picture. I didn't understand how he could remember the awful events of that night so accurately and still laugh affectionately about Vinny, the perpetrator. I realised my own strategy had been to block it out completely. Knowledge, without first-hand sensual memory, isn't hard to bury. Perhaps shockingly, I found it easy to shut out anything that didn't relate directly to my love for Tony.

'Would you still love me if I went to prison?' he asked.

'Tony, you're not going to prison! You mustn't tell the police!'

'So you wouldn't,' he concluded.

'Of course I would.' I blinked back tears. 'Tony, I'll love

310

you whatever happens, you know that. But . . . there's no need to tell the police. Everything's fine as it is.'

After some persuasion I got him to agree, but his words lingered in my mind all afternoon and evening. What had Tony meant about Mark Ryder's head? I couldn't stop myself from wondering and imagining the possibilities.

I felt ill as I struggled to cook Alistair's tea. We were having chicken curry, courtesy of Patak's sauces, on which I had been relying heavily since my life descended into polygamous mayhem. Delia Smith is obviously faithful to her husband; those of us who have lots of men to juggle don't have time to mash spices to a pulp with a pestle and mortar.

'I need to talk to you later.' Alistair appeared at the kitchen door as I numbly stirred chicken flesh in a murky yellow sauce.

My heart skipped a beat and then I told myself I was being silly. There was no way he could know anything. 'What about?' I asked.

'Well . . .'

'Not Phil again?' Phil Douglas seemed to have replaced Bill Gates as Alistair's moaning target.

'Well, sort of.'

'Oh, God, Alistair. Does it have to be tonight? I'm knackered. I don't think I can take another Phil diatribe.'

Alistair looked vaguely disappointed and wandered back into the lounge. I wondered whether Phil could sense that Alistair was going off him rapidly. Hayley hadn't said anything, but then I hadn't said anything to her either.

When the food was ready I carried it through to the lounge and slumped down in front of the television. Alistair tucked into it enthusiastically, saying, 'Mm, this is delicious, thanks,' but I couldn't bring myself to eat more than a few mouthfuls. Every time I chewed a piece of chicken I thought of Mark Ryder and wanted to vomit.

# Chapter Nineteen

## Gripless

'Look at this,' Darryl burst into my office the next day, waving several sheets of paper. 'I don't fucking believe he's starting again, after everything that's happened. Just when I was beginning to relax.' His glasses steamed up within a few seconds of his entering the room and, in a flustered attempt to restore clear sight, he ended up dropping both his glasses and the papers he was carrying all over the floor.

'What's up?' I asked, picking up his glasses and placing them safely in his chubby hand.

'Seth! Look at this letter he's sent me.' Darryl passed it to me with the tips of his fingers as if it were hazardous nuclear waste.

I took the letter and began to read. Clearly Seth had ignored everything I said about keeping it short. There were eight sides of A4 here. I skim-read them quickly, groaning whenever I hit a particularly awful paragraph. Darryl circled the room angrily as I read, occasionally hitting the wall. I remembered Seth thumping the arm of my chair the day before and hoped he and Darryl would resolve their difficulties without further assaults on my office.

Seth had done everything I told him not to do, from openly declaring his undying love for Darryl on page one ('I know it would be foolish to hope that you could ever feel the same, but I beg you not to cut me out of your life altogether. Seeing you is what I live for.') to inserting random references to past family tragedies ('I don't know whether I've ever told you this, but my sister threw herself under a Piccadilly Line tube train when I was only three.'). On page seven, line twenty-three, he had written, 'I can't think of anything I want more than to be inside you', which I took as a blatant disregard for my advice.

I let the crumpled sheets of paper drop on to my desk. 'I don't know what to say,' I said. 'He said he was going to write to you but . . .'

'You knew about this?' Darryl yelled, his face creasing with outrage. 'Why didn't you warn me?'

'I had no idea he was going to do this! He told me he was just going to write you a short letter, apologising for what had happened. I told him not to . . . say all this.'

'I can't believe you didn't tell me.' Darryl stared at me in disgust. 'This is typical of you. Don't tell anyone anything that might upset them.'

'I didn't want to worry you,' I said. 'I thought you'd panic if you knew he was in love with you.'

'Too bloody right I'll panic. I'm taking this straight to my solicitor.' Darryl's face burned with anger.

'Hang on a minute,' I said. 'Just sit down and think about this rationally. What Seth did before, that was harassment. This is just a letter.'

'Just a letter! Just a letter!' he squealed, pushing his sliding glasses up the slope of his perspiring nose.

'Okay, it's a letter that's upset you,' I qualified, 'and I can completely understand why, but . . . well, from Seth's point of view, he's just trying to explain why he did what he did. If he loves you as much as he says he does, he has to try, doesn't he? At least once.'

'I don't fucking believe this.' Darryl looked around the room as if to gather support from non-existent spectators. 'You think I should have to put up with letters like this? I feel sick just thinking about it and you want me to . . .'

'No, of course I don't think you should put up with it. Darryl, just calm down. Sit down. Listen for a minute, okay? I know what it's like, remember, being someone's sexual fantasy when they repulse you. You have to write back to Seth and tell him that you forgive him, but that there's no way you're interested in . . . any kind of sexual relationship with him and you'd prefer it if he didn't send you any more letters. Say you're willing to let bygones be bygones, but in return he must keep his behaviour towards you on a purely professional basis.'

'I don't want to write to him.' Darryl threw up his hands in exasperation. 'Why should I have to? I don't want anything to do with him. And it wouldn't work anyway. You think he'd just go "Oh, okay" and leave me alone? Not Seth. He'll probably be sending me obscene letters till the day I die.'

'If he sends you another you can go to your solicitor. Then it would be harassment. But at the moment, well, it's just one love letter. I know it seems obscene to you, but that's because you don't fancy him. He hasn't actually done anything wrong. I mean, he's just telling you how he feels, which he's entitled to do. Now, if you tell him you're not interested and he carries on hounding you, that's something he's not entitled . . .'

'Why are you sticking up for him?' Darryl looked bereft. 'I thought you were on my side.'

'I am, Darryl,' I said honestly. 'It's just . . . it's because I now know he's in love with you. I feel sorry for him. I know how that feels.'

'Being in love doesn't give you the right to send people pervy letters.' Darryl stamped his foot on the carpet, shaking my bookshelf. 'Love doesn't justify everything. I suppose you think it does, don't you?'

'Yes,' I admitted.

'So what about what Carl's doing to you? Is that justified?'

'That's all over.' I dismissed Carl with a wave of my hand. 'I wrote him a letter. Seth knew all along. He doesn't care.'

'He doesn't care? He doesn't care?' Darryl hopped up

314

and down furiously. 'Well, he should care! He's the director of the school, for fuck's sake!'

'You want him to sack me?' I was offended.

'No! But . . . oh God.' His voice tailed off despondently.

'Nothing matters to him except you,' I explained.

'Oh God! Three months ago I didn't have a care in the world, and now I'm conspiring in fraudulent marriages and being pursued by a nymphomaniac!' He saw the look on my face and said, 'Well, not fraudulent, then. You know what I mean.' Darryl wandered aimlessly around my office, opening and closing his mouth occasionally without saying anything. I decided to let him get this new trauma out of his system and opened the top drawer of my desk. There was my wedding certificate. I stroked it fondly, warmed by its Conjugal GLOW.

'Oh my God.' Darryl's voice brought me out of the pink bubble in my head. He was standing beside my bookshelf, reading a spare copy of my letter to Carl which I had forgotten to throw away. Damn, I would have to get my act together. Little moments of carelessness like that could ruin everything.

'Belinda,' he said ominously. 'Please, please tell me you haven't sent this yet.'

'I sent it yesterday,' I said. 'Why, what's wrong with it?'

'I take it the plan is to let him wait around for a year and then ditch him, when he's no longer at Beasley?'

'Got it in one.' I grinned triumphantly.

'How can you be so . . . barbaric?' Darryl looked as if he could weep. 'This won't do you any good. He could still tell everyone he had an affair with you while he was a student.'

'I'll just have to make sure he doesn't,' I said. 'Meanwhile I've bought myself nine months to think about how to handle it. The imminent danger has been averted.'

'It's so cruel,' said Darryl. 'Making him wait for a year when you've got no intention of getting back together with him.'

'Darryl, what the fuck else am I supposed to do?'

'Well you should have . . .'

'Thought of that before? Is that what you were going to say? I can predict a lot of things, but I can't be expected to anticipate a total personality change, from cool, hard lad to sensitive love poet. Listen, Darryl . . .' I looked at my watch, bored by the subject of Carl Sillery past and present. 'I have to go and pick Tony up and take him home from the hospital.'

'Can I come with you?'

'Yeah. I'm surprised you want to. Oh, I get it – you're scared of bumping into Seth,' I translated.

'I'm not scared,' said Darryl indignantly. 'I just don't want to see him and I'm aware that lunch-time is dangerously close, a whole hour and a half in which he'll have nothing to do but hunt me down.'

'Come on then.' I grabbed my jacket.

We went outside, with Darryl using me as a sort of human shield, clinging with both hands to the back of my blouse and positioning me between him and possible Seth-attack until we had safely reached my Nova.

As we drove down the school's long gravel driveway we passed a wide turquoise Mercedes on its way in and I had to drive half on the grass to pass it comfortably.

'Belinda,' said Darryl tentatively when we got on to the main road.

'Mm?'

'What do Carl Sillery's parents look like?'

'Why?'

'I just wondered.'

'His mum looks a bit like him and his dad's got a red, bloated face. Why?' I demanded, beginning to feel uneasy.

'Thought so. They were in that car we passed on the way out.'

'So?' I challenged Darryl to put my fear into words.

'So . . . I wonder why they were going to the school in the middle of the day. Don't they work?'

'I don't know.'

'You don't think . . . ?'

'No, I don't think,' I agreed, speeding towards the hospital.

# Chapter Twenty

## Parental Guidance

'I'm sorry, Belinda. I don't see that I have any alternative.'
The increasingly grey-haired Seth avoided my accusing
stare. 'I'm not firing you. I'm just asking you . . . begging
you . . . to help me out of a tricky situation by resigning.'

It was Monday 20 October and Seth's office looked as
appalling as he did. In addition to the usual carnage of unfortunate students' desecrated manuscripts and penicillin-
breeding coffee mugs, there was a large jagged hole in one
of the cupboard doors and the coffee table that had once
been in the middle of the room was now resting in pieces
against the wall. John and Hilary Sillery had paid a visit.

Luckily I hadn't been on the premises at the time. I was
at the Princess Margaret hospital, which no doubt was
where both Sillery parents have would put me, given half a
chance.

'And if I refuse to resign?' I said angrily. 'You'll sack me,
right?'

'What else can I do? Look, it took me nearly two hours
to calm Carl's parents down. You're lucky I got them to
agree to this much. At first they were threatening to go to
the papers. The school would have been ruined. I can't let
that happen.' Seth's expression implored me to make this
easier for him.

'So instead it's just my career that gets ruined?' I said
stonily.

'I'll give you a glowing reference, Belinda. You'll have

no problem getting a job teaching Creative Writing some-where else.'

'I don't want to work somewhere else!' I snapped, sounding spoiled because I was. Someone who can get Tony Lamb naturally expects all other things to go her way. 'I want to work here.'

'Well, you should have thought of that before you started seeing Carl.'

'Oh, and I suppose you never make a mistake?' I couldn't believe this was happening to me. I wanted to shout and scream at the injustice of it all.

'Yes, I do,' he said lugubriously. 'But at least I know when I'm beaten. I'm going to have to accept the fact that I can't have Darryl. Have you seen the letter he sent me?' Seth pushed a discouragingly stained piece of paper across the desk at me.

I flicked it straight back to him. 'I'm not in the mood,' I said.

'Look, I think you've got off lightly.' He sighed. 'The Sillerys aren't going to go to the papers, they aren't even demanding that I sack you. All they want is to get you away from Carl. You can resign, make up some other reason why you're leaving. No one needs to know the truth. Alistair doesn't need to find out.'

'How come the Sillerys are willing to give me an easy way out? Aren't they after my blood?'

'They were when they first arrived,' said Seth. 'Well, you should be able to see that from the state of the office. But I managed to talk some sense into them. I told them any publicity would be as harmful to Carl as it would be to you and the school. I persuaded them it'd be in all our best interests to hush it up.'

'I suppose that's something, then. All I need is Alistair finding out. But . . . I'll have to tell people why I'm leaving. What will I say? Everyone knows I love this job.' Saying that made me realise how true it was. I dug my fingernails into my palm to stop myself from crying. 'I just can't

319

believe this is happening to me. Why me? Oh, don't answer that. I know why.'

'At least you've got Tony,' said Seth. 'I've got nothing.' He stroked Darryl's letter lovingly for a few seconds, then ripped it up viciously, spit flying from the corners of his mouth.

I turned to leave, unable to muster the energy to console Seth. I felt so sorry for myself that I had no sympathy left for anyone else. The sound of his substantial head thudding against some item of furniture followed me along the corridor.

I went back to my office, where I sat at my desk and sobbed quietly for half an hour. I tried to convert my pain into rage, to get angry with myself for setting off the chain of events that had led to this tragedy, which was what I felt it was, but no matter how hard I tried, I felt like the victim rather than the perpetrator. Ever since this whole thing started, since I first laid eyes on Tony, I had been swept along on a current of obsessive passion. There was no element of rational choice in any of my actions, I now realised. I had been taken over by a devastating force that was slowly ruining me.

I turned on my computer. Writing my letter of resignation would be the hardest thing I had ever had to do. I tried to activate my defence mechanisms. If my life were a Tom Cruise film, I told myself, this bit wouldn't be a tragic ending; it would just be the set-back.

Darryl popped his head round the door. 'Well?' he asked. I'd phoned him over the weekend to tell him Seth had requested a meeting with me this afternoon, assuming Darryl would be the subject. How I wished he had been!

'Not exactly,' I said, and told him how the Sillery artillery was gunning for me. 'It seems Carl is more intelligent than I thought. He saw through that letter. He knew he was being dumped.'

'I can't believe he told his parents.' Darryl was aghast. 'He's a seventeen-year-old boy. When I was seventeen, I

320

never told my parents anything, especially not stuff like that. What are you going to do?' His horrified tone made me feel worse. How was I supposed to pretend things weren't so bad if Darryl looked at me like that?

'Nothing I can do. Resign. Look for another job.'

'This is all my fault,' Darryl groaned. 'I should have tried harder to stop you.'

'When do I ever listen, Darryl? Never. There was nothing you could have done. Look, I have to write my letter of resignation.'

'When will you . . . actually leave?' he asked.

'I have to give a month's notice. I wish I could leave straight away. I don't want to have to see Carl again. Seth's taken him out of all my classes, but I'm bound to see him around.'

'I could kill the bastard.' Darryl clenched his fists as rage took over from shock.

'Why?'

'Why? Because of what he's done. Blackmail, telling his parents – what right has he got to do all that, on the basis of . . . a few meaningless shags?'

'They weren't meaningless to him,' I said. 'None of this is his fault, Darryl. It's all my fault. He's only done everything he's done because he loves me and he's miserable.'

'But . . . I mean, will you be all right?'

'Of course I will,' I said with a lot more confidence than I felt. 'Tony is all I really need. And, who knows, I might get an even better job. Seth says he'll give me a brilliant reference and I won't have to work with the Bu . . . with Carmel-Marie any more.'

'What? What were you going to call her?'

'Oh. Nothing.' I turned away. From the moment Carmel-Marie admitted to her crime, I had changed her nickname from Celia Johnson to the Butcher of Windsor.

'Ah,' said Darryl, thinking he'd guessed. 'You thought she and Tony were having an affair. Were they?'

'No.' I fidgeted uneasily in my chair.

321

'Did you ever ask him why he was sneaking out of her office that day?'

'Darryl . . . just drop it, okay?'

'What's going on, Belinda? Is it this thing you haven't told me?'

'Yes.'

'Are you ever going to tell me what it is?'

'I doubt it. You're practically the only friend I've got. I don't want to make you hate me.'

.'Hate you?' Darryl looked alarmed. 'I thought it was something about Tony. Why would I hate you? Is it something you've done?'

'It's something I haven't done, I suppose,' I said cryptically. Any normal person would despise me for not insisting Tony went to the police.

'Oh, this makes no sense to me, none whatsoever.' Darryl sighed.

'Good,' I said, starting to type my letter of resignation.

'Look, do you want to go for a quick drink?' he suggested. 'It might cheer you up.'

'I'm supposed to be going round to Tony's in a bit,' I said defensively.

'This seems to be turning into a daily routine,' said Darryl. 'Tony's after work for a couple of hours, then back to Alistair . . .'

'Darryl, the last thing I need now is another lecture.' I slammed my mouse down on the desk. 'If you were about to ask me what I'm going to do long-term, I have no idea. My definition of long-term is getting shorter and shorter. I can't even think as far as this evening.'

'Okay, I'm sorry.' Darryl backed off, too polite to criticise me when I'd just been sacked. 'Come on, let's go for a drink. Ring Tony and tell him you'll be a bit late. You'll feel better once you're out of here.' I looked around at my lovely office, imagining how painful it would be to leave it for the last time. Choking on the lump in my throat, I dialled Tony's number.

'Yep?' Vinny answered the phone with his customary nasal efficiency. I wondered whether he had ever considered a career advertising Tunes.

'Vinny, it's Belinda. Can I speak to Tony?'

'Nah. He's gone out.'

'Gone out? Where? I'm supposed to be coming round.'

'Well, he's gone out. Some bloke phoned and he's gone to meet him.'

'But he should be resting!' I wailed. 'What was the bloke's name?'

'Dunno. Tony said he was from that play you all did.'

'Was it Carl?' I felt bile rise in my throat.

'Oh, Jesus.' Darryl sat down heavily in a chair.

'Yeah, that was it,' said Vinny.

'What did he say?' I demanded. 'This is really important, Vinny. Did Tony say where they were meeting?'

'In Ledgrove Park,' said Vinny. 'Don't know where, though.'

'Thanks.' I slammed the phone down. 'Darryl, we've got to . . .'

'. . . go and find Tony.' Darryl was already getting up. 'Before Carl kills him.'

'Or before he kills Carl,' I said as we ran across the carpark.

'Does Tony know anything about Carl? Does Carl know you and Tony are married?' Darryl shouted as he leaped behind the wheel of his car and started the engine.

'No, of course not. But they'll both know everything pretty soon, unless we can get there before too much damage has been done. I can't believe Carl phoned Tony. He doesn't even know I'm still seeing Tony, not for sure anyway.' I felt a cold, swelling horror take possession of my body.

'He's probably just desperate to blame someone,' said Darryl, wiping sweat from his forehead with one hand and steering with the other. 'Jesus, how come you look so calm?'

'I think,' I said slowly, 'because I'm on the verge of total calamity. If anything happens to Tony . . . well, I might as well die. I feel as if I'm dead already. I wonder if my heart's still beating.'

'Well, mine sure as fuck is!' said Darryl, clutching his side as if to prove it.

# Chapter Twenty-One

## The Park

Ledgrove Park is where people in Slough go when they want to see trees. We pulled into a lay-by near the main entrance on Ledgrove Road and jumped out of the car. Darryl had got us there in twenty minutes. I was amazed we hadn't been stopped for speeding. We ran around the park like maniacs, Darryl's short legs struggling to keep up with my longer ones. Mothers and toddlers stared after us with interest as we sprinted between the swings and slide, the quickest route to the next field. Darryl nearly knocked over a hotdog stand by the side of the bowling green. The whole scene was like a grotesque parody of an episode of *Cagney and Lacey*.

I saw two figures by the duck pond as we raced towards it. One of them was wearing a checked shirt. I heard raised voices. 'That's them.' I gasped for breath. 'That's Carl's voice shouting.'

It seemed like hours before we reached them although it couldn't have been more than a few seconds. Tony didn't register our arrival. He was mumbling incoherently and shaking violently, and Carl was walking round him in tight circles, crying and clenching his teeth. There were a couple of bystanders loitering at a safe distance, but I barely noticed them.

'Tony!' I tried to hug him, but he wouldn't keep still. 'Tony, are you okay?'

'Growarowa. Grinerowa.' That's the closest I can get to

describing what he was saying.

'You bitch!' Carl yelled at me, snot streaming down his face. 'You're still seeing him, aren't you? That's why you finished with me.'

'Shut up, you little turd,' I growled. 'What's wrong with Tony? What have you done to him?' I struggled desperately to glean what had happened so far. Had they hit each other or, even worse, exchanged damaging pieces of information?

'Let's all calm down.' Darryl bobbed up and down, purple in the face. He looked like the leading grape in the Ribena advert. 'Let's try and talk about this like civilised human beings. Look, no harm's done. Everyone's okay.'

'Tony, you've got blood all over your shirt,' I cried, trying to grab hold of him. 'We've got to get you to a hospital.'

'Love is God and love is free,' Tony chanted vacantly. 'True love never dies. Love means immortality. Sleeping Lions rise.'

'Stop it,' I cried.

'Grownaryer,' he grunted. 'Mark Ryder. Mark Ryder.'

'Is he saying Mark Ryder?' Darryl asked me.

'No.' I put my hand over Tony's mouth but he struggled free.

'He's been saying that since he got here.' Carl waved his arms in front of Darryl's face, trying to re-establish himself as the centre of the drama. 'He says he killed Mark Ryder.' A couple of riveted bystanders took a step back.

'Darryl, take Tony and wait with him in your car,' I said firmly. 'Get him to lie flat on the back seat. He's bleeding.'

'But what about . . . ?'

'Never mind me and Carl. Just get Tony out of here. I want him safe.'

Darryl grasped the elusive, mumbling Tony and proceeded to lead him away, looking back at me anxiously every few seconds to check I wasn't being stabbed by Carl. I could hear Tony burbling faintly as Darryl propelled him along: 'There's no authority she'll recognise. No individual, no church or court, Whose will trumps hers, whose petty rule applies . . .'

'What did you do to him?' I yelled at Carl. 'You've got to tell me.' I was terrified that Tony would never recover, never make sense again.

'I don't have to do anything for you!' Carl's face convulsed greenly. 'You don't give a shit about me and you never have. Tony reckons you're still seeing him. He says he loves you and you love him.' Thank God, I thought. At least he knows that. 'I started hitting him,' said Carl proudly, strutting aggressively in my direction. 'Then he started mumbling, saying he killed Mark Ryder. Is it true?'

'No, of course it isn't. He's ill, Carl. He suffers from schizophrenia. You hitting him must have . . . made him have some kind of fit.'

'Good!' Carl wept snottily. 'I hate him. I hate you.'

'Well, I hate you too,' I said venomously, finally able to express my true feelings. 'I've lost my job because of you!'

'I'm sorry.' He sank to his knees, grabbing me round the shins. 'I'm sorry for everything. Just give me another chance. If you knew how much I love you . . .'

'Fuck off.' I struggled to get away. 'I don't love you, all right? I never have and I never will.'

I bent down to assess the mucus damage to my trouser legs and my face met Carl's clenched fist that was travelling upwards. He punched me hard, knocking me over. I heard my head thud against the fence as I fell to the ground.

# Chapter Twenty-Two

## Damage Limitation

'Ow,' I said, opening my eyes. 'Where am I?' My hair felt wet and my eyelids were heavy.

'In my car,' came Darryl's glum reply. 'On Ledgrove Road.'

I looked out of the window, running my hand over the large lump on my head. It felt as big as a grapefruit. The right-hand side of my face was throbbing painfully. I tried to sit up straight, but Darryl put a hand on my shoulder.

'Keep still. How do you feel? Have you got any . . . concussion?' He tried to sound suitably medical. It was dark outside. My head was pounding and my neck felt stiff.

'I'm fine,' I said. 'Where's Tony? What time is it?'

'Tony's asleep on the back seat.'

'But he's bleeding! He needs to get to a hospital.' My words sounded slurred and too slow.

'He's okay,' said Darryl. 'I had a look at his . . . sinus thing. It's not too serious, just the usual post-op weeping. Our Lee had a lot of that. I've taken off his dressing and put a new one on.'

'What . . . where did you get a dressing from?'

'I improvised with some tissues,' said Darryl. 'It's not ideal, but he'll be fine until the nurse next sees him.'

'Tony let you do that?' I was amazed. Sometimes he wouldn't even let me touch him and I was his wife.

'He was completely out of it. He was . . . going on in a mad way. I don't think he knew what was happening.'

'Did you try to talk to him?'

'Talk to him? He was incoherent, Belinda. You saw what he was like. I just listened to him until he stopped and fell asleep. Then I came to look for you and found you conked out with your head in the pond and Carl sitting next to you, crying.'

'Oh God. Where's Carl now?' I jerked my head up, setting off another round of agonising throbs. 'Aagh!' I moaned.

'Gone home. I don't think you'll be hearing from him again. I pointed out to him that he'd committed two serious assaults and asked him to give me one good reason why I shouldn't go to the police.'

'Nice one.' I sank back in my seat with relief. 'Poor Carl.'

'Don't,' said Darryl miserably. 'I've never felt so low in my life. I even told him how ashamed his parents would be if he got a criminal record.'

'What time is it? Alistair . . .'

'Don't worry. After Carl went home I phoned Alistair on my mobile. I told him there was some trouble at school and you'd be late back. Then I carried you back to the car, since when I've just been sitting here,' he said resentfully, 'waiting for you to come round.'

'Thanks,' I murmured.

'Tony killed Mark Ryder, didn't he?' said Darryl quietly. 'Don't deny it. That's it, isn't it, what you wouldn't tell me?'

'He didn't lay a finger on him,' I said. 'He was involved, yes, but . . . he didn't do it.'

'What does involved mean?'

I gave Darryl a brief synopsis of the story and he listened in silence, shaking his head in disbelief and disgust at the whole thing. 'You won't say anything, will you?' I pleaded.

'I don't know.' He shivered. 'I might. Tony asked me to take him to the police station, you know. He kept mumbling about having to tell someone. Sounds to me like he wants to confess.'

'But you didn't take him. Why not?'

'I couldn't just go off and leave you, could I? To be honest, I don't know what the fuck I'm doing. I can't think straight.'

He could think a lot straighter than I could. He'd even remembered to phone Alistair.

'What did Alistair say?' I asked.

'Not a lot. Belinda, this has got to stop. You're losing it. I'm losing it. This is murder we're talking about. Carmel-Marie . . . I can't believe it, it's so foul! Things can't just . . . carry on as normal now, you know. Something's going to have to be done about this. I'm not blaming Tony, I mean, he's quite clearly mad, but . . . I suppose you've tried to talk him out of going to the police?'

'Of course I have.'

Darryl turned on me aggressively. 'You're so fucking selfish, I can't believe it. All you can think about is what you need, what you want. What about him?'

'Oh, you think prison would do him the power of good, do you?' I closed my eyes, wishing everything would disappear, everything except me and Tony.

'I think if he wants to tell the truth you've got no right to stop him. Mark Ryder's dead. There are people out there who killed him, walking around free. Doesn't that bother you? Vinny! You made me spend an afternoon with a murderer!' Darryl sounded angrier than I had ever heard him, even on the subject of Seth.

'Of course it bothers me,' I said, feeling deeply misunderstood, 'but not as much as losing Tony would bother me.'

'If you make him keep this bottled up for ever he really will go mad, properly mad,' Darryl whispered fiercely. 'He needs to tell the truth, Belinda, or it's going to ruin his life. Can't you see that?'

'No. The truth is what ruins people's lives, more often than not.'

'Ah, what crap! Look, he'd be bound to get off lightly.

330

He's clearly not fully . . . in control of his actions.'

'I'm not risking it.'

'It's not up to you,' said Darryl coldly. 'You don't own Tony. He's a person in his own right as well as being your . . .'

'Husband is the word you want.'

'He wants to do the right thing. Don't stop him. How can you do that?'

'Are you going to go to the police?' I asked coldly.

'Is that all you're worried about?'

'No, it's not *all* I'm worried about. There are about a billion other things . . .'

'No, I'm not going to go to the police,' Darryl interrupted. 'But if you don't, if you stop Tony . . . Belinda, I'm not sure . . . how things are going to be between us. In the future.'

'Fine,' I said. 'Can you give me and Tony a lift home, please?'

We drove to Sandlea Court in silence. When we arrived I pulled my aching body out of the car and went to open the rear door. Tony was still sleeping soundly on the back seat. I was glad he'd missed my horrible row with Darryl. I tapped him gently on the shoulder, shaking him slightly harder when he didn't wake up straight away.

'Tony. We're here.' His glazed eyes opened gradually. 'Come on, you're home. Are you okay? How do you feel?'

'Leave me alone,' he said. 'Stop fucking with my head. Everybody always fucks with my head.'

'What?' I started to cry. 'I'm not. What are you talking about?'

'This!' he said, with a look in his eyes that I'd never seen before. 'I didn't ask for any of this. I warned you to keep away from me. You're all the same! You're just like my stupid slut of a mother and my bastard stepfather and my stupid whore sisters! Everyone always tries to fuck with my head.' Sisters? Tony had sisters? This was the first I'd heard of it. I was crying with frustration.

'Marvellous.' Darryl got out of the car and leaned against it.

'Darryl, why's he saying these awful things?' I wept. 'Why's he attacking me? He's never been like this before.'

'Because he's mad, Belinda.' Darryl sighed quietly. 'He's mad, okay? Look no further for an explanation.'

'Tony, I'm not trying to fuck with your head,' I said patiently, stroking his hair. 'I'd never do anything to hurt you. Me and Darryl are looking after you. Darryl's put on a new dressing for you.' Tony shoved me away violently. I tried not to take it personally but failed. I couldn't bear this. It was as if he didn't recognise me.

'I don't want to go there.' He pointed at the hostel. 'I don't like it there. I'm not going.'

'But Tony, it's where you live.'

'No!' he screamed. 'I'm not going there.'

'Okay, okay.' I addressed the portion of Darryl's back that was pressed against the car window. 'You'll have to take him back to yours,' I said.

'No, I won't. I want out of this fucking mess,' said Darryl. 'I don't want anything to do with you or him.'

'Darryl, please!' I begged. 'I can hardly take him back to mine, can I?'

'That is just not my problem,' said Darryl. 'He is not coming back to mine, do I make myself clear? No way.'

'Let him sleep in your car, then.'

'Oh, Christ. This is a nightmare. Please, somebody, tell me this isn't happening.'

'Just for one night, Darryl. I'll come and get him first thing tomorrow. I'll sort everything out, I promise. Just one night is all I'm asking.'

'Fine,' Darryl snarled. 'Just make sure you show up tomorrow and take him away. And this is the last . . . the very last . . . thing I'm doing for you, ever.'

'That's not very nice.' My voice trembled. 'I'm worried about Tony. I don't need you being horrible to me, okay? You heard him before. What if he never goes back to normal? What if he's had some sort of breakdown?'

'Just get in the car,' said Darryl more gently. 'I'll take you home. If I were you I'd tell Alistair the truth. The complete, unabridged truth.'

'You're not me,' I said.

# Chapter Twenty-Three

## The Douglases and the Downfall

'Where have you been?' Alistair shouted as soon as I got through the door, following me down the hall. 'What's going on at the Beasley madhouse? Why does your hair smell?' He sniffed as if to prove his point. Anger was Alistair's way of expressing concern.

'I've resigned,' I said. 'I'm leaving.'

'Well, good, if this is the sort of state you come back in. It's nearly midnight. Where've you been? What's been going on?'

'Alistair, we've got to talk.'

'You're telling me. I've been waiting all evening to talk to you.'

'Why? What is it?'

'Phil,' he said.

'Oh, Alistair . . .' I rubbed my aching head.

'No, listen. It's important. It involves Hayley as well. I've got to tell you. I've been trying to for days but you've seemed so preoccupied. In the end I just decided to . . . make a unilateral decision. It is my house,' he added defensively.

'What? What unilateral decision?' I sat down numbly on the sofa. All I wanted was to crawl into bed and forget that I existed. I wanted it to be tomorrow so that I could rush round to Darryl's and make Tony become his old self again.

'I've had to increase Phil and Hayley's rent. Substantially.'

'What? Don't be ridiculous. We can't make them pay any more.'

'We have to. Especially if you're leaving Beasley.'

'I can get another job.' I yawned.

'Belinda, please listen to me.' Alistair looked worried. 'We've got no money. We're in debt up to our necks.'

'But . . . how can we be? We earn enough.'

'We spend too much. We have been for ages. I could get five hundred pounds a month for that house at least, now Phil's done it up. We can't afford to let them live there for two hundred and fifty pounds for ever. That was a reduced rate, even when they first moved in, if you remember. It was supposed to go up once Phil had finished decorating.'

'Yes, but it never did, did it? We can hardly put it up now, out of the blue.' I did my best to look interested but my mind was elsewhere. I wondered how soon I would be able to make an excuse and go and ring Darryl, check if Tony was okay.

'Why not?' asked Alistair. 'They've been lucky to get it so cheap all these years.'

'They're skint,' I said.

'So are we. Anyway, there's no use arguing. It's done now.'

'What do you mean, "it's done"?'

'I mean, it's done. I phoned Phil before.'

'What?' I leaped out of my chair, feeling dizzy and weightless. 'You didn't? Please, say you didn't!' I had assumed this was all still at the hypothetical stage.

'I did. Why are you so bothered?'

'What did they say?' I leaned over Alistair threateningly.

'They weren't in. I left a message on their answerphone. God, calm down. I've never seen you like this before.'

'What did you say? In your message?'

'That we were going to have to put the rent up. To four hundred pounds a month.'

'Oh my God! Oh my God!' I turned away from him and banged my head slowly against the wall, hoping to be rescued from this disaster by a brain haemorrhage.

'Belinda, what's wrong? Stop acting like a mad person. I think that's a reasonable . . .'

'Did you say "I" or "we"?'

'What?' Alistair looked confused.

'In your message?' I spun round to face him. 'Did you say "I" or "we"? Did you make it sound as though it was both of us who'd decided this?'

'Well, yes. I didn't think you'd object this strongly. I said "we". Why are you so keen to dissociate yourself from me all of a sudden?'

'You must phone them back straight away, leave another message saying you didn't mean it, it was a joke. That's it, say it was a joke.' I grabbed his shirt-sleeves and tugged pathetically.

'No chance.' He pushed me away. 'Why should I?'

'Just do it!' I yelled.

'What's got into you? I'm not being ordered about by you or by anyone. It's my house, not yours.'

'I'm going to phone them, then,' I said, running into the hall. 'I'll say we've changed our minds.'

Alistair pulled me back. 'Don't bloody dare to phone them. It's not up to you. Is four hundred pounds a month so unreasonable?'

'Oh, God,' I muttered, trying to calm down and think logically, but failing miserably. What could I say to Alistair? It was his house. If he was determined to put up the rent, how could I stop him? 'It's Hayley,' I said. 'I don't want to fall out with her, Alistair, I really don't.'

'She won't fall out with you, will she? I'm sure she'll understand.'

'Well, I'm not! I'm not sure at all!' I couldn't believe his naïve attitude. 'I think it's highly unlikely. She's got money worries as it is. This is going to make them a thousand times worse and who do you think she's going to blame, hey?'

'I've never seen you in such a rage before.' Alistair held

both my arms firmly. 'Stop it. You are not phoning them. If Hayley doesn't understand that's her problem. She can't be that good a mate if she'd let something like this come between you.'

'Alistair, please. Please. Look, I'll get another job. I'll cut down on my spending. I'll get two jobs. There's another way, I know there is, we just need to think about it.'

'Look, forget it, okay? Forget it. You always get your way about everything. I'm not giving in this time. It's my house and my decision. Maybe we could economise, but why should we have to when that Douglas bastard's taking the piss, living in my house for next to nothing?'

'Oh, so it's not about money at all!' I said triumphantly, thinking that if I could get Alistair on to shakier ground he might back down. 'It's about your petty squabbles with Phil in the office.'

'No, it isn't,' said Alistair. 'I just don't see why I should be a mug.'

'It's not Hayley's fault you don't like Phil. She can't be blamed for what he does. What's Hayley ever done to you?'

'Nothing.' Alistair gritted his teeth. 'Which is why I'm letting her live in my house – *my* house – for the reasonable rent of four hundred pounds a month!'

'Look, okay.' I tried to free my arms from Alistair's grasp, which was beginning to hurt. 'Whatever you say, but let me phone Hayley just to . . . you know, check that there are no hard feelings.'

'What? So you're giving in?'

'Yes, yes, just let me ring her, please,' I squawked hysterically.

'You won't say it was a joke?' Alistair's eyes narrowed suspiciously.

'What would be the point?' I sighed. 'You could just ring them back and say it wasn't a joke. As you say, it's your house.' Reluctantly Alistair let go of my arms and I went to the phone. All I needed to do, I thought, was somehow

337

signal to Hayley that the decision about the rent had been nothing to do with me before she decided to tell Phil about my undercover marriage.

I dialled the Douglases' number. Alistair stood two inches behind me, poised to bundle me off into the lounge if I said the wrong thing. There was no answer. I let the phone ring and ring.

'They're not answering. The machine's not even on,' I said angrily to Alistair, although I knew none of this was his fault. 'What time did you phone them?'

'I don't know. Half an hour ago.' There was a sudden loud banging on the front door.

'It's them,' I shouted over the thumping, feeling the dragging weight of inevitability.

'How do you know?' Alistair looked puzzled. 'Why would they come round at this time of night? Jesus, are they trying to break the door down?'

It was nice to be right for a change. It was indeed the Douglases. This must have been how W B Yeats felt when he wrote 'Things fall apart, the centre cannot hold'. He must have had the equivalent of Phil Douglas banging on his door in the middle of the night, just about to ruin his life.

'Belinda, I'm sorry, I'm really sorry, I tried to stop him.' Hayley sobbed as Alistair reluctantly opened the door. Phil fell in, landing in a heap on the carpet and springing up again immediately like a hideous Jack-in-the-Box. Hayley's hair was wet, although it wasn't raining. She was wearing a yellow pyjama top with blue elephants on it and grey jogging pants.

'Did you know she's married to someone else?' Phil asked Alistair. 'Serves you right, that's what I say. You two deserve each other. Tight bastards! After I did the whole house up as well!'

'Married . . . what are you talking about?' For a moment Alistair looked like a confused little boy who had woken in the middle of a disturbing dream.

338

'She's married.' Phil pointed to me without looking at me.

'Oh, God, Belinda, I'm really sorry, I didn't mean to tell him, it just came out,' Hayley spluttered, shivering and hugging herself on the doorstep.

'Belinda, what are they talking about?' Alistair asked me.

'I'll tell you later,' I said. 'Let's just . . . get rid of them first.'

'No, tell him now,' said Phil. 'I want to hear you tell him the truth.'

'Fuck off, you pathetic waste of skin,' I spat in Phil's face. 'Why don't you concentrate on your own marriage instead of other people's? I suppose you know Hayley's bored stiff of you.'

'Oh no, Belinda, please,' Hayley squealed pitifully. 'Don't do this.'

'You started it!'

'You started it by putting our rent up!' She wept, doing her best ever victim act. Somehow she managed to give the impression that she might be irretrievably damaged unless I backed down immediately. 'You knew we couldn't afford that much. You're trying to kick us out!'

'I didn't know anything about it until Alistair told me he'd left a message on your machine. It was nothing to do with me, Hayley! As if I'd do that without warning you.'

'Well, how was I supposed to know that?'

'What the fuck is going on?' Alistair shouted suddenly, as if the full horror of the crisis on his doorstep was only just beginning to sink in.

I could hear windows opening nearby. Good, I thought. My life might have been facing imminent disintegration, but at least I was providing some vicarious entertainment for my neighbours with my valiant and tireless attempt to lead three lives while most people skive off from leading even their paltry allotted one.

'Some people are trying to sleep,' our next door neighbour Mrs Cutler yelled unimaginatively.

'Bore me later,' I yelled back.

'I can't afford four hundred quid a month,' Phil barked, jabbing a finger angrily into Alistair's chest. 'I'm not paying that, no way.'

'Fine.' Alistair wrinkled his nose the way he did when he smelled cheap wine. 'Go and live somewhere else, then.'

'There's laws against this. You can't do this.'

'Look, this is ridiculous. You were only supposed to be getting the cheap rate while you did the house up,' said Alistair. 'You should be grateful I've not put the rent up before.'

'This isn't putting the rent up,' Phil spluttered. 'It's putting it up a hundred and fifty quid a month. Where are we going to find that kind of money?'

'Look, you're not the only one with financial problems.' Alistair glowered at him.

'Why don't we go inside?' Hayley suggested. 'Talk about this quietly.'

'What's there to talk about?' I stared at her coldly.

'You fucking cow,' Phil yelled. 'You . . . you bigamous!'

'I think you'll find the word is "bigam*ist*",' I smirked. 'And I'm not one.'

'Belinda isn't married,' said Alistair. 'Don't be ridiculous.'

'Yes, I am,' I said. 'But don't worry, it isn't what you think. I can explain.' I said this matter-of-factly. I almost believed it. Trainee liars take heed: act as though everything is perfectly straightforward and natural, and you will have a better chance of convincing others. If people see you panicking they panic.

Alistair looked at me oddly. 'Get out,' he said to Phil and Hayley. 'Go home.'

'I'm seeing a lawyer about this.' Phil wagged his finger at the closing door. 'You can't do this, I'll show you!'

'What a pair of revolting specimens,' said Alistair, once they'd gone. 'What the fuck did you mean, you're married?'

340

'Come and sit down,' I said, 'and I'll explain. There's one condition, though. You've got to promise not to get annoyed.'

'What the fuck . . . is this some sort of joke? Not get annoyed! Not get fucking annoyed, when you're sitting there telling me you're married?' Alistair's cheeks flushed bright pink.

Sounds very bad at this point, doesn't it? But what I know about Alistair that you don't is that, despite his incendiary temper, he hasn't got much stamina. If someone does me a serious wrong, I'm capable of holding a grudge for years, but Alistair can be angry one minute and perfectly cheerful the next. Ten minutes after we've had a row, he'll have forgotten what it was about. I only hoped his anger would follow its usual curve on this occasion.

'Alistair, this is a very long story,' I said. 'I can't tell you unless you calm down. Please sit down and listen to me.'

He perched uneasily on the edge of a chair. 'Well?' he said.

'I'm married. But it's only a marriage of convenience. Wait! Don't say anything. Let me finish. Let me explain and then you can say whatever you want. It's a bloke called Tony. He was one of the sound engineers for *Lions*. He . . . he was really ill. Have you heard of a pilonidal sinus?'

'No.' Alistair looked as if he didn't want to either.

'Well, that was what he had. Usually they're quite harmless, but this was a particularly bad one. He needed an operation urgently or else he might have been paralysed for life,' I exaggerated considerably. 'He couldn't get a hospital bed, though, and he might have had to wait for up to a year. So I married him so that he could be covered by my BUPA insurance.'

'What BUPA insurance? You decided not to do that.' The distraught expression on Alistair's face spurred me on to invent new and better lies. I had to make him happy again and soon. I couldn't bear to have misery in my house.

341

'I did it, Alistair, I just didn't tell you. I knew you'd go mad and start lecturing me about . . . left-wingness. That's why I couldn't tell you about Tony and our marriage of convenience, because I would have had to admit that I hadn't told you about BUPA and . . . well, you know how it is. You tell one lie and it leads to another.'

'I can't believe this.' Alistair shook his head slowly. 'My girlfriend is married to a guy called Tony who I've never even met. Did he pay you or what?'

'No. I did it to help him, no other reason. I don't know, maybe I felt a bit guilty about the whole BUPA thing. Carmel-Marie had been going on at me about selfishness and queue-jumping, so when Tony got ill I thought here's my chance to help someone else, not just myself. He might have been paralysed.'

'Most people pay through the nose for a marriage of convenience and this Tony just gets one for free!' Alistair enunciated each syllable to emphasise the injustice. He was very financially minded all of a sudden.

'Don't be so materialistic,' I said. 'Tony hasn't got any money. If he had, he could have paid for his own BUPA cover.'

'How could you do something like that and not tell me?'

'What would you have said if I'd told you? Would you have let me do it?'

'Of course I bloody wouldn't!' Alistair roared.

'Well, then. That's why I didn't tell you. Tony might be paralysed now, if I'd told you.'

'Stuff Tony! People get ill all the time. Doesn't mean my girlfriend has to fucking marry them behind my back. This guy's a stranger.' He got up and punched the wall viciously. A framed Magritte poster fell to the floor, its glass clip-frame shattering. Neither of us made any move to clear up the mess.

'Is it so wrong to want to help a stranger?' I said.

'Don't twist things . . .'

'I'm not twisting anything. I was just helping someone,

342

that's all. It doesn't affect us.'

'How can you say that? Of course it affects us! What if I want to marry you?'

'You don't,' I said. 'Come on, you know we've always agreed that living together's just as good. You've never been arsed about marriage.'

'That was before I knew you were married to someone else! Just imagine how I felt, Belinda, hearing that from Phil Douglas of all people. If Phil Douglas knew about it, I think I had a right to know. Everyone must think I'm a right mug. Who else knows?'

'No one, honestly. Just Hayley. I had to tell her because she's in charge of all the BUPA stuff at school. Look, I'm sorry. I should have told you a lot sooner, I know. I was just scared . . . of this. Can't you understand that?'

'No!' he shouted. 'I don't give a shit. I feel like a total idiot.'

'Well, don't,' I said simply. 'Listen, Alistair. I love you, right? I don't love Tony.' I crossed my toes inside my shoes as I told my biggest lie ever. 'I hardly know him.' At least this was true, I thought grimly, remembering Tony's mysterious reference to his stupid whore sisters. 'I was just doing what I thought was right.'

'You've never . . . done anything with him, slept with him or anything?' Alistair eyed me suspiciously.

'Of course not. He's been too ill to sleep with anyone or even think about it. Alistair, please just try to have a bit of compassion.'

'Why? If this operation was so urgent, couldn't he have had it done on the NHS?' His tone was stabilising, I noticed. His questions were beginning to sound as if he might actually listen to the answers.

'You would have thought so, wouldn't you?' I went on, encouraged. 'But there's a shortage of beds, as always. His doctor said he'd do his best, but there were no guarantees. He couldn't take the risk. I mean, put yourself in his position. If you thought you might be paralysed for ever, wouldn't you do anything, absolutely anything, to stop that happening? If you were Tony, wouldn't you want someone to do what I did?'

'I don't know.' Alistair sighed miserably.

'You know you would. Anyone would.'

'But why did it have to be you?' He was running out of steam for sure.

'I was the only person at Beasley who wasn't already married,' I said, in a flash of inspiration. I love it when that happens. Sometimes you find that a bit of truth is just waiting there to be slotted conveniently into a lie, like the last slice of the Trivial Pursuit pie. 'Carmel-Marie's married and anyway she's boycotted the school's BUPA scheme. Rosie's married. So is Hayley. So are all the female staff except me.'

'Have you ever been unfaithful to me, Belinda?' Alistair looked at me earnestly. 'Tell me the truth.'

'No,' I said easily. 'Never.'

'You've never had an affair, a one-night stand?'

'No, I haven't.' We sat in silence for a while.

'Well, you'd better not,' Alistair said eventually. 'Has he had his operation now?'

'Yes.'

'When can you divorce him?'

'I don't know,' I said, kicking myself for not having anticipated this question.

'Well, you'd better find out.'

'Does that mean you forgive me?' I risked a tentative smile.

'No. I don't know.' Alistair looked confused. 'I want to, but . . .'

'Then do. I was only doing what I thought was right.'

'I want you to divorce him as soon as you can. And then we're getting married,' he said defiantly.

'What?'

'You heard. If you can marry him, you can marry me.'

'Alistair, I'll get angry with you in a minute. I know

344

you've had a shock and I'm sorry I didn't tell you sooner, but this is totally out of order. If we get married it should be for a better reason than you having something to prove. If you marry me just because you're annoyed about Tony, that would be worse than a marriage of convenience. It would be ... a marriage based on resentment and ... punishment. Can't you see that?'

'I suppose so.' Alistair looked away. 'I just feel I need to ... do something. Maybe I'll go and marry someone else as well.' He scowled.

'I wouldn't mind, if you did it for the same reasons I did,' I said, wondering whether this was true. 'Look, can't you just ... stop being so conventional about this? It doesn't affect us, the thing itself, I mean. It's just the idea you don't like. But why not, really? Tony's benefited from it and we haven't lost anything. Just separate marriage from love in your mind and you'll see I'm right.'

'Okay, okay.' Alistair put his hand up to stop me. 'I'm trying. I'll try. It's going to take some getting used to, though.'

'Of course. I know that.' I got up and started to gather together shards of clip-frame. 'But the most important thing is that we love each other, isn't it?'

'I never said it wasn't,' Alistair snapped.

'We'll probably be laughing about this next week.'

'Don't push it, Belinda. You're lucky I haven't thrown you out.'

'Do you want to?' I asked.

'No, not particularly.'

'Good. Neither do I. Want to be thrown out, I mean.' I smiled at him. He grimaced at me and reached for the television remote control.

# Chapter Twenty-Four

## And Then at the End You're the Best Again

Alistair and I spent most of the night arguing, but I think I eventually managed to talk him into seeing things from my point of view, or at least the point of view I adopted for his benefit. Luckily Alistair isn't one of these irritating truth-above-all types. He has lied to me on several occasions, which prevented him from claiming as much moral high ground as he might otherwise have done. I knew I was extremely lucky that the main crisis had passed and left us relatively unscathed. Well, not just lucky. I'd put in a lot of effort as well. The one problem was that Alistair was still insisting I divorce Tony as soon as possible. I had yet to think of a way round that one.

I got up first thing the next morning and set off to Darryl's, having made a suitable fuss of and breakfast for Alistair first. I knew I should have been feeling exhausted and unable to function for another second, but from the moment Phil Douglas had banged on our front door I had gone into Superwoman mode. I could feel the adrenalin like a drug rushing through my body, spilling out of every pore in my skin.

'How is he?' I asked as soon as Darryl answered the door. He was wearing an old navy dressing-gown and looked less than thrilled to see me.

'A lot better,' he said. 'I'm all right too, thanks for asking.'

'Sorry, Darryl. Can I see Tony?'

'I'm not his mother. He's in the kitchen.' I ran past

Darryl into the kitchen. There was Tony, looking alert and gorgeous, wearing Darryl's baggy red shorts and a black T-shirt. He was sitting at the table eating a bowl of corn-flakes.

'Hi,' I said hesitantly. 'How are you?'

'All right.' Tony looked at me shyly. 'Sorry about last night. I went off on one, didn't I? Darryl says I wouldn't go home.'

'Don't you remember?' Only now was I beginning to take Tony's schizophrenia seriously, to realise how vastly different his mental landscape was from mine.

'No.' He shrugged.

'Do you remember anything?' I sat down next to him, basking in the GLOW of proximity.

'Not much. That Carl rang me. I went to meet him.'

'I know. Me and Darryl were there. Don't you remember that?'

'No. I'm sorry.'

'What for?'

'Everything. Now you know what I mean. My head's fucked.'

'I love you anyway.' I stroked his arm.

'Do you? Still?' He looked at me as if I were seriously unhinged.

'Of course I do. I always will, Tony, whatever happens.'

'I love you too.'

'Tony, I'm sorry to bring this up now, but ... do you still want to go to the police?'

'I thought you didn't want me to.' He stared into his cereal bowl.

'Well, it's up to you. If you want to, I won't stop you. If you think it would make you feel better.'

'It would,' he said.

'Okay then. That's what we'll do.'

'How come you've changed your mind?'

'Darryl talked some sense into me,' I said.

'Some,' said Darryl from the doorway. 'Only some.'

347

Despite the sarcasm in his voice, Darryl sounded friendlier than he had the night before. I turned round and looked at him and he condescended to flash an irritated smile in my direction.

'Can we go now?' Tony asked.

'Yes. I don't see why not.'

'I'll go and get my stuff. Thanks for the breakfast,' he said to Darryl.

While Tony was upstairs I filled Darryl in on what had happened with Alistair and the Douglases.

Darryl shook his head 'So, you delayed the inevitable for a bit longer,' he said. 'What about when Tony goes to the police? It might be in the papers.'

'Alistair only reads the sports page. I'll have to try and make sure he doesn't see it,' I said happily. I was so relieved that Tony was back to his old self that I was determined not to let anything get me down.

'Doesn't he watch the news?'

'I'll have to see to it that he doesn't. And if he sees or hears anything, well – I'll just have to explain, won't I?'

'Explain what? The truth?'

I took Darryl's renewed enthusiasm for interrogating me as a sign that he still wanted to be my friend. 'No, you fool.' I smiled. 'About Tony's . . . mental problems. Just because he's schizophrenic doesn't mean he deserves to be paralysed.'

'Paralysed! What a load of bollocks! How could you say all that with a straight face? How could Alistair fall for it?'

'Or else I'll just say I didn't know anything about it. That's possible as well.'

'Belinda, when are you going to give up?'

'Never,' I said.

Tony came back downstairs carrying a Thresher's plastic bag. 'I'm ready,' he said. 'I'm scared.'

'Don't worry.' I smiled at him, even though I was probably more frightened than he was. 'You're doing the right thing. Everything will be fine. Come on, let's go.' I turned to Darryl. 'I'm never going to give up,' I said.

# Chapter Twenty-Five

## Four Massive Loans, Three Grand Bail, Two Men in my Life and a Partridge in a Pear Tree

*Christmas Day 1997.* SETH BEASLEY *is sitting in his office with his feet up on the window-sill, swigging Teacher's whisky from a large bottle. There is an empty bottle of Teacher's beside him on the floor and a parcel wrapped in Christmas paper on the desk in front of him. Suddenly the door opens and* BELINDA NIELD *enters.*

SETH   What are . . . what do you want?

BELINDA (*sarcastically*)   Merry Christmas to you too. I popped round to your house. Natasha said you were here. (*She sits down opposite* SETH.)

SETH   I couldn't face her today. I've got a present for Darryl. I was going to take it round to his house . . .(*His voice tails off*) What do you want, anyway?

BELINDA   Oh, you know. Just wondering how you were feeling, whether you were feeling short-staffed at all, what with Carmel-Marie in prison . . .

SETH (*stifling a hiccup*)   Carmel-Marie . . . none of us could believe it . . .

BELINDA   . . . because, you know, I'd be happy to come back if you needed me.

SETH   Don't be ridiculous. You can't teach dance. Anyway, we've been through this. You know it's impossible. Hirrally Sirrally . . .

BELINDA (*laughing*)   You mean Hilary Sillery. Hey, that'd make a great drunk driving test. I must remember to mention that to the police. I see so much of them these days. Come on, Seth, surely you're not still scared of the Sillerys. The school's name's been thoroughly tarnished anyway, what with Carmel-Marie. Alistair says he knew as soon as he met her at your place that she was a crazed killer.

SETH    Oh, God, I wish I was dead!

BELINDA    Seth? My job?

SETH    What . . . what job?

BELINDA (*impatiently*)    Is there any chance of you giving me my job back?

SETH    No. Of course not. I can't, Belinda. We're already known for our murderers. The last thing we need is a reputation for child molestation.

BELINDA    Oh, cheers!

SETH    You know what I mean. Anyway . . . how are you?

BELINDA    Up to my neck in debt. And working as a secretary again.

SETH    Why?

BELINDA    Because you made me resign, remember?

SETH    No . . . why in debt?

BELINDA    Tony's bail. I had to get four separate loans, can you believe that? Four! Two from gullible family members, one from the Halifax and one from some dodgy company. I'm going to be in debt for the rest of my life.

SETH    Oh dear. How is . . . everything, apart from that? What about Alistair? Why aren't you with him now . . . or Tony . . . I mean, it's Christmas Day!

BELINDA (*smiling*)    Thank you for taking a drunken interest. Alistair's fine. He's been promoted actually. I have been with him all morning and I'm off to see Tony this afternoon. I'm dividing my time, as published authors always say on their cover blurbs.

SETH (*distractedly*)    Do they? I haven't read anything for ages.

BELINDA    I couldn't live if I didn't read. I need something more boring and less dramatic than my life to escape into. I make a point of only reading books in which bugger all happens.

SETH So ... Alistair knows about the Mark Ryder business?

BELINDA Of course he doesn't. Tony's name hasn't been in the papers and I certainly haven't said anything. Alistair's still pestering me about divorce, though. I don't know what I'm going to do about that.

SETH Has Darryl ... said anything to you? About me?

BELINDA No, Seth, he hasn't. He never mentions you.

SETH He's so distant these days. I've got him a Christmas present, you know.

BELINDA Yes, you said. Seth, Tony's solicitor's bills are huge. I could really do with having a well-paid job at the moment. I'm sure the Sillerys wouldn't do anything, not after all this time. They wouldn't want their son's name in the papers, would they?

SETH I don't know, Belinda. If Tony goes to prison ... well, no offence but ...

BELINDA ... you don't want the wife of a convicted murderer on your staff?

SETH Well, no. I've ... well, after Carmel-Marie ...

BELINDA Tony won't be convicted of murder, Seth. His solicitor's virtually certain of that. He reckons it's a case of diminished responsibility. And Tony confessed to his part in it. There's a strong chance he won't get a custodial sentence.

SETH But ... there'll be a trial. His name will be in the papers then and so will yours, probably. What will happen then? What will you tell Alistair? Oh, it's all impossible!

BELINDA No, it's not. I don't know what I'll tell Alistair. I'll think of something. Actually, I've already got a sort of plan. Do you want to hear it?

SETH Yes. No. I can't concentrate on anything ...

BELINDA All the times me and Alistair have rowed about

my being married, Alistair's never once asked what Tony's surname is. So if his name does get in the paper at some stage, or on the news, who's to say it's the same Tony?

SETH   What? But his name's in the *Lions* programme . . . and what about your wedding certificate?

BELINDA   Seth! This is Alistair we're talking about. He doesn't know there is a *Lions* programme and it wouldn't occur to him to ask to see a wedding certificate. He hasn't yet, anyway, and if he does suddenly, I'll just say I've lost it, you know, because the wedding was so unimportant to me, just a marriage of convenience. If he ever asks me Tony's surname, I'll just say it's Smith or something. Alistair doesn't need to find out any more than he already knows. I just have to hope that when I pretend to get divorced, Alistair'll take my word for it. Darryl says . . . (*She stops suddenly.*)

SETH   (*leaning forward eagerly*)   Darryl? What? What did he say? About me?

BELINDA   No, no, about me pretending to get divorced. He says Alistair, if he's got any sense, will ask to see the divorce papers. I need to get to know some talented forgers. Vinny could have done it but . . . well . . .

SETH   Who? Who's Vinny?

BELINDA (*sadly*)   Never mind. So, your answer's definitely no, then?

SETH   Maybe after the trial . . . if there's not too much scandal. If your name doesn't get into the papers. If the juicy story of your weird marriage isn't plastered all over the tabloids.

BELINDA   It won't be. It had better not be, otherwise I can say goodbye to Alistair.

SETH   How do you know it won't be?

BELINDA   I don't know. I'm just going to have to make sure it isn't, aren't I?

SETH   It's so risky, though. It could all go so wrong.

BELINDA   I know that, Seth. I'm not a complete idiot. But

I can't just give up, can I, not when I've got this far. If I can make it through the trial and . . . whatever happens afterwards, well, there's no reason why I shouldn't be able to get away with it for ever.

SETH But what if Tony goes to prison? If Darryl ever went to prison I'd kill myself.

BELINDA There's no chance of me doing that.

SETH It's bad enough being virtually ignored by him every day, but not to see him at all . . . oh, God!

BELINDA If Tony goes to prison, which I don't think he will, I'll do what normal wives of unjustly imprisoned people do – visit him as often as possible, appeal, and wait for him to get out.

SETH I wish I could be like you.

BELINDA Give me my job back and I'll train you. How about that?

SETH I can't, Belinda. This place is all I've got. I can't risk any more dirt being raked up . . . look, have a drink. Have a Christmas drink with me.

BELINDA (*standing up*) Sorry. Got to go to Slough, for the second of today's Christmas dinners. Still, at least I don't have to eat the same thing twice. Tony's idea of cooking Christmas dinner is opening a tin of corned beef and mashing a couple of potatoes. Badly. Whereas Alistair, of course, does it properly: home-made gravy, three different kinds of stuffing . . . Seth? Are you asleep?

SETH (*opening his eyes suddenly*) Hm?

BELINDA Bye, Seth. Merry Christmas.

SETH Yeah, sure. Bye. Take care.

BELINDA *leaves.* SETH *takes another swig of whisky and falls asleep again.*

CHORUS Only a fool gives up. The wise
Ascend the higher leagues of lies,
Acquiring, as they climb, more skill,
Rewriting truth and fact until
Their stories have grown tall enough
To elevate and smooth the rough

353

Realities that can be found
Crouching, ungainly, on the ground.

And who will win and who will lose
Is unaffected by our views,
And who will rise and who will sink
Will not be changed by what we think.
If things do not work out her way
At least she knows the world will say
That, knowing the potential cost,
She tried to win until she lost.

# Epilogue

Perhaps you would have preferred, readers in all categories, a neater ending. Cats A and E, you probably wanted Alistair, the schizophrenia and the Mark Ryder incident to disappear so that Tony and I could live happily ever after, whereas Bs and Cs might have hoped I would realise how much I preferred Alistair and leave Tony. Category F readers must be fuming because I haven't learned my lesson. I hope they've learned theirs and won't read this book again. I did try to warn you, Cat Fs, so don't say I didn't. Maybe only those in Category D, the free-thinkers, will appreciate that there is no other logical way for a story like this to end.

But it hasn't even ended, some of you will say. Every-thing's so unresolved, so up in the air. Anything could still happen. Isn't it terrible? Doesn't it make you want to scream? At least it's only a book for you. Imagine how I must feel – this is my life.

*Also available from Arrow*

**NAMEDROPPER**

Emma Forrest

*I don't see what's so good about being genuine. Clog dancing is genuine. Isn't being fake more of an achievement? At least it takes some inspiration.*

At the start of the summer, sixteen-year-old Viva Cohen has a blissful home life with her gay uncle Manny, a best friend who eats a pound of lettuce a day because she likes the taste, a tune she can't get out of her head and a lot of Elizabeth Taylor posters. At the end of the summer she has a lot of Elizabeth Taylor posters. When Viva rejects a happy successful rock star for a miserable, unsuccessful one, Elizabeth is there. When she runs away with a sickly celebrity who wears an anorak in ninety-degree heat, Ava and Marilyn help out. Follow them all, from Edinburgh to Brighton, from L.A. to Vegas, as Viva uncovers the icon in everyone.

Willy, insightful and fresh, *Namedropper* is a must for anyone who's ever felt nostalgic for something they've never experienced.

'The most delightful comic heroine to have watched TV in fluffy mules since Bridget Jones. If there's any justice, Forrest's star turn will do for post-pubescent angst what Helen Fielding's creation did for thirty-something neurosis. Forrest has a sharp eye for idiosyncrasies, allied to a wicked way with words'   *The Big Issue*

'Shrewd, cool, sure and insightful'   *Independent*

# TRUTH OR DARE

## Sara Sheridan

*Crime is easy once you get started, you know. It's the initial break with respectability which is difficult.*

Libby and Becka are two ordinary girls. They've both got things in their lives they'd like to forget. But when the owner of the flat they're borrowing (without her permission) goes missing, things start to spiral and the girls take to the road on what might be the trip (the last trip) of a lifetime.

They break the rules. They make up their own. They lie, cheat and panic in equal measure. It's a story about London, Glasgow, Belfast and Dublin. Drink, drugs, bleached hair and bad disguises. Idle fun, stolen millions and running for your life.

*Truth or Dare* is a rollicking road movie of a book, an exhilarating, funny and poignant novel of female friendship, family . . . and premeditated murder.

'It made me laugh out loud, but it also nearly reduced me to tears' *Express*

'Darkly comic and compassionate' *Daily Telegraph*

# CHLOË

### Freya North

Chloë Cadwaller is in a quandary.

Jocelyn, her godmother, has died leaving Chloë a letter instructing her to give up her job (lousy) and her boyfriend (awful) to travel the four countries of the United Kingdom during the four seasons of the year.

Heavens. How can Chloë deny a godmother's last wish?

Off she goes, with a tremor of doubt and a letter marked Wales, to a farm deep in the Black Mountains where she finds an assortment of animals in varying states of mental health and the best looking man she's ever laid eyes on.

As the seasons unfold, so does Chloë's journey. From Abergavenny to St Ives, from the Giant's Causeway to the shores of Loch Lomond, with sex, sculpture, ice-cream, egg sandwiches and a potter called William thrown in on the way, Chloë encounters love, lust – and a man for each season. Travel with her in the warm and witty story of one girl's quest for a place to call home.

'An original, direct, funny new voice' *Independent on Sunday*

# CONCERNING LILY

## Sally Brampton

*Three friends, three relationships . . . and one young woman without a conscience.*

When Elisabeth Delaware, bored of her comfortable life, invites young, friendless Lily Clifton to meet her husband and friends, she cannot imagine the terrible consequences the invitation will have. For Lily is not just a stranger to London, she is a stranger to conscience.

Elisabeth does not see Lily for what she is, nor can she see that her marriage to solid, dependable Charles is slowly crumbling. Even Elisabeth's good friends, Bella and Daisy, both intent on salvaging the wreckage of their own relationships, are powerless to resist as Lily moves through all their lives wreaking quiet but careless havoc.

'As fascinating as as being a fly on the wall of your neighbour's Smallbone kitchen. I enjoyed it hugely'  Kate Saunders, *Observer*

'An entertaining tale of modern friendships, lovers and wives'  *Elle*

'A modern morality tale of marriage and discontent . . . shrewd, intense and, in a there-but-for-the-grace-of-God way, compulsive'  Elizabeth Buchan, *Mail on Sunday*

'A savage entertainment'  *Independent*

# RECKLESS DRIVER

## Lisa Vice

'Concise, resonant prose . . . From the first propulsive words of Lisa Vice's debut novel, readers know they're in for a breathtaking ride with a powerful stylist. Sometimes sweetly lyrical, at others quietly foreboding, *Reckless Driver* is always fascinating' *San Francisco Chronicle*

Lana Franklin's house is full of mysteries: Why does 'remodelling the house' involve her father tearing it apart yet never doing it up? What do her mother and sister find so exciting about boys? What's it like being dead? The adults around her don't seem to have the answers, nor the time to listen to her questions. As Lana grows up, she has to seek her own solutions.

Told in Lana's piercingly honest and lyrical voice, *Reckless Driver* hauntingly captures a young girl's struggle to make sense of the chaos of her world. Unsparing and yet deeply compassionate, this highly acclaimed novel is beautifully written, moving and insightful. It is a novel you will not forget.

'Poignant' *Prima*

'Ominous, concise, relentless' *The Times*

'This beautifully written novel has a very real voice narrating it. The author has a true understanding of human nature . . . It's an everyday story and it's a unique story. You won't forget it easily' *Tatler*

## OTHER TITLES AVAILABLE IN ARROW